SECRETS

OTHER BOOKS AND AUDIO BOOKS

BY ERIN KLINGLER

Between the Lines

kM/4

SECRETS

A NOVEL

Erin Klingler

Covenant Communications, Inc.

Cover images: *Huey Helicopter Land in Desert* © Blair Bunting, *Business People in a Modern Building* © caracterdesign, *Graphene* © Andrey Prokhorov, all courtesy of istockphoto.com.

Cover design copyright © 2013 by Covenant Communications, Inc.

Published by Covenant Communications, Inc.
American Fork, Utah

Printed in the United States of America
First Printing: August 2013

19 18 17 16 15 14 13   10 9 8 7 6 5 4 3 2 1

ISBN 978-1-62108-398-6

For Leslie Schwieder, for spending your precious free time reading this for me, cheering me on, and catching some rather embarrassing oversights. You're not only an amazing editor, you're a great friend.

And for Jaime Scott, for always making me laugh through the stress of writing this and for always demanding the next chapter—and for bribing me with M&M McFlurries when the writing got tough. I love you!

ACKNOWLEDGMENTS

Many thanks go out to my helpful friends:

To Abby Nielsen, for reading this and motivating me to keep writing by continually asking for more, and for giving me invaluable suggestions and feedback.

To Tori Harrigfeld, for being my eyes and ears of Denver and answering way more questions than you wanted to, I'm sure!

To my husband, for his cyber security knowledge and helping me with the technology of this plot.

And to my kids, for putting up with me for all the time I spend at the computer, knowing how important writing is to me.

CHAPTER ONE

He's coming.

The words pounded through Dan's head in a repetitive, frantic rhythm that matched the drumming of his heart. Adrenaline rushed through his body as he stood behind his desk, his shoulders bunched and tensed, his fingers flying across the keyboard.

He only had a minute—maybe less—before the man would be here. It had been pure chance that he'd been looking out the wall of windows along the back of his office just as the familiar silver Mercedes had pulled into the parking lot. He didn't need to see through the darkly tinted windows to know who was behind the wheel. Two encounters with Benton's henchman had been two too many. Dan knew what the man was capable of.

A bead of sweat formed on his brow and trickled down his temple. His refusal to play ball had only infuriated Benton, and the man was clearly done playing nice. He should have seen this coming. Now there was only one thing left to do. He had to hide the data.

With urgent, shaky movements, Dan typed in the keystrokes that would keep the information out of the wrong hands. What he'd developed had been with his best intentions. He'd wanted to help, to make a positive impact for once in his life.

But his intentions were clearly not the same as everybody else's. In the right hands, his work over the past few years could mean safety and protection for the American people. In the wrong hands . . . death and destruction.

The *tick tick tick* of the clock on the wall to his right sounded like gunshots, threatening and deafening, reminding him that time was running out.

He completed the last three keystrokes and slapped the Enter key.

There. It was done.

A sense of relief like none other swept through him as he pulled the far left thumb drive from the wireless hub next to his monitor. Making sure to grab the right one, he slipped it inside his suit jacket pocket. They'd never find the information now.

He turned and grabbed the file folders behind him, frantically flipping through them to make sure he'd shredded all the evidence. Nothing remained. It was as if the work he'd accomplished had never existed.

"Working hard, I see. I'd never expect anything less from you."

Dan's head jerked up, his eyes widening with alarm. He *knew* that voice. And it wasn't the one he'd been expecting. Looking up in astonishment, he saw a familiar man in his office doorway. The dark-haired, lean-figured man leaned casually up against the doorframe.

How many times had this man come in for a talk or discussion in just that same manner? He was comfortable, confident, a team player.

Well, Dan had never suspected it—his colleague was playing for the other team.

Pushing off from the doorframe, the man eased the door shut and sauntered toward him. "I heard you found the solution to the problem. I knew you would. That technology is going to change everything. You should feel proud."

The thumb drive seemed to burn against his body from where it lay in Dan's jacket pocket, safely concealed. For now. He'd planned to give it to Cambry. If anything happened to him, she'd be able to follow the clues he'd left. She was a smart girl. Brilliant, actually. He couldn't attribute any of that to himself. He'd been worthless as a father.

Agony ripped through him. It hadn't been until the last couple of years that he'd realized how much he'd screwed up, and by then . . . Well, he guessed he couldn't blame Cambry for ignoring his recent attempts to reconcile. If only he had more time . . .

That was exactly what he was up against right now. Lost time. Surely this man was here for one reason and one reason alone.

Dan looked back up at the man now standing before his desk. The singleness of purpose was etched in every muscle of his colleague's face.

"I'm sure you know why I'm here."

"Why are you doing this?" Dan asked in a strangled whisper. "I didn't put in all this time—years—to have this technology used in any way but how I intended."

"You wanted to make a difference. I understand that. It's altruistic. Noble even. But you've been in this business long enough to know that altruism doesn't pay. That's the difference between you and me—I know which wheels to grease to make the big bucks. You understood that too until you had that inconvenient change of heart a couple of years ago. Now it's all about reconciling with your daughter, isn't it?"

Dan's throat tightened as he watched the man pick up the framed picture on his desk and study the pretty, petite redhead.

"She's beautiful. I wonder . . . How much is she worth to you?"

The implications made Dan's stomach roil. "She has nothing to do with this."

"Doesn't she?" He set the frame back down and leaned forward, placing his palms on the desk. "If you'd played ball when you learned what we wanted, it wouldn't have come to this. Benton thinks you need a little motivation. I tend to agree."

Seeing the sadistic gleam in his colleague's eyes, Dan found his mind scrambling for a way out. His eyes flickered to the other thumb drive protruding from the wireless hub next to his monitor. Nothing of consequence was stored on it—only a handful of password-protected files containing old projects. But if he could make his colleague think differently, maybe he could just come out of this encounter unscathed. At least long enough to get out of here and warn the authorities. And Cambry.

When he looked back up, Dan saw that the man was scrutinizing his every movement. That could definitely play to his advantage. With a more deliberate motion, he looked down at the thumb drive.

His ruse worked.

"Is that it?" Hunger sparked in the man's gaze as he reached across the desk and pulled the thumb drive from the hub. He held it up expectantly with a cocked eyebrow. "See how easy that was?"

"Easy enough that you'll leave my daughter out of it? Leave *me* out of it?"

The answering chuckle erased any hope from his mind. "We can't leave you out of this. You designed this technology. We're going to need your help with the prototypes and demonstrations we've set up for the buyers."

Dan felt his eyes widen at the demand. "You can't expect me to do that! I want no part of this."

"But see, that's what you don't understand. You *are* a part of this. Willingly or not." The man reached inside his coat and pulled out a gun. "This is where you decide if you're a team player. Or not."

So it had finally come to this. Nothing he could say was going to make this end well. He didn't know much about guns, but he knew that the extension on the end was a silencer. It definitely meant business.

He backed up a step.

"Not so fast," his colleague said. "Benton's man is outside waiting with the car. Let's take a drive. Benton's going to want to talk to you." He gestured with the gun toward the closed door. "Let's take the stairs."

Deciding to do what he was told for now and wait for an opportunity to escape, he lifted his hands and slowly skirted the desk. His colleague's eyes never left his. When Dan reached the door, the man pulled it open, peered out to make sure nobody was around, then gave a little jerk of his head toward the hall. Dan obeyed and stepped through.

A darting glance up and down the hallway confirmed that the hall was devoid of people.

It was past quitting time, and everybody had gone home for the night. Anticipating Dan's hesitation, the man shoved the gun against the small of Dan's back to urge him along.

Dan moved right to the stairwell door and opened it. They slipped through and started down the stairs. Every footfall made by their dress shoes echoed through the enclosed space, ringing off the metal steps. The march down the five flights of stairs seemed to take forever, but even so, by the time they reached the bottom, Dan still hadn't come up with a viable escape plan.

Stepping off the last metal stair onto the gleaming marble floor, he decided he was out of time. He had to try something. *Reasoning* was the first thing that came to his mind. "The building's not empty," Dan reminded his colleague, his voice not as steady as he would have liked. "People are going to see us as soon as we walk out there. You have the thumb drive. Why don't you just take it and leave?"

His colleague smirked. "We're still going to need your help with the prototypes. And I have a feeling that with the added incentive of keeping your daughter safe, you'll help us." The man's expression grew serious, and he leveled the gun at Dan's chest. "Let's go."

The sound of a couple of coworkers calling out good-nights to each other through the lobby door made them go still. His colleague's eyes flickered to the door, and a moment of indecision crossed his features.

Realizing this may be his only chance to escape and get to the police, Dan forced himself into action. He grabbed for the gun and bent his captor's hand backward. The man let out a startled grunt, then grabbed the gun with a second hand to try to regain control.

Using brute strength, Dan shoved the man up against the stair railing and held on to the gun for all he was worth, knowing that if he didn't win this wrestling match, his life would be over. The gun wobbled around between them, and Dan gave one more lurching push, hoping to unbalance his opponent. With a cry of alarm, his colleague stumbled to the left, catching his foot on the railing. He went sprawling.

The gun was wrenched from Dan's hand, and a single, muted pop echoed through the stairwell. Something slammed into his chest, followed almost instantaneously by a blinding pain. He stumbled backward and clapped a hand to his chest. Realization settled heavily over him.

He'd been shot.

Looking down, he saw a slow, expanding red stain seeping through his fingers. Shock made him numb. His legs gave out, and he dropped to the floor. As he stared up at the ceiling from his supine position, the light overhead spun in a nauseating circle.

Somewhere through the haze moving over his mind, another set of voices, greetings exchanged, sounded from right outside the door. His colleague bit out a muffled curse and then scrambled to his feet. Fear of discovery fueling his movements, his attacker jumped over him and started pounding up the stairs. A moment later he was gone.

Dan let out a hitching breath. He was alone. And alive. But for how long?

He tried to take inventory of his situation. Even breathing hurt. Getting up was out of the question. Turning his head slowly to the right, he glanced at the door a few feet away. Could he find the strength to pull himself through it?

Knowing it was his only option, he gritted his teeth and forced himself to move. Agony ripped through him as he sat up and managed one excruciating scoot backward. Then another. Then another. The door was beside him, and he managed to reach the handle and tug it downward.

It took every ounce of his dwindling strength to wedge his elbow in the door to keep it open and haul himself partially out of the stairwell. He only managed to pull himself another few inches out into the lobby before the pain became too much. He collapsed.

His thought processes felt labored, but he considered the impossibility of his situation. The stairwell was at the far end of the lobby, around the corner from the reception desk and elevators. He wasn't in easy sight from the building's entrance. But he was halfway out, his body keeping the door open. Surely that would catch somebody's attention quicker than not.

With that last scrambled thought, he sent up prayers that what he'd managed would be enough. Breathing heavily and gasping at the pain and darkness closing in on him, he hoped that he could manage to stay alive until somebody found him.

CHAPTER TWO

CAMBRY GLANCED BOTH WAYS, CHECKING for oncoming traffic, then hurried across the street. Around her, downtown Denver was hopping. The nighttime breathed a different life into the city, an energy that was pulsating and electric. She loved the hustle and bustle of the late dinner crowd and late-season tourists that filled the streets. The high-rise buildings that bordered the streets were fronted by panes of glass that caught the lights from neighboring buildings and streetlights and reflected them back, bouncing from building to building like a larger-than-life pinball game.

She shoved her hands into her overcoat pockets and kept her pace brisk. The fitted, knee-length black business skirt made long strides a challenge, but she did her best. She wanted to get where she was going and be done with it. It was bad enough that she'd felt guilted into meeting with her father, but he had asked—demanded, really—that she meet him at his office building. That meant she didn't even have the convenience of neutral ground for this meeting.

Her mouth drew into a tight line. It was the last place she wanted to be. And he was the last person she wanted to see. Too much had happened between them. Bridges burned and all that. But over the past several months, he'd been reaching out to her. Asking to see her. Wanting to talk. Nothing had swayed her—until his unsettling phone message that her assistant had handed her after her meeting tonight. *In trouble. Need to talk to you. Urgent.*

Something about the tone unsettled her. How was he in trouble? And why should she care? After all he had done to her and Mom . . .

Shoving those unpleasant thoughts aside, she slowed her steps and joined the group of people waiting for the light rail transit at the station. A fairly attractive man in his late twenties standing next to her smiled down at her, and she felt her cheeks flush as she smiled back. Feeling a little self-conscious, she surreptitiously glanced at the reflective wall of glass beside her. She pulled a hand from her overcoat pocket and discreetly pushed at some of the irritating red curls that had escaped from what, a couple of hours ago, had been a very professional looking chignon. But then, her hair had always been the bane of her existence. Long, thick, and naturally curly, it refused to be tamed. More often than not, she resorted to a fancy up-style secured with a lot of bobby pins to make sure she looked nice for work. Professional. Stylish. Older.

Her work as a rep for a technologies firm sent her around the country to help new research companies set up their labs. The problem was those firms expected somebody capable and knowledgeable to walk into their offices. When *she* walked in, they took one look at her tiny five-foot-three, one-hundred-and-ten pound frame and assumed she was a lost middle-schooler, rather than a twenty-six-year-old professional.

It also didn't help that she had a smattering of freckles across the bridge of her nose that stood out against her light, creamy complexion, making her look young and fresh faced. Too young to be able to manage the multimillion dollar research labs' setups. Now that she'd established a name for herself, it wasn't nearly as bad. Her clients knew her to be efficient, organized, and tough as nails. They respected her, referred her to others, and spoke highly of her.

People told her she'd be thankful one day for her youthful looks. Somehow she doubted it. Who cared that you looked a dozen years younger when you were sitting in a wheelchair in some retirement home playing bingo with an eccentric, blue-haired lady who did nothing but argue the merits of the best denture creams? She'd rather be taken seriously now while it still mattered, thank you very much.

The rumble of the approaching light rail caught her attention, and she joined the crowd of fellow commuters shuffling toward the loading area. Once on, she took the first open seat available and watched the city lights flash by her window.

When the light rail finally stopped a block from her father's building, she got off and started walking. Traffic at this hour was steady but lighter now that she was away from downtown. It was after eight, and most of the offices had closed down for the day.

Soon the five-story brick and stucco building belonging to Saville Enterprises came into view, with its bold architecture and landscaping—complete with twin stone fountains flanking the paved path to the front doors.

She crossed the elaborate courtyard and climbed the handful of steps to the mirrored-glass double doors. Pulling one of the heavy doors open, she walked into the brightly lit lobby with its gleaming marble floors and elegant cream-colored walls with crisp white trim. She approached the front desk to sign in, remembering that visitors were required to do so, but no guard sat at the station.

She hesitated. That was unusual. Wondering if she should find the clipboard and sign in without checking with the security guard, she finally decided to just head to her father's office. She didn't want to delay this meeting any longer.

Walking through the reception area, her heels echoed through the hall as she strode toward the bank of elevators. To her frustration, one of the two elevators had a Closed for Servicing sign affixed to the rope stretched across the front of it, and the other elevator's light showed it to be at the top of the building. She punched the button a couple of times, but the elevator didn't start a descent.

Forget it, she thought as she turned on her heel, clicked back down the hall into the lobby, and hung a right, heading for the stairs around the corner. She knew where her dad's corporate offices were on the fifth floor. She could just as easily use the stairs.

She turned the corner, gasped, and jerked to a halt. A man in an expensive looking suit lay crumpled on the floor, his back to her, his body half out of the stairwell door.

Panic skittered across her spine as she took a few steps back toward the lobby and shouted, "Somebody help! There's a man hurt here in the stairwell! Call 911!"

Without waiting to see if somebody came running, she rushed back toward the man and crouched down beside him. Putting a hand gently on his shoulder, she gave a slight squeeze to alert him to her presence.

"Sir! Sir, are you okay? What happened?"

The man groaned and rolled slightly, shifting from his side to his back, swinging his head toward her with a pained moan.

Her heart lurched in recognition. The familiar dark brown hair was now grayer than she remembered, and deep creases around his eyes and mouth made him look haggard and weathered. It may have been years since she'd seen him, but there was no mistaking the man's identity.

It was her father.

A quick assessment showed a deep cut that could likely have come from a fall down the stairs. It started at the hairline and disappeared into his somewhat thinning hair. His pallor was gray and his brown eyes glazed, but a flicker of recognition darted through his eyes when he looked up at her.

"The picture," he struggled to get out, his voice raspy and labored, "of us."

"What?" Her eyebrows drew together. "What picture? What are you talking about?"

"Isaac . . ." he managed and then coughed. It was a weak, feeble sound.

A cold chill settled in her stomach. "Hang on, okay? Help is coming."

"In my coat pocket," he rasped.

She reached inside the pocket he'd gestured toward and pulled out a small, nondescript thumb drive.

Her father's large hand closed around hers, sealing the thumb drive between their palms. He swallowed with great difficulty then said, "Don't give it to anybody. Don't let them find it."

"Find what?" she asked, her hands starting to shake. "What's going on?"

"Password . . . Nicknames . . ." He struggled to say more, but his eyes fluttered and then drifted closed. The hand clutching hers went limp.

With shaking hands, she reached out and placed her fingertips against his throat. Relief took the edge off her panic when she detected a faint pulse. He was only unconscious.

The sound of footsteps running toward her drew her attention, and she slipped the thumb drive in her overcoat pocket. Whatever that was all about, she'd deal with it later. She looked up to see a security guard rushing toward her. His eyes widened in shock at the scene.

Without taking his eyes off her father, he pulled out a cell phone and dialed 911. Cambry tuned out the conversation as she turned her attention back to her father, a jumble of thoughts ricocheting in her head.

It seemed like an eternity before the distant sound of sirens cut through the lobby. She heard screeching tires and slamming doors just before the lobby erupted with activity. Police officers and paramedics rushed over and immediately started asking questions. Shakily, Cambry answered: Yes, she had found him. No, she didn't know what happened. No, she hadn't seen anybody suspicious leaving the scene.

Her mind screeched to a halt at that one. Suspicious? Hadn't her father simply fallen down the stairs?

For the first time, she noticed the puddle of blood seeping out from beneath her father's dark suit jacket. Surely that couldn't have all come from the cut, though she knew head wounds tended to bleed heavily. Just then she heard one of the paramedics call out something about a gunshot wound. Cambry felt all the blood drain from her face, leaving her feeling light-headed and dazed. Gunshot wound?

It only took seconds for her to put this new information into the equation. The startling sum clearly meant one thing. Her father hadn't fallen down the stairs. He'd been shot.

"Miss? Miss? Are you okay?"

Cambry looked up, the jerky movement causing the officer before her to blur and then sway. The next thing she knew, the officer had lunged toward her and shoved her head between her knees.

"Take deep breaths," he ordered, his grip tight on the back of her neck as he held her in place.

She struggled to do as he instructed, but her lungs felt constricted, every breath painful. It seemed like forever before breathing became easier and the world stopped whirling by at a dizzying speed.

The sound of thundering footsteps drew her attention, and the grip on the back of her neck eased. She looked up to see a crew of EMTs rushing toward them with a gurney. A paramedic dropped to the ground beside her, asking questions and trying to assess her condition. Did she really look so awful that he would think she'd been hurt?

Cambry pushed him away, insisting she was okay. A blanket was thrown around her shoulders, and she watched as the paramedics slipped an oxygen mask over her father's face and applied pressure to his gunshot wound. An IV was hooked up, and he was finally lifted onto a stretcher and wheeled toward the waiting ambulance.

She scrambled to her feet but barely managed to stay upright as the world tilted beneath her. After a steadying breath, her head cleared, and she hurried to her father's side just as they reached the sidewalk.

"I'm his daughter," she said in a voice that sounded weak even to her own ears. "I want to ride with him to the hospital."

The EMT nodded and then helped her into the ambulance. As they sped off toward the hospital, Cambry watched the EMTs continue to work on him, tossing around words and terminology she didn't understand. *Pulse thready. Need to get him stable.* She'd watched enough *Grey's Anatomy* to know that wasn't good.

It seemed like hours before the ambulance finally screeched to a halt in front of the hospital, and the back doors were thrown open. There was a scramble of people as the EMTs jumped out of the vehicle and pulled her father out on his stretcher, barking out instructions. Cambry did her best to keep up as they rushed him toward the ER.

The sliding glass doors whooshed open into chaos, with doctors and nurses swarming toward them like locusts, talking and calling out orders and assessing her father's condition. The smells of disinfectant and day-old coffee assaulted her senses.

The next thing she knew, the doctors had whisked her father through a set of double doors and off to parts unknown. Cambry moved to follow them, but a pretty young woman in scrubs put a hand on her arm to stop her. She was in her early thirties, with thick, light brown hair pulled back in a ponytail that fell almost to her waist.

"I'm sorry, miss, but you can't go in there." Her tone was gentle and sympathetic. "Were you with him when this happened?"

Cambry nodded. "He's my father. I went to his office to see him . . . I don't know what happened. Or who did this."

"I'm so sorry," the woman repeated. "I'm Jaime. Why don't I show you to the waiting room, and I'll let you know how he's doing as soon as we know anything."

Cambry managed a grateful smile and followed the nurse down the hall to the waiting area where several other people sat. She was guided to an empty seat near the far wall, where she sat numbly for a few minutes before a container of juice appeared in her hand. She looked up to see Jaime standing before her with a reassuring smile.

"Drink that," Jaime said. "You look like you could use a little something." Then, after a kind pat on Cambry's shoulder, she headed back to the nurses' station.

She didn't know how long she sat there, staring at nothing and unable to process her jumbled thoughts, when Jaime approached once more with a scrub-dressed woman wearing a stethoscope around her neck. When Jaime introduced the woman as the ER doctor, Cambry straightened.

"How's my father?"

The doctor's face was grim. "The bullet is lodged near his spinal cord, and we rushed him up to surgery. We need to remove the bullet and determine what kind of damage it's done. But you need to know that a lot can happen with a surgery this delicate, and there are definitely risks. The best thing I can tell you to do is to stay positive until we have more information for you."

"How long will he be in surgery?"

"Likely a few hours, and then we'll have a better idea of his prognosis. We'll keep you posted, okay?"

After the doctor hurried away, Jaime gave Cambry's arm a squeeze. "Is there anybody you should call? Your mother? Brothers or sisters?"

Cambry shook her head. "It's just me. My mother passed away several years ago, and I don't have any siblings."

Jaime's brow furrowed. "Is there anybody you could call to come sit with you? A friend, perhaps? Having somebody with you would help make the wait more bearable."

As soon as Jaime suggested it, Cambry latched on to the idea. She needed somebody with her. And she knew exactly who to call. Cambry thanked the woman, and Jaime left her.

Pulling her cell phone from her coat pocket, Cambry hit the first speed dial key. The phone rang once, twice, three times. Then a woman's familiar voice answered.

Cambry's eyes misted with tears of relief. "Janette?"

"Hey, sweetie," came the voice. "What's wrong? You sound upset."

"I'm at the hospital with my father. Somebody shot him . . ."

An audible gasp sounded across the line. "Cambry, no! Is he okay?"

"I don't know. He's in surgery right now, and it's going to be a while." She hesitated. "I was kind of hoping . . ."

"Cambry, you don't even need to ask. Dean and I will be there as soon as we possibly can. Which hospital?"

Cambry gave her the information and then hung up. Glancing at her watch, she sighed and leaned back in her chair, trying to look more relaxed than she felt. It could be a half hour before they got there. She might as well make herself comfortable.

Her gaze moved across the room, taking in the bland walls and standard-issue plastic waiting room chairs. A flat-screen TV, high on the far wall, droned on softly, and an aquarium bubbled quietly in the corner while a few dull, gray fish swam around inside. They did nothing to cheer the heavy atmosphere in the room.

Cambry stared down at her half-finished juice, wondering how she should feel. She didn't feel bereaved or inconsolable. Mostly she just felt . . . numb.

She pondered that for a long time. *Maybe it's just the shock of it*, she reasoned, *of finding him like that. Maybe my brain simply hasn't finished processing everything.*

She sipped some more of the juice, trying not to force herself to feel something she didn't until, about a half hour later, right on schedule, Janette and Dean appeared in the entrance of the waiting room. Dean—six feet tall and wearing faded jeans and an old, stained Henley over his thin, wiry frame—was a remarkable contrast to his curvy, plus-sized, five-foot-four-inch wife—who was impeccably dressed in tan dress slacks and a rich blue blouse. Mismatched in appearance, sure, but their love for each other wasn't.

Janette's startlingly green eyes—an exact match of her son's, which was something Cambry had tried to put out of her mind over the past five years—were warm, vibrant, and assessing. She rarely missed anything, and she didn't miss anything now.

The instant her gaze landed on Cambry, relief and concern swept across her face. She bustled over to Cambry while Dean limped along behind on his bad knee. Janette promptly commandeered the vacant chair beside her and drew Cambry into her arms.

The sense of relief Cambry felt at their presence was immeasurable. Over the years they had become her surrogate parents of sorts, and she knew that with them at her side, she could get through anything.

When Cambry pulled away, she turned to give Dean, who'd slid into the chair on her other side, a grateful smile. "I'm impressed that you almost managed to keep up with your wife in that race across the waiting room. Is she trying to wring every last ounce of usefulness out of your bad knee before it gets replaced next week?"

Dean chuckled and gave her leg a fatherly pat. "You know it. She's a cruel, harsh woman, my Janette."

Janette glowered around Cambry at him. "Oh, stop." Then she turned her attention back to Cambry and began to fuss over her. "Honey, you're about fifteen shades of pale. How's your father? And how are you holding up? Are you okay? Have you had anything to eat?"

"Which question do you want her to answer?" Dean asked his wife with playful recrimination. "Stop firing questions so quickly at the poor girl that she can't answer them."

Cambry smiled. Their loving bantering always made her feel better. "I haven't heard anything since I called you. They said his surgery could take a few hours."

She explained about getting her dad's message and arriving at his building to find him near the stairwell. "I don't know how to feel," Cambry admitted. "You know what happened between me and my father. We haven't spoken in six years. He's in an OR fighting for his life, and I should probably be crying or scared out of my mind or something. But I think I'm just . . . numb. What's wrong with me?"

Janette gave her arm a squeeze. "It's a tough situation, for sure. Don't beat yourself up about not feeling the 'right' thing."

Dean put a gentle hand on her shoulder, his eyes kind. "What can we do to help?"

She gave him a shaky smile. "Just having you here is enough."

"Nonsense." Janette went into take-control mode and got to her feet. "We're here to help, and that's what we're going to do. Why don't I go find out if the nurses have any new information? Then I'm going to see about rounding you up something to eat. You look like you could use some fortifying. I'll be back in a few minutes."

While Janette was gone, she and Dean made small talk, and he didn't say one thing about her father, for which she was eternally grateful. Then Janette bustled back into the waiting room with a wrapped sandwich and a container of milk.

"I checked with the nurses at the nurses' station. They're going to talk with the surgeon and get an update," she said, shoving the food and drink into Cambry's hands and giving her a stern look. "Now eat that right away. If I know you—and I do—you ate a Pop-Tart for breakfast and something fast at your desk for lunch. You need something healthy in you to get you through the next few hours."

Tears rose unbidden in her eyes at Janette's mothering. "Thank you," she said sincerely. "But what about you two?"

"We had an early dinner with Emma and Nick," she said, referring to her daughter and son-in-law. "We're fine."

Cambry devoured the sandwich and downed the milk, not having realized how hungry she was until that moment. She had just finished off her milk when a uniformed police officer appeared in the room with a nurse at his side who pointed in their direction.

Uneasiness raced up Cambry's spine. The officer—a middle-aged man with thinning, dark hair and a world-weary expression—walked toward them, his softly crackling radio drawing the attention of everyone in the room. Cambry felt horribly conspicuous when he stopped in front of her.

"Are you Cambry Saville?" he asked, his voice quiet and discreet.

"Yes. Is something wrong?"

"I'm Officer Miller, from Denver PD." He gestured toward the hallway. "I need to ask you a few questions."

CHAPTER THREE

CAMBRY ROSE TO HER FEET just as Dean reached for her hand. "You want us to come with you?"

She shook her head and attempted a weak smile. "No, that's okay. I'll be right back."

Once in the hall, away from prying eyes—for which Cambry was thankful—the officer told her he needed to get her statement and pulled a worn notebook from his uniform's shirt pocket. She told him what had happened, how she'd found her father in the stairwell, barely conscious. The officer wrote furiously as she spoke, trying to keep up.

"The security guard says he didn't see you come in," he said, referring to his notes. "And we didn't see your name on the sign-in sheet. Why is that?"

She gave the officer a perplexed look. "When I arrived, there wasn't anybody at the desk. I decided just to head up to my father's office."

"And what time was that?"

Thinking back, she said, "About eight fifteen, I think."

One bushy eyebrow lifted. "You think?"

"I didn't check my watch when I arrived. Just when I got off the light rail a block from his building."

He gave her a long look that made her feel uneasy, then he jotted the information down in his notebook.

Cambry shifted her weight from one foot to the other as he continued to write. What was his deal? Why was he asking her these kinds of questions? She didn't know anything about who had done this.

"Did he say anything to you?" His eyes were intent on hers as he waited for her answer, his pen hovering over his notebook. "Like who may have done this to him? Or why?" Cambry suddenly remembered the thumb drive, which she had forgotten in the chaos. Now it seemed to burn a hole in her pocket, as if reminding her of its possible significance. Her father's last words to her had been to not give it to anybody. Why? It was clearly something he was willing to die for. What was on it?

She wasn't about to turn it over to anybody until she knew what it contained and why he was willing to die to protect it. Her father may have been terrible to her, but he was in the hospital undergoing a surgery he may never make it through. If he died, it would have been his dying wish. She couldn't give it to anybody until she knew what it contained that was so important. She owed him that much. As soon as she knew what her father had been talking about, she'd pass it along to the authorities.

Then something else leaped into her mind. "Isaac," she muttered, remembering the name her father had mentioned.

The officer watched her, his expression unreadable. "What?"

"I just remembered, my father said something about somebody named Isaac."

"No last name?"

She shook her head. "Sorry."

He made a disgruntled noise and scribbled on the page. "Anything else?"

"No." She prayed that temporarily withholding information would be a forgivable offense. "I'm sorry I'm not more help."

He flipped his notebook closed with a frown. "I may have more questions later."

Before he could rush off, she asked, "Do you have any leads?"

"Not yet. We questioned the janitor who'd been working on the fifth floor at the time, as well as the other employees still in the building, and nobody in the vicinity saw or heard anything. Not even the security guard at the front desk, who didn't know you were there until he heard you yell for help." He tucked the notebook back into his pocket. "We'll be in touch."

Cambry stared after the officer retreating down the hall, feeling both irritated at the officer's attitude and guilty for (temporarily, she told herself) withholding information that could maybe help the police in their investigation or might at least be relevant.

Hoping she'd made the right decision, she returned to the waiting room where Dean and Janette still sat, looking anxious. She told them the officer had only needed to get her statement, and their expressions relaxed. She purposefully left out the part about the officer being testy. They didn't need to know that. They'd just get all protective, and right now she just wanted to forget about it.

The rest of the evening passed slowly, but Janette and Dean kept her from complete boredom by sharing that day's tales of Jessica, their eighteen-month-old granddaughter, and how everyone was making idiots of themselves getting two-month-old Camille to practice her newly discovered smile on them.

At last, a doctor in scrubs, a mask dangling from his neck and a colorful surgical cap on his head, approached them. "Ms. Saville?"

Cambry nodded and looked up at him anxiously. "Is my father out of surgery?"

"He is. We were able to take the bullet out and repair the damage. Another inch and the bullet would have hit his heart and killed him. He hasn't regained consciousness since being taken to the ICU, and that's causing us some concern."

Janette spoke up. "Has he not regained consciousness because of the anesthetic he was given for the surgery?"

"I don't think so. Usually patients start to come out of it by now, but he hasn't." He turned to Cambry. "I understand you found him. He was talking and conscious when you got there?"

"Yes. But he lost consciousness shortly after that."

The doctor's lips tightened. "We'll monitor him closely for the next few hours and see how he responds. Until then, all we can do is wait."

"Can we see him?"

The doctor directed them to the ICU, where a nurse pointed them to a room a few doors down from the station. Feeling apprehensive, Cambry pushed open the heavy door and led Janette and Dean inside.

Her father was lying motionless in the bed, his eyes closed and his breathing even. Cambry forced herself to cross the distance to his side. She grasped the cold metal bed railing and studied him. He looked pale and frail against the white bed linens, so different from the hardened, domineering man who had so easily pushed her aside and abandoned her and her mother so many years ago.

She looked down at the white tape on the back of his hand that held the IV needle in place, and it brought back a flood of memories. But then it had been on the hand of the mother she had loved, not the father she'd come to despise.

A gentle hand slid onto her shoulder. "You okay?"

Cambry nodded as she glanced up at Janette standing beside her. "I don't know what to do now," she admitted. "Do I stay here with him? Wait for more news?"

"It's up to you, of course," Janette said patiently. "But more than any-thing, I think you could use a little sleep. You've been through a lot tonight.

Why don't we give the doctor our home number, and he can call us first thing in the morning with an update. By then you will have gotten some sleep and will be better able to handle whatever comes next."

Cambry gave her a look of confusion. "Don't you mean that I should give him my cell number?"

Janette shook her head. "No, you're coming home with us tonight. You can borrow some of Emma's old pajamas, and we'll run you home in the morning after a nice, hot breakfast."

"But I don't want to impose," Cambry spoke quietly, the soft tones seeming appropriate in the hospital room. "Could you just drop me off at home tonight?"

Janette gave her a stern look. "Cambry, you know as well as I do that when you're distracted you don't eat and then you get sick. Can you really afford that right now? You need your strength."

Dean chuckled beside her, the sound comforting in the bleakness of the sterile room. "You know better than to argue with her," he said with a twinkle in his brown eyes. "She always gets what she wants. Why not humor her? Besides, when was the last time you had a good home-cooked breakfast and not one of those breakfast burritos from Taco Bell or some such thing on the way to work?"

Cambry had to admit he had a point. She looked back at her father's haggard face with the tubes in his nose and running into his body. There was nothing to be gained by waiting here. And Janette was right—she needed some sleep. She was exhausted. Janette and Dean had to be as well.

"Okay," she finally agreed, taking a step back from the bed. "Let's give the nurses at the ICU station our numbers and get out of here."

***

By the time they pulled into their neighborhood a half hour later, any adrenaline in Cambry's system had vanished. The night's events had taken their toll on her, and she struggled to keep her eyes open.

As they passed her house, she stared at the large, dark, empty home and was suddenly grateful she wasn't staying there alone tonight. Farther down the street, they pulled into the Reeces' driveway. Cambry picked up the cardboard box sitting on the seat next to her—the one an ICU nurse had handed her on their way out that contained the clothes her father had been wearing, his keys, and his wallet—and opened her door.

She picked up her leather messenger bag and balanced the box under one arm as she climbed out and followed Janette and Dean inside. They passed through the mudroom and into the great room, and she took a moment to pause and breathe. No matter what challenges she'd faced over the years, the Reeces' home felt as much an oasis as her own home did, probably because she'd spent half her life there as part of the family.

The spacious two-story home's great room, with its soaring ceilings and tall windows, was decorated with a charming hominess that invited visitors to come in and sit for a while. There were deep leather armchairs and comfortable fabric sofas arranged to define a family living space while separating it from the beautifully crafted kitchen beyond.

Janette set her purse and coat on one of the kitchen barstools before turning to Cambry. "Where would you like to sleep? We're still working on turning Emma's old room into a guest room, so there are stacks of boxes in there. But you could take Ethan's old room or the hide-a-bed in the downstairs den."

"I'll take the den," she said without hesitation.

Janette's brief flash of sympathy let Cambry know the woman understood the quick choice, even after all these years. "The den it is. Let's get clean sheets and blankets from the linen closet."

Cambry set her things down and followed Janette down the hall to the linen closet. "Do you guys need any help packing up Emma's things? I know Dean's not able to do anything strenuous with his knee. Can I help you carry boxes to the storage room or run them over to Emma's house?"

"You're amazing to offer," Janette said, opening the closet, pulling out what she needed, and setting the linens in Cambry's outstretched arms. "Right now, though, *you* are the one who needs the help. Don't give it another thought. We'll get to it when we get to it."

Cambry opened her mouth to argue, but Janette had closed the closet door and bustled back down the hall toward the den before Cambry could even speak. Cambry smiled and shook her head. The woman was a walking cyclone. Always had been.

Cambry hurried after her. When they reached the den, they pulled out the hide-a-bed and started putting the sheets on the mattress.

"This reminds me, I need to change the sheets on Ethan's bed and air out his room before he gets here," Janette said, almost to herself. She opened the flat sheet with a flick of her wrists.

Cambry froze. "Ethan's coming home?"

When Cambry didn't grab her side of the fluttering sheet, Janette looked up and caught Cambry's startled expression. A look of apprehension crossed her face. "I'm sorry. I thought you knew."

Cambry shook her head. "I had dinner with Emma and Nick the other night, and they didn't say anything."

"He's coming to help out when Dean has his knee surgery. He'll be here for about ten days." She frowned and put her fists on her ample hips. "Knowing how protective that daughter of mine is, she probably thought you'd be more upset by the fact that he was coming to visit than the fact that she hadn't bothered to tell you." She studied Cambry for several moments, worry in her eyes. "You're *not* upset, are you? I mean, with what just happened with your father, the last thing I'd want to do is—"

"No, no," she cut off Janette and busied herself by pulling the sheet across the mattress. "Why should it upset me? He is your son, after all. He has every right to visit." She pasted on a smile that she was afraid looked more like a grimace. "I'm glad he's coming. It's been a long time since you've seen him, hasn't it?"

"It has," Janette said. "I'll never understand why he makes such an effort to stay away from his family. I know he's been in Afghanistan and heaven knows where else over the past five years, but he's been out of the forces for almost a year and has been working in Baltimore. Why hasn't he come home to see us?"

Cambry knew it hurt his parents that he didn't visit, but personally, she was glad he stayed away. Things hadn't ended well between them. She wasn't exactly thrilled at the possibility of running into him.

"Baltimore's a long way away too," she offered diplomatically.

Janette snorted. "There are such things as airplanes."

Cambry didn't have a response to that. She kept silent as she finished tucking in the sheet and helping Janette spread the blankets.

"At least we've been able to talk to him on the phone and through e-mails," Janette went on. "Even used that Skype thing. Though without Emma's help, I'd never understand how to use that confounding technology." She chuckled and shook her head. "But it has been nice to at least see him that way. When he said he was planning to take some vacation days and come home to help with Dean's recovery, we were all thrilled."

"I'm thrilled for you too," Cambry said, her tone neutral. The truth was she was glad. For them. As for herself—well, she definitely appreciated the warning. She would stay away while Ethan was home. Far away.

When the bed was made up and Janette had managed to rustle up a T-shirt and an old pair of Emma's pajama pants for Cambry to sleep in, exhaustion was setting in once more.

"Well, I'll leave you to change and settle in for the night," Janette said. "Is there anything else you need? Something to eat before you turn in, maybe?"

Cambry shook her head. "No, I'll be fine, thanks. I'm too tired to eat. I think I'll just crash."

Janette gave her a smile. "I understand. Get a good night's sleep, then, and we'll see you in the morning."

"Good night," Cambry said, giving her a hug. "And thanks for everything tonight. I don't know what I would have done without you and Dean at the hospital."

"We're just glad you called. I would have hated for you to have gone through that alone. Sleep well."

When Cambry was alone, she changed into her borrowed pajamas. Because Emma was a tall and willowy five-foot-ten with an athletic build, the pajama pants dwarfed her both in height and waist. She rolled the hems up several times and pulled the drawstring to cinch the waist. Then she pulled on the T-shirt, which was huge on her tiny frame. She had to smile. She probably looked ridiculous, but it beat sleeping in her work clothes. When she sat down on the edge of the bed, she let her mind consider Janette's news. Ethan was coming home.

The realization created a knot of anxiety in her stomach. Sometimes everything that had happened between her and Ethan seemed an eternity ago; other times it felt like yesterday. It had made things easier that since Ethan had left, he'd never been back. It meant no painful reunions, no awkward conversations. No extra tubs of Ben & Jerry's. It had helped her keep the past in the past, but now it looked like she would actually have to deal with it.

If she had to choose between her surrogate family's support and protecting her heart, her heart won hands down. She would get through this on her own. Once Ethan arrived in town, she would keep her distance.

That decision made, she let her thoughts drift back to her father. A burst of adrenaline shot through her as she remembered his last words to her and the thumb drive he'd given her.

Standing up, she walked over to the coat that she'd draped on the back of the chair and rummaged in the pocket. She pulled out the thumb drive and stared at it for a long moment. What had her father said? Something about a picture of them and a man named Isaac. And what had that been about a password and nickname?

Needing answers, she walked over to the computer on the desk in the corner. Making sure the room's door was shut so the noise wouldn't disturb Janette and Dean, she turned on the computer and heard it hum to life.

She sat in the rolling chair, scooting it up to the desk as she waited for the computer to boot up. When it did, she inserted the thumb drive into the USB slot. She moved the mouse to open the folder to view the contents of the drive. More than a dozen files appeared, as well as several folders.

Seriously? she thought with a frown. *How am I supposed to find whatever my father was mumbling about in this mess?*

It felt like looking for a needle in a haystack, especially when she had no idea what she was supposed to be looking for. She clicked on the first few files, only to find that they were password protected.

Yeah. That's helpful.

She continued clicking on various files, looking at the ones she could open. They seemed to be notes, schematics, and various hypotheses for current or future projects that the scientists from his labs had been working on. Some of the files that she opened, however, seemed to be encrypted, and gibberish filled her screen.

With a frustrated sigh, she'd punch the Back button and move on to the next folder.

The fact that several of the files were password protected and many were encrypted didn't surprise her. Her father's scientific research and development corporation was renowned for the work they did and for the groundbreaking technology they produced. It made sense that whatever work he took home would have security measures to prevent against possible misplacement of the drive or, worse, corporate espionage. R&D was an extremely competitive market and had a history rife with espionage. Her father would have been careless and stupid to transport work without such measures.

When she finished going through the files, she didn't feel any closer to understanding what he'd been trying to tell her. The only thing that seemed out of place was a folder that contained a single image. A photograph of them—of Cambry, her mom, and her father.

It had been taken at their cabin when she was about ten or so. She remembered summer days spent hiking, picnicking, and animal watching, and winters spent snowmobiling and cross-country skiing.

But then her father's corporation had exploded onto the scene with several breakthroughs in microtechnologies that resulted in widespread applications, including energy, transportation, and even space technology.

He became the darling of the R&D and business world, his success being splashed on magazine covers such as *Fortune*, *Newsweek*, and *Forbes*, and his life became all about work.

He became an absentee father—missed Christmases and holidays, and birthdays went by without acknowledgment. If it hadn't been for the Reeces' involvement and support in the things she did, her life would have been all about her and her devoted mom. When her parents finally divorced a few years later, she remembered feeling somewhat relieved because it meant she wasn't subjected to her parents arguing late into the night and the hurt she often saw on her mom's face during that difficult time.

In the years that followed, she could honestly say she and her mom were happier than they'd been in a long time. They'd been inseparable, and her mom had supported and encouraged Cambry in whatever she wanted to do. She'd loved those years when it had been her and her mom against the world.

But then her mom had gotten sick, and Cambry's world had come crashing down. What little had been left of her relationship with her father had been destroyed when he hadn't bothered to show up for his ex-wife's funeral.

Looking once more at the picture, at her mom's laughing eyes and bright smile, Cambry could once again feel the gaping hole her mother's absence had left in her heart. With a weary sigh, she closed the picture file, pulled the thumb drive from the computer, and leaned back in her chair.

What do I do now? she asked herself, dangling the thumb drive from her fingers.

She replayed her father's last words in her mind, but it brought her no closer to figuring out what they meant. He specifically mentioned something about a picture. The cabin picture was the only picture on the drive, so that had to be the one he was referring to. But what significance did an old family snapshot have? Did it have something to do with the fact that he'd been trying to reconcile with her? He'd known how much she'd loved going to the cabin. Was that it?

Maybe. But that didn't explain what he'd been saying about not letting anybody find . . . something. What didn't he want someone to find? And who wasn't she supposed to give it to? And who was Isaac? Something continued to nag at her that the answers were locked in these files.

A sudden burst of inspiration made her sit up and reach for her cell phone. If anybody could get through the passwords and encryptions and tell her what, exactly, was on the drive, it was Alisa.

She and Alisa had met in college, and they'd become fast friends in spite of their career interests—Cambry in research technology, and Alisa in computer science specializing in cyber security. After college, Alisa had been recruited by the CIA to do some kind of hacking work. She'd always said she couldn't talk about it. Security clearances and all that.

After two years with the CIA, Alisa had been in a bad car accident which left her with some rather serious physical problems. Unable to walk without the help of a cane, she'd quit the CIA and come home to Denver to start her own freelance computer security business. Utilizing the contacts she'd made in her two years with the CIA, her business had taken off. Now she had a very healthy bank account and could afford to only take the jobs she wanted.

Her fingers flew across the keypad as she texted Alisa, telling her friend she needed some help with something and asking to stop by in the morning.

It was only seconds before she got a reply. Cambry smiled. Even with it being almost one in the morning, she'd known her friend would be up. She wasn't much for sleeping.

Sure thing. Text me when you're on your way over. I'll make sure I listen for you buzzing at the gate so I can let you in.

Feeling a sense of relief that she'd figured out what to do next, she turned her phone off for the night to preserve the battery until she could charge it when she got home, then she climbed into bed.

She was asleep almost before her head hit the pillow.

***

The sky's inky blackness draped itself like a heavy curtain across the wide-open Texas horizon. It served as a backdrop for the glimmer of landscaping lights curving artfully around the blue waters of the pool, making it a glowing turquoise oasis in the night.

With sure, steady strokes, Isaac Benton propelled himself to the side of the pool. He surfaced, swept his hair back from his face, and then climbed out onto the travertine edging. His cell phone alerted him to an incoming call, and he slung a towel around his neck and sauntered toward the poolside table where the phone sat. He checked the caller ID before answering.

"Do you have it?" he asked in gruff tones.

"I got his thumb drive, but the project isn't on it."

"What?" Isaac's hand tightened around the phone.

"I cornered him in his office and gave him your ultimatum. He told me it was on the thumb drive. He obviously lied."

Isaac swiped the towel across his dripping hair. "Then track him back down, and this time make sure he gives you what I want. Use force, if necessary."

"Well," his man said, stalling. "That's the problem. After I got the drive, we struggled, and the gun went off. The bullet hit him in the chest. Before I could do anything, I heard somebody coming and ran. I checked with a source later and learned that he was taken to the hospital."

"And?"

Pause. "He's in a coma."

"That's just great." Isaac jerked the towel from his head and pitched it onto the table. "You need to get back in there and finish the job. We can't have him waking up and IDing us."

"I thought of that. But the hospital is crawling with security."

Benton clenched his hand around the phone. This wasn't happening. This deal was going to make or break him. Navarro's connections and financial resources were legendary. If this sale went without a hitch, Isaac stood to make a substantial amount of money. Not only that, but future dealings with Navarro and his contacts ensured Isaac a position as one of the premier technology dealers. He would have the money, power, and notoriety he'd always dreamed of, and more. This was the deal of a lifetime. It was going to go down on time or else.

"You get back down to the office and comb through his hard drive. Get me that file *tonight*," he said into the phone. "Do you understand?"

Silence. Then, "That's going to be a problem. There are police all over the building. There's no way I can get in and go through his computer right now."

Isaac closed his eyes and pinched the bridge of his nose, fighting for control. "So give the police the chance to do their thing, then get into his office. And check his home computer. Every workaholic does work at home. It's got to be somewhere."

"And if it's not?"

Losing what was left of his patience, he yelled, "I don't care how you do it, just get it! I need that file!"

Isaac jerked the phone from his ear and thumbed the End button. His aggravated growl met with a response.

"Bad news?"

Isaac looked up to see Garrison standing on the travertine terrace just outside the French doors. His arms hung loosely, almost casually, at his sides. But Benton knew there was nothing casual about Richard Garrison. That's why Benton had wanted him on the team. Benton himself didn't have the stomach for the dark side of this business. Garrison, however, lived for it.

Not a tall man, maybe only five-eleven, Garrison had a thick, burly build and darker skin that hinted at a South American heritage. He'd had his share of run-ins, as the deep scar running from the corner of his mouth almost to his ear attested. His threatening appearance always sent fear through the people he targeted.

He didn't share much of his past or where he'd come from. All Benton knew was that Garrison was a man he wanted on his side. He'd proven his worth over the last couple of years, and Benton now looked to the man as a kind of right-hand man. If it needed done, Garrison was the man to go to. His contacts were endless, his ethics nonexistent. The rest of the team followed without question. Benton didn't know if that was because they were loyal or because they were terrified of him. Whatever the reason, Garrison was the perfect person to have at his side.

"What are you still doing here?" Isaac asked, returning his cell to the table and lowering himself into a chair. "I thought you left a couple of hours ago."

"I was waiting for a call. Trouble?"

Benton nodded, his mouth stretched in a grim line. "The Saville technology. Our man was supposed to get it from Saville one way or another, and he choose 'another.' Now Saville's in a coma, and the technology is nowhere to be found."

The scar at the corner of Garrison's mouth stretched as he frowned. "Do you want me to go in and take care of it?"

"Not yet. Our man's already in place, so we'll give him another day or so. I'm having him check Saville's work and home computers as soon as he can access them. If this guy can't come up with the goods, I want you to get it done. I need that file. I'm meeting with Navarro in a little over a week to sell him the technology, and you know how much we stand to make on this deal."

One corner of Garrison's mouth twitched. Almost a smile. "I know. I have plans for that money."

"So do I." Isaac stood up and finished toweling off what moisture the heat from the Texas night hadn't taken care of. "When we recruited this guy, I had my doubts. But he said he could get it done. Now I'm not so sure."

"Don't worry, boss. If he can't get the file, I will."

A deadly undertone rumbled through the words, and Isaac had no doubt the man would. But he didn't want any unnecessary changes in their plan yet. Only when things veered completely off track would he send Garrison in. Bodies were usually left in his wake. And he didn't want to go there just yet.

Isaac nodded as he headed inside. "I'll keep you posted."

CHAPTER FOUR

CAMBRY WOKE THE NEXT MORNING to find the house still silent. She got up, put the hide-a-bed away, and then crept through the house so she didn't wake anybody. It was only a block to her house, and she could easily walk. She'd let Dean and Janette sleep.

She walked up the wide cement steps of her house a few minutes later and typed in her code on the front door's keypad. The familiar beep told her that her code had been accepted, and she pushed the front door open. A pronounced silence greeted her.

As she shut the door and toed off her pumps, she glanced around the spacious living room to her left. She'd inherited the house upon her mom's death, and she'd remodeled shortly afterwards in an attempt to make the space feel less empty and lonely. She'd redone the floors, putting in hardwood instead of the tile and carpet in the main living areas, and she'd remodeled the kitchen. Everything was shiny and new. She'd also chosen a warm yellow for the walls, jewel-toned throw pillows for the overstuffed leather furniture, and rich burgundies and greens for the rugs covering the hardwood.

Sometimes it worked. Sometimes it didn't.

The quiet was almost palpable as she walked through the two-story entry and into the kitchen beyond. She set her leather messenger bag on the gleaming granite counter and reached for a glass. Then she shuffled across the room, enjoying the feel of the smooth hardwood floor beneath her bare feet. The stainless-steel side-by-side refrigerator was covered in to-do Post-Its and grocery lists.

Ignoring the reminders of things she needed to do, she pulled open the door and reached for the apple juice. She poured herself a tall glass and drank it while standing at the sink, looking out through the window at the flagstone pavers making up the expansive patio and at the lush green lawn.

The quiet moment evoked a surge of doubt and vulnerability. Flashes of her father lying on that gurney and being rushed into the OR, followed by the appearance of a questioning police officer made her frightened about what might come next. She'd never been involved in a police investigation, and the thought of dealing with this alone scared her.

Dean and Janette were there for her. She knew that. All she had to do was ask. But Ethan was coming home. How could she lean on them when their tall, handsome son, whom she'd loved more than life itself, would be there, his presence threatening to rip open old wounds and destroy her heart?

Distance had helped her cope. And cope she had. Whenever times had gotten tough the past few years, she'd reminded herself she was tough. She could handle things. And she could. And did.

But there were times when she was so tired of being capable and responsible, of proving she could handle everything on her own. She'd spent so many years proving to everybody that she could handle anything that somewhere along the way she'd lost a piece of herself. Of her dreams. Of the hope of somebody to love. A family. Children. Laughter and silliness.

Somehow her life had become all about responsibility and sensibility. She'd spent all her time trying to please professors, then bosses, then the people she'd been sent to work with on her contract jobs. She often felt so weighed down by all that responsibility that her dreams had long ago taken a backseat. Now she wasn't sure how she was ever going to find her way back to those again.

Draining the last of the juice, she set her glass on the counter next to the sink and headed upstairs to her room to shower and change.

Forty-five minutes later, she'd texted Alisa to let her know she was on the outskirts of Denver and close to Alisa's house. When she pulled off the freeway, she soon left the subdivisions behind, and the area became less populated and more hilly.

She drove another few miles before she reached a quiet gated community. She typed in the code at the gate, waited for it to swing open, then continued on. She'd always loved this area. Large homes with stately architecture occupied perfectly manicured two- to three-acre lots that were set back farther off the road. She navigated through the maze of tree-lined streets until she reached the end of a quiet cul-de-sac at the rear of the community. The last home was tucked even farther back off the road, all but hidden by carefully planted trees and bushes that softened the presence of an impressive, ornate iron fence that surrounded the front half of the property. Cambry knew the rest of the acreage was protected with electric fencing, lights, and alarms, and that the house itself was wired with state-of-the-art security.

She didn't understand why Alisa felt a need for such thorough security, though she suspected it had something to do with the time her friend had spent working for the CIA. Alisa wouldn't talk about it, and Cambry never pried.

Cambry eased to a stop in front of Alisa's private iron gate decorated with elaborate scrollwork. She rolled down her window and reached out to push the call button beneath the security camera. Moments later she heard Alisa's voice through the speaker. "Hey, Cambry, come on in," she said.

The gates swung open from the middle, and she drove through. The asphalt driveway at the entrance and down the private lane eventually gave way to red pavers that stretched the length of the driveway and led to the classical beauty of the Spanish-style home. Alisa had always been an admirer of the Spanish style, and Cambry had to admit, the architecture was gorgeous.

The large two-story house was designed in perfect symmetry, with arched doorways and windows, small and inviting balconies, curved red roof tiles, and white stucco exterior walls. The courtyard boasted young trees and bushes around its perimeter, lending a relaxing and welcoming feel.

As always seemed to be the case, she spotted two men with rather impressive builds wearing emerald green T-shirts that sported the name of a local landscaping company. They were moving along the paved garden paths with hoses and other gardening equipment, their minds obviously on the tasks.

She smiled and shook her head. If she could ever afford a landscaping company to take care of her yard, she would definitely ask Alisa for the company's number just so she could have guys like that showing up to do the work.

Pulling up to the front walk, Cambry turned her car off and climbed out. She was only halfway up the walk when the door opened, and Alisa appeared in the entrance with a smile.

What Cambry had always thought was hilarious was the fact that nobody ever believed Alisa when she told them she was a freelance computer security specialist. Most people had this preconceived notion about what computer nerds looked like—thick, ugly glasses, pocket protector, mismatched socks . . . Alisa blew all those preconceived notions right out of the water. She was five-ten and slender, with brown eyes and short brown hair cut in a chin-length A-line that framed her face perfectly. But what generally caught people's attention was her outgoing, bubbly personality. She started up conversations with strangers in grocery store lines, was the first to volunteer to be "it" in group games like charades, and loved wearing bright colors that made her stand out in a crowd.

"Hey, Cambry," Alisa called out, her lilting voice almost musical as she took a shuffling step forward with the help of a flashy, bright pink cane with lime green stenciling down its length.

Cambry couldn't help but smile. All Alisa's canes were flashy and made a statement, but she'd never seen this one before. She glanced pointedly at the cane and then back up at Alisa with an arched brow. "New?"

Alisa's grin kicked up a notch. "My physical therapist's teenage daughter is going into design, and she customized it for me. What do you think?"

"Gotta love it." Cambry gave her friend a hug. "How are things?"

"Good. Busy." Alisa closed the door behind them. "I have a new client who wants his stuff last week. He's pretty pushy." She made a wry face.

"Clients like that make me crazy," Cambry sympathized.

"So what do you have for me?" Alisa asked as she led the way through the high-ceilinged living room with its dark wood accents and arched cutouts in the walls, carrying the Spanish architecture throughout the house.

They took a seat on the leather couch in the living area, and Cambry pulled out the thumb drive and held it up. "I have something for you that might be a bit of a challenge."

"Ooh, fun," Alisa said with a smile as she reached for the drive. "A new mystery. Tell me what I'm looking for."

Cambry grinned at her friend's enthusiasm. "There are a few encrypted files on this, and I need to know what they are. Do you think you can do whatever magic you do and find out?"

"Sure," she replied. "Who is it for? One of your clients?"

Cambry hesitated. How much should she tell Alisa? It wasn't like this was stolen, but even so, her father had told her not to give it to anybody. That meant he was worried about somebody in particular acquiring it. Possibly the person who had attacked him in his building last night? And if that's what had happened, the person was probably still looking for it. She didn't want to put Alisa in any danger, but she really needed to know what was on this thumb drive. It would help her know if she should share it with the police.

Deciding to be as honest as she could without getting Alisa in any deeper than necessary, she said, "It's not for one of my clients. It's for me."

Alisa's enthusiasm faded into a look of concern. "What's going on, Cambry? Does this have to do with what happened with your dad?"

Cambry froze. "How did you hear about that?"

"It was all over the news last night and this morning."

"Great," Cambry groaned, rubbing a hand across her forehead. "This whole thing is just such a nightmare." After a moment, she looked back up at her friend. "I don't know if what's on this thumb drive has anything to do with what happened," she admitted, "but I'd like to find out."

"Okay." Alisa gave a concerned nod. "Anything for you, you know that. I'm assuming this means you need it as soon as possible?"

Cambry sighed. "Kind of. But I know you're on a deadline with your client, so I'm not expecting you to drop everything for me. Just as soon as you can get to it would be great."

"I should be able to finish up my project in the next couple of days," Alisa said. "And I'm flying out to Atlanta on Friday night so I can work with their techs over the weekend to get it all set up. I should be back early next week, but I can at least take a quick look while I'm working on the stuff for my client. How long it will take to decrypt, though, will depend on what kind of encryption we're dealing with. It could be hours, days, or weeks. It just depends. But I'll focus on these the second I'm back from Atlanta and do my best to get back to you as quickly as I can."

"Thanks," Cambry said, giving Alisa a hug. "I really appreciate it."

"I wish I could just drop everything and do it now, but this contract—"

"It's okay. You're up against a deadline, and I understand that. I just appreciate your help."

Cambry left a few minutes later, feeling like a load had been lifted off her shoulders. If anybody could find out what those encrypted files were, it was Alisa.

It was a beautiful morning, with only a bit of fall chill, so Cambry opened her Honda's sunroof and let the fresh air wash over her, helping to ease her tension. The traffic moved along smoothly, and before long, she was turning back into her subdivision. She had just made a right-hand turn onto her street when she saw an unfamiliar dark blue sedan in her driveway. As she drew closer, she noticed there were two men sitting inside.

Uneasiness raced up her spine. Who were they and what did they want?

As she pulled into the driveway, she decided against opening the garage door to pull inside. The last thing she wanted was to give these men easy entrance to her home. She needed to find out who they were and what they were doing here first.

As she pulled to a stop beside them, the two men looked up. The dark-haired driver with a bushy mustache gave her an intimidating, steely-eyed stare before climbing out of the car. Her eyes darted around her surroundings, taking note of the activity in the neighborhood. Even though it was a weekday morning, it wasn't deserted. She spotted John, her retired neighbor across the street, mowing his lawn, and his sweet wife, Margaret, standing on the doorstep watching closely.

Their presence was reassuring. She knew all it would take was a scream and the cavalry would come charging.

Cautiously, Cambry opened her door and climbed out. By then both men were out of the car and walking toward her. "Can I help you?" she asked, her voice wavering slightly.

The mustached man who'd glowered at her from the driver's seat looked even more intimidating up close. He stood about six feet tall, had a bit of muscle on him, and looked to be in his early fifties. And he'd clearly perfected that scowl.

"Ms. Saville?" he all but growled. When she nodded, he pulled a badge from his jacket pocket. "Detective Dalton, Denver PD."

Conflicting emotions swept through her at the announcement. On the one hand, there was relief. These men were police officers, not men who'd tried to kill her father and decided to come after her now. On the other hand, the officer who'd introduced himself as Dalton didn't exactly give her a sense of security. He looked downright mean.

Still, they were outside. The fact that they could talk in the driveway with neighbors looking on gave her a little peace of mind. Besides, maybe they had learned something. Could they have even caught the person who'd attacked her father?

She studied the two men, trying to ascertain what might have happened. While Dalton looked intimidating, grouchy, and had a mouth set in a perpetual frown, his Hispanic partner's expression was neutral and made him look more approachable. But the slightly shorter, gentler man wasn't talking. He seemed as uncomfortable with Detective Dalton as she was.

Swallowing her apprehension, she asked, "What can I do for you?"

"We need to bring you to the precinct—ask you some more questions about what happened yesterday." Then he turned on his heel, walked the few paces to his car, and opened the back door for her. He lifted one of the burly eyebrows sitting over turbulent, steel-gray eyes. "Shall we?"

She stared at him in disbelief. She'd already told the officers at the scene everything, and she'd reiterated it for the officer who came to the hospital. What else did they think she knew?

As Detective Dalton stood there holding the door open for her in stoic silence and staring at her reproachfully, she wondered what this guy's problem was. He certainly seemed to have more than just *one* chip on his shoulder. Did he honestly think she was going to submit to him like a meek lamb? She knew her rights. He couldn't push her around.

Feeling a rush of righteous anger, she met Dalton's angry gaze with her own determined one. "I'd rather follow you there in my car, thanks. Which precinct?"

A smile resembling a sneer twitched beneath that bushy mustache. "That's not the plan. We're taking you there in our car."

Her gaze held his in a silent show of stubbornness. After several moments, she realized they were at a stalemate. She turned to look at his more humane partner for help. The other officer's expression held a look of compassion, but he didn't look as if he'd be taking her side. He took step toward her.

"Please, Ms. Saville," he began, his tone unthreatening. "If you could just come with us, it would make everything easier. We just want to ask you some more questions."

Her anxiety and anger softened. *See?* she thought, glaring at Detective Dalton. *Was that so hard? A little kindness could have gotten me in that car a lot sooner.*

She nodded at the partner. "Okay, Detective . . . ?"

"Hernandez."

"I'll come with you," she said, "but I need to pull my car into my garage first." She got back into her car without waiting for a response, then hit the garage door opener and pulled in. Moments later she was walking back to the police car with the garage door closing behind her.

She bit back a triumphant smile as she saw that Dalton hadn't moved from his spot holding the car's rear door open. He looked irritated and put out. At least she'd made the man wait, which clearly peeved him. That was something.

Adjusting her backpack strap on her shoulder, she moved to the open car door. She glanced up to see that Margaret was still standing on the step, watching closely, and John had stopped mowing and was looking on with concern. Cambry waved at them, reassuring them that she was okay. The kind couple returned her wave. It felt good to know somebody had her back.

She slid into the backseat, and they were off moments later. As they left her subdivision and merged with traffic, Cambry couldn't help but wonder what all this was about. What else could they possibly ask her?

Then a shiver went through her. Could this be about the thumb drive? Had they discovered she'd left out that little tidbit? A strained silence filled the car, and Cambry was relieved when they pulled into the precinct's parking lot. The police station was bustling when they walked inside, and more than one set of eyes turned to watch their arrival. Was it just her imagination or did several conversations stop as well?

She turned her head to study the scene, and a prickle of apprehension skittered down her spine. She wasn't imagining things. Several people had stopped to stare and were whispering to each other as they watched her walk past. What on earth was going on?

The detectives led her down a hall and stopped in front of a door with a single slit of a window. Dalton opened it and gestured her in. A table with four chairs sat in the middle of the room, a mirror covered most of one wall, and a single fluorescent light fixture was mounted on the ceiling.

Just then something clicked in her mind. This was an interrogation room. She was about to be interrogated.

CHAPTER FIVE

WITH WIDE EYES, SHE STARED at Detective Dalton. He'd just been handed a file, and when he looked back at her, his mustache twitched, betraying his eagerness.

Fear lodged in her throat, and she struggled to breathe around it. They'd brought her to the station to interrogate her? And Detective Dalton was going to be doing the interrogating?

"Have a seat, Ms. Saville," Detective Dalton ordered.

Cambry's gaze darted over to Detective Hernandez, who stood in the doorway looking both grim and sympathetic. She opened her mouth to plead with him to be the one to ask whatever they needed to ask, but no sound came out. She doubted her request would be honored anyway. Dalton looked like a pit bull with a bone. There was no way he was letting it go.

"Ms. Saville?" Dalton prompted, gesturing to the chair on the far side of the table.

It took every bit of her self-control to walk calmly around the table and sit down. To her dismay, she watched Hernandez discreetly leave the room, pulling the door shut behind him. She glanced over at the wall-length mirror to her left. She had the sneaking suspicion she was not alone. Although, knowing she had to face Dalton's simmering aggression from across the scarred wooden table, the realization was comforting.

She swallowed past the tightness in her throat. "Do I need an attorney present for this?" Like a lion sensing fear, Dalton's eyes gleamed. "If you feel like you want one, Ms. Saville, you're welcome to call one. But you're not under arrest, so you don't need one . . . yet."

That *yet* struck fear into her heart.

Dalton made a big production of pulling out a digital recorder from his pocket, pushing the record button, and setting it on the table between them. Then he started in.

"What do you do for a living, Ms. Saville?"

She answered slowly, measuring her words. "I'm a business executive with Global Technologies."

"And what exactly do you do there?"

"I'm a client solutions director. I'm contracted out to various upstart technology firms around the country to help them set up their R&D labs. I help hire staff, order the necessary equipment . . . basically, get the labs up and running. I help them dot their *i*'s and cross their *t*'s."

"And how does that kind of work pay these days?"

She blinked. "I'm sorry?"

His steely gray eyes stared into her anxious brown ones. Speaking slowly, as if he were talking to a two-year-old, he asked, "Do you make a good living?"

She met his gaze for a long moment, trying to decide where this was going. Finally, she answered. "Yes, it pays well. I'm good at what I do."

"Enough to retire well?" he persisted. "Or do you have a plan B on that ten-year career plan?"

Cambry's brow furrowed. "I'm sorry, I don't understand the question. What exactly are you asking me?"

Like a predator just having lured its prey into its trap, Dalton bared his teeth in an imitation of a smile. He flipped open the file in front of him and lifted the top paper to better read the writing.

"We've done a little nosing around after your father's attack last night, and we've managed to find out something rather interesting," he began. "Apparently, your father recently revised his will. Did you know about that?"

She looked at him in surprise. "No, I didn't know that. My father and I have been estranged for six years. I haven't spoken to him in all that time."

"Well, that's interesting," Dalton drawled, carefully setting the paper back on top of the others, "because we managed to learn that when your father revised his will recently, he named you as sole beneficiary. That means that upon his death, you stand to inherent not only the millions of dollars in his bank accounts, but his properties around the globe, his corporate and personal holdings, and all his patents, potentially worth millions."

Cambry stared at him, dumbfounded. Dalton had to be kidding. Why would her father do that? Wouldn't he have realized she would have turned it all down? Accepting anything from him after what had transpired six years ago would be like waving the proverbial white flag, and she wasn't about to do that.

She met Dalton's predatory gaze with a determined look of her own. "Detective Dalton, I don't know why my father changed his will. He certainly didn't say anything to me."

The detective stared at her long enough that she started to squirm. Finally, he asked, "That kind of money and power would be nice, don't you think?"

She shrugged. "For some people maybe, but I don't need it. I own my house free and clear, I have a manageable car payment, and I don't own any credit cards. And my job pays a nice salary. What would I need all that money for? And I certainly don't have any desire to run my father's companies. I like what I do."

He snorted. "I don't believe that, Ms. Saville. Not for a second. If there's one thing I've learned in this profession, it's that everybody always wants more. Why don't you just come clean and tell me what really happened last night with your father?"

Cambry felt the blood drain from her face. In that moment it became clear what Dalton was after. He thought her father's recently revised will gave her a motive to kill! Compound that with the fact that their past was ugly, followed by a lengthy estrangement, and the fact that she'd been the first at the scene of the crime . . .

"Detective Dalton," she began, feeling nauseated and slightly faint. "I didn't do whatever it is you're implying. My father had been trying to contact me over the past few months for a possible reconciliation, but I didn't have any interest in returning contact. I haven't talked to him, and I certainly didn't know about the will. We may have been estranged, but I have no reason to want my father dead."

Dalton slapped a hand down onto the table, making her jump. "You're not telling me what I want to know, Ms. Saville!" he yelled as he rose to his feet. Bracing himself on his fisted knuckles on the table, he leaned toward her threateningly. "Now, you can make this easy, or I can make it hard. Which would you prefer?"

They were interrupted by the door swinging open, and Detective Hernandez's blessed reappearance. Cambry closed her eyes and let out a slow breath. *Thank heavens.*

"Ms. Saville, I brought you this."

She opened her eyes to see Detective Hernandez holding a container of juice. He walked in and placed it in front of her before retreating to the corner. Cambry reached for it and murmured her thanks. Had the detective been watching from behind the glass and seen how violent Dalton was becoming, or had he been planning on bringing her something to drink all along?

Deciding she didn't care, she opened the container and took a long drink. The sugars gave her a much needed jolt. She finally looked back up at Dalton still hovering over her. "I didn't do anything wrong," she insisted with a vehemence that rang loud and true. "And I've already told you everything I know. You have my statement, so if it's all the same to you, I'd like to go home now."

Dalton's eyes met hers in a silent battle of wills. "I don't think you understand what kind of trouble you're facing here, Ms. Saville. There's no doubt in my mind that you tried to kill your father, and here's how I think it went down. I think you found out about his revised will, realized just how much money you stood to inherit, and decided to take advantage of it. You found out when he would be leaving work, went to his office, and shot him. Isn't that so?"

Tears of panic and frustration welled up in Cambry's eyes. "No, you're wrong! I didn't try to kill my father!"

"I think you did." If possible, Dalton's voice became even lower and more menacing. "Everything points to you, Ms. Saville. There are no other suspects at this point. Only you."

Cambry's heart stopped as her gaze flew to his. "I'm officially a suspect?"

Hernandez moved in, his expression somewhat comforting. "No, Ms. Saville, you haven't been named as a suspect at this point."

Cambry caught the lethal look Dalton shot his partner. Then Dalton turned back to her. "Because we don't have enough yet to arrest you, Ms. Saville, we are only considering you a person of interest. But in my mind, it's only a matter of time before we find out you were behind this. And the second I find out you've been lying to me, that you've had more to do with this than you're saying, I promise you, I will personally throw you behind bars and leave you there to rot for the rest of your life."

Cambry's eyes widened as she looked at the two detectives. Seriously? She was going to remain under intense scrutiny until something else came up in their investigation? *If* something else came up in their investigation. Dalton didn't seem inclined to look any further than her. If he was so convinced she had done it, would he even bother to look anywhere else?

And if her father died, this became a homicide investigation.

The room seemed to close in around her, and she found it difficult to breathe. How could this be happening?

Just then the door opened again, and another man appeared. He was older and had an air of authority about him. When she heard him ask to speak with Detective Dalton immediately, Dalton didn't argue. But he wasn't happy about it. He shoved back from the table and followed the man out into the hall. Hernandez joined them, leaving her alone.

The silence upon their departure was a suffocating one. Before she could let her thoughts wander back to the what-ifs, she was distracted by the sounds of loud arguing—Dalton's angry voice followed by another low, rumbling voice, calm yet resolute. There was more anger, then the sound of someone storming off down the hall. A few moments later, the door opened, and the man reappeared in the doorway.

"Ms. Saville, I'm Chief Mahoney," he said in a low, neutral tone. "That's all we need from you today, so you're free to go. Detective Hernandez can drive you home."

She gave him a shaky nod as she leaned over to pick up her backpack. At least she wouldn't have to face Detective Dalton any more today.

When she stepped out into the hall, Detective Hernandez was waiting for her. They didn't speak as she walked with him back through the building and toward the front doors. She kept her eyes averted to avoid the curious stares she was sure were following her, and tried to block out the whispers. Right now she didn't care what the people in the station did or said. She just wanted out of there.

Not soon enough, Hernandez was helping her into his vehicle and pulling out of the parking lot. Something about her appearance must have concerned Hernandez because he glanced back at her over his shoulder when they stopped at a red light.

"You okay?" he asked, his tone caring.

It was all she could do to nod. If she spoke, she knew the dam holding back her tears would burst. Once she lost it, she doubted she'd be able to stop. Better to see herself safely home first. When they finally pulled into her driveway, the world seemed changed. Life was harsh and loud and ugly, full of menacing accusations and terrifying predictions.

Detective Hernandez let her out of the backseat, and all she could do was nod her thanks as she hurried past him and up the front walk. She didn't wait to see if he was still watching her as she unlocked her door and let herself in. All she wanted to do was put a solid door between them, as if that door would protect her from everything that had just happened.

The tears she'd been working so hard to contain finally started to flow. Leaning back against the door, she slid down until she felt the floor beneath her. Then she wrapped her arms around her legs, buried her face in her knees, and started to sob.

What am I going to do? she thought. *How am I supposed to get myself out of this mess?*

She was going to have to come up with a plan. But what? Her thoughts turned to the thumb drive, now in Alisa's possession. How did that thumb drive play into her current situation?

Detective Dalton's threats were still ringing in her ears. The man was absolutely certain she had tried to kill her father, and there would be no changing his mind. All it would take was one small misstep, one piece of withheld information, and he would pounce.

That fact made her even more determined not to mention the thumb drive to him, or anybody else, for that matter. She didn't dare. She didn't want to give Dalton any reason to think she'd lied to him. He'd love nothing more than an excuse to toss her in jail and throw away the key, and he'd made it no secret that they would be watching her every step, probably questioning her again. Maybe even repeatedly.

He was planning on wearing her down. The problem was she had no confession to give him. She hadn't attacked her father. So where did that leave her? He was going to torment her, stalk her, and beat her down emotionally until she told him what he wanted to hear. How was she going to be able to stand up under that kind of pressure?

Pray. The word came silently yet firmly into her mind, and a measure of peace settled around her heart.

Could it be that simple? She shook her head. Nothing about this situation was simple, but prayer was maybe the only thing that would make it bearable. She'd had enough hard experiences in her life when prayer had seemed to be the only thing that got her through. She had faith that her Heavenly Father knew everything she was going through, and He was there and eager to help her. And if she'd ever needed help, it was now.

Pushing off from her place against the front door, she stood and went upstairs to the sanctuary of her bedroom, where she knelt beside her bed. She prayed with all her heart and soul, pleading with her Heavenly Father to help her get through this and to give her the strength and clarity of mind to handle whatever came. She also asked to be guided and directed to make the right decisions.

Peace settled over her like a comforting blanket, shielding her from the terrifying events of the morning, and her mind started to settle. At that moment the loneliness fled, and a feeling that she wasn't ever alone permeated her soul.

With tears of gratitude, she rose and took a deep breath. It was going to be okay. Somehow. She just had to move forward with faith and wait to be led through this trial.

She only hoped the end would be soon.

***

Isaac Benton was going through his files at his desk when his cell jangled to life. He reached for it. "Yeah."

"It's me," came the gravelly voice.

Benton's interest in the work on his desk vanished. He leaned back in his leather chair and swiveled toward the darkened windows behind him. "Did you get it?"

The man's hesitation gave him his answer.

Tightening his fingers around his phone, he ground out, "Do not tell me you failed. You won't like the consequences."

"We've looked everywhere," his man said. "We searched Saville's computers. Our guy inside searched his office computer, and I searched his home one, but we didn't find anything."

"Great," Benton growled into his phone. "What now?"

"I think we should turn our attention to Saville's daughter like we discussed before. We know he was conscious when she found him. Our source inside the police department confirmed that. I think he told her where the technology is. She's the key."

"Did you share our discovery with the police?" Benton asked.

"I did. The news about the recent change in Saville's will worked perfectly. The police are going after her hard. Motive and all that. I don't think it'll be long before she's scrambling to cover her tracks. If she knows where the technology is, she'll lead us right to it."

"Perfect," Isaac said in clipped tones. "Put round-the-clock surveillance on her. I want to know where she goes and who she talks to. Maybe she'll lead you someplace you haven't thought to look."

"You got it."

CHAPTER SIX

SPECIAL AGENT ETHAN REECE KNOCKED on his supervisor's door. Almost immediately, he heard a booming voice call out, "Come!"

Ethan walked in and spotted his stocky, broad-shouldered, fifty-something boss sitting at his desk, scrawling his signature across a stack of papers.

In the years before Special Agent in Charge Chris Natoni had taken the supervisory position in the FBI Baltimore field office, he had been one of their top agents—gruff, intimidating, and able to see things in a way people didn't. Those skills now benefited him as he directed the agents under him, demanding respect but also giving it when earned.

"You wanted to see me?" Ethan asked, stepping up to the desk.

"Agent Reece. Have a seat." When Ethan did, Natoni went on. "I know you're taking a little time off starting next week. Going home to Denver, right?"

Ethan nodded. "My dad's having knee surgery, so I thought I'd go help out."

"I'm sure he appreciates that." Natoni fell silent, and Ethan saw hesitation dart across his supervisor's face. Ethan had always been good at reading people, and it was clear Natoni had something to say but wasn't sure how to approach it.

Ethan cringed. "I'm not going to like what you have to say, am I?"

A look of amusement lit Natoni's eyes. "Why do you say that?"

"You get that same look every time you're about to assign me to something dicey."

Agent Natoni chuckled. "Nice to know my agents pick up on the little things." Then he sobered. "I'm hoping to have you look into something while you're in Denver."

Ethan barely suppressed a groan. He definitely counted himself as a team player and had set his personal feelings aside for work these past several years, but he wasn't sure he was willing to do that this time. He hadn't been home in five years. He hadn't seen his parents and sister, or even met his two young nieces. This trip was all about trying to mend fences. How was he supposed to do that if he was on assignment?

Natoni picked up on his hesitation. "Look, I know your family is the reason you're going home and that you haven't seen them in a long time, but I wouldn't ask if it wasn't important."

"What's the problem?"

His boss pulled out a folder and slid it across the desk to Ethan. "A threat to national security. Isaac Benton. Showed up on the radar two years ago with ties to several terrorist organizations."

Ethan looked at the picture clipped to the front of the file and felt his mouth firm into a thin line. "I know this guy."

Natoni leaned back in his chair and studied him. "Tell me what you know about him."

"He was one of the higher-ups for International Dynamics—a market leader in aerospace and defense, information systems and technology, and combat systems. The company holds hundreds of military contracts but caters to civilian markets as well. Benton decided to take his contacts and step out on his own, forging alliances with the shadier characters in the field. When he branched out into corporate espionage across international lines and started selling off technology to the highest bidder, my Special Forces counterterrorism unit made him a priority. We went after him on two different occasions. We grabbed several of his men, but we never caught up with Benton himself."

Natoni nodded. "Yes, he's been a hard man to corner. But this time we can't let him slip through our fingers. He's after something in the field of nanotechnology that one of the military's contractors developed. The potential military applications of his discovery are endless—miniature computers and sensors for biological warfare agents that could provide better protection against terrorist attacks, better threat detection and neutralization, and surface and structural coatings for both vehicles and uniforms that could withstand weapon fire.

"The downside is it has weapon applications as well, which is why Benton wants it. There are any number of organizations around the world who would love to get their hands on this. Selling it to the highest bidder would make Benton a very wealthy man. I don't have to tell you that there will be devastating consequences if this technology falls into the wrong hands."

"And Benton's are definitely the wrong hands," Ethan agreed. "His ties to Al-Qaeda make him a dangerous man."

"Exactly. Our intel says Benton contacted the contractor on two occasions last month. We assume he was trying to buy the man off and acquire the technology. Seems this man turned Benton down. But three days ago the contractor was attacked in his office building and left for dead."

"So Benton sent one of his men to get rid of the contractor and simply steal what he wanted," Ethan finished.

"That's a very real possibility." Natoni's expression was grim. "The man survived, but he's in a coma. To make things more complicated, it appears the technology has gone missing."

Ethan lifted an eyebrow. "Missing?"

"We have a man inside another organization who learned that the same night the contractor was attacked, Benton set up a meeting with a buyer. The next day Benton pushed the meeting back, no reason given. Obviously, something went wrong. His man could have stolen the wrong files, or maybe somebody else managed to steal it from Benton.

"We've already talked to the contractor's firm, though we made sure to keep details to a minimum. We told them of our suspicions that somebody attacked their colleague in order to steal their latest technology. We were able to keep terrorism out of it by letting them think this was a violent act of corporate espionage, which is unfortunately common in the competitive field of research and development. They've been cooperative and even did a search for the research on their computer systems, but there's no sign of the technology. That just seems to confirm that Benton's man must have managed to steal the files. Where it is right now is anybody's guess. But there is one other possibility we're pursuing."

"Other than Benton?"

"Or maybe working with Benton. It's hard to say."

Ethan's brow furrowed. "I think you've lost me."

"When we were running down leads," Natoni explained, "we came across something interesting. The contractor has a daughter. Estranged. She still lives in Denver, close enough to her father to keep an ear to the ground, to know what he's working on. She's made a name for herself in a similar field in research technology, so she knows what this kind of groundbreaking technology is worth.

"The day after her father was attacked, some interesting details came to light. Even though they were estranged, her father recently changed his will, not only putting her back in it but naming her as sole beneficiary. She stands to inherit millions—in bank accounts, patents, companies, and international interests. She lives a pretty simple life, and you know as well as I do how motivating that kind of wealth and power can be. It can make people do unspeakable things."

"So you think she somehow found out about this change in his will and tried to kill him?"

"That's what the local police think, but I think there's another possibility. True, she stands to inherit an awful lot of money, but the police don't know about this technology. I think it's possible that this woman found out about her father's technology, stole it, tried to kill him, and is in collaboration with potential international buyers—or possibly with Benton—and is trying to sell it herself. Combine that with the inheritance she stands to get if her father dies, and she'd be more than set for life."

Ethan closed the folder and set it on the desk. "So where do I fit in with all this? Do you want me to investigate the daughter?"

Natoni nodded. "We want you to get close to her and find out what she knows, if she has the technology, and what her intentions are."

Ethan stared at his boss in disbelief. "Look, I'm flattered you think so much of my skills that you'd task me with an assignment this important, especially since I've only been with the FBI for a year. But I was only planning on being in Denver for ten days. How could I possibly get close to this woman and learn anything in that short a time?"

"It should be easier than you think," Natoni said. "According to my sources, you grew up with her. We want you to get back in touch with her while you're there, reestablish a friendship. I understand that you two were close."

"Oh? What's her name?"

"Cambry Saville."

Ethan felt a chill move down his spine. Knew her? He'd almost married her. And she still haunted his dreams to this day.

When he'd recovered from his initial shock, Ethan said, "We *were* close. We grew up together, practically lived at each other's houses. But we"—he searched for a nicer way to spin it—"parted ways after my brother was killed in Afghanistan five years ago. We haven't spoken since."

"I understand it won't be easy, but you're smart and intuitive. Besides, you already know her, which makes you the perfect man for the job. It would take another agent too long to try to get close to her and learn what we need to know. In our search, she's a great first place to look. We need to know if she has the technology, or knows where it is, and if she tried to kill her father and is planning to sell it to the highest bidder. Ms. Saville could be behind everything."

"She's not," Ethan insisted. "She's not that kind of person."

His boss leveled him with a look. "You said yourself that you haven't spoken with her in years. Is it possible that she's not the same woman you knew all those years ago?"

Ethan hesitated. It was true that he hadn't known her in a long time. Did he know for sure she wouldn't do this?

But his parents knew her. Trusted her. Loved her like a daughter. In the sparse communication he'd had with his family over the years since he joined the marines, that was one thing that came through loud and clear. She was considered family.

Natoni went on. "The local law enforcement has been notified about our jurisdiction over this case, so they've turned the investigation over to us with a promise of continued cooperation should we need it. The detective on the case—Dalton—is a real piece of work though. He wasn't about to give up this case without a fight. There's no doubt in his mind that Ms. Saville tried to kill her father. To him, she had the motive and was even at the scene, which makes this is an open and shut case."

Ethan frowned. "So much for innocent until proven guilty."

"Yeah. Like I said, the guy's really something."

"Do you really think she could have the technology?"

"When we sent two of our Denver agents to talk to her two days after her father's attack, she seemed genuinely surprised to hear that her father was working on nanotechnology for the military. They asked her if she knew anything about his work, but she assured them she didn't."

"And they don't believe her?"

Natoni hesitated. "They're not certain. They said it was impossible to get a good read on her because that local detective has her so rattled. They couldn't tell if she was nervous because she was hiding something or because that jerk of a detective has been breathing down her neck. From what I understand, he threatened her within an inch of her life and continues to hound her, even though jurisdiction has been turned over to us. He's so convinced she killed her father that he's refusing to look for other suspects."

"That's not going to help her confide in us."

"You're right. She did admit that her father had been trying to contact her recently about a possible reconciliation. Apparently, he e-mailed her through her company account once or twice in past weeks, but she deleted them unopened. When the agents told her to see if those e-mails could be retrieved and asked her to check for possible e-mail attachments that could have contained the research, she seemed willing enough to look.

"The truth is, that detective did such a number on her that it's possible she'd be too scared to tell us even if she *did* turn up anything, for fear of repercussions from that bloodthirsty cop. We need to go about this a different way. I don't think she's going to confide in our agents. Having somebody she knows get close to her to find out what she knows or what her intentions are could make all the difference. That's where you come in."

"You want me to betray my friend," he said, feeling grim.

Natoni shook his head. "I'm not asking you to betray anyone. I just want to know if she's a lead to pursue. Just be a concerned friend. Maybe she'll talk to you. Ms. Saville told police that when she found her father in his building, he was still conscious and talking. Maybe he told her where the technology is. If she knows, *we* need to know. We have a race on our hands. The person who gets to it first wins. And if Ms. Saville *is* innocent, we need her on our side."

Ethan leaned forward to rest his forearms on his knees as he contemplated what Agent Natoni was asking. It seemed cut and dried, but it wasn't. After the way he'd left Cambry all those years ago, she wasn't likely to be happy to see him. And while Natoni didn't consider it a betrayal, it came dangerously close to one in his own mind.

The actual undercover investigation was pretty easy considering some of the others he'd been involved with. The end results of this one, though, were much more critical. They were talking terrorists and connections to Al-Qaeda. He wasn't happy about the circumstances, but he finally found himself nodding.

"I'll do it."

Natoni smiled. "Good. You're scheduled to leave Monday, right?" When Ethan nodded, he said, "The bureau will be reimbursing you the cost of your plane ticket, and a rental car will be waiting for you at Denver International. And I'm extending your vacation time in exchange for your help."

That perked up Ethan's spirits. "How long?"

Natoni smiled. "Depends on how good a job you do. Consider it extra incentive."

"Right."

"Check in when you get there, and I expect daily phone reports. We need to stay up to speed."

"Understood."

After going over a few more details, Ethan left the office to go back to his own. It was Friday, and he needed to finish his paperwork that afternoon before leaving for Denver on Monday.

After finishing up for the day, he left the office. The hint of an early fall clung to Baltimore's air as he left the office. After years spent abroad in desolate places like Iraq and Afghanistan, Maryland's beauty was like heaven. He loved Baltimore's history, charm, and beauty, but the idea of enjoying fall in the Rocky Mountains got his blood pumping. There was nothing quite like the majestic, rugged beauty of the Rockies, and he could hardly wait to be back home.

Even though it came with complications.

He let out a weary sigh. This visit home was hardly going to be a vacation. It was all about righting wrongs. He wanted to somehow prove that he was sincere in his desire to be back in his family's lives. And to be honest, he wasn't sure how one went about that.

When he reached his car, he climbed in and steered out into the early evening commuting traffic. It would take him a while to get home, and that gave him plenty of time to think—something he really needed to do. He needed a plan.

How *did* a person rejoin his or her family after disappearing from their lives for five years? Did he just show back up and pretend nothing had happened? Did Hallmark make a card for that? With possibly some prodigal son reference?

His sudden disappearance from their lives had hurt them, probably more than he could imagine. His parents, his sister . . . And especially Cambry.

He'd tried to justify his actions to himself over the years, mostly to assuage his own guilt. He supposed that if he'd explained his reason for leaving, Cambry and his family might have understood. But at the news of his older brother's death in Afghanistan, he'd been so lost and heartsick and in a cloud of grief so black that he'd been oblivious to everyone but himself. The roadside IED had killed not only the brother he had worshipped but an entire platoon of soldiers who Ethan had come to know as friends through his brother's e-mails and video calls.

Blind to all else, Ethan had rushed off and enlisted the very next day, set on revenge against the terrorists who'd killed not only his brother and his brother's friends but the hundreds of thousands of others who had died in the war against terrorism.

It hadn't taken him long to realize he'd rushed in blindly, foolishly. He'd found himself in basic training that felt anything but basic, in sweltering heat, covered by insects, and being yelled at and challenged by drill sergeants with chips on their shoulders. As he lay in bed one night, exhausted and battered both physically and emotionally, reality hit. What had he done, and how had he gotten there?

After a brutal stint with his combat unit in Iraq, he'd found his way into a Special Forces counterterrorism unit. There he'd started forming bonds and feeling like he was making a difference. His years in the marines had been life altering, mostly for the better. He wouldn't trade those years for anything. But that fact still didn't assuage his guilt for how those years had come to be. The cause was good, but the price had been too high. He hardly knew his family anymore. He had two little nieces he had never seen in person. And he'd lost the woman he'd loved almost his entire life.

From the time they were little kids, her four and him five, they had been best friends. He didn't have a single childhood memory that didn't have her in it. She was a part of him, and he'd just up and left her. He'd said good-bye in a note consisting of three meager lines. He still felt like a monster.

He'd shattered her heart, and he knew he would never forgive himself for that. What was worse, he still loved her.

He shook his head. He was glad his boss didn't know the whole story. Sure, Natoni had been able to find out they'd been close. But he obviously hadn't known they had been only a ring-shopping trip away from being officially engaged. If Agent Natoni had known, he might have balked at the idea of sending Ethan in undercover. Objectivity was something Natoni valued highly, and Ethan wasn't sure if he could stay objective on this one. It could get messy.

Natoni had said the local police were looking at her as a person of interest in the case, but the thought turned his stomach. Cambry was kind and sensitive and had a huge heart. This had to be killing her. He couldn't imagine her breaking the law or doing something as terrible as trying to kill her father for his inheritance. True, he hadn't spoken to her in years, but people didn't change that much over the course of five years. Did they?

What really bothered him was that he'd planned to get in touch with her while he was home, to try to make amends and see if they could at least be friends again. The fact that the decision had been taken out of his hands made him slightly ill. He wanted to make amends for *himself*, not because the FBI had told him to. Something about that seemed inherently wrong. It felt like a blatant betrayal.

But this was his job. He'd joined the FBI knowing there would be cases he'd be working on that were less than ideal. This was just going to have to be one of them.

Drawing a deep breath to fortify his resolve, he decided he would do what he had to do. Natoni had entrusted him with this, and he would do his best not to let the bureau down. No matter how messy it got.

CHAPTER SEVEN

CAMBRY WAS GETTING READY FOR work Monday morning when her doorbell rang. Wary about who was stopping by so early, she went to the front door and peered cautiously through the peephole. Relief flooded through her when she saw that it was Emma.

She opened the door and smiled at her friend's rumpled appearance—stained sweats, bulky jacket, no makeup, and her shoulder-length brown hair pulled up into a messy bun. She was Ethan's twin sister, and the resemblance was obvious. It had often made it harder to get over Ethan when she had to stare into shockingly green eyes so like his.

"Hey," Emma breathed as she hurried inside, shoving a warm, foil-covered plate into Cambry's hands. "Cinnamon rolls. I know how much you love my homemade ones. They're fresh out of the oven."

Cambry looked back up at Emma with a lifted eyebrow. "You've been up baking? It's seven o'clock. Shouldn't you still be asleep from that eight-week-old baby keeping you up all night?"

Emma grimaced. "Yeah. About that. Camille woke me up at four thirty this morning and refused to go back to sleep. So I put her in the baby swing in the kitchen and made cinnamon rolls. And since you aren't answering anybody's calls," she said pointedly, "I decided to leave the kids with Nick and just bring some over. I figured you'd answer the door, even if you won't take my calls."

Cambry shifted uncomfortably as guilt crept in. It was true. She'd been avoiding Emma, Dean, and Janette like the plague.

She opened her mouth to apologize, but Emma gave her a quick once over and scowled. "You look terrible."

That made Cambry feel even worse. Unfortunately, she couldn't blame her friend for telling the truth. She'd looked into the mirror this morning and seen the same thing Emma had—the dark shadows under her eyes, weariness etched into her features, and a few pounds lost in spite of the fact that she hadn't gone to the gym in days. Severe stress did that to a person.

"Gee, thanks," Cambry drawled, trying not to sound as hurt as she felt.

Emma's tone softened. "How's your father?"

"The same." Cambry shrugged. "No change. The doctor says that's good though. He's holding his own."

"Good." Emma studied Cambry for a long moment. "How come you're not answering my calls?"

Cambry did her best not to squirm. "I'm sorry. I've been . . . busy."

"Busy working? Or busy hiding?"

Leave it to Emma to get to the heart of the matter.

"Friends are supposed to be there for each other in times of need. But you won't let me."

Cambry sighed. "Emma, please don't take it personally. It's just . . . this is how I've been coping. It's been really hard, especially when I see things about it on the news and hear my name mentioned as a 'person of interest.' I can feel everybody staring at me when I go to work or church or even to the store. Do you have any idea how awkward that is?"

Emma stepped forward and drew her into a hug. "I'm sure it must be. But those of us who know you know that you're completely innocent."

The sympathy in Emma's voice soothed some of the anxiety and stress that had been a constant companion over the past several days. "Thanks."

When Emma released her, she fixed Cambry with a look. "Cambry, you need help. Why won't you let us do more for you? Mom says you haven't returned her calls either. Or accepted her dinner invitations. She thinks you're avoiding her. She says the few times you've talked, you tell her you're fine. But you're not fine. You're clearly not eating or sleeping, and I'm willing to bet you've stopped answering the door whenever somebody comes over." At Cambry's guilty look, Emma smiled wryly. "I know you too well, don't I?"

"Maybe," she admitted grudgingly. "But can you blame me? The situation is out of control."

"Did you talk with that attorney friend of your dad's? About whether you need a lawyer?"

"I did. He said that because I was only a person of interest in the case and not a suspect, I don't need an attorney yet. In fact, hiring one might work against me and make me look guilty. But he said if the police decide to question me again and I feel uncomfortable, or if I get named as a suspect in the case, I should call him immediately."

"Well, that's something good, right? That things aren't even bad enough that you need to hire an attorney?"

"I guess," Cambry said, "but now I have two FBI agents asking me questions, and a camera crew from a local news station has been camped outside my house for three days. I'm not sure I can handle much more of this."

"I know. That's why you need our help."

Cambry rubbed her aching temples. "You're right. I know that. But I just can't be around you guys right now."

Emma's gaze narrowed. "And why is that, exactly?"

Shifting uncomfortably, Cambry hesitated. "Your mom mentioned last week that Ethan was coming home."

Emma's eyebrows shot up. "So you've avoided me and my mom and dad—the people you need most right now—because my brother is coming to visit?"

"It's *Ethan*."

"And?"

"And . . . we were going to get married. I loved him more than anything. And then he broke up with me. In a *note*. I know it was years ago, but a lot of the hurt and anger is still there. I don't want to see him."

"But what about what you need?" Emma asked, her tone gentle. "I understand why you don't want anything to do with Ethan. I do. Yes, he's my twin and I love him, but he deserves to be hung over a pit of fire ants in the hot sun for what he did to you."

The corner of Cambry's mouth twitched. "Nice image."

"And not that it's an excuse," Emma went on, "but Adam's death really hit him hard, harder than even Mom and Dad. He was acting irrationally. Ultimately, I'm hoping you can get past that, Cambry, because frankly, you need us. For all intents and purposes, we're your family. Let us help you. Just ignore my stupid brother if he shows up when you're around."

"I don't know . . ." she hedged.

"Don't say no," Emma said firmly. "And tell me you'll come to dinner tomorrow night. Dad's anxious about his surgery on Wednesday, so we're having a family dinner to help take his mind off things. Mom said to tell you that you don't have to bring anything except yourself."

When it came to Dean, Cambry knew she couldn't say no. Dean had done so much for her over the years that she couldn't *not* return the favor. "Okay, I'll be there," Cambry agreed reluctantly.

"Thank you," Emma said sincerely, squeezing Cambry's hand. "Now I'd better let you finish getting ready for work."

After another hug at the door, Emma left, and Cambry went back into the kitchen to snatch one of the warm cinnamon rolls off the plate. Just as she sank her teeth into the warm, doughy mixture, her cell phone rang. She pulled it out of her skirt pocket and checked the caller ID. To her surprise, *Saville Enterprises* flashed on the screen. Who would be calling from her father's company?

"Cambry, this is Jim Stafford." The pleasant voice came across the line when she answered. "It's been a long time."

"Jim," she said in surprise. "How nice to hear from you."

She'd always liked her father's business partner. It had always puzzled her, though, how a genuinely nice man like Jim Stafford had put up with such a leech like her father. They had been in the research field together when her father had started the company, and he'd brought Jim on as senior vice president and managing partner from the get-go.

She'd gotten to know Jim and his sweet wife, Leslie, during her middle and high school years, and she'd come to think of him as her honorary uncle during that time. He was fun and easygoing, and she'd loved having him as one of her mentors during her internship at the company in high school. Sadly, she hadn't had much contact with him or his wife since her mother's funeral.

"I'm sorry about your father," Jim said, his voice sober, "and for what you must be going through right now. How are you doing?"

"I'm okay," she said after a moment's hesitation. "You know me—tough as nails."

He chuckled. "Hey, listen. I have something I'd like to talk to you about. Do you have some time today to come to my office?"

The question surprised her. "I could come in now before I head to work," she said.

"That'd be great. See you in a few minutes."

Cambry hung up, then set about gathering up her things. She put everything in her leather messenger bag, grabbed her keys, and headed for the garage. As she backed her car out, she looked up and down the street warily. Ever since her father's attack, news crews had camped outside her house, and news footage and pictures of her had become so widely used that people often recognized her in public. Mostly people just stared, but a few people went as far as calling her names and telling her they hoped she rotted in prison.

Lovely.

And then there was Detective Dalton, who was still stalking her like a lion waiting to pounce. She'd spotted him sitting in his car on several different occasions, parked across the street from her house or at her office, watching her. How could Emma possibly blame her for hiding away inside her house?

At least the FBI agents she'd talked to a couple different times were less threatening. Yeah, it was intimidating to talk to federal agents, but it was different. With them, she didn't feel like she was being ruthlessly hunted.

She'd been surprised to hear from them that her father had been working on nanotechnology for the military, but obviously there was a lot she didn't know about him these days. The fact that somebody was going after him for his technology made her uneasy. It made sense of the attack; it wasn't just some random act of violence.

She was more anxious than ever to find out if the missing technology the FBI was looking for—and that somebody had attacked her father for—was on the thumb drive her father had given her. Was that what he'd been talking about? Warning her not to give to anybody?

Alisa should be back from Atlanta now, and Cambry hoped her friend would be able to solve that question before life went any more downhill. If there was nothing of importance on the drive, there was no harm, no foul. But if there *was* something there, what then? The FBI was searching for her father's missing research. Did she turn it over to them just like that?

The truth of it was, she was still too scared to say anything to the FBI—or anybody else, for that matter—about the thumb drive, even if she did find something important on it. She didn't know how the law worked. If she confessed to the FBI that her father had given her the thumb drive, would they be required to share that info with Detective Dalton? Would he then arrest her and throw her in jail for withholding evidence or something? It was definitely something Dalton would see as a deception. That would be all it would take to drive that final nail in her coffin.

Turning on some soothing music to try to ease her tension, she settled back in her seat and tried to relax on the drive into the city. The drive downtown took longer than usual, with the morning traffic backed up, but finally she pulled into the parking lot behind Saville Enterprises. As she stepped out of her car, she stared up at the tall building that she hadn't seen since her father's attack the previous week. She wasn't sure she was prepared to be back inside, but for better or for worse, here she was.

As she started for the doors, a sudden feeling of being watched set her pulse skittering.

She looked around the parking lot, but the parked cars were all empty, and nobody was walking past. Trying to shrug off the feeling, she continued on her way with quick steps and was soon stepping through the glass doors into the lobby. She paused and looked back outside, but she still didn't see anything.

"Miss Saville?"

The voice made her whirl. She felt a little sheepish when she spotted the stocky security guard standing behind the reception desk.

"Everything okay?" he asked with a lifted eyebrow.

She forced a smile onto her face. "Yes. Sorry. I'm here to see—"

"Mr. Stafford," he finished for her with a kind smile. "Yes, I know. Mr. Stafford instructed me to send you up as soon as you arrived."

"Thank you." She returned his smile and then headed across the lobby to the elevators. She reached the fifth floor before she was ready. The moment she stepped out into the reception area, eyes turned her way. Feeling self-conscious, she forced herself to ignore the curious stares and continue on down the corridor to the right.

As she turned the corner leading to the management wing, her thoughts shifted from the stares to whatever it was Jim wanted to talk to her about. She hoped it wasn't anything bad. She didn't need any more stress right now.

Offering up a prayer that she would have the strength to handle whatever was coming next, she approached his office.

***

"She just went inside the building," the man reported into the cell phone pressed against his ear. He rolled down the car's window and let the cool morning air brush past him. "What do you want me to do?"

"Stay there." Isaac Benton's voice rumbled across the line. "Our eyes inside can take over. But when she leaves the building, I want a full report of where she goes and what she does. Every single move. Understand?"

"Understood."

When the call disconnected, the man turned off his car's engine and sat back to wait.

CHAPTER EIGHT

"You want me to do *what?*"

Cambry stared in disbelief at Jim sitting across the desk. He was still as tall and broad shouldered as she remembered, now carrying a few extra pounds and his light brown hair thinning a bit. His brown eyes were still kind, but they stared back at her without a hint of the good-natured teasing she remembered him for. He was serious.

"We would like to offer you a job as chief operations officer," he repeated. "As such, you would monitor the daily operations of the company and report to the board of directors—"

"I *know* what a COO does," Cambry cut him off. "What I don't understand is why you're asking *me*. You know what happened between my father and me."

Jim leaned back in his chair. "Cambry, I know this is a shock, but I want you to hear me out, okay?"

After a moment, she nodded.

"Your father has changed, Cambry," he said, his tone solemn. "In the years since your mother's death, especially the past couple of years, he's really been struggling. He started to realize that by burying himself in his work and putting all his focus on success and money, he'd not only lost your mother, but he'd lost you. That's when he started making an effort to change. He recommitted himself to the things that are important and has worked to set better priorities. He started going back to church, and the idea of family really started to become important to him again. That's why he's been trying to reconnect with you."

His eyes became soft, his expression gentle. "He wanted to make amends, Cambry. He wanted to be a part of your life again."

"And I wouldn't let him."

He nodded. "And he understood why and didn't blame you. But that didn't stop him from trying. He knew he'd been terrible to your mom—and to you. But he wanted a second chance." He paused. "Now this has happened. I really hope he pulls out of it so you can both have that second chance—for both your sakes."

Cambry remained motionless in her chair, trying to decide how to feel about this new insight into her father's life over the past few years. She could understand how life could alter one's perspectives and priorities, but he'd hurt her so much. And he had hurt her mother. How could she possibly forgive him for all the horrible things he'd done?

Jim hurried on, his tone persuasive. "We recently had our longtime COO retire, and we haven't yet hired a replacement. Your father had been seeing to the job until we found the right person. Between you and me, I think he was holding out for reconciliation so he could convince you to take the position. He's talked about you and your skills for years. He really wanted you on board."

"He did?" Cambry asked skeptically.

Jim smiled. "He did."

Cambry's mind whirled back to those days she'd interned with the company. She remembered her father boasting to his colleagues about her full-ride scholarship to Northwestern and how she was going to set the business world on its ear. She'd also heard him brag to a visiting dignitary that he was going to snatch her up after her master's program and make her a partner at the company since he knew her "outside the box thinking" would revolutionize the company. At the time, she'd written it off as him just trying to get back in her good graces after her parents' divorce. But maybe there'd been more to it than that.

"But what about the board of directors?" she asked. "A decision like this would have to be approved by them."

"They've already approved the idea," he told her. "Your advanced business degree and your specialty in the field make you more than qualified to take this position, more so than most candidates that would apply. Plus, they knew your dad wanted this in the long run. They just saw this as an opportunity to have you step up sooner. You have your own unique talents and qualifications that could really help this company, Cambry, and I know your father saw that too. He always said you were capable of great things."

She blinked in surprise. Her father had said that?

"You know by now about your father's will," he went on, "giving you controlling interest of his company in the event of his death. And this may be entirely premature since I hold every hope he'll pull through this, but I know your father, and I know his wishes. He would want you to keep his company and be personally involved by overseeing things. I know you've been estranged, but he wanted that to change."

"It's a lot to think about—" she began.

"We're offering a great salary and benefits package," Jim interrupted, sliding a large packet across the table to her.

Curious, she picked it up and pulled out the contents. The figures proposed nearly made her gasp. The salary was almost double what she was making at her current job. She was sure the benefits package would be just as tempting.

Eager to drive the deal home, Jim continued. "Look, Cambry, I know this isn't an easy decision. You're dealing with a lot right now, with your father in the hospital and the police investigation, but keep in mind that this could be a great career opportunity for you. I bet somewhere on that ten-year career plan of yours, COO is on the list?"

Cambry knew Jim was right—this was something she'd hoped for someday. She just hadn't planned on it being with her father's company.

"I can tell you have a lot to think about," Jim interrupted her thoughts, his tone gentle. "Why don't you sleep on it? But please let me know your decision as soon as possible. We've been without a COO for a couple of months, and now that your father hasn't been able to fill in, things are really piling up. If you decide you don't want to do this, we need to start interviewing people, maybe even as early as tomorrow."

Cambry's mouth dropped open in surprise. He needed an answer in the next twenty-four hours? How could she possibly make a decision of this magnitude so quickly?

Jim reached for a business card on the corner of his desk and scribbled across the back of it. "Here's my cell number. Just let me know what you decide."

She nodded and was about to get out of her chair when something else occurred to her. "Can I ask you about something else?"

"Anything."

"I had a couple of FBI agents talk to me last week about some missing nanotechnology my father developed. Have they been by to talk to you too?"

"They have," he said. "We've been going through our computer systems searching for your father's missing research, but we can't find it. Our contract date for the project was up a couple of weeks ago, and we've been anxious to deliver it to our liaison. But it sounds like whoever attacked your father was looking for it too. They must have found it."

Silence fell over the room as they considered that. Then Cambry got to her feet. "Well, I'd better head into my office. I'll think about your offer and call you as soon as I've decided."

"Please do. And if there's anything at all my wife or I can do for you, please ask."

She gave him a grateful smile. "Thanks."

She left the office in a daze and stepped out into the fall sunshine. As she went about her tasks at work, Cambry couldn't stop thinking of the pros and cons of the job offer. Five o'clock rolled around, and for once, Cambry didn't work late. She packed up her things and got into her car, where she put on her Bluetooth headset and phoned Emma. Emma had always been her sounding board, and right then she needed just that.

She told Emma about Jim's offer to take the COO position at her father's company and that she was considering it. Emma asked pointed questions and helped her go through the pros and cons. By the time she'd finished talking with Emma, she felt more calm and objective. It made her realize that the decision needed to be made with her head and not her heart. If her father hadn't been involved, would she have taken the job?

Definitely, she realized. The company was stable and profitable, the employees were top-notch, and the salary and benefits were great. All of those factors were slotted nicely in her *pros* column. The only thing in her *cons* column, Emma helped her to see, was the fact that it was her father's company. And maybe it sounded callous, but her father didn't even work into the equation at the moment. She had time to settle in with the company and establish herself right now without that dynamic. She had every hope that her father would recover and that she'd get to see this supposed changed man Jim had claimed him to be. That alone might make it worth sticking around.

When she reached her turnoff, she signaled then glanced over her shoulder at her blind spot. As she did, a familiar car pulled into the exit lane behind her. She frowned. Wasn't that the car she'd seen parked outside of her office today?

She knew there were a lot of black cars on the road, but she distinctly remembered admiring this foreign import's smooth black paint and gleaming chrome as she'd walked across the parking lot to get into her car.

Funny thing was, now that she thought about it, she remembered seeing movement in the driver's seat behind those darkly tinted windows.

She hadn't thought anything of it at the time, but now, seeing what appeared to be the same car behind her, her nerve endings tingled.

Why would somebody be following her?

She continued to glance up into her rearview mirror as she pulled off the highway. Her alarm grew when she turned right and then left into her subdivision, and the black car continued to follow her. When she turned onto her street, she held her breath and watched in the mirror.

The car drove past.

Her body sagged with relief. She shook her head, scolding herself for letting her imagination run away with her. Once she was safely in her garage with the door closed behind her, she let her head to fall back onto the headrest.

She needed a vacation. Or a less stressful life.

Gathering up her things, she climbed out of the car and went inside. She walked into the kitchen, dropped her bag onto the end stool, and opened the freezer. She took out one of the TV dinners and popped it in the microwave.

While it cooked, she went upstairs to change. She pulled on her most comfortable pair of jeans and an old, soft, pink T-shirt that hugged her small figure. Emma always laughed when she wore the combination because she said it made Cambry look twelve years old.

Cambry smiled wryly. Oh, to be twelve again and not have to face adult problems.

She let her hair down from the French twist and brushed it until the loose curls fell tangle-free down her back. When she heard the microwave timer beep, she went back downstairs to eat. As she sat down at the table, she offered a blessing on her food and asked if her decision to accept the position was the right one. She closed her prayer and then ate in silence as she continued to contemplate the decision.

As the evening wore on, she continued to feel increasingly better about the COO position until she decided to take Jim up on it. Really, it was the opportunity of a lifetime. She'd be crazy not to jump at it.

Knowing Jim was in a hurry to get somebody in place, she fished out his business card and dialed his cell. He answered on the second ring. When she told him that she would take the position, he was thrilled.

"You won't regret this, Cambry. I promise."

He went on to ask her if there was any way she could start tomorrow, even for a half day, and she told him she could. She'd go into her office in the morning to talk to her boss and tell him that she was resigning.

She had a ridiculous amount of vacation time coming, and she knew it wouldn't be too big a problem to farm out her current client list to other directors while they hired her replacement.

She could hear the smile in Jim's voice as she told him she'd see him tomorrow afternoon, and Cambry hung up feeling like she'd made the right decision.

Deciding she wanted to celebrate, she went to the freezer. This definitely called for ice cream. She opened the freezer, and her eyes widened in dismay. While she had plenty of TV dinners, it looked like her ice cream stash was gone. It was no wonder, after the week she'd had.

For long moments she stood in the middle of the kitchen and deliberated. The thought of running to the store and having people staring at her was almost enough to produce an anxiety attack. But what was she supposed to do? Refuse to grocery shop? Besides doing a little restocking, she could really use some more comfort food.

She weighed her options, and the ice cream won hands down. She grabbed her wallet and keys and fled through the front door. It wasn't until she was standing on the front porch that she realized two things.

First, her car was in the garage, not the driveway. She'd gone out the wrong door. Second, while her car wasn't in the driveway, another one was. And somebody was climbing out of its driver's side.

That's when she realized who that somebody was, and it was all she could do not to run back inside.

It was Ethan.

CHAPTER NINE

SHE'D KNOWN ETHAN WAS COMING home and that she might end up running into him sooner or later, but she hadn't counted on it being in her driveway.

The first thing she noticed was that he'd bulked up and filled out in the five years since she'd seen him. He stood his familiar six-feet-four, but he'd been maybe 170 pounds when she'd last seen him, and he was easily close to 200 pounds now. Most of that looked to be hard muscle. It was obvious the marines had turned him into a man.

He wore faded jeans that hugged his muscular legs and a dark green fleece pullover that was almost the exact color of his thickly lashed green eyes. His light brown hair was short but looked rumpled, as if he'd been running his fingers through it—a habit of his when he was upset, she remembered with a pinch in her heart.

He had his hands shoved into his front jeans pockets, making him appear casual and relaxed, but the tiny wrinkles around the corners of his mouth and eyes hinted at all he must have seen and done in Iraq and Afghanistan. The responsibility had surely changed him.

He looked at her assessingly with those sharp, intelligent eyes—a gesture that unnerved her. He'd always had a gift for reading people in a space of moments, something she was sure the military had put to good use. Then he frowned, as if he didn't like what he saw.

Defensiveness flooded through her. So maybe she wasn't as appealing as he remembered. She was tired and stressed and haggard looking. But could anybody blame her for that after everything she'd been through?

"What are you doing here?" she asked, annoyed.

A corner of his mouth kicked up. "Nice to see you too, Bree."

The old nickname surprised her. He'd been the only one who had ever called her that. The happy childhood memories it evoked warred with the more recent—and apparently still unresolved—pain of her broken heart.

"Don't call me that," she warned, glaring at him.

He flashed her a heart-stopping, unrepentant smile, and that dimple she'd always loved appeared in his right cheek. "Why not? You used to like it."

Cambry's hand started to hurt, and she looked down to see that she had a death grip on her keys, which were biting into her skin. She made a conscious effort to relax her hands.

Taking a step toward her garage, she jangled her keys pointedly. "I'm on my way out, if you didn't notice. You have two seconds to tell me why you're here before I get in my car and run you over."

The corners of his mouth tightened, and he lifted one of those big, muscular shoulders in an all-too-familiar shrug. "I got into town tonight and thought I'd stop by. See how you were doing."

A surge of anger started to boil and rise inside of her. "Five years after you dumped me—*in a note*," she added tightly, "and tonight you just decide to stop and talk to me? I haven't heard a word from you in five years, Ethan. Did you think I'd be happy to see you?"

He had the decency to look embarrassed. "I'm sorry about that," he said quietly. "The last thing I ever wanted to do was hurt you."

"Well, you did," she bit out. "Now if you'll excuse me, I have somewhere to go."

Without another word, she walked over to the keypad on the garage door, typed in her code, then quickly ducked under the rising door, all the while aware of Ethan's intense gaze following her every movement.

Her hands were shaking as she opened the door and climbed behind the wheel. When she backed out, she caught a glimpse of him watching her, his lips compressed in a tight line and his expression unreadable.

An invisible hand clenched her heart. As much as he had hurt her all those years ago, she realized that in some remote corner of her heart, she still loved him. He'd been such a huge part of her life ever since they were little, and when he'd left, it had felt like losing a large piece of herself. It had taken her a long time to feel whole again.

As she drove around the corner out of his line of sight, she drew a deep, calming breath. So much had happened this week, but seeing Ethan standing in her driveway, so achingly familiar, had possibly been the hardest thing she'd had to deal with yet. As she'd stared into those familiar green eyes, she'd felt a lifetime of memories tumbling down around her.

What a source of strength he'd been in her life. He'd always been there for her, no matter what. She needed somebody's strength so badly right now, but the very last thing she wanted to do was fall victim to the man who had all but destroyed her heart five years ago.

What they'd had was gone. She had to remember that. If she could do that, maybe she stood a chance of getting through his visit with her heart intact.

***

Ethan steered his car through the streets of Denver and in his mind replayed the scene in Cambry's driveway. To be honest, it hurt to think about it.

Cambry had looked exhausted. She still looked very much a little girl, with that tiny figure, the creamy complexion sprinkled with freckles, and those tumbling chestnut curls gleaming with red highlights. But lines of worry and fear were etched around the corners of her mouth and eyes, and the weight of the world was clearly on her shoulders. There were deep shadows under her eyes from lack of sleep, and the once happy, vibrant woman he remembered seemed to have vanished beneath a veil of vulnerability.

Underneath all that wounded pride, bluster, and attitude, he could see she was frightened. She was pale, exhausted, and barely managing to hold it all together, and if he had to guess, he'd say she hadn't had a good meal or a good night's sleep since this ordeal with her father had begun. And knowing her as he did, he suspected she wasn't letting anybody shoulder the burden.

She needed help. His help.

Seeing her so fragile and vulnerable had sent a rush of protectiveness through him. He'd wanted to sweep her into his arms and kiss her and hold her until all the hurt went away. But he'd managed to keep his distance, recognizing that the tough shell she was wearing was probably the only thing holding her together.

He shook his head and frowned. He'd been naive to think he could maintain objectivity with this assignment. He knew it would have its complications and might be a little difficult emotionally, but this . . .

For the first time since talking to Agent Natoni, he seriously considered backing out. How could he do this? Cambry was a mess, and she certainly didn't need another complication in her life. Taking advantage of the quiet roads, he pulled out his cell and pressed a speed dial button.

"Natoni here."

"I know it's late out there, but you said you wanted me to check in," Ethan said.

"I'm glad you did. What's the status?"

"I'm on my way to the Denver field office to talk to the agents in charge, but I stopped by Ms. Saville's house first." Somehow calling her by her last name helped him maintain his professional distance.

"And?"

Ethan hesitated. One of his most useful skills was assessment, and Natoni knew that. He'd always been able to assess situations and people at first glance with deadly accuracy, and it was a skill he'd used to his advantage over his years in the military. He could size up a person in seconds, dissect a situation, and gain knowledge before most people had even finished introducing themselves. One look at Cambry had given him their answer.

Ethan let out a troubled breath. "She's a mess, Natoni. There's no way she tried to kill her father or is conspiring with terrorists. I only talked to her for a few minutes, but she's coming apart at the seams. Those aren't the nerves of somebody engaged in corporate espionage or dealing with terrorists."

"Okay." Natoni seemed to consider that. "So let's work off the assumption she didn't go after her father and that she's not involved with Benton. She might still know where the technology is. Keep on her and see what you can find out."

Ethan gritted his teeth. *Easier said than done.*

With a promise to check in later, Ethan hung up and drove the rest of the way to the field office in Stapleton. At last he pulled into the parking lot of the tall, formidable-looking, state-of-the-art glass and steel building that had been recently constructed on the old Stapleton airport tarmac. He didn't have any problem finding a close parking space for his rental car at this time of night.

After showing his credentials to the guards stationed in the front, he was directed up to an office on the third floor where the agents assigned to help him were waiting.

The two agents in charge greeted him. Agent Lawford was a stocky, capable-looking man in his early fifties with brown hair and matching mustache. His partner, Agent Arehart, was younger and more athletic looking, maybe just slightly older than Ethan's twenty-seven years, with curly black hair and wire-framed glasses. They were both friendly and accepting of his presence as a new agent assigned to the case.

They offered him a seat in a large open office space where a dozen or more desks were neatly arranged throughout the room. Together they brought him up to speed, sharing their files, notes, and observations.

"What's the situation with the local police?" Ethan asked.

"We're continuing to work with them as they look for suspects, but they understand that we have jurisdiction. One of the detectives has been hostile, though, and might continue to be a problem."

"Is that Detective Dalton? Natoni told me he was a loose cannon."

Lawford nodded. "Even though we have jurisdiction, he's still going after Saville. He has it in his mind that she's guilty, and he's not going to rest until he wrenches a confession from her. Let us know if he continues to be a problem, and we'll file an official complaint with the chief of police."

"Will do." Ethan rose. "I've been traveling since early this morning, so I'm going to call it a day. I'll touch base with you tomorrow."

Ethan left headquarters and headed to his parents' house. He was tired enough that all he really wanted to do was climb into bed and crash, but his parents had other plans. His mom had been so excited about his arrival that she'd put pies in the oven and invited Emma, Nick, and the girls over to see him.

He had mixed emotions about this little reunion. While he was excited to see the family he hadn't seen in five years, he was apprehensive as well. He'd been away for so long he didn't even feel like a member of the family anymore. Not really. His twin sister, Emma, now had two daughters. He hadn't met either one of them.

The guilt he'd harbored for the past five years upon his departure continued to feel overwhelming. He suspected they'd welcome him back with open arms, but would things ever be the same? He wasn't sure he deserved their forgiveness for what he'd done. For how much he'd hurt them. He needed his family, but did he deserve them?

When he finally turned into his parents' driveway, he climbed out of his car and was halfway up the walk when the front door flung open. Emma stood in the doorway. She looked as pretty and vibrant as ever, with her light brown hair and bright green eyes—both still the exact same shade as his.

The only thing wrong with this reunion was the fact that she wasn't smiling.

She stalked out of the house, down the two steps to the front walk, and came to an abrupt halt in front of him. Then she utterly surprised him by punching him in the bicep. Hard. The blow actually made his bare arm sting a little.

He stared at her, startled. When she started to move again, he flinched as he prepared for another blow, but instead she threw her arms around him, buried her face in his chest, and started to cry.

Completely caught off guard, he stood frozen for a moment before he folded his arms around her and pressed his head against hers. "Hey, Em," he managed through the suspicious thickness in his throat. "Long time no see."

"And whose fault is that?"

"Mine." His voice came out strangled, and he tightened his arms around her.

When Emma pulled away, she grabbed his arm and pulled him toward the door. "Mom! Dad! Look who I found!"

The next few minutes were filled with hugs that left him feeling loved, if not more than a little squished.

"Let's go on into the kitchen," his mom urged, happily leading the way. "I just pulled the pies out of the oven, and they're best when they're warm."

As the crowd followed, his dad pulled him into yet another bone-crushing embrace followed by a thump on the back. "So how are you, son?"

"I'm good, Dad," he said, trying not to get emotional over his father's obvious delight to have him home. "How's the knee?"

"About to be a whole lot better after this surgery Wednesday." Dean grinned. "I can't believe how good you look. Welcome home, kid."

The endearment almost undid him. Before he unmanned himself completely by crying in front of his family, he distracted himself by going and helping his mom cut and dish up the pies.

For the next hour, they all talked and laughed and caught up with each others' lives, and Ethan couldn't remember the last time he'd felt so happy. All his fears at facing an awkward reunion had gone, and he reveled in the feeling of belonging that he'd thought he'd never feel again.

He enjoyed talking to Nick, Emma's husband, whom he hadn't seen since Emma had gotten married. He also spent a good deal of time making a fool out of himself to entertain Emma's darling toddler and baby. The two girls were adorable and looked so much like Emma's baby pictures that it brought back fresh waves of guilt for all that he had missed out on in the last few years.

Needing a little distance to compose his thoughts, he excused himself to go to the bathroom. On his way back, he stopped in the living room to look at pictures adorning the mantel and set around the room. Some were old school pictures or were ones taken on favorite family vacations. There were several that he hadn't seen of Emma and Nick and their two little girls, so he spent some time looking at those.

Then there were some of Adam.

His heart pinched a little when he looked into the familiar face of his brother, two years older than he and Emma. He had idolized his brother, and it had been the worst day of his life when they'd gotten the news that Adam had been killed in Afghanistan.

A noise in the entryway made him look up. His mom smiled as she came to stand beside him.

"I wondered where you disappeared to. You okay?"

He nodded and inclined his head toward the pictures. "Just feeling nostalgic, I guess."

His mother smiled and picked up a frame from a lower shelf in the corner and handed it to him. "This one was always my favorite."

Ethan groaned in dismay. In the picture, he and Emma were six and Cambry was five. The girls had been playing dress-up, and they'd bribed him to let them dress him up. One giant Hershey bar was all it had taken. Then his mother had swooped in, laughing, and snapped the picture he was looking at now, with him in a flowing Cinderella gown with gleaming white bows in his hair and bright pink lipstick on his mouth.

He had never looked at a Hershey bar favorably since.

"You guys always had so much fun together," she said wistfully. "That picture is only one of hundreds of precious memories I have of you three."

Ethan smiled softly as he stared at the image of a young Cambry, so vivacious and full of life. She'd been a force to reckon with. Nobody had ever been able to make her do anything she didn't want to do. That brave, conquering smile, so apparent in the photograph, had been missing from her face tonight.

"How is she?" he asked his mom, his voice soft.

His mom gave a troubled sigh. "It's been really hard for her, though she'd never admit it. It was hard enough that she was the one to find her father in his building, but to be taken in for questioning and hounded by media . . . The poor girl's been through too much, and frankly, your dad and I are worried about her."

"I stopped by her house tonight."

"Did you?" Janette's eyebrows arched with curiosity.

He shook his head at her hopeful expression. "It didn't go well."

"I guess that's to be expected," Janette said with a sigh. "Truth is she's miserable even if she is putting on a brave face. We've been trying to help her, but she's been avoiding us the past few days."

"Why?"

Janette hesitated. "She learned you were coming home."

"So she stayed away."

His mom nodded.

The realization hit him hard. She needed somebody to support her and fuss over her, and the fact that she wouldn't let the closest thing she had to a family do that told him just how bitter she was about facing him.

"I'm especially concerned about her after Emma told me something else," his mom continued.

Ethan's brows furrowed in concern. "What now?"

"Cambry's apparently starting a new job tomorrow, which I'm not sure I approve of because it's just one more tumultuous change among all the others right now."

"What new job?"

Janette briefly explained the circumstances. "The decision to take the job at her father's company couldn't have been an easy one. You know as well as I do what transpired between her and her father."

He remembered.

After long moments, his mom clapped her hands in an effort to change the subject. "Well, should we go back in and see if anyone's ready for another slice of pie?"

The rest of the evening went by in a blur, and by the time Emma, Nick, and their girls had gone home, he felt more hopeful about his future with his family. It wasn't until he climbed into bed and had nothing else to distract him that his thoughts once more turned to Cambry.

Things were looking up with his family. Could he somehow make things right between him and Cambry? He knew he had to try. Undercover assignment or not, he needed to be there for her. He owed it to her. He hadn't been able to be there for her six years ago, when her mother had passed away, because he'd been half a world away on his mission, but he could be there for her now.

Just as he was drifting off to sleep, a long-ago memory surfaced, giving him an idea how to take that first step. It was something he'd always done to show her he cared. It was their special thing. If there was anything that would soften her heart, that was it.

With his next move planned, he gave in to his exhaustion and slept. There would be enough to do tomorrow.

CHAPTER TEN

CAMBRY FELT LIKE SHE WAS running a marathon at work the next morning as she darted from one director's office to the next, reassigning her workload in preparation for her departure. By the time lunch rolled around, everything was taken care of, but Cambry was ready to drop.

She left the office, stopped for a sandwich, then headed in to face her new job at Saville Enterprises. Jim greeted her warmly and personally showed her around the new areas of the building. She was surprised at how much had changed since she'd interned there.

"I have an office ready for you in the east wing," he told her as they stepped out of the elevator into the reception area of the fifth floor.

She'd been there the day before, but this time she allowed herself a moment to take in the details. It was a welcoming area, with neutral carpeting, cream-colored walls, elaborate crisp white trims around the doors and floors, and plush leather sofas and armchairs.

While she hadn't recognized either of the two people behind the granite-topped reception desk yesterday, she recognized one of them today. "Shanice!" she exclaimed happily as the woman came around the opening of the desk to greet her with a warm hug. "It's so good to see you!"

Shanice was a lovely, dark-skinned woman in her late fifties who had been with her father's company for the past fifteen years. Cambry remembered her from when she'd interned.

"It's so good to see you too, Cambry," Shanice said. "When Jim told me you were going to be working for us, I was thrilled."

"Thanks. I'll probably need a lot of help familiarizing myself with the company and the things I need to do."

"I can go over a lot of that with you. Don't worry. You'll settle right in."

Jim spoke up. "And if you have any questions or concerns, feel free to come to me. You know where my office is."

Jim excused himself to make some calls, leaving Shanice to show her to her office. It was at the end of one of the halls and had large windows that overlooked the city and the distant Rocky Mountains. A gleaming, two-tone cherry desk was positioned near the windows while a small, round table in matching cherry with two upholstered chairs sat in the near corner. A plush-looking, small leather sofa sat along the wall a short distance away. Two tall, carved-wood filing cabinets sat along the back wall and shelves ran the entire length along the wall to her right. The furniture and décor were a little dark and masculine for her taste, but it was well-appointed.

Shanice spent some time with her, going over everything she needed to know. After going through the client lists, contracts under negotiations, projects in development, and lab equipment requests, Cambry's head was spinning. Thanks to her years of training and experience, she understood what needed to be done to accomplish each task, but to have them all thrust at her at once was overwhelming.

"You'll do fine," Shanice said, giving her a motherly pat on the shoulder. "Just take things one at a time, and if you run into problems, let me know."

Only moments after Shanice left, a knock sounded on the door. "Come in," Cambry called.

Her door opened, and a grinning man appeared in the doorway. "Hey, shortie."

"Kurt!" She jumped to her feet and rushed over to give him a hug. "I haven't seen you in years! How are you?"

The summer she'd been interning, Kurt Kunde had been hired as the new chief financial officer. Part of her internship had dealt with business finance, so she had spent a lot of time working with him. Even though he was seven years older, they'd become good friends. They'd spent many lunch hours together and even went to an occasional Colorado Rockies game.

"I'm good," Kurt said, returning her hug. "I hear you're stepping in as operations officer. That's wonderful." Then he sobered and stepped back. "I'm sorry to hear about your dad though. How's he doing?"

"The same."

"Is there anything I can do?"

"Thanks, but all anybody can do is wait."

He nodded and then shifted his gaze to her desk. "Yikes. It looks like you have your work cut out for you."

With a sigh, she turned back to look at the stack. "It's not pretty, is it? I'm beginning to wonder what I've gotten myself into."

"You can handle this," he said, giving her shoulder a squeeze. "Jim wouldn't have asked you if he didn't think you were right for the job."

"I'll keep repeating that to myself until I believe it."

Kurt laughed. "You should. Well, I'll let you get to it. Would you like to grab some takeout or something after work? We could catch up."

"I'd like to, but I have plans tonight," she said, remembering her promise to join the Reeces for dinner. "Could I take a rain check?"

He smiled. "Absolutely. Just let me know when."

For the next few hours, she brought herself up to speed on the company's clients and went through the project and productivity reports. Just as she was turning her attention to the lists of projects in development, Shanice knocked on her door.

"This was just delivered for you by a very handsome young man who refused to give his name." She held up a small yellow gift bag and winked. "I think he figured you'd know who it was from."

When Shanice left, pulling the door shut behind her, Cambry opened the bag and pulled out two items: a bag of miniature Reese's Peanut Butter Cups and a tube of Reese's Peanut Butter Cup–flavored lip gloss.

Cambry smiled, even as her heart constricted. *He remembered.*

Reese's Peanut Butter Cups had been her and Ethan's running joke from the time they were young. She'd always loved them, but the day they realized the similarity between Ethan's last name and her favorite treat, it had become "their thing." Ethan started teasing her when she was in third grade that she had a "thing" for Reese's, which obviously included him. So she gave him a Reese's Peanut Butter Cup T-shirt for Christmas that year—proving him right.

For her tenth birthday, he gave her a bag of miniature Reese's Peanut Butter Cups stuffed into a mug with the Reese's Peanut Butter Cup logo. When he'd gotten his driver's license and his parents had bought him a junky old truck—which he'd loved—she'd bought a Reese's lanyard and hung it on his rearview mirror with a "Congrats!" button pinned onto the end.

When he'd left for his mission in Brazil, he'd given her a fringed throw with the Reese's Peanut Butter Cup logo woven into it. "To wrap around you and hug you when I can't," he'd written in the note she'd read after he'd checked into the MTC.

She'd cried for a week.

And she still had the blanket.

Overwhelmed by her feelings of nostalgia, she hunted for a note. She spotted it taped to the candy package.

Cambry,

Saying "I'm sorry" may never be enough. I don't expect you to ever forgive me, but I still care about you. I wasn't able to be there for you when your mom died, but I can be here for you now.
Will you let me?

Ethan

Tears swarmed her vision. *Darn the man!* He may have stirred up a lot of wonderful memories with his gift, but she wouldn't let him off the hook that easily. If he wanted any kind of contact with her, he was going to have to earn her trust all over again.

Setting the bag aside, she went back to work. The rest of the day was a lesson in perseverance as she slogged through her workload, all the while trying not to think about Ethan.

By five o'clock, she was more than ready to go home. The stress of wrapping things up at her job at Global that morning, then diving into her new position at Saville Enterprises had left her physically and mentally drained.

She shut down her computer, turned off the lights, and then headed downstairs. Several people shot her looks of recognition and curiosity, but she only gave them a closed-lipped smile in response and continued on her way.

She was outside and almost to the parking lot when she was once more startled by the sudden sensation of being watched. Unease skittered across her skin as she looked around. She looked around the parking lot, but it was far from empty. At least a dozen people were in the lot, getting into cars, exchanging pleasantries, and calling out good-nights. There was nothing to suggest anything out of the ordinary.

Picking up her pace, she walked quickly to her car and started for home. Her nerves remained on edge as she navigated the heavy stop-and-go traffic, and she continually glanced in her rearview mirror. Still, nothing unusual caught her attention.

As she neared her turnoff, a glimpse of black and chrome in her mirror caught her attention. A feeling of panic swept through her. Was it the same car? She steered onto the exit ramp, her eyes continuing to flit to her rearview mirror. To her relief, the black car two lengths back maintained its speed and continued on past.

Her hands were shaking, she realized, as she pulled up to the red stoplight at the end of the exit ramp. She closed her eyes briefly and drew a deep breath. It had been her imagination, right? It couldn't have been the same car. If somebody really had been following her, they would have taken her same exit.

The light turned green, and she made a right-hand turn into the subdivision. As she neared her own street, she signaled and slowed. A car was approaching from the other direction, and it signaled and slowed as well. Then she saw the driver.

It was Ethan.

Their eyes met, and he lifted his hand in a tentative wave. Not knowing what else to do, she returned his wave and finished making her turn. A glance into her rearview mirror told her that Ethan had also turned and was now behind her.

A flutter of apprehension filled her stomach. He was probably on his way to his parents' house down the street, but would he stop at her house? And if he did, what would she say to him?

When she turned into her driveway, Ethan pulled in behind her.

She was so preoccupied with trying to decide what she'd say to him that she hadn't noticed the car parked along the curb in front of her house or the man sitting behind the wheel until she'd stopped in her driveway.

Instantly, she went on alert.

Deciding not to pull into the garage just yet, she cut the engine. She'd just grabbed her leather messenger bag off the passenger seat and was getting out of the car when she saw that her visitor at the curb was doing the same thing.

Recognition hit, and her heart dropped down to her toes.

It was Detective Dalton.

CHAPTER ELEVEN

ETHAN FROWNED AS HE THREW his car into park and turned off the ignition. Judging by Cambry's tense stance and paling complexion, the man approaching her wasn't somebody she wanted to see. That was all it took for him to jump out of his car and put himself between them.

"I want to know why you lied about your place of employment, Ms. Saville," the man started in just as Ethan reached Cambry. "Lying to a police officer is a punishable offense, you know. I should take you down to the station right now."

"I don't know what you're talking about," she said, the quaver in her voice putting Ethan on alert.

He moved to stand beside her, their shoulders almost touching. She gave him a quick glance, and instead of hostility, he saw immense relief in her eyes.

"You told us, on the record, that you worked for Global Technologies," the man continued, seemingly unconcerned by Ethan's presence. "But it's come to my attention that you're actually working for Saville Enterprises. Care to tell me why you lied, Ms. Saville?"

Her eyes widened. "I didn't lie, Detective. When we talked I wasn't working for my father's company. The managing partner offered me a job yesterday."

"Really." The detective took an intimidating half step closer. "Didn't you stop to think how this would look in our investigation? The guilt it implies? Your next step in taking over your father's company?"

Cambry's jaw dropped in an openmouthed gasp at the accusation, and Ethan had had enough. This man wasn't going to show up and start harassing Cambry. Not when he was around to do something about it.

Stepping in front of Cambry, he crossed his arms over his chest and asked with quiet authority, "Is there a problem here?"

Now that the man's eye contact with Cambry had been broken, he looked up the few inches into Ethan's face and glowered. "I didn't catch your name."

"I didn't give it." Ethan kept his tone cool and lethal. "How about I see some credentials?"

The man bristled and whipped a badge out of his pocket. He flashed it in Ethan's face.

Ethan caught the name *Dalton* on the badge, and suddenly it all made sense. This was the detective who'd been refusing to back off the case. Well, that was going to stop right now.

"I'm a detective, not some beat cop," Dalton bit out, his tone just as abusive as it had been to Cambry, "so you'd better watch your mouth before I run you in for interfering with a police investigation."

Ethan felt anger build at this man's insolence, and it was all he could do not to plant his fist in the man's face. "I was told you were out of the investigation," Ethan said, his voice firm and controlled. "You're overstepping your bounds."

Rage flashed in Dalton's eyes, and his lip pulled back into a sneer. "How dare you tell me what to do! If you're not out of here in two seconds, I'm hauling you downtown."

"I'd like to see you try." He reached inside his jacket and pulled out his own credentials. "Agent Reece. FBI." He drew great pleasure from watching the man pale. But Ethan didn't back off. "Local law enforcement no longer has jurisdiction in Ms. Saville's case, Detective Dalton. So unless you want me to report this to your superiors, I want *you* off Ms. Saville's property in two seconds or I'll remove you myself."

Dalton's gaze met his in a silent standoff, but Ethan didn't flinch. At last, Detective Dalton backed away and fixed Ethan with a hateful glare. Then his gaze swept back to Cambry's. "I'm not through with you yet, Ms. Saville. Don't think you're going to get away with everything you've done."

Ethan took a threatening step toward Dalton and snarled, "You stay away from her or I'll have your badge."

Cambry remained silent behind him as Dalton turned and stormed back to his car. The engine roared to life, and the tires squealed as the car shot away from the curb and sped down the street.

Good riddance, Ethan thought, his anger still dangerously close to the surface.

When he turned back to Cambry, her frightened gaze was still following the car's departure down the street.

"Are you okay?"

Her jerky nod made her look anything but. "I think so." She gave an unsteady laugh. "I really hate that guy."

Ethan's jaw tightened. "I can see why."

She looked up at him as if viewing him in a new light. "I knew you'd left the military, but I didn't realize you worked for the FBI."

His mouth went dry. When his instincts to protect her from Dalton's harassment had taken over, he hadn't stopped to consider that flashing his credentials might tip her off about his involvement in this case. Especially since he'd told Dalton that he knew the FBI had jurisdiction. How would he know that unless he was involved?

Stupid, stupid, stupid, he chastised himself.

At least Cambry appeared too rattled to have picked up on those clues. He was going to have to be more careful in the future not to do anything to make her suspicious.

"I accepted a job offer with the Baltimore field office when I got out of the marines. It seemed like a good fit."

"Do you enjoy it?"

He smiled. She'd just been harassed by an abusive detective, and she wanted to make small talk? He had to love her resilience.

"Beats Iraq's 120-degree temperatures and sand storms that leave sand in every crevice of your body." He reached for the leather messenger bag dangling from her fingers and put a hand on the small of her back to guide her up the front walk. "Come on. Let's get you inside and get you something to drink. You look a little shaky."

The house was quiet as they stepped inside, and Ethan shut the door behind them. It had been five years since he'd been inside Cambry's house, and what he saw impressed him. It was Cambry's childhood home—he knew it as well as his own—but it wasn't. Almost everything had been remodeled and updated.

The soaring two-story ceiling of the spacious entry way and its downward slope into the living room were awash with light from new can lighting overhead, shedding warmth on the soothing earth tones of the wall paint and decor done in rich browns, golds, and burgundies. The old tile flooring in the entry way had been replaced with warm, walnut-colored hardwoods that flowed into the kitchen, making the space seem unified and open.

"I love what you've done in here," he said as he set her bag down by the front door.

"Thanks. I had a friend who was an out-of-work contractor, and because I was thinking of remodeling anyway, I hired him. He did a great job."

He walked with her through the foyer and into the kitchen, then crossed over to the fridge. She needed something to get some color back into those cheeks and ease the shaking in her limbs.

"Let's see what you've got in here." He opened the fridge and spotted some apple juice in the door. He smiled. It always had been her favorite.

Grabbing the container, he pulled it out and set it on the brown-flecked granite countertop that separated the kitchen from the informal dining area. He moved automatically to the cupboard where the glasses had been when they were growing up, but the cabinet was glass fronted, and he could see there weren't any glasses in there.

Deciding not to play hide-and-seek, he looked over at her and lifted an eyebrow. "Glasses?"

The hint of a smile touched her lips. "Corner cupboard."

He opened the cupboard and grabbed a glass. He poured her some juice and thrust it into her hand. "Here. Drink this."

When she'd drained the juice, he took the glass from her, set it in the sink, then leaned back against the opposite counter to study her. He took in the dark bruising under her eyes and the strain evident on her face.

"When was the last time you slept?"

She looked startled by the question. Then she fixed him with a testy glare. "What are you saying? That I look terrible?"

He deliberated over that for a moment and decided to go for honesty. "Would you boot me out of here if I said yes?"

To his horror, her eyes filled with tears. Muttering at himself for being an insensitive jerk, he closed the distance between them and drew her into his arms. She started to cry in earnest, her tears wetting the front of his shirt. She felt so tiny and fragile in his arms, and he cursed himself for being the one to send her over the edge.

He stroked a hand lightly over her hair, smoothing back the strands that had escaped from the fancy bun-thing positioned near the nape of her neck. It felt amazing to have her in his arms again. He would have reveled in the experience had she not been sobbing. Unable to help himself, he pressed a gentle kiss to the top of her head and whispered soothing words as she cried.

When her tears diminished, he loosened his hold and reached for her hand. Hoping she wouldn't protest the contact, he led her into the living room where he guided her down onto the couch. Once she was sitting, he lowered himself to his haunches in front of her.

Her eyes were red, and her nearly transparent skin was blotchy. Even so, she looked beautiful to him. A contradiction in vulnerability and toughness. "I'm sorry," he said, feeling contrite. "You know I've always had foot-in-mouth disease."

She swiped at her cheeks and took a calming breath. "It's not that. It's just been a really hard week, you know?"

All he could do was nod. When a couple more tears leaked out to replace the ones she'd swept off her cheeks, his heart twisted painfully in his chest.

"Bree," he said softly. "You know I don't handle tears well, especially yours. How can I help? What can I do?"

She shook her head but remained silent as she struggled for composure. Unable to stop himself, he lifted a hand and brushed it along the side of her face. To his surprise, she closed her eyes and leaned into his palm. His heart skipped unevenly. It had been so long since he'd touched her that he'd forgotten the power of the connection they shared. Had it always been this strong? Or had the years apart only made him more aware of it?

As much as he wanted to comfort her, he also knew he had a job to do. He let his hand fall from her face and forced himself to back off emotionally. Getting to his feet, he sat beside her on the couch.

"I'm so sorry you've had to go through all this, Cambry," he said. "Why were you heading to your father's office that night anyway?"

She looked down at her clenched hands. "We still weren't talking, but he'd been trying to contact me the past few weeks. His managing partner told me yesterday that my father had changed and that he'd wanted to make amends."

Ethan recognized an opening. This was the perfect opportunity to find out what she knew without asking a lot of questions and making her suspicious. "So had you talked with him?"

"No. I'd ignored his attempts to contact me. But the last message I got from him made it sound like he was in some kind of trouble. That's what made me decide to go talk to him."

"So what happened then?"

"When I got there, I decided not to wait for the elevator, so I headed for the stairs. That's when I found him. He was conscious, and he recognized me. He said something about somebody named Isaac. And a picture . . ."

Ethan frowned. A picture? That piece of information hadn't been in his briefing. He knew about Isaac Benton and the role the man was playing in this, but this was new.

He reached for her hand and gave it a gentle squeeze. "What picture?"

Something flashed in her eyes. Wariness? Guilt? Before he could analyze it, it was gone.

"I don't know," she said, shaking her head. "I don't know about any of this."

He watched her for a long moment, and his instinct told him there was something about the encounter she wasn't telling him. What had gone on in those moments before Dan Saville had lost consciousness? But pushing her for the answers right now would only drive her away, he realized. Already she was putting her guard back up, and he wouldn't get anywhere if that happened.

Deciding to come back to that later, he moved on, gentling his voice. "And then what?"

"The next day, the police interrogated me. And the day after that, two FBI agents showed up, asking about some missing technology my father had been working on for the military. They were worried about it falling into the wrong hands," she explained. "Something about weapon capabilities. They wanted to know if I knew where it might be, or if my father could have gotten it to me without my realizing it."

Ethan quirked a brow. "Did he?"

"I deleted the e-mails from him, so if he did, it's not there anymore." She shrugged. "After I told the agents that, I didn't hear from them again. I wish I could say the same for Detective Dalton."

"I'm so sorry," Ethan said softly. "I can't imagine going through everything that you have. But you need to know you're not alone in this. You have my family to help you through it. And you have me."

Cambry stiffened. Their gazes met and held, and he could see the uncertainty in her eyes. After a few moments, she said, "I got your gift today. And your note."

He paused. "And?"

She exhaled and rubbed a palm across her forehead. "Look, Ethan, I appreciate you wanting to be there for me, but to be honest, the offer really threw me." She shook her head in confusion. "I loved you. You were everything to me. But you left. And I never saw or heard from you again."

He winced. "Cambry—"

"If you look at this from my perspective, you have to admit that it's a shock to have you show up like this and decide to be my friend again. Not that I don't appreciate it, but it leaves me feeling . . . a little confused."

"I know." He sat back and dragged a hand through his hair. "I'm not sure where to start."

"How about at the beginning? What happened with us, Ethan? For years I've wondered if it was something that I said . . . that I did . . ."

The words felt like a blow. "Cambry, no," he said, reaching for her hand once more. "I never meant for you to think it was something you did."

"Then what?"

Ethan considered his next words. "When we got the news that Adam had been killed in Afghanistan, I think I went a little crazy. Maybe it was a coping mechanism. Maybe it was shock. I don't know. My first instinct was to rush out and avenge my big brother's death. I know that doesn't make any sense now, but it was all I could think about then—joining the marines and rushing over there to kill the scumbags who had taken my brother from me. It wasn't until a few months later, when I found myself on a battlefield in Iraq in the middle of insurgent fire, that I realized what I had done. I'd not only deserted my family, but I'd deserted the only woman I've ever loved. And for what? Some foolish notion that I could somehow make Adam's death mean something?

"Not that I didn't think I was making a difference in the military," he continued. "It felt great knowing I was defending our country and helping people. But I had done it for all the wrong reasons. I felt so much guilt over what I had done, though, that I couldn't bring myself to come home and face the people I'd hurt. I finally figured out nothing was going to change if I stayed away. So when Mom told me Dad was going in for knee surgery, I scheduled the time off. I wanted to try to make things right." He paused, then met her gaze intently. "Maybe even between us."

Her lips parted in surprise. "Ethan," she said, shifting uncomfortably in her seat, "I do miss you. I miss what we had. You were my best friend." When she spoke again, pain and weariness filled her eyes. "But you broke my heart. You can't just expect me to forget that or pretend it never happened."

"I know," he said solemnly. "And I don't."

It was quiet for a minute as they let the words settle around them.

Then Ethan let out a deep breath. "I understand your feelings, Bree; honestly, I do. You think it's too late for us, and maybe it is. But whatever we were before, and regardless of what we are or aren't now, I want to be here for you. You're facing the battle of your life, and you're facing it, for the most part, alone. I don't like it."

She looked a little uncomfortable, no doubt thinking she didn't need what she considered to be charity. "I appreciate you saying that, but there's not much you can do—"

"That's ridiculous and you know it," Ethan bit off, his brows narrowing. "There's a lot I can do, that my family can do. Family dinners. Game nights. Anything that helps you laugh and distracts you from what's going on. I'll challenge you on that game system my parents just bought. I'll even let you beat me once."

That drew a smile out of her. "Just once?"

"Okay, maybe twice, but don't push your luck." He grinned, but a moment later, he sobered. "My point is, you don't have to go through this alone. Whatever I've done, however I've handled things, I want to put that in the past. You need us right now, Bree, and I don't want to be the reason you turn down help. Could we call a truce? Even for a little while?"

He watched as she considered, her emotions warring in her eyes. At last she nodded. "A truce."

A happiness he hadn't expected to feel swept over him, and he smiled. "Good." He glanced down at his watch. "My parents are expecting us for dinner in forty-five minutes. Do you still feel up to going?"

Cambry groaned and buried her face in her hands. "I'd love nothing more than to climb into a hot bath and soak away some stress, but I did promise your mom and Emma."

Ethan nodded and got to his feet. "I'll tell you what. Why don't you jump in a hot shower and relax a bit. I'll come back to pick you up at seven. Then all you have to do is sit around my house and let my mom fuss over you."

"When you put it that way . . ."

He chuckled as she got up and followed him to the door. When he pulled it open, he turned back to her. "See you at seven." He gave the dead bolt a light thump with his fingers. "Lock up behind me, okay?"

At the instruction, she blinked rapidly a couple of times, and he was startled at the sheen of tears that he saw in her eyes. Had it really been that long since somebody had shown concern for her well-being? The thought made him angry. She deserved that and more.

"I will," she said, her voice sounding thick.

"See you in a while."

"Thanks, Ethan."

The words were spoken with caution, but he wondered if that was a crack he saw in the protective wall around her heart. He hoped it wasn't just his imagination.

CHAPTER TWELVE

CAMBRY SHUT THE DOOR BEHIND Ethan and headed upstairs. She wiped at the moisture clinging to her eyelashes, both surprised and alarmed that she'd almost cried at Ethan's request to lock up behind him. She didn't know why his concern for her welfare had touched her so much. She had friends, and Janette, Dean, and Emma were doing nice things for her all the time. But for some reason, having Ethan show that he cared in such a subtle, instinctive way touched her deeply.

With weary feet, she climbed the stairs and got into the shower, letting the hot stream pound across her shoulders and loosen her muscles. When the water started to run cold, she got out and dried off. She shrugged into her fuzzy bathrobe and walked out into her bedroom. A glance at the clock told her she still had twenty minutes.

Crossing over to the TV, she turned it on and pressed the buttons to queue up the DVD in the player to where she'd left off two nights ago. She smiled as the next episode of *Doctor Who* flashed onto the screen. The BBC series had always been a favorite of hers, and she had recently splurged on the latest season's disc set. She was slowly working her way through the episodes, enjoying the light banter and campy themes she'd always loved. The humor was the perfect remedy for her mood.

She pulled clothes out of her closet and dressed as she watched, surprising herself by even laughing a little. Deciding to leave her hair down made getting ready easier, so all she did was apply a little concealer to her freckles, some mascara to her light-colored lashes, and a touch of lip gloss.

Just as she was turning off the DVD to head downstairs, her cell phone alerted her to a new text message. Her heartbeat accelerated when she saw it was from Alisa.

I'm back in town, so I'm turning my attention to your files. Sorry it took me so long. I'll run them through decryption programs and tell you what I find.

Cambry let out a relieved breath. She didn't know what Alisa would uncover, but knowing what was or wasn't on the drive would sure help. She replied to Alisa's text with one of her own, thanking her and asking her to call her day or night with whatever she found.

As she headed downstairs, she felt a new sense of unease. She had let the tidbit about the picture slip, but she hadn't told Ethan about the thumb drive. She'd been so grateful to unload her burdens that she'd almost confessed to that detail, but she still wasn't ready to tell anyone about it—not until she knew what it contained.

The thumb drive had fallen to the back of her mind the past few days, ever since the FBI had stopped checking in with her. Maybe they'd found the technology. That would explain why they hadn't been back in touch. But if they had the technology safely in hand, what was on the thumb drive that her father wanted to protect? Until she got to the bottom of the mystery, there was no reason to go against his last wishes and tell somebody about it. And that included Ethan.

Her thoughts turned back to the evening ahead as she looked out the window and watched for Ethan to arrive. A rush of butterflies invaded her stomach at the thought. While she was grateful she and Ethan had cleared the air a bit, she wasn't convinced things wouldn't still be awkward between them. She just hoped Dean didn't pick up on it. With his surgery tomorrow, she didn't want to give him more stress.

All you can do is stick it out, she told herself. *And hope for the best.*

***

Ethan left his parents' house at a quarter to seven to pick up Cambry, but thoughts of betrayal and duty warred in his mind.

He meant what he'd said to her. He wanted to make things right between them, to be her friend. But that didn't change his directive. In spite of what he wanted to do to help Cambry, he still had a job to do. And Agent Natoni was expecting an update.

Ethan climbed into his car but didn't start it. He dialed Natoni's number and got him on the second ring. "I've got a few things for you," Ethan said without preamble.

"Great, let's hear it."

Ethan started off telling him about his encounter with Detective Dalton. "I'd like you to call Dalton's superior and have him make the detective back off. He's going to compromise our investigation."

"Done. What else did you learn?"

"She mentioned a picture."

"A picture?" Natoni sounded confused.

"Yes. Her father mentioned Isaac's name and something about a picture before he lost consciousness."

"Did you ask her for more details?"

"I did, and she immediately got fidgety—like she hadn't meant to say anything and it had just slipped out. I was afraid that if I pushed her, I'd scare her off. But I definitely got the impression that there was more."

Natoni's agitation bled across the line. "I understand you not wanting to scare her off, but you're going to have to start pushing, Reece. Time's running out. We can't afford to let Benton beat us to this."

When they ended the call a few minutes later, Ethan let out an aggravated growl. Why couldn't this trip home have been all about getting back on track with his family and Cambry, like he'd intended, rather than about investigating the woman he loved? This was the first vacation he'd taken in years, and it certainly wasn't feeling like much of one.

He started the car and drove down the block to Cambry's house. Pulling into the driveway, he walked up the front steps and rang the doorbell. He shoved his hands into his jeans pockets and waited. As he did, he reminded himself of tonight's objective. He wouldn't have a chance to talk privately with Cambry about the picture she'd mentioned, but tonight would go a long way to gaining her trust again.

The door opened then, and he turned his attention to Cambry standing in the doorway.

"I'm just looking for my shoes," she told him. "I'll be just a minute."

He smiled reassuringly as he stepped inside. "Take your time. Dinner's not quite ready yet, anyway."

As Cambry looked around the living room for her shoes, he allowed his gaze to take in her appearance. She was wearing jeans that flattered her petite figure and a fitted, emerald-green shirt that complemented her warm chestnut coloring perfectly. Her hair had deepened in color since he'd last seen her—not quite as red, but a subtle auburn—and hung in thick, loose waves to almost the middle of her back. She still looked young and innocent, but she had grown up into a lovely, capable woman.

Why hadn't some man realized how amazing she was and married her? A part of him was relieved that nobody had, and another part wondered if he stood any chance with her now.

Investigation. National security. Missing technology, he reminded himself, forcing his appreciative gaze away from her. As much as he wanted to reestablish things between them, he reminded himself that he had a job to do.

"Ah-ha!"

Her exclamation brought his gaze back to where she stood just inside the kitchen. She walked over to him with leather clogs on her feet.

"Found 'em," she told him with a sheepish smile. "You'd think I could remember where I put my shoes, but I never do."

He remembered that about her. Not feeling quite comfortable enough to razz her about it, he only smiled as she got her sweater and shouldered an expensive-looking leather backpack she must have been using as a purse. He held the front door open for her and followed her out.

They drove to his parents' house, and as soon as they'd stopped in the driveway, she reached for her door handle.

He stopped her with a little growl. "Don't even think about. I'll come around and get it for you." He hurried around to her side and opened her door, receiving a genuine smile of gratitude as she stepped out.

"Trying to be my knight in shining armor?" she teased.

His mouth twitched. "What is a knight if not chivalrous?"

They walked up to the front door, and Ethan let them in. The second they stepped inside, Janette bustled into the foyer. Her eyes were warm as she spotted Cambry with Ethan.

"I'm so glad you came," she said, giving Cambry a hug.

They went inside and greeted Emma and Nick, then Dean, who sat in the corner lounger with two-year-old Jessica curled up in his lap as they read a book.

"You ready for surgery tomorrow?" Cambry asked.

"Is anybody ever ready for surgery?" he grumbled. "All that poking and prodding . . . I'll just be glad to have it done."

Ethan guided Cambry to the unoccupied sofa and sat down beside her while Emma moved to take her fussing younger daughter from Nick. She then settled into the armchair next to the couch.

"Oh!" Cambry exclaimed suddenly, reaching down for the backpack she'd dropped at her feet. "Emma, I wanted to return your book."

Cambry unbuckled the flap, and Ethan watched, amused, as she started to rummage around in the deep pouch. She pulled out her wallet, a notebook, a pack of gum, a checkbook, a Maglite, and a travel-size bottle of hand antiseptic before she let out an *Ah-ha!* and extracted a thin, hardback book that she held out victoriously to Emma.

Ethan laughed. "Do you have dinner in that bag as well? Good grief, Cambry, that thing is a TARDIS."

"Nice comparison!" Cambry said, grinning broadly and obviously pleased that he'd remembered her love of all things *Doctor Who.*

"What's a TARDIS?" Emma asked.

"Remember that show Cambry likes, *Doctor Who*? It's about this time traveler known as 'the Doctor,' who explores the universe in a kind of space ship/time machine called the TARDIS. From the outside, it looks like this small 1960s London police box, but when you walk inside it, it's enormous—practically endless. Kind of like Cambry's backpack."

Emma grinned. "Ah. It fits. I'm always teasing Cambry about that backpack. A Boy Scout would be proud to carry that bag around with everything she has in it."

Ethan peeked at the cover of the book Cambry was holding. "*Sense and Sensibility?*"

"We were reading it for our book club," Emma told him.

As his sister and Cambry started discussing the book, Ethan went to help his mom set the table. Soon, dinner was ready, and they all moved into the dining area. It was quite a production as Emma strapped Jessica into the high chair and set a now-sleeping Camille in her infant seat away from the commotion.

After a blessing, they started passing around the food. Ethan was glad to see Cambry relaxing now that she was surrounded by his family. They talked and laughed about simple things, including the changes Ethan noticed around Denver and how he liked living in Baltimore.

When they finished eating, everybody went into the family room to watch some television and talk. Ethan walked over to the couch and was about to sit beside Cambry when Jessica wandered over to him with a shape sorter.

"Unca Efan," she said, her version of *Uncle Ethan* melting his heart every time she said it. "Shapes?"

"You want me to do the shapes with you?" he asked his curly-haired niece, pleased that she was warming up to him so quickly. When she nodded, he lowered himself to the floor beside the couch, his shoulder brushing up against Cambry's leg.

He turned to smile at Cambry over his shoulder, and she smiled back, but he couldn't help noticing the somewhat wistful look in her eyes. As Jessica plunked herself into his lap with her toy, Ethan couldn't help wondering if Cambry was thinking about the children they'd talked about having together. Four, they had decided. She'd wanted two girls and two boys, but he'd wanted four girls. All with auburn hair and brown eyes, just like their mom.

Regret settled like a rock in his stomach. Because of him, she was still single and alone. She worked long hours and went home every night to an empty house. What kind of life was that?

He knew that hadn't been her plan, but his impulsive decision had changed all that. Did she have regrets that her future hadn't been what she'd wanted? That she was living a very different life from the one she'd dreamed of?

Jessica tugged at his hand to recapture his attention, and for the next few minutes, he forced himself to focus on helping his niece fit stars and squares and letters through the proper holes.

They had dessert a while later, and afterward, everybody decided to call it a night. His dad's knee surgery was early the next morning, and Janette announced, over her husband's protests, that he needed his sleep.

While Cambry went to get her backpack and sweater, Ethan managed to persuade Emma to give him Cambry's cell phone number. Just having the number made Ethan feel better, knowing that he could call or text her at any time to make sure she was okay.

When they finished saying their good-nights, Ethan herded Cambry out the door. They were almost to his car when he caught her glancing up and down the street, her expression wary.

"What's wrong?"

"It's probably nothing," she said. "For two nights now I've thought somebody was following me home from work, but it was probably just my imagination."

Ethan fought to keep his expression neutral. "What does this car look like?" he asked, his tone low and serious. "Did you get a look at the driver?"

"No, I couldn't see the driver through the tinted windows, but the car was a black import, four-door, lots of chrome." Then, as if to reason it away, she shrugged and said, "That description fits a lot of cars, I know, so it could have been a totally different one both times."

Deciding not to scare her, he gave her his best casual shrug. "Could have been. I wouldn't worry too much about it. If you see it again, though, let me know."

She nodded, and they were soon driving back to her house, where he insisted on walking her to the door.

"I'm glad I went tonight," she told him as he walked her up her front steps. "You were right. It was just what I needed."

They stopped on the porch in front of her door, and Ethan was relieved to see that some of the tension had left her face.

"See you tomorrow?" she asked as she unlocked her door.

He nodded. "I'm not sure when because I'll be up at the hospital with my dad, but I'll call you and let you know how he's doing."

"That would be great. If he's feeling well enough for visitors, I'd love to go see him after work."

"I'm sure he'd love that too."

Then, in a gesture borne of years of habit, he leaned over and gave her a quick kiss.

It was the barest brush of lips on lips, more a peck than a kiss, but almost the instant their lips touched, Ethan jerked back in mortification. What was he doing?

Cambry looked startled. Then a lovely tinge of color suffused her cheeks.

"Sorry," he murmured, taking a quick step back. "That was . . . um . . ."

She smiled and lifted one auburn brow. "Habit? Don't worry, Ethan. I understand." Then she said a quick good-night and vanished into her house.

He stood on the doorstep for a long minute, battling the warmth engulfing his heart. Wow. It may have been a mistake, but it was one he wouldn't mind making again.

He climbed into his car feeling agitated with himself. He hoped this wasn't going to put her at arm's length again, just when she was getting comfortable with him. As he backed out of her driveway, his thoughts turned to what she'd told him a few minutes ago. *Was* she being followed? If so, why? And by whom?

Reaching for his cell phone, he hit a speed dial button and had Agent Natoni on the line moments later.

"We might have a problem," he told his boss. He explained about Cambry's suspicions and gave him Cambry's description of the car. "We need to look into this. Maybe put a discreet tail on Cambry to see if we can see this car for ourselves and run a plate. It could lead us to Benton."

"Agreed," Natoni said. "What's your assessment of the situation?"

"I think whoever tried to kill her father thinks she has his technology and could be watching to see if she'll lead them to it."

"And does she have it?"

"I'm still working on that. She knows *something*. I just haven't found out what it is. But I will, I promise you that."

Natoni's voice softened. "Good. I have faith in you, Agent Reece. I know this can't be easy, working with her like this, but remember why you're doing it and how important it is."

Ethan's lips firmed. "I know. I'll be in touch soon."

He disconnected his call and soon pulled into his parents' driveway. He didn't like this black car business. Benton was capable of anything, and he had no doubt the person driving the car was one of Benton's men.

Starting tomorrow, he'd make sure he saw her safely delivered everywhere she needed to go. He wasn't about to let anyone hurt her.

He just hoped that included himself.

CHAPTER THIRTEEN

CAMBRY WAS STANDING IN FRONT of her closet in her robe the next morning, trying to decide what to wear to work, when her cell phone rang. She went over to pick it up off her nightstand and saw an unfamiliar number.

"Hello?" answered warily.

"Cambry, it's Ethan."

Her forehead creased in confusion. "How did you get my number?"

"Don't be mad, but I begged it off Emma last night."

A slow smile worked its way across her face. "It's okay," she said, unable to be angry. It wasn't like Emma had handed it around to a bunch of strangers. "Why are you calling? Is your dad okay?"

"He's fine," he hurried to reassure her. "They haven't taken him in for surgery yet, but Dad said I was making him nervous, so he kicked me out. He said to come by with you this evening instead. Mom promised to call with updates. Are you almost ready for work?"

Cambry stalled on the abrupt change in conversation. "Almost. Why?"

"Because I'm waiting for you in your driveway. I came by to drive you to work."

"You did? Why?"

"Bree," he said with an aggravated growl. "Will you stop with the twenty questions? I'd forgotten how much that annoys me."

"Yeah, well, you're not making any sense, and that's annoying the heck out of me," she countered.

He chuckled. "Just hurry up, will you? I'm out here waiting."

"Well, there's no sense waiting out there," she said, moving back to her closet and pulling out clothing. Just come inside and wait in the living room. I'll be down in a few minutes."

She gave him the keypad combination on the front door so he could let himself in, then she hung up. Hurrying to get dressed, she pulled on a flouncy, jade green, knee-length skirt and simple white blouse. The whole time, she tried to suppress the butterflies in her stomach, knowing Ethan was downstairs waiting for her.

That kiss last night had really thrown her. She'd just been starting to get used to the idea of having Ethan around as a friend, and then he'd kissed her. Granted, it had been one done out of years of habit. She got that. But it didn't help her in the battle to keep the walls up around her heart.

Hurrying to finish getting ready, she pulled her hair up into a simple but professional twist and added some makeup. Then she grabbed her leather messenger bag and went downstairs.

Ethan was lounging on the couch, and the sight of him made her traitorous heart do a flip. He wore a dark blue T-shirt that was stretched taut across a wall of solid muscle and tucked into a pair of comfortably worn jeans. He looked right at home flipping through her favorite coffee-table picture book on the sights of Scotland.

He looked up at her and smiled. "You look nice."

"Thank you."

"Let's go, then." He stood and pulled his car keys out of his jeans pocket.

"Just hold on," she said, heading for the kitchen. She held up one finger and quoted, "'First things first, but not necessarily in that order.'"

Ethan laughed. "What?"

She grinned over her shoulder at him as she walked to the pantry. "*Doctor Who*. Don't you remember that line?"

"No, but it sounds like something The Doctor would say. Still able to quote from the show, huh?"

Pulling a small box from the pantry, she turned and gave him an indignant look. "Of course. Best show ever. I especially love the new episodes on BBC."

"Believe it or not, I've seen most of them."

A heady rush of pleasure filled her as she recognized they still had that in common. "You have?"

"What can I say?" He shrugged one large shoulder. "It grew on me after all those years that you made me watch the original show's reruns with you."

She grinned. "Perfect. Another person corrupted." She pulled a foil package from the box, opened the fridge, and pulled out another item for her breakfast.

Ethan looked at her in dismay. "Seriously? An apple and a Pop-Tart? What kind of breakfast is that?"

She ripped open the foil package and took a bite of the unwarmed processed pastry, enjoying his look of mortification as she did so. In fact, the whole interaction was making her heart feel lighter than it had in a long time. There was just something about the old, familiar banter that made everything seem right with the world again.

"You can at least warm it up, for crying out loud," he protested. "That's just nasty."

She gave him a taunting smile. "Believe it or not, I still prefer mine warm."

"Then why are you eating it cold?"

"To annoy you," she announced as she sashayed past him to the front door. "Why else?"

She was rewarded with a deep chuckle, one that lightened her heart even more.

When they arrived at Saville Enterprises, Ethan pulled up to the curb to let her out. "What time are you going to be done with work tonight?" he asked. "I thought I'd pick you up so we could go by the hospital."

"I'd like that. Why don't I call you when I have a better idea of what's going on?"

"Okay." He nodded toward the large glass doors of her building, visible from where they sat. "I'll wait until you get inside."

Realizing that he was intent on seeing her safely delivered made her feel cared for and protected. Thanking him for the ride, she got out of the car and hurried inside.

"Morning, Shanice," she said with a smile as she stepped out of the elevator on the fifth floor and spotted the woman at the reception desk. To Cambry's surprise, Shanice looked frazzled. That was something she'd rarely seen.

"Morning, Cambry." She hurried to pull a stack of papers and packages off the counter, but the top cellophane-wrapped item bounced to the floor.

Cambry hurried over to pick it up. When her hand curled around the familiar item, she looked up at Shanice with a laugh. "What are you doing with a Kong?"

It was a large, red, rubbery ball-shaped dog toy, hollow inside, designed for a large dog's chewing habits. She recognized it from the years she and her mom had spent training and showing German Shepherds.

Shanice let out a troubled sigh. "My son took a construction job in Texas that was only supposed to last two weeks, so he conned me into watching his Old English Mastiff while he was gone. I agreed, even though I'm not a dog person. But two weeks turned into a month, and last night he called to tell me the job became permanent. He can't have Willoughby there because he's working eighteen-hour days and living in a small apartment, so he asked if I could keep him."

Shanice grimaced. "There's no way I'm keeping a dog. All my things are going to be destroyed at this rate. I'm going to have to find him a new home."

The spark of an idea lit in Cambry's head. She loved dogs. She'd had as many as four German Shepherds at a time growing up. She had fond memories of the hours she'd spent with them and her mom, training and showing.

She hadn't really thought about it until now, but she'd missed having a dog around. And with the house so empty and feeling especially lonely as of late, this was possibly the perfect solution. "I might be interested," she heard herself saying to Shanice. "Could I maybe come by tonight and meet him?"

"Oh, heavens, yes!" Shanice gushed, the tension in her body visibly easing. "That would be amazing. Are you sure adding another thing to your plate is a good thing though?"

Cambry smiled. "I think it might be just the thing, actually. I live in that big house by myself, and a furry friend underfoot might be nice."

"He's not exactly a toy poodle," Shanice warned. "He's big and pushy, and he drools. Everywhere."

She laughed. "I know all about mastiffs. I think I could handle it. I've always preferred big dogs to little ones anyway."

"Well, you'd be saving my sanity, that's for sure." Shanice shuffled a bunch of papers and then handed Cambry a stack. "These are for you. Let me know what time you'd like to come by and meet Willoughby."

"I will."

Cambry headed to her office and got to work. Ethan called late morning to let her know his dad had come out of surgery and was doing well. Knowing that everything had gone smoothly was a big relief. She told Ethan he could come pick her up at five, and he said he'd see her then. Just talking with him made her feel happy.

The rest of the day, however, wasn't so nice. She had to deal with disputes on lab time, complete several reports, and talk to one of the project managers about some new high-tech pieces of lab equipment he wanted ordered. Because she was familiar with it, she knew that the equipment was in high demand and was back ordered. The manager wasn't happy.

When a knock sounded on her door at the end of the day, she seriously considered pretending she wasn't there. "Come on in," she called out in a less-than-enthusiastic voice.

Kurt popped his head into her office. "Are you in the middle of something?"

She laughed. "Always. But come on in."

He did and made himself comfortable in the armchair in front of her desk. "I had a few minutes, so I thought I'd come by and see how you're settling in."

"Good, I think," she answered. "I have the feeling I'm going to be overwhelmed for a while before I get the hang of everything."

"Anything I can do to help?"

"Thank you, but no. I'm okay." She looked at Kurt for a moment, considering. "Kurt, you've been here a few years. Do you still like the executive position? Is it worth the frustration?"

Something shifted in Kurt's expression. "It depends what you're in it for." He shrugged. "The job pays well, and it's definitely the place to be because a company like this gives you a lot of opportunities to network. But you know me. I've always been a climber. I never was planning on making this my permanent stop."

She lifted an eyebrow in question. "What are you hoping for next, then?"

"My goal was to springboard from here to a Fortune 500 company, but the economy went south, and those jobs are harder to come by. I've had to stick it out a while longer until the right opportunity came by."

Kurt's cell phone rang, and he gave her an apologetic look as he answered the call. "I'll be just a second," he mouthed.

She smiled to let him know that it was fine. As he talked, she stretched and rolled her head on her neck. Her muscles felt so incredibly tense. Stress was definitely wearing her down. What she needed was a soak in a hot bath. Maybe she should invest in a hot tub. The idea was actually appealing.

Just then another knock sounded on her door, and the sound jarred Cambry back to reality. Her groan slipped out before she could stop it.

Kurt ended his call and laughed. "That bad, huh?"

"If that's one more hostile person coming to gripe at me, I quit." She lifted her fingers to her temples to rub at the increasing tension there as she called out, "Come in!"

The door swung open, and to her surprise, Ethan walked in.

***

Ethan felt his body tense when he walked into Cambry's office and noticed she wasn't alone. A man was with her, and he looked just a little too comfortable for Ethan's liking.

"Ethan," Cambry said, looking surprised. Her eyes flew to the clock on the wall. "You're early."

"Only by twenty minutes," he clarified with a smile. He watched as her hands slid from her temples, and he frowned in concern. He detected tension in the creases between her eyes and in the tightening around the corners of her mouth. He didn't have to be a genius to pick up on the fact she was feeling stressed and overworked.

"If you're not done, I don't mind waiting," he said.

His gaze fell on the man seated in the chair in front of her desk. He did a quick assessment of the guy: Slender. Almost too good-looking. Not very substantial. Smart but a bit insecure. Self-absorbed. And sitting in front of Cambry's desk like he had a right to.

Ethan wasn't impressed. Turning to Cambry, he asked, "Am I interrupting anything?"

"No, Kurt and I were just talking."

"Kurt?" Ethan arched one dark eyebrow.

"Oh, I'm sorry," Cambry said. "Ethan Reece, Kurt Kunde. Kurt is the company's chief financial officer."

"It's nice to meet you." Kurt rose from his chair to shake Ethan's hand, and Ethan exerted more pressure than necessary when their hands met. He took pleasure in seeing Kurt wince.

Out of the corner of his eye, he caught Cambry's disapproving scowl. He gave her a look that said, *What?*

She rolled her eyes.

Fighting a chuckle, he focused once more on the man before him. In his best interrogator voice, he crossed his arms over his chest and asked, "What brings you by Ms. Saville's office?"

He ignored the warning look Cambry shot him.

Seemingly oblivious to his alpha male routine, Kurt smiled. "Just a little conversation."

As if sensing upcoming conflict, Cambry stood up. "I'm actually at a good stopping place with work," she said, gathering her things. "Let's go."

Ethan's gaze softened as he looked at her. "You look tense. Are you okay?"

"Just a rough day." She turned to smile at Kurt. "Guess I'm heading out. I'll talk with you later?"

"I haven't forgotten about our rain check for dinner," he said as he followed them out of the office. "I'll talk with you tomorrow and see when we can get together."

Ethan glared at the man's retreating form. *Over my dead body.*

Cambry turned off the lights and shut her office door. "I just need to give these to Shanice on the way out," she said, indicating a handful of papers.

They stopped at the reception desk on their way past, and Cambry handed Shanice the papers. "What time is good for me to come over to see Willoughby?" she asked.

Shanice smiled. "Anytime. I'm heading home in a few minutes, and I'll be there all evening."

As they walked to the elevator, Ethan had to ask. "Who's Willoughby?"

Cambry looked both smug and excited. "A dog I might be adopting."

"Really?" He watched her in surprise as she punched the elevator button.

She shrugged. "It would be a win-win situation. Shanice's son can't keep him, so Shanice needs to find a home for him. And it's been pretty lonely at my house. With all that's been going on, it would sure make me feel better to have a big, scary-looking dog around."

Ethan inclined his head. He could see the wisdom in that.

Cambry looked at him hopefully. "Want to come with me to see him?"

"Sure." Ethan put a hand on the small of her back to guide her into the elevator when the doors opened. "I've always liked dogs. It's been awhile since you've had your shepherds, hasn't it?"

She nodded. "Since I graduated and moved away to college. Having a big dog around again would be nice."

When they got off the elevator, they crossed the lobby and stepped outside. Cambry looked over at him. "So how's your dad? Tell me how the surgery went."

"It went well," he said as they rounded the corner of the building and headed for the parking lot. "They still plan on releasing him tomorrow morning, and he'll start physical therapy soon after. Right now he's just anxious to go home." Ethan gestured to the side of the parking lot nearest the corner. "I'm parked over there."

He again put his hand on the small of her back to guide her, and warmth from his hand radiated through the thin fabric of her blouse. A tingle of awareness swept through her. She'd forgotten how much she loved the protective, comforting touch of his hand on her back.

They'd almost reached the parking lot when movement from the street corner caught her attention. She glanced to her left, and that's when she spotted it.

A black import, four-door, lots of chrome, parked across the street.

She froze. This time she got a good look at the car, and there was no doubt about it. It was the same one she'd seen before.

Because he had his hand on her back, Ethan stopped the second she did. "Cambry?" he asked, his tone concerned. "What is it?"

She nodded imperceptibly toward the car. "That's the car."

Ethan's gaze flew to where she was looking, and she glanced up at him. His face had become a hardened mask. "Are you sure?"

"Yes."

When Ethan took two steps forward, she gasped and grabbed his arm. "Wait! What are you doing?"

"I'm going to go have a little talk with the driver." The steely menace in his voice sent a shiver along her spine.

Without a word, Ethan started walking toward the street in determined, confident strides. The driver must have realized the game was up because the engine roared to life. With a squeal of tires, the car peeled away from the curb, barely missing the bumper of the car it was parked behind.

Ethan took off. With powerful strides, he sprinted across the street and caught up to the car just as it squealed into the road. His hands thumped against the back rear quarter as it fishtailed past, and Ethan had to jump out of the way to avoid being knocked over. Horns blared as the driver swerved into the oncoming lane of traffic, narrowly missing an approaching car, then swerved violently to the right, nearly colliding with a car merging into traffic.

The erratic maneuver slowed the driver's escape, and Ethan gained the advantage. He was closing in when the car's wheels squealed yet again as it rocketed around the corner then shot off down the street.

With the car's taillights fading into the distance, Ethan's long strides slowed then stopped. He stood in the middle of the road staring after the car, his hands on his waist as his chest heaved. Finally, he turned and started walking back.

The crowd that had gathered on the street corners to watch the chase started to disperse, but Ethan continued to draw a few stares as he walked back toward where Cambry was still standing. His breathing was only slightly labored when he reached her, and his gaze was murderous.

"I need a piece of paper," he all but growled, staring off in the direction the car had gone. "I need to write down the plate number."

Impressed that he'd had the mental clarity to memorize it while running after the car, she fished her notebook out of her bag and handed it to him with a pen. He took it from her and scribbled the information down.

"Did you get a look at the driver?"

He shook his head. "The windows were too dark. But at least this is a start," he said, holding up the notebook.

"Do you want me to call somebody with it? Those FBI agents that talked to me last week, maybe?"

"I'll take care of it." His voice was terse as he ripped the page out of her notebook, folded the paper, and shoved it into his jeans pocket.

For a frightening moment, she managed a glimpse of what he must have been like as a soldier in battle. The single-minded determination and hardness in his face told her he was used to pushing everything out of his mind and focusing solely on the mission. He would have been a force to be reckoned with.

When Ethan snapped her notebook closed and handed it to her, the menacing expression on his face eased. "Do you know if your father's building has security cameras outside?"

"I'm not sure, but I would think so. Let's go back in and check with the security guard. He would know."

Ethan shook his head. "No, I'll take care of everything. For now let's go see my dad. I'll make some phone calls while you're talking to him."

She let Ethan guide her to his car and help her inside. She sat, her body tense, as Ethan shut the door and went around to his side. When he climbed in, he looked preoccupied, his expression hard.

"Ethan, what's going on?" she managed, her chest tight. "Why is somebody following me?"

Ethan's hand stilled on the key in the ignition. He seemed to consider her question for a long moment. Then he let out a troubled breath and sat back in his seat. "Cambry, somebody tried to kill your father, likely for the technology he developed. These same people could be after you, thinking you have it."

Cambry tensed. "Why would they think I have it?"

"You were there with him when he was still conscious. Think. Did he say anything?"

"No. I told you what he said." Cambry started to fidget, and she looked up to see Ethan watching her carefully, his eyes catching and assessing every movement. It made her feel like he could see right through her.

Ethan shifted in his seat to turn slightly toward her. "Cambry, listen," he said, his expression and tone serious. "If your father said *anything* that might help the police or the FBI get to the bottom of this, you have to tell them. Your life could be in danger."

Her lips trembled, and she pressed them together in a tight seam. "He didn't say anything about that missing technology. I don't know anything about it."

His gaze, steady and unnerving, remained on her another minute. Then he turned wordlessly in his seat and started the car. The drive to the hospital was made in silence, which only made Cambry feel more on edge.

When they arrived, Cambry crossed the parking lot with Ethan, feeling unsettled by the black car and by Ethan's explanation. Was her father's attacker really stalking her? Waiting to see what she did and where she went? She couldn't help glancing around for signs of somebody watching her.

A warm hand touched hers, and she jumped. She looked up to see Ethan walking beside her, concern and understanding in his eyes. A lump lodged in her throat. For a traitorous moment, she felt extraordinarily grateful to have this man beside her. She felt safe and protected, which surprised her considering he'd been the one to shatter her heart five years ago.

But the man had just chased a car for her. Who knew if the driver had been armed? Surely Ethan would have known the possible consequences of such an action. He'd been in the war, for crying out loud. He knew how to assess risks. Yet he'd still taken off after that car like a man possessed. That practically earned him a Get Out of Jail Free card.

When they reached the hospital room, they pushed open the door to see Dean sitting up in bed, arguing with Janette about watching another home improvement show. Ethan released her hand, but not before Cambry caught the quick flash of pleasure that darted into Janette's eyes. She clearly hadn't missed the gesture.

"You visit," Ethan said quietly. "I'm going to go make a call."

Cambry caught Ethan's eye, and she knew he was referring to the security tapes and doing what he could to get to the bottom of the person following her.

Thank you, she mouthed as he backed toward the door.

One corner of his mouth lifted, and he gave a slight nod. Then he turned and stepped out into the hall.

When he was gone, Cambry turned back in time to see Janette and Dean exchanging a look. Not wanting to elaborate on the recent events and worry them, Cambry said, "So how did everything go today?"

CHAPTER FOURTEEN

ETHAN DISCONNECTED HIS CALL WITH a frown. His first call had been to Agent Natoni to report the car. Then he'd called Agent Lawford to have him and Agent Arehart research the plate number and get the security tapes from Cambry's building and review them. It was enough to keep the Denver FBI agents busy, but he hoped they would have at least some information as soon as tonight. They didn't have time to waste.

Time. It all came back to that. They didn't know how close Benton and his men were to beating them to the technology, but if Cambry's tail today was any indication, they were as desperate to learn its whereabouts as the FBI was. They wouldn't be watching her if they knew where the technology was.

Cambry was clearly the key. He didn't think she had it. But the fact that Cambry had started to fidget in the car when he'd asked her about it hadn't escaped his notice. She knew *something*. He just needed to find out what it was.

Frustrated, he raked his fingers through his hair and pushed off from the wall. He hated this. All the deceit and half-truths. He just wanted to sweep this all aside and focus on his family. And on Cambry.

Walking back to his dad's room, he tried to put his assignment out of his mind. He heard Cambry's laughter and saw his dad smile. It was clear Dean was enjoying her company, but Ethan could tell his father was getting tired.

Cambry must have picked up on it too because when she saw him walk into the room, she stood up from her chair next to the bed. "We should get going," she told Dean, putting a hand on his arm. "Get some rest. I'll come by the house tomorrow after work, though, to see how you're settling in."

"I'll look forward to it," Dean said, giving Cambry's hand a pat.

They said their good-byes, and Ethan shepherded Cambry out of the hospital. When they were in his car heading home, Cambry asked, "What did you find out?"

He took a moment to construct an elusive answer that would satisfy her. "I made a couple of calls, and I hope to hear something tonight."

"Part of me wants to know who's following me and why, but another part doesn't."

Ethan hated hearing the vulnerability in her voice. She desperately needed to get out and do something to take her mind off all this. "What about Shanice and Willoughby? Should we swing by there before going home?"

Cambry's expression brightened. "Oh! I'd forgotten about that. Let's do."

She gave him directions to Shanice's house, and before long they pulled up in front of an immaculate split-level home with beautiful landscaping.

The inside of the house turned out to be another matter.

When Shanice welcomed them in and went to go get Willoughby from one of the back rooms—she said he'd been put in time out, which made Cambry laugh—Ethan's eyes widened as he looked around at what he could tell would otherwise be an immaculate living room.

A bright, fabric-covered dog bed nearly the size of a tractor tire lay in front of the fireplace, and various dog toys—most of them chewed into unrecognizable shapes—were scattered over the floor. A laundry basket was tipped over on its side near the TV cabinet, and socks were strewn everywhere around the room—several of them unmated and looking a little soggy. One of the wingback chairs near the fireplace had been overturned, and various throw pillows littered the room.

"It looks like a war zone."

"Shh." Cambry elbowed him in the side, but he could hear her suppress a snicker.

Shanice returned a moment later, clinging to an enormous dog's collar and being towed down the hall toward them. She finally released her grip, and the dog rushed forward to greet them.

"Cambry, meet Willoughby," Shanice said with exasperation in her voice. "Willoughby, this is my friend Cambry. Do. Not. Eat. Her."

Cambry laughed as the dog the size of a small pony started wagging his tail and shoved his broad muzzle into her palm, demanding attention.

Shanice gave a weary sigh and sank down onto the couch. "He eats everything else. Why wouldn't he eat you too?"

As Cambry knelt in front of the dog, Ethan took a good look at the beast. The mastiff was enormous, with a giant, squared head that was easily bigger than Cambry's. His coat was a light fawn color, but his ears, muzzle, and the fur around his eyes were almost black. The dark accent coloring on his head made him look even more threatening.

Cambry reached down and started rubbing Willoughby's ear. He promptly let out a moan of pure delight and bent his head, his large dark eyes now looking up at her in adoration.

"Oh, don't do that!" Shanice suddenly sat up and raised a hand toward her. "He'll—" She broke off as they all saw the pool of drool slip from beneath an enormous jowl and dangle like a shoelace for a moment before it dripped down onto the carpet. "Drool."

While Cambry found that enormously funny, Shanice groaned and reached for an old towel draped across the arm of the couch, probably for this very purpose.

Willoughby dropped to the floor at Cambry's feet, leaning his massive weight up against her legs. Cambry shifted a little before he cut off her circulation. "He's fabulous," she said with a laugh. "I'll take him."

Shanice looked at Cambry in surprise. "Just like that?"

Cambry grinned. "Just like that. We're already best friends, aren't we, Willoughby?" She bent over to rub the dog's ears, and he rolled over to expose his belly, which she scratched.

"Cambry, you are heaven-sent," Shanice said. "You can have all his things, which should make it easier. No trip to the pet store for supplies."

Ethan caught Cambry's eye as she straightened. "Are you sure about this?"

She nodded, and he couldn't help thinking she looked happier than he'd seen her since he'd arrived. "It'll be great."

He was skeptical himself, but he figured Cambry must know what she was getting into. He only hoped the dog would fit in the back of his rental car. Or maybe they should rent a horse trailer.

Ethan was a good sport and hauled Willoughby's bed, food, and box of supplies out to the trunk of his car. When he went back inside, he smiled at Cambry.

"I barely got that fifty-pound bag of dog food and his bed into the trunk, and there's no way I'm fitting the bag of toys and leashes in there with them. It'll have to ride on the floor in the backseat with Willoughby."

Cambry looked down at the dog sitting at her side, staring up at her with soulful eyes. "You'd better not make me regret this," she mock scolded him.

"Oh, you will," Shanice told her with a laugh, going over to hug her. "But I will never be able to thank you enough for saving my sanity."

Cambry hugged her back. "It's no problem."

"My son had him microchipped as a puppy, and I'll let you know who to call to change that contact information."

They said good-night and headed outside. Willoughby practically leaped into the backseat when they opened the door for him. Apparently he loved cars. When they got to Cambry's house, Cambry climbed out and opened the back door for Willoughby. She barely caught the end of his leash as he barreled out.

"For a big dog, he's sure got a lot of energy," Ethan said with a grin. "You're going to have your work cut out for you."

"He won't stay this energetic." Cambry reached down to pat his shoulder as he walked beside her to the front door. "Mastiffs are generally pretty laid back and lazy. He's just excited about a new adventure."

Cambry opened the front door and let them in, and Willoughby walked right inside. She left his leash on as she walked with him through the house, giving him the grand doggie tour. When they got back to the kitchen, Ethan took the leash from Cambry's hand.

"Why don't you go on upstairs and change? While he's checking out the downstairs some more, I'll go get his things from the car."

"That'd be great." She paused, then put a hand on his arm. "And thanks for not arguing with me about the spontaneous decision to adopt a dog. I was half expecting you to tell me I was stupid or not giving it enough thought. It's just something I really wanted to do."

Her smile warmed his heart. "I know it was," he said. "I actually think this is a good thing for you. It will be fun. I think you've spent so many years being sensible and proving to yourself and others that you're capable and responsible that you've forgotten how to have fun."

Cambry's jaw slid open in protest. "I have fun. Ask your sister. Ask my other friends. We have fun girls' nights all the time."

"But I'm not talking about *planned* fun, like book clubs or dinners out," he said. "I'm talking about spontaneous fun. Like dancing to the radio just because you like the song. Like playing a practical joke on someone. Like sliding across your gorgeous hardwood floors. Remember how we used to do that at my house when we were growing up?"

The memory brought a smile to her face. "Like the time you overshot and hit the sliding glass door? You were lucky it didn't shatter. I thought your mom was going to skin you alive."

He chuckled. "She was tempted, that's for sure. I never slid that direction again, just in case. But that's what I'm talking about. When was the last time you did something spontaneous like that?"

Cambry's smile faded, and he realized he'd hit a sore spot. Before things could go downhill, he nudged her toward the stairs. "Go. Change. I'll take care of the pony."

She hesitated but then nodded and disappeared upstairs.

Ethan released Willoughby and went out to the car to bring in the dog's things. He stacked them in the entry and then straightened and looked around for Willoughby. That's when he noticed the big puddle in the middle of the kitchen floor.

Ethan groaned. Either Willoughby wasn't housebroken very well, or he just hadn't been able to wait until they took him out back.

With a resigned sigh, he went into the kitchen, skirted the puddle the size of Lake Superior, and opened the cabinet under the sink to look for cleaning supplies. He'd just finished the unpleasant task and sprayed something to combat the smell when his phone rang.

He quickly washed his hands and answered the call. "Reece here."

"I've got some information for you," Agent Lawford reported.

"Can you hold on a minute?" Ethan asked, making a grab for Willoughby, who had just come in to investigate the interesting new smells on the kitchen floor. He glanced up at the stairs, knowing Cambry could be down any second. "Let me get somewhere I can talk."

He opened the sliding glass door, shooed Willoughby outside, then stepped out onto the paved patio. When the door was shut, he continued. "What did you find?" he asked, keeping his voice quiet in case Cambry had a window open upstairs.

"The plate we ran belongs to a vehicle in a corporate fleet here in Denver. At first glance, the corporation doesn't appear to have any ties to Isaac Benton, but we'll keep looking. It was signed out to a man named Joseph Patterson, but according to the supervisor I spoke with, Patterson's in Washington at a conference. Charges on the man's credit card seem to back up that claim, so he couldn't have been the driver."

Ethan frowned. "I didn't think it would be straightforward, but I'd hoped. What about the security at Saville Enterprises?"

"There were two outside cameras—one covering the parking lot and the street running along the north, and one covering the front of the building and a little of the street in front. I have two agents reviewing them as we speak. What exactly should we be looking for?"

"Anything that gives us information about the vehicle in question. I want to know if the driver parked somewhere around the perimeter all day or if there were frequent drive-bys. Maybe we'll even luck out and see the driver get out at some point so we can ID him. Call me with what you find, day or night."

"You got it."

"One more thing. I'd like you to task an agent to start following Cambry and keep an eye out for a tail. I might have scared the guy off tonight, but then maybe I didn't. If we can find out who's following her, it could get us the break we need."

After Lawford assured him they were on it, Ethan hung up. With help from the local field agents, he hoped they could get to the bottom of this quickly. They had to find Benton. He only hoped they'd catch up with Benton before Benton caught up with Cambry.

***

As Cambry changed out of her work clothes and into jeans and a T-shirt, she felt surprisingly melancholy. Ethan's words had hit a nerve.

The depressing thing was that she suspected he was right. She couldn't remember the last time she'd done anything spontaneous, something just because. Her whole life since her mom's death had been about proving herself—proving to her estranged father that she didn't need him or his money, proving to her friends and family that she was able to stand on her own two feet, proving to everyone—including herself—that she didn't need anybody or anything.

When had she become so focused on proving herself capable and responsible that she'd forgotten to *enjoy* life? When had everything become all about responsibility and to-do lists? Deadlines and promotions? Somewhere along the way, she'd forgotten to enjoy the journey.

She finished dressing and then sat down on her bed to put on her favorite comfy wool socks to ward off the chill of the hardwood floors downstairs. Wiggling her toes inside the soft socks, she got up and opened the bedroom window a little to air out the stagnant room.

Ethan's voice drifted up to her, and she guessed he was taking a call out on the patio. She could see Willoughby moving around the yard, happy for some space.

She stared at her old swing set out in the corner of the yard. Even as teenagers, she and Ethan had used it, laughing and having contests to see who could swing the highest. She hadn't thought about doing anything like that for a long time. Or anything else silly or spontaneous, for that matter.

She left her bedroom and went back downstairs. The first thing she saw was the pile of dog things in her entryway. But there was no sign of Ethan or Willoughby. They were probably still out back.

She turned around, and her slick wool socks slipped a little on the hardwood floor. A memory flashed into her head. Hardwood floors and new socks. Hadn't Ethan just reminded her of that? Her eyes moved speculatively across the large expanse of shiny hardwood floor stretching from the entryway all the way through to the other side of her kitchen.

Did she dare?

The previously suppressed kid in her leaped at the prospect. Ethan had said she needed to be spontaneous, to enjoy the simple things. What had been more fun than sliding across glossy hardwood floors in slippery socks?

Her stomach jangled with excitement as she straightened and braced one foot slightly behind her for traction. Then, before she could chicken out, she took off. She took three energetic strides and then planted.

Her momentum carried her forward through the kitchen doorway, and she squealed as she widened her stance slightly to keep her feet beneath her. She'd just reached the area in front of the fridge when disaster struck.

The smooth floor suddenly seemed to have turned to ice. She started to go down. Her legs scrambled for purchase as her arms windmilled. She made a frantic grab for the handle of the fridge but only succeeded in knocking off several of the magnets holding papers on the door. The magnets went shooting across the floor like hockey pucks, and papers fluttered down like confetti. Before she could brace herself, her bottom connected with the floor with a painful thump, then the back of her head connected with the fridge.

The silence that followed seemed to reverberate through the empty room as she lay there in shock. Then a loud moan filled the silence. It took her a moment to realize it was hers. The sound of the sliding glass door opening reached her ears, and a moment later, Ethan stepped inside. His eyes widened when he saw her sprawled across the floor.

"Cambry, are you okay?" he asked, shutting the door behind him and rushing over. "What happened?"

As he crouched down beside her and put a steady arm behind her back to help her sit up, she put a hand to the back of her head. "I came downstairs, and after everything you'd just said, I looked and saw that wide expanse of hardwood floors . . ."

He started to laugh as he helped her gingerly to her feet. "You slid!" he cried out happily.

"Yes, I slid." She straightened, grateful for his hand around her waist, then reached for the sore spot on her tailbone. She groaned. "My body will never be the same again, thank you very much. Why did you have to put such an idea back into my head?"

He was still laughing as he tightened his arm around her. "Are you all right?"

She nodded as she stood gingerly on her feet. "I think so. Just remind me never to do that again."

"I'm sorry," he said, suddenly looking repentant. "This is my fault. That walking mountain of a dog wet on your kitchen floor while you were upstairs, so I put him outside and cleaned it up—you owe me big time for that, by the way. After I cleaned up, I looked for some kind of air freshener, but the only thing I could find was the can of lemon Pledge in your basket of cleaning supplies under the sink."

She stared at him in openmouthed disbelief. "You sprayed furniture polish on my hardwood floor?"

He grimaced. "And apparently turned it into a skating rink. Sorry."

She started to laugh, and he soon joined in. When their laughter faded, he said, "Regardless of the outcome, this is a good thing. In the last hour you adopted a wildebeest and slid across your floor like a teenager. I can see a hint of the old you peeking out from underneath that serious exterior. There's hope for you yet."

"Thanks, I think," she answered with a wince as she touched the throbbing spot on the back of her head.

He shook his head, but there was still the hint of a smile hovering around the corners of his mouth. "How bad is it? Let me see."

He closed the distance between them and pushed her hand aside. Then he cradled her head in his large hands and ran his fingers lightly over the back of her head. She winced again when his fingers found the tender spot.

"You have a nice goose egg going here, but I doubt it's anything serious. Think you'll live?"

The corners of his mouth twitched, and it was all she could do to keep from slugging him.

"No thanks to you," she scolded, looking up into his face.

It wasn't until then that she realized just how close they were, their faces only inches apart. The air around them suddenly felt charged, electric. The brilliant green of his eyes seemed startlingly bright in the gleam of the fluorescent lights overhead, the sudden intensity of his gaze mesmerizing.

His amusement faded, and something in his expression made her breath catch in her chest. His eyes roamed over her face, taking in the tumble of red curls, pausing at her lips, then drifting back up until his eyes met hers again.

Her heart felt like it was going to explode from her chest. He wasn't going to kiss her, was he? Did she even want him to?

His hand slid around from the back of her head to her cheek, and he trailed his fingertips lightly along her cheekbone. She stood still and tried to control the sudden hitch in her breathing. But even as she tried to shore up those walls around her heart, the soft touch of his palm made her traitorous heart waver. It had been so long since somebody had touched her like this. Since she had wanted somebody to touch her like this.

And then, before she could even draw a breath, his lips were on hers.

His kiss was painfully tender at first, barely there, as if feeling out her acceptance. Then, as if they had a will of their own, her lips softened against his. That was all the encouragement he needed.

Pleasure ripped through her as his lips moved over hers slowly, deliciously. She savored the warm softness of her lips against his, the absolute rightness of kissing him. That hadn't changed. So many things between them had but not that. Everything else, the past and the present, fell away. The heavy weight was gone.

When at last he pulled away, he didn't go far. She could still feel his breath on her lips as she opened her eyes. Their gazes met and held, and she saw something lurking in his eyes. Yearning. Hope.

Ethan backed away, a look of gentleness in his expression that made her heart melt. "I'd better go," he said. "Do you want me to put Willoughby's stuff anywhere in particular?"

"No, just leave it. I'll put things away later." She walked stiffly with him to the door, her hand braced on her lower back. "Oh, I meant to ask. Who were you on the phone with earlier? Was it something about the security cameras?"

Something flickered in his eyes. Wariness. Maybe even guilt?

Before she could analyze what he might feel guilty about, he shook his head and said, "No news yet. I'm still looking into things."

A bark sounded, and a look of relief crossed Ethan's features at the interruption. "Sounds like he wants back in. I'll see you tomorrow, okay?"

He reached up to trail a finger down her cheek, his eyes meeting hers in a moment of connection. Then he was gone.

Cambry locked the door behind him. Relief at avoiding her questions? Possibly guilt? What was going on?

She turned and walked carefully across the kitchen to the back door, her tail bone and head still smarting from her earlier attempt at spontaneity.

In the future, maybe she should ease into spontaneity a little more carefully. And that included the spontaneous kissing of handsome men.

***

Garrison walked into his hotel suite and shut the door firmly behind him. He pulled his cell phone out of his pocket and dialed.

"You'd better have good news," Benton growled.

He was tense. Garrison got that. But this wasn't his fault, and he wasn't about to take the fall.

"We have a complication. Santos reported in. He's seen Ms. Saville several times in the past couple of days with one man in particular. That man caught sight of the tail this afternoon and chased down Santos's car. Santos managed to get away, but the guy must have gotten the plate number because we got a hit that somebody ran the plates. The paper trail is nonexistent, so nobody will trace the car back to us, but Santos ditched the car anyway. I asked around and learned that the man's name is Reece. Preliminary reports say he's FBI."

"That's all I need. I know the FBI has been nosing around, but having one suddenly getting all chummy with Saville is a problem."

"Want me to take care of him?"

"No, just sit tight until I get there. We're out of time. If I don't have the technology by this weekend, my buyer walks. I'm going to take the jet and fly in early tomorrow morning. Get the helicopter ready. I'll take it to the ranch and meet you there. I expect to hear a full report on this Reece guy when I arrive."

"Understood. See you then." Garrison clicked off the call and then tossed the phone onto the bed. He could make the arrangements after he checked out and was on his way to the ranch. He'd already told his man to have both the helicopter and ranch ready in case Benton needed them, and he was glad he had. Benton often rented out the five hundred–acre guest ranch northwest of Denver to colleagues for retreats, and it would have been occupied if he hadn't anticipated every eventuality.

This did present a slight problem for him though. He was going to have to make some last-minute changes to his own plans.

CHAPTER FIFTEEN

CAMBRY FINISHED APPLYING HER EYELINER and then put all her cosmetics back in her bag. She glanced at her watch. If she hurried, she would have just enough time to eat some cereal before she left for work.

She was in the process of putting her cell phone into her slim, black, knee-length skirt's miniscule pocket when Willoughby sauntered into the room, tail wagging, mouth curled into what appeared to be a satisfied smile.

A bright white, *drippy* smile.

She gasped. What was dripping from his mouth?

As she stood staring at him in shock, white drool dripped from his jowls and landed in a puddle on the floor. That jarred her out of her shock and spurred her into action.

"Willoughby, what have you done?" she exclaimed in a panic, rushing over to him and grabbing his massive head in her hands. She did her best to hold his head still as she tried to determine what the substance was. One of her cleaning chemicals? Soap?

She sniffed. It smelled . . . minty.

What on earth . . . ?

With a jerk, Willoughby dislodged his head from her hands, turned, and loped out of her bedroom.

"Willoughby! Get back here!"

She took off after him, running down the hall and stairs and into the kitchen, where he stopped near the sink. She skidded to a stop in her panty-hosed feet, trying to keep her feet beneath her this time. She didn't want a repeat of last night.

Willoughby grabbed for a white-coated item on the floor, happily situating it in his mouth, and chomped down. More white gushed from the object.

Cambry made a grab at his collar and gave it a firm jerk. "Drop it!"

He stared up at her rebelliously. The tilt of his head gave her a better look, and realization dawned. His dog toothpaste. Vanilla mint, to be exact.

"Willoughby! Did you take this from the mudroom bathroom?" she asked. "This was a brand-new tube!"

White paste oozed with every movement of Willoughby's jaws, and white drool was starting to puddle on the hardwood floor at their feet. She tried to pull the tube of dog toothpaste from his mouth, but her efforts only became a fun, new game of tug o' war for Willoughby. When her hands grew slick from the fight, Cambry gave up with a snort of exasperation. Willoughby's eyes gleamed with satisfaction, and his tail wagged as he waited for her next move.

"Don't you dare look pleased with yourself," she reprimanded as she tried to figure out her next course of action.

Opening his mouth to chomp down again, Cambry thought quickly and made a grab for the tube before his jaws could close. She succeeded in ripping it away.

"Hah!" she exclaimed victoriously, holding it up out of his reach. Ignoring his efforts to jump up to grab the tube again, she inspected the remains. Willoughby had managed to split the tube down the middle and had flayed it open. It looked like gutted African roadkill.

She glanced down at Willoughby, who was sitting and looking up at her in eager anticipation. "Don't even think about it," she said, glowering at him. "Where else did you smear this stuff?"

She looked around the room for more of the substance. There were traces of it on the floor, on the fridge, and on a few of her lower cupboard doorknobs. Soon it would crust over, and then it would take a bucket of hot water and a sponge to clean up.

"You're in big trouble, buster. How am I supposed to find time to clean all this up? I'm supposed to leave for work in fifteen minutes!"

Just then her cell phone rang. She rushed to the sink to wash the toothpaste and drool off her hands before answering. Then she yanked the phone out of her pocket, clicked the Talk button, held the phone to her ear, and snapped, "What!"

A low chuckle came across the line. "Good morning to you too, Sunshine."

She groaned inwardly. *Ethan.*

"Sorry," she mumbled, feeling contrite. "You caught me at a bad moment. Willoughby just gutted a tube of his doggie toothpaste, and it's *everywhere.*"

Judging from his sudden bout of coughing and throat clearing, he was doing his best not to laugh. "Hmm," he said noncommittally. Then, "Maybe he's just trying to christen your place?"

"Not funny, Ethan."

He didn't bother apologizing. "I'll help you clean it up. In the meantime, though, I called to ask a favor."

"Hold on just a sec." Cambry walked over to the kitchen garbage can and dropped the destroyed tube into the can. Then, thinking ahead, she picked up the garbage can and shut it in the mudroom bathroom around the corner. Knowing dogs as well as she did, Cambry figured Willoughby would be Dumpster diving for it as soon as her back was turned.

Willoughby followed her, looking forlorn once the bathroom door was shut.

"Okay, what's the favor?"

"My mom went up to the hospital early this morning to be with Dad, so I was hoping I could get a ride with you into the city. I wanted to help my dad get checked out and then drive him and Mom home in their car."

"Sure, no problem."

He thanked her and told her he'd be over shortly, and true to his word, he arrived not five minutes later.

When Cambry let him in and they went into the kitchen, he looked around at the toothpaste drying on the knobs, floor, and fridge, and his face creased in amusement.

His gaze moved over to Willoughby, who was lying in the corner on his huge pillow, his chin on his knees, looking like he'd lost his favorite toy. Maybe he had. "Willoughby, I think you're in serious trouble."

"That he is," Cambry said as she walked back to a bucket of water and picked up the sponge to resume wiping toothpaste from cabinet knobs.

"Here, let me do that." Ethan walked over to take the sponge from her. "Go finish getting ready for work."

She straightened and handed him the sponge, a look of gratitude on her face. "Thank you. I need to change my clothes. I'll be down in a minute."

It only took a few minutes, and when she came back down, Ethan was finishing rinsing out the sponge.

"There's no way I'm leaving him inside unattended all day, that's for sure," she said with a frown. "I'm going to put him in the garage until I get home. It's going to be cooler today, so he'll be fine. Could you possibly carry his bed out there so he has somewhere comfortable to lie?"

"Sure thing."

After letting Willoughby outside for a few minutes, Cambry shooed him into the garage with his bed and a large bowl of water. Then she and Ethan headed into town.

When they pulled up in front of the hospital, Ethan said, "Thanks for the ride. You sure you'll be okay today without me around? If you see anything suspicious—strange cars or people hanging around—call me. Don't even wait."

Memories of yesterday stopped her from downplaying his concern. "I will."

When she got to her office, she had a stack of messages waiting and several reports to go through. It was more than enough to distract her. Strangely, she was grateful for that.

***

Garrison pulled into the parking area in front of the ranch's front lodge and stopped beside two four-wheel-drive vehicles and an unmarked black van with tinted windows. Two large, formidable-looking men dressed in camo and clutching sidearms appeared in the lodge doorway. When they saw Garrison, they relaxed.

Garrison grabbed a folder from the passenger seat and climbed out of his car. He followed the two men through the lodge's front room and then down a long hallway that eventually led to an office at the back of the structure.

When they knocked and Benton's deep voice responded, they opened the door and gestured for Garrison to go in. When he did, they quickly closed the door behind him, leaving him alone with Benton.

Benton looked up at him expectantly. "Did you get it?"

"Yeah." Garrison tossed the folder onto the desk in front of Benton. "The man's name is Ethan Reece. He's FBI, and before that, marines. Special Forces. I had my guy at FBI headquarters look into it. He was able to grease a few palms and learn that Reece has been sent in undercover to get close to Ms. Saville. Find out what she knows about her father's missing technology. Reece and Saville were apparently involved a few years ago, and the agent in charge thought he'd be their best chance to get inside and find out what she knew."

"Clever." Benton's mouth stretched into a grim line. "We both decided the girl could be the key. Problem is they got to her first."

"There's been no indication they're any closer than we are," Garrison said. "Reece's presence is a complication, but it's nothing we can't handle."

"If the feds have somebody on the inside, we're going to have to get this done *now.* No more tiptoeing around, no more waiting for Ms. Saville to make a move. Our buyer is antsy, and I stand to lose millions on this deal if he bails. Break into her house and look hard. I want it found."

Garrison thought about that. "Our surveillance man tells us she goes to work and then home. She doesn't go out much in the evening, at least not long enough for us to handle a search of her house. Maybe a quick run to the store or something."

"Then our best chance is to set up a diversion," Benton said. "Get with our man inside and have him arrange to get her out of the house for a while tonight. Even for a couple of hours. That should give you and your team enough time to get in and dig. She's got to have that research somewhere."

Garrison nodded and took a step backward toward the door. "I'll call you as soon as we're finished."

***

Cambry's busy workday was broken up by a pleasant lunch with Kurt. He talked a lot about the latest Fortune 500 companies he was applying to and the palms he planned to grease to make his climb up the ladder of success. Cambry had never been interested in making it to the top, so to speak; she'd always been more interested in enjoying the work she was doing and the people she worked with. Good for Kurt for pursuing his own dream though.

They finished lunch and then drove back to the office together. "We should do this again," Kurt told her as they rode the elevator up to their floor. "I had a good time."

"I did too."

As soon as they stepped off the elevator, Shanice smiled. "Oh, good, you're back," she said to Cambry. "The lab manager needed to talk to you. Apparently, the wrong equipment was delivered, and they need your authorization to make a rush order on the correct ones."

"Sounds like you have work to do," Kurt said, touching her arm lightly. "Thanks for lunch."

He lifted his hand in a parting wave and moved off down the hall opposite hers. When Cambry turned back to Shanice, she saw the woman looking at her expectantly with the beginnings of a smile hovering on her lips.

"What?" Cambry asked with a grin. "Don't start."

"Lunch with Kurt? And yesterday with Ethan? You've got men coming out of the woodwork."

Cambry snorted. "Hardly. Ethan and Kurt are both friends. Nothing more."

"Mmmhmm," Shanice murmured, holding out Cambry's messages.

Cambry bit back a smile as she snatched the messages. "You're a menace."

Shanice's laugh followed her down the hall. Cambry headed into her office to get back to work, but Ethan called just a few minutes later. He told her that he and his mom and dad were home, and that other than feeling tired, Dean was doing well.

"Are you sure you're okay driving home tonight?" Ethan asked.

"I'll be fine," she assured him. "I didn't see anything out of the ordinary on my way to work or when I went out to lunch with a friend just a little while ago."

"Who did you go out to lunch with?"

"Kurt," she said. "Caught up on old times. You know."

A pause. "Old times. Really."

The note of jealousy in Ethan's voice was unmistakable. Why that pleased her so much, she didn't know.

After they hung up a few minutes later, Cambry turned her attention back to work. It was a busy afternoon, and by five thirty she was more than ready to call it a day. She was just packing up her things when a knock sounded on her open door. She looked up to see Jim standing in her doorway, looking concerned.

"I hadn't heard back from you about tonight, so I thought I'd stop in and make sure you got the memo."

Cambry's hands stilled in the process of straightening a stack of papers. "Uh-oh. What memo?"

"The staff and board meeting tonight? The change in time?" When she only continued to look at him blankly, he blew out a breath. "Oh boy. I should have talked to you earlier."

"What meeting? Fill me in."

"We have a monthly meeting with the executives and board members," he explained. "It's normally on the last Thursday afternoon of the month, but one of our board members was flying in late and couldn't make it in time, so we agreed to push the meeting back until seven o'clock tonight so everyone could be there. We have two big contracts to make decisions about. Are you able to come? It's really important."

She gave a resigned sigh and nodded. "I'll be there."

After Jim left, Cambry reached for her phone. She got Ethan on the second ring.

"It turns out that I have a staff meeting at seven, and it doesn't make sense for me to drive all the way home just to turn around and come back."

"That stinks."

"I know. Could you do me a favor and run over and let Willoughby out back for a while? And give him his dinner? He's been cooped up all day."

"Sure, no problem. Do you want me to just put him back in the garage before I leave?"

"That'd be great. Thanks, Ethan."

She hung up the phone feeling grateful that Ethan was such a good sport. Any man who would willingly go deal with a two-hundred-pound mastiff was indeed a good friend.

Cambry spent the next couple of hours working, consoled by the fact that at least she was catching up on her paperwork. She was on her way to the boardroom when she got a text message from Ethan.

Willoughby's fine, all shut back in. I'm riding into the city on the light rail to run a few errands. Can I ride home with you after your meeting?

Cambry stared at his message suspiciously. Ethan needed to come into Denver to run errands tonight? It sounded suspiciously like an excuse for him to play bodyguard.

Is that such a bad thing? the voice in her head challenged. *What's wrong with having a handsome man looking out for you?*

Texting Ethan back, she typed, *That's fine. I'll text you when the meeting is over.*

Cambry greeted the other executives in the boardroom and sat down at the long table. She pulled her cell phone out of her pocket to silence it, but just then another text came in. Seeing that everyone was still talking and getting settled, she opened the message. Her heart lurched when she saw it was from Alisa.

I'm on a job tonight or else I'd call, but can you come over first thing tomorrow morning? I ran into a few problems with your project that I want to discuss.

Cambry's palms turned clammy as she reread the text. What problems exactly?

Jim called for everyone's attention, so Cambry silenced her phone and put it back in her pocket. The first order of business was ordering in food, but because she wasn't picky, she let the others decide. Her thoughts were too occupied with Alisa's cryptic text message and what it could mean.

CHAPTER SIXTEEN

ETHAN'S HEAD JERKED UP AT the sound of heels clicking across the marble tile, and he saw Cambry coming across the lobby. She looked tired. Not that he blamed her. It was almost nine thirty—well past the hour she should be home.

He stood up from his armchair near the front doors, where he'd been waiting. "You okay? You look exhausted."

"I'm okay. Just very ready to get out of here."

He fell into step beside her. "How was your meeting?"

She shrugged. "A meeting. Jim apologized for it running late and told us we could come in a couple hours later in the morning."

"That's something."

She looked down at the large bag he was carrying, eyeing it curiously. "What do you have?"

Ethan smiled, feeling very proud of himself. "Banana cream pie," he announced, spreading the handles so she could peek inside. "I stopped by the bakery on my way here. My mom told me it was still your favorite."

Tears appeared in Cambry's eyes. "You stopped to buy me a pie?"

"Yeah." His forehead creased in concern. "Was that okay? I figured you might need a pick-me-up, and I thought we could share it at your place before I go home."

She surprised him by throwing her arms around him. It was a neat trick, considering they were still walking. He laughed and gave her a one-armed hug, trying to keep the pie from being demolished. "I take it you approve."

"Thank you," she said, some color coming back into her cheeks. "That was amazingly thoughtful."

When they stopped next to her car, Ethan held out his hand. "Give me your keys."

Cambry looked up at him in surprise. "Why?"

"I'm going to drive. You're dead on your feet."

She handed them over without hesitation. He got her into the car, and before long they were pulling up to her house.

"Don't open the garage," she told him. "Let's leave my car out here until I get Willoughby outside."

When they got out of the car, Ethan could hear Willoughby barking ferociously.

"What's gotten into him?" Cambry asked as Ethan came around the front of the car. "Mastiffs generally aren't barkers." Then she directed her next words at the garage door. "Willoughby, enough!"

There was a moment of silence. Then Willoughby whined plaintively a couple of times before starting to bark again.

"Let's get inside so we can let him out before he makes the neighbors nuts," Ethan said as they walked briskly toward the front door.

They'd just mounted the first step to the porch when Ethan put a hand on her arm to stop her. She looked over at him, her brows drawing together. "What?"

He nodded at the door. It was open a couple of inches. "I shut that when I left at six," he told her in a low voice.

Cambry's throat tightened, making it difficult to breathe. "Could you have maybe not pulled it shut all the way? With the new weather stripping, it can be hard to shut."

He shook his head and set the bag containing the pie down by the door. Then he reached for his weapon in the ankle holster under his jeans. Cambry's eyes widened as he smoothly pulled out the 9mm.

"What are you doing?" she whispered, staring in shock at his weapon.

"Stay there." He pointed to the far end of the porch where the house met the protruding angle of the garage. It was away from windows and made a nice hidey hole. She'd be safe enough there while he checked the house.

"But—"

He cut her off with a look that made her back up a half step. "Just do it!" he hissed. "If you see anything, holler. If not, don't make a sound. Just sit tight until I come back for you. Understand?"

"But what if—"

"Cambry." He bit out her name in a harsh whisper, his patience gone. "Just do as I say."

Her mouth stretched into a taut line, but she backed away, looking equal parts petulant and frightened.

Turning back, he took a silent step that put him right next to the door. He listened. Everything was silent.

With his gun at the ready, he put a flat palm on the door and eased it open. He crept forward, stepping gingerly over the threshold. He glanced once more in Cambry's direction and was satisfied when she remained unmoving. She watched him with anxious eyes as he disappeared through the doorway.

Turning his attention back to the interior, his gaze swept through the shadows. A knot formed in his stomach as he took in the condition of the room. Even in the dark, he could see the evidence of a search. Books had been pulled off the shelves by the fireplace and were now littering the floor. The coffee table contents were scattered and strewn.

He moved on. The kitchen looked relatively untouched, but the downstairs bedroom Cambry used as an office was a disaster. Papers had been scattered, CD jewel cases lay open and devoid of their contents, and the bookshelves and the hutch over the desk were in complete disarray. Even pictures on the wall had not been spared, as if somebody had made the effort to look behind them for a possible wall safe. A framed BBC *Doctor Who* poster had been knocked from the wall and was lying askew on top of the couch against the wall.

Backing out of the room, he checked the spare bedrooms and found them relatively untouched. Cambry's master bedroom, however, was another matter. Drawers had been upended, and clothes were scattered around the room. The closet had been gutted. The boxes on the shelf in her closet had been opened and dumped. There wasn't a square foot of empty floor space anywhere in the room.

His last stop was her bathroom. Other than vanity drawers having apparently been gone through, it checked out. Lowering his weapon, he turned and left the room. Whoever had been in the house was long gone.

The break-in had to be connected to Benton. But what did they think Cambry had? Judging from the thoroughness and haste of the search, they were looking for something very specific, and they knew they only had a limited amount of time.

Ethan went back downstairs and stepped out onto the front porch. To her credit, Cambry hadn't moved. Her expression was tense and anxious, and she waited for him to nod before she approached him.

"Whoever was here is long gone, but your house is a mess. Somebody was looking for something." He lifted one eyebrow and gave her a hard stare. "The question is what do you have that's valuable enough for somebody to come looking for?"

Something unreadable flashed across her face. His mouth pulled into a firm line as he leaned down to slip his 9mm back into its ankle holster. When he straightened, his eyes met hers with dogged determination.

"Cambry, I know there's something you're not telling me. Don't you think it's about time you leveled with me about whatever it is?"

Her face paled. "I don't know what somebody could possibly be looking for," she said, her movements nervous as she pushed past him and headed for the door. "Maybe it was just a random break-in."

He could tell from her tone that even she didn't believe that. Fighting back his frustration at being continually rebuffed, he picked up the bag containing the pie and followed her inside. After he set the pie down on her counter, he pulled out his cell phone. He didn't bother calling the police. He wanted his own team on this.

When Cambry headed through the mudroom to the garage and out of earshot, he dialed Agent Lawford.

"Yeah, it's me," he said when the agent answered his call. "We have a problem."

As he moved back into the entryway, he explained in a low voice about the break-in. He heard the garage door open, followed by the sound of canine claws scrambling for purchase. Then Willoughby came barreling into the kitchen, where he stopped and immediately began sniffing every inch of the place.

Lawford promised to have a forensics team over in half an hour. Ethan hung up and walked down the hall to the office. He stopped in the doorway and watched Cambry bend over to pick up a plant that had been knocked off the desk. She set it off to the side and surveyed the mess, her expression somber.

"Don't touch anything," he said. "Someone's coming over to dust for fingerprints and look around."

"Please tell me Detective Dalton won't be in the group."

He shook his head. "Not a chance. I used my contacts. An FBI forensics team is on the way over."

She looked at him in astonishment. "You must have a lot of pull."

He pressed his lips together. *You have no idea.*

"Your bedroom's a disaster too," he said, changing the subject. "It might be a good idea to look around and see if anything is missing."

When Agent Lawford arrived a short time later, he was with two other men. They all stared warily at the huge dog on Ethan's heels.

"Don't worry, he won't bite," Ethan said.

He ushered the men inside and shut the door behind them. Agent Lawford instructed them to start at the front door and work their way through the areas Ethan said had been searched. The men nodded and went to work.

Agent Lawford turned to Ethan. "Is she okay?"

He nodded. "A little shaken up, but she's coping. She's upstairs putting clothes away. I told her not to touch anything else."

"Good. If these guys left any prints, we'll do our best to find them. You know that's a long shot though."

"I know."

"Has she told you anything yet?" Lawford's gaze swept the ransacked room. "It's obvious this wasn't a typical break-in. Somebody was looking for something, and my bet's on Benton's men. They must think she has her dad's research, and they're getting desperate."

"My thoughts exactly. She hasn't told me anything, but if these people didn't find whatever it was they were looking for, they're going to be coming for her next. Her life could be in danger. I don't think she realizes the gravity of the situation."

"Then tell her," Lawford said, looking a little agitated. "It might scare her enough that she'll come clean about whatever information she's withholding."

He thought about that and realized Lawford was right. He certainly wasn't getting very far tiptoeing around her. But he had to tread carefully. If he let on why he wanted to know what she was hiding, the game would be up.

He stepped away from the commotion to call Natoni and give him an update. Afterwards, Ethan found Agent Lawford in Cambry's office. "Natoni wants surveillance on the house tonight," he said in a quiet voice so Cambry wouldn't overhear if she came downstairs. "We need to make sure whoever did this doesn't come back."

Lawford nodded. "I'll set it up."

Cambry appeared in the doorway a few moments later. "Anything?"

Ethan shook his head. "Not yet. It could be a while, though, if they find anything at all." He put his hand on her arm and nudged her away from the door. "Let's let these guys do their work. How about we take Willoughby out back for a while?"

She followed without question, and soon they were seated on the lounge chairs on the back patio eating slices of the pie Ethan had bought earlier. The sound of the sliding glass door opening drew their attention, and Ethan looked over to see Agent Lawford standing in the doorway.

"I'll be right back," Ethan told Cambry as he swung his leg over the lounge chair and climbed to his feet. He crossed the patio and went inside, shutting the door behind him.

"We're finished here," Agent Lawford said. "No prints, no indication who was involved."

"It's what we expected. Natoni would have had my head, though, if we hadn't looked. Thanks for the rush job."

"I made arrangements for surveillance. Two teams of agents will be trading off watching the house tonight."

"I appreciate you being so on top of all this."

Lawford shrugged into his jacket. "It's what I'm here for."

After showing the agent out, Ethan went back through the kitchen. He met Cambry as she came in through the sliding glass door juggling the empty dessert plates.

He hurried over to take the plates from her. "The agents just left. They didn't find anything."

Her face fell. "I was hoping they would. Then maybe this part of my nightmare would be over."

Ethan's jaw tensed as he set the plates in the sink. When he turned back to her, he leaned back against the sink and folded his arms over his chest. She looked tired, and he knew she'd had a long, stressful day. But he had to have his questions answered, once and for all. He wasn't leaving empty-handed.

"What's that look?" she asked suspiciously.

"It's my *I'm out of patience* look." His tone was firm. "There's something you're not telling me, and I'm not leaving until you tell me. What were those guys looking for when they broke into your house? And don't tell me you don't know because I get the feeling that you do."

She shifted uncomfortably. "Ethan, it's late. Can't we do this tomorrow?"

"Uh-uh." He shook his head. "We're doing this right now. Whoever came here tonight was looking for something specific. If they didn't find it, their next step will be to come after you. They could do to you what they did to your father, Cambry. Tell me what they were looking for."

"I don't know!" she yelled, standing her ground. "And that's the truth! It's just . . . complicated."

"Then *un*complicate it for me, Cambry, because I need to know. What were they looking for?"

She glanced toward her bag sitting near the kitchen doorway, then back at him. In that second, she seemed to make a decision. She walked over to her bag and pulled something out. Stalking back, she shoved it at him.

"I think they were looking for this, okay? Well, not this one in particular, but one like it."

He looked down at the item in his hands. It was a USB drive attached to a pink butterfly lanyard. Hardly threatening.

But he knew she was talking about what the drive contained. His heart started to pound. Had she had her father's work all this time? His fingers closed around the drive, the plastic biting into his skin. "What's on the drive, Cambry?"

"I don't know." When he opened his mouth to protest, she held up her hand to silence him. "I promise, I don't know."

"How can you not know? You plug it in, open the files, and look at them. How hard is that?"

She gave him a withering look. "The files are encrypted. They could be his taxes, for all I know. I just didn't know if anything on that drive would be relevant to the investigation—"

"Cambry, *everything* is relevant right now! Somebody tried to kill your father, and somebody is after you! You have to give it to the FBI. Have their computer forensics guys take a look. They can decrypt the files and see what they are. I just don't understand why you would keep this from them! Help me understand, Cambry, because I'm at a loss here."

"Because he told me not to."

Ethan stared at her in confusion. "Who did?"

"My father. Just before he lost consciousness."

"Wait a minute." Ethan held up a hand, struggling to make sense of what she was saying. "Your *father* gave you a USB drive? And he told you not to give it to the FBI?"

"Yes."

"Did he say anything else?"

She began hesitantly. "When I found my father, he gave me the thumb drive and told me not to give it to anybody. Not to let *them* find it, whoever *them* is. Then he said *password* and *nickname* and lost consciousness. I have no idea what he was trying to tell me about a password or a nickname. He was so insistent when he told me not to give it to anybody," she whispered, her voice faltering. "I was so scared, Ethan. I didn't know why it was so important that his last words were not to give it to anybody. So I didn't even tell the FBI about it. I couldn't be sure that somebody in the agency wasn't the one he was trying to keep it from. I just didn't know who to trust. I plugged the drive into the computer to see if I could figure out what was so important, but all the files were encrypted. All except one. A picture."

"Tell me about the picture." Ethan's tone was gentle, prompting.

"It was taken up at the cabin we owned up in the mountains, about an hour from here. We used to go there several weekends a summer, do you remember?" When he nodded, she went on. "I have really good memories of that cabin. But once my dad started being more interested in business and success than in his family"—a hint of sarcasm crept into her voice—"we stopped going. I don't know why he had that picture on the same drive with the encrypted files." She shrugged. "Maybe he'd been carrying it around with him to remember how good things used to be."

"Maybe," Ethan said. "If he was trying to reconcile with you, maybe he mentioned the picture before he lost consciousness as a way of letting you know how important those memories were to him."

Cambry thought about that. "I guess that's possible. But then most of what he was saying didn't make any sense and seemed so random. I wondered if he was delirious and just saying whatever popped into his head."

"I don't think so." Ethan closed the distance between them and took her hands in his. "It definitely sounds like he was trying to tell you something. That's what tells me this drive could be the key to this whole thing. But we won't know until we have somebody look at those files. Let's take it to the FBI. I trust them, and so can you."

"I already have somebody looking at it," she admitted quietly. "A friend who's a computer security contractor. Alisa Munro. I've known her since college, and she used to work for the CIA in cyber crimes. If it turns out my father's research is on it, I'll give it to somebody who can keep it safe from whoever is after it."

"How far has Alisa gotten on decrypting the files?"

"I got a text from her just before my staff meeting, saying she needed to talk to me about it first thing tomorrow morning. I told her I'd be by before work. Maybe she's found something."

Ethan felt a spark of hope. Finally. Something solid to run with.

"I hope so," he said, giving her hand a squeeze. "Thanks for telling me." He glanced up at the clock and got to his feet. "It's getting late. Why don't you get some sleep. We can talk with Alisa in the morning and decide what to do about it after hearing what she has to say."

Cambry cocked an eyebrow at him. "You're not mad? I just told you I've been hiding something from the police, the FBI—even you."

He sighed. "What do you want me to say, Cambry? That I don't understand why you didn't just turn it over to the authorities? I know you've been faced with impossible decisions and challenges this past week, and some of those have definite shades of gray. I can't fault you for that."

"Thanks. It's just . . . I didn't know what to do. Or who to trust."

Ethan felt as if a knife buried itself a little deeper in his chest. He hoped she would never learn how unworthy he was of her trust.

He took a few steps toward the door, and Cambry and Willoughby followed. "Let's just see what Alisa has to say about it tomorrow, okay?"

He said good-night to Cambry and stepped out into the night. As soon as he was in his car, he pulled out his phone and dialed Natoni.

"Yeah, it's me," Ethan said when his boss answered. "Turns out Cambry's father gave her a USB drive before he lost consciousness. He told her not to give it to anybody, so she's been too scared to tell anyone because she didn't know who her father was trying to keep it from. Apparently, the drive contains a bunch of encrypted files, so she gave it to a friend of hers, a freelance, ex-CIA cyber specialist named Alisa Munro, who's working on decrypting it."

"And?"

"And Cambry and I are going to visit this friend of hers in the morning to see what she's found."

Natoni's excitement bubbled over into his voice. "I want that drive, Reece. It could be our key to everything."

"Understood, sir. I'll call you after the meeting."

***

Garrison called Benton. "We didn't find anything, and we were thorough."

"She's got to have it," Benton said. "But we're out of time. It's time to grab her and make her talk."

"I have no problem with that. What about the agent following her around?"

"If necessary, grab him too. I'm meeting with Navarro on Monday, and I need that technology *now.*"

"Do you want to interrogate her yourself? Or are you leaving this to me?"

"No offense, Garrison, but leaving this to you will just turn up a lot of dead bodies. I'll take care of this personally."

CHAPTER SEVENTEEN

CAMBRY HURRIED OUT THE FRONT door the second she saw Ethan pull into the driveway the next morning. She was a little surprised when he didn't get out and come around to get her door as he always did. When she slid into the seat, she looked over at him. He was brooding. She could see it in the wrinkles between his brows and the set of his jaw.

They exchanged brief greetings, and she told him how to get to Alisa's house. After that, a tense silence fell between them until they finally pulled through Alisa's gates.

Alisa met them at the door, smiling welcomingly at them as she leaned on a canary yellow, bejeweled cane. "Hey, Cambry," she said with a hug. Just before Alisa pulled back, she whispered into Cambry's ear, "Who's the eye candy?"

Cambry introduced them as they went inside. Once they were sitting, Alisa began. "Okay, here's the deal. I was able to decrypt the files, and they don't seem to be anything of importance—just old project files. Most were dated months ago, even up to a year ago, with notes on patents, contracts, and things like that. But that doesn't mean I haven't missed something. Decryption is tricky. If I decrypt the files with a certain set of keys, I get one set of files. If I decrypt them with a different set of keys, I could get a different set of files. I went at this logically, starting with the most obvious methods first. But that logic failed, apparently."

Cambry made a wry face. "Well, you know what they say about logic. 'Logic merely enables one to be wrong with authority.'"

Alisa looked at her contemplatively. "Spock?"

"Doctor Who."

"Ah. I should have known." Alisa smiled. "Listen, if you want me to keep working on it, try different decryption keys, maybe something important will turn up."

"Well . . ." Cambry hesitated. "I don't want to keep you from your work."

"It's no problem. I don't meet with the people for my next contract until next week."

"Then that would be great. Thanks so much, Alisa."

"Hey, like I said, it's no problem. Anything for a friend."

Ethan spoke up. "Could you make us a copy of everything on that USB drive? Cambry and I can take a look through the files and see if anything jumps out at us."

"Sure," Alisa said, standing up. "I'll just burn it all onto a disc. It'll only take a few minutes. I'll be right back."

After she walked out of the room, Cambry sighed and leaned back in her chair. "I was prepared for a yes or no. I just want this thing to be over. I don't know what to do." She turned to look at Ethan. "What do I do?"

"I know what we should do," he said. "But you might not like it."

Cambry looked at his guarded expression. "What is it?"

"We need to take the drive to the FBI."

"I already told you why I'm not ready to do that. Besides, Alisa couldn't find any evidence that it's tied to my father's attack, so what would be the point in giving it to the FBI? For them to waste their time looking through old project notes and patent information?"

"Just because Alisa didn't find anything in her first go-round doesn't mean your father's missing technology isn't still on that drive somewhere," he argued. "I say get the FBI involved. Let them choose whether or not they want to spend time on it. But I can tell you right now this will become their top priority. With more people working on this, this whole nightmare could be over fast. Don't you want that?"

Cambry's control fractured. "Yes, I want that!" she said. "But you weren't there when my father was pleading with me not to give it to anybody! I'm sure he had a very good reason for it. How am I supposed to just disregard what I know nothing about?"

A muscle jumped in Ethan's jaw. "Cambry, there's a time to hang on to loyalty, and a time to save your own neck. It's time to save your neck. Give it to the FBI. Be done with it."

"Everything okay?" a voice intruded.

They both looked over to see Alisa standing in the doorway with a disc case in her hand. Cambry blew out a breath. "Yes, everything's fine."

Alisa wisely decided not to press the issue. "Here's the copy of the drive," she said, holding up the disc and walking toward them, her cane thumping on the tile. "I'll keep working on the decryptions and let you know if I find anything."

"Thank you." Cambry took it, slipped the disc into her leather messenger bag, then gave Alisa a hug. "I really do appreciate this."

"Just let me know if there's anything else I can do."

Cambry and Ethan got back into the car. The drive to her office was made in more uncomfortable silence, and Cambry was relieved when they finally pulled into her building's parking lot. She did her best to ignore Ethan's brooding as they made their way upstairs to her office. When they stepped out of the elevator, Cambry forced a smile onto her face for the sake of the receptionists at the desk.

"Oh, good! You're here," Shanice said. She handed Cambry a couple of phone messages and then tapped a large stack of manila folders. "I hate to be the bearer of bad news, but this stack of paperwork is for you."

Cambry's eyes widened. "All of it?"

Shanice nodded. "Jim wants you to review the start-up inventory lists to make sure everything checks out. Then he wants you to sign the forms and get them back to him no later than noon."

"By noon?" she choked out. "Is he serious?"

"I'm afraid so." Shanice gave her a sympathetic look. "He needs time to give them his final approval before his assistant faxes them out at lunch."

With a sigh, Cambry started to reach for the stack, but holding on to her bag made it difficult to juggle.

"Here, let me take that." Ethan suddenly reappeared at her side and took her bag.

Cambry had a hard time feeling gracious after their argument and his brooding silence. "Thanks," she mumbled.

She collected the folders and headed to her office with Ethan on her heels. When she made it into her office and managed to get the files onto her desk without dropping any, she breathed a sigh of relief. Ethan wordlessly handed her her bag. She took it and set it down next to her desk.

When she looked up at him, his expression was hard and unreadable. Their eyes met and held for a long moment. Then he took a step back toward the door.

"I've got to go make a phone call," he muttered and then turned on his heel and was gone.

"Fine, go," she mumbled after he was out of earshot. Trying to put Ethan's grumpiness out of her mind, she sat down and opened the first folder from the stack.

***

"It's me," Ethan said in a low voice when Agent Natoni answered the call. Ethan looked around the landscaped courtyard in front of Cambry's building to make sure he was alone.

"What did you learn?" Natoni asked, sounding anxious.

"Cambry's friend just found a bunch of old project files, notes, and patent information. But apparently there are a lot of ways to encrypt things, so it's very possible there's still something on there. I got a copy of it." Ethan shoved aside the flash of guilt and feelings of betrayal the announcement caused. "I snuck it out of her bag just now. What do you want me to do with it?"

Natoni's voice was softer, as if he knew what the deception had cost Ethan. "Good work, Agent Reece. Take it in to the Denver office immediately and give it to Agent Lawford. The cyber team will go through it with a fine-tooth comb. With the manpower we have on this, they'll get through that decryption in no time flat. Then we'll know for sure what's on it."

Ethan ran his free hand distractedly across the back of his neck. "There was one other thing though," he said, sitting down on the nearby bench. "She said her father mentioned something about a password and a nickname before he lost consciousness. He might have been trying to tell her that she needed a password and username to decrypt the files."

"As much as I hate to do it, we may have to bring her in on that if the team runs into problems."

A feeling of coldness converged in his chest. "I'd rather use that as a last resort. If she ever finds out I was assigned to get this information . . ."

Natoni's tone sobered. "I understand. We'll try to keep you out of it. For now, get that copy over to Agent Lawford. We'll go from there. Good work."

Ethan ended the call and slipped the phone into his pocket. Then he leaned forward with his elbows on his knees and put his face in his hands. He'd just stolen from the woman he loved. What kind of man did that? He understood it was his job, but that only made him feel worse. That he'd choose his job directives over her.

But we're dealing with possible terrorist threats. Homeland security, his voice of reason argued in his head. *You're doing it for the good of your country.*

He sat up and let out a long breath. That helped a little but not enough. Getting to his feet, he headed for his car.

***

Cambry pulled her attention away from the inventory lists she was going over when her cell phone rang. She was confused to see Ethan's name displayed on the caller ID.

"Hey," she answered. "Where'd you go? I thought you were just stepping out to make a call."

It took Ethan a moment to answer. "I did, but it turns out I need to run a quick errand. Stay in your building while I'm gone, okay? You'll be safe as long as you don't leave."

She frowned at Ethan's strange tone. "That's a little creepy. Why do you say that? Is there something I should know?"

"Just do what I ask, okay?" Ethan's tone was matter-of-fact and not very reassuring. "I'll talk to you when I get back."

He hung up, and Cambry glared at the phone as she pulled it away from her ear and set it back down on her desk. This whole business was doing a number on her nerves. If only Alisa had found something one way or another. It would have made it easier for her to decide on the next step she should take. Her father had almost died trying to protect whatever was on that drive. Or whatever it might lead somebody to.

Lead somebody to.

She dropped her pen and sat up in her chair, her heart pounding.

The picture! What if Alisa was right, and the files on the drive were just old files? What if the key to this whole thing was that picture? Her father had seemed adamant about it. What if he'd been trying to tell her that the technology was hidden *up at the cabin*?

Dropping her pen, she shoved her chair back from her desk and hurried out of her office. Shanice looked up as she approached.

"Shanice, I have a question for you. Do you know if my father still owns that cabin in the mountains west of Denver? The one he used to take the other executives up to for hunting trips?"

"He does," Shanice answered readily. "He went fishing up there with a few business associates a few weeks ago. Why do you ask?"

Cambry felt a surge of excitement. "Just something that occurred to me. Thanks!"

She hurried back to her office, pulling her cell phone out of her pocket as she went. She went into the office and shut the door, then she dialed Ethan's number. As much as she hated the possibility of getting grumped at again, she had to tell him what she suspected. This could be the break they'd been looking for! She didn't know why she hadn't thought of it before.

Ethan's phone went straight to voice mail. After a moment's hesitation, she decided not to leave a message. Instead, she'd wait until he got back from his errand. She forced herself to sit at her desk and focus on her work, and at ten minutes before ten, she finished filling out the last form for Jim. Signing her name with a flourish, she sat back in her chair. There. Now she could get these to Jim and have that off her plate. She rolled her shoulders, trying to work out the tension.

Just then a dark form appeared in her doorway. She jumped a little and then realized it was Ethan. "You scared me."

"Sorry." He looked rather grim as he walked in.

"You okay?"

His jaw tightened. "Fine. Just got something on my mind. Did anything happen while I was gone?"

She raised an eyebrow. "No. Was something supposed to?"

He let out a weary breath and shook his head. "No. Sorry. I guess I've just been on edge since that break-in last night."

Cambry decided to let his odd mood go. "Listen," she said, getting up and walking over to him. "While you were gone, I had a thought."

She explained to him the theory about the picture, and her idea about searching the cabin. "What if he mentioned the picture on the drive because he was trying to tell me the missing technology was at the cabin? Maybe we've been on the wrong track, thinking the technology is on the drive. He was very specific about mentioning the picture of the cabin. It makes sense."

A noise in the hall caught her attention. She looked over Ethan's shoulder and then crossed to the open doorway to look out into the hall. Nothing. A prickle of unease swept across her skin. She'd been so sure she'd heard somebody.

"What's wrong?"

She shook her head, telling herself she was being paranoid. "I thought I heard somebody out here."

When Ethan looked and didn't see anybody, he turned back to her. "Do you think your father still owns the cabin?"

"Shanice says he does and that he was up there recently. Maybe he has a computer at the cabin, or maybe he stashed it in the little office he used to use up there. I think we should go check it out. I'm done with Jim's paperwork, so I could come up with an excuse to tell Shanice why I'm cutting out early. Maybe about needing to talk to the police again about the break-in or something. You up for a little road trip?"

Ethan nodded. "It's worth a shot. You'll want to change though. Office attire is hardly something you'll want to wear into the mountains."

Just then somebody tapped on her door. Cambry spun around to see Jim standing in the doorway.

"Sorry, am I interrupting anything?"

"Oh no, you're fine," Cambry insisted. "Did you need to talk to me?"

"I was just coming by to see if you'd finished that paperwork yet."

"Yes, it's all ready for you." She went to her desk to get the stack of files.

"I'm sorry for the rush," he said as he followed her to her desk. "I know we had a late meeting last night, but this paperwork was supposed to have arrived by courier yesterday. When it didn't arrive until this morning, it really put us in a crunch."

"It happens," she said, handing him the files. "Don't worry about it."

Jim thanked her again and hurried out of her office. When he was gone, Cambry turned back to Ethan. "If you're done with your errands, let's go. If we leave now, we'll still have plenty of light when we get there."

***

Garrison ended his call and headed up the lodge steps. He found Benton inside, growling at two of the men. Garrison hung back in the doorway, waiting for him to finish. When he did, Garrison stepped forward.

"Our source inside Saville Enterprises just called. Ms. Saville is cutting out of work early, and she and Agent Reece are heading up to her father's cabin. Ms. Saville said something about her father's technology. Maybe her daddy stashed it there."

Eagerness lit Benton's eyes. "Then I say we beat them there. Where's this cabin?"

"About an hour and a half west of Denver. It's isolated. Perfect for us to go in unseen. They have a head start on us though. We might not beat them there."

"What about the helicopter?"

Garrison shook his head. "After your trip here, it went in for servicing. Something about needing a part."

Benton's jaw clenched. "Rush that along. I want to be ready for anything. In the meantime, let's get up to that cabin as fast as we can so we can pay Reece and Saville a visit away from prying eyes."

Garrison nodded. "We can intercept them before dark. We're going to need the vans and some backup vehicles. I suggest taking your computer equipment as well as your tech guys. If the technology turns out to be at the cabin, you'll want to be able to verify that's what it is. And have your field medic bring sedatives in case Reece gets out of hand."

"What would I do without you?" came Benton's snide comment, his tone biting and filled with impatience. Not expecting a reply, Benton spun and walked into the next room of the lodge, shouting orders to his men.

Garrison frowned at Benton's back. "You'd be back in the little leagues, pilfering office supplies and probably getting caught," he muttered under his breath.

He shook his head and forced himself to focus. He'd paid his dues, worked his way up. Soon he'd be at the top of this food chain, and Isaac Benton would be history. He just had to bide his time.

With determined strides, he headed to his lodgings to pack a bag. It looked like they had a long night ahead of them.

CHAPTER EIGHTEEN

CAMBRY LOOKED OVER AT ETHAN, taking in the firm set of his mouth and the stress lines around his eyes. He continued to stare straight ahead as he drove, oblivious to her gaze. Or at least pretending to be.

When another few miles of strained silence slipped by, she couldn't stand it any longer. "You know, it's been almost an hour since we left Denver, and you've barely said two words to me. Are you mad at me for arguing with you about the thumb drive? Is that what this is about?"

The muscle in his jaw bunched. "Cambry, it's not anything you did, okay? I just have a lot on my mind." He slid his gaze over to hers, and she caught a glimpse of guilt there before he turned his attention back to the road.

She considered that. He was feeling . . . guilty? What was he feeling guilty about?

Okay, well, other than acting like a complete jerk most of today, she amended.

Willoughby whined from the backseat and shoved his head between them. She grimaced and shoved his enormous head away from hers. The last thing she wanted right now was dog drool down her neck.

After she and Ethan had left her office, they'd gone to her house so she could change into jeans and a T-shirt. She'd also pulled on an old hoodie, knowing the mountains got chilly in the early evening. Ethan already had on jeans and a fleece pullover, so a stop by his parents' house wasn't necessary. But Willoughby had seemed to sense they were going somewhere, and he'd sat at the front door and whined until they finally decided to take him. A run in the mountains couldn't hurt.

After another twenty minutes of uncomfortable silence, they turned onto a familiar side road. They wound through the trees on the well-maintained dirt road, and a short time later they pulled to a dusty stop in a clearing surrounded by towering pine trees. A stately, two-story log cabin stood in the clearing, boasting an abundance of huge windows and a wide wraparound deck.

Just seeing it stirred up a well of emotion in Cambry's chest. It had been years since she'd been there, and the memories of her family's vacations there filled her with nostalgia. Getting out of the car, she closed her eyes and breathed deeply. This was what she remembered. The smell of fresh earth and pine trees. The call of birds. The sound of the wind in the trees.

Better yet, peace. Isolation.

She found herself wishing that she'd thought ahead and decided to make a weekend of this. *No phones. No TV. Just peace and quiet . . .*

A car door shut.

And Ethan.

She sighed. Yeah, that wouldn't have worked.

She opened her eyes and watched as Ethan walked around the front of the car and came to stand beside her. She waited for him to speak, but he only leaned back against the car with her. He must have let Willoughby out because the dog went trotting happily past them toward the edge of the meadow, his nose to the ground.

"I'm sorry I've been surly," Ethan offered quietly. "I'm not mad at you. I'm just distracted with work and feeling a little stressed about it."

Work. Okay. She could live with that.

She looked over at him. "Apology accepted."

He offered a reluctant smile, but she could still see the tension around the corners of his mouth and eyes.

A distant bark caught her attention. "Willoughby's probably treed a squirrel," she said, breaking the awkward silence. "I'd better go get him."

Ethan looked toward the woods. "Why don't you let me do that? You can head inside and start looking around."

"No, I'll do it," she said. "I'm perfectly safe. Besides, I know the area better than you do, so I won't get lost."

"Okay, but come right back. Where's the key to the cabin?"

"We always kept it in the hidey hole rock behind the first step of the porch. I hope it's still there."

"Don't worry, I'll find it."

Leaving Ethan to open up the cabin, Cambry set off after Willoughby. She entered the woods and breathed in the damp, earthy smell. Daylight struggled through the dense canopy of foliage overhead, creating dark patches and a kaleidoscope of patterns along the forest floor as she shuffled through the dense undergrowth.

As she rounded a familiar tree stump, a memory flashed into her mind, causing a spark of excitement. *Was it still there?*

Her steps quickened as she weaved along the familiar path. Soon she found herself staring up at a tree, delighted to see the old, shabby birdhouse hanging from a lower limb. With a nostalgic smile, she reached out to finger the peeling, faded blue paint and the lopsided pink heart over the round entrance on the front.

She'd forgotten about it until now. She and her father had built it together. The birdseed was long gone, but the memories remained. Those had been good times, when her father had still cared about quality time with his family. So much had changed.

Maybe things were still changing. At least Jim had said they were. According to him, her father had been trying to change again—this time for the better. It almost hurt to hope.

But then, it might not matter. His prognosis was guarded. Would he even get the chance to tell her what his intentions truly were? If he came through this, was it possible that their relationship might not be completely lost?

A bark in the distance reminded her of her purpose. Letting her fingers trail along the weathered wood of the birdhouse roof, she stepped back and turned to look for Willoughby.

A slight breeze kicked up, and Cambry shivered, pulling her hands inside her hoodie sleeves. "Willoughby!" she called. She didn't hear an answering bark, so she called again, this time louder. Nothing.

She shook her head. "Blast, that dog. He'd better not get so far away that we have to go searching for him by car."

She started walking, her pace quick. It got dark early in the mountains, and it was already chilly. She didn't want to be caught without a flashlight, compass, and jacket. She'd only gone a few steps when she heard a twig snap somewhere off to her left. She froze. Her heart hammering, she looked around, searching the woods for the source of the noise.

Some other animal?

For another long moment she remained still, straining to hear any other sounds, but the woods were silent.

Too silent.

A shiver slithered up her spine. Something wasn't right.

Feeling a sudden spike of adrenaline, Cambry started back toward the cabin at a half walk, half jog. Her pace soon brought her within sight of the cabin through the dense trees, and she'd never been so glad to see anything in her life.

But then she jerked to a halt. She and Ethan weren't alone. Several vehicles were parked at the edge of the clearing, and several camouflage-clad figures were silently approaching the cabin's front door, guns in hand.

Ethan!

Cambry's heart started to pound. Ethan wasn't on the porch, which meant he'd found the spare key and gone inside. He'd never see the men coming.

She ducked behind a tree twenty paces from the edge of the clearing, hoping she hadn't been detected. Her mind whirled as she tried to decide what to do. With shaking hands, she pulled out her cell phone and held it in front of her face. She waited a moment and then saw *No Service* flash on her screen.

Great.

She looked back at the cabin as fear lodged in her throat. There were at least eight armed men. No matter what training Ethan had in special ops or what action he'd seen, he'd be no match for that many men. They needed help.

She glanced back over her shoulder at the trail she'd been following. It led farther down the mountain, and an offshoot trail led to a section of the road not far from the little town a couple of miles away. If she could find her way there in the dwindling light, she could get to a phone. Call for help.

Taking a deep breath, she turned and hurried back the way she came. She'd only taken a dozen strides when a noise behind her made her jump. She started to whirl, but a muscular arm snaked around her waist and a large, strong hand clamped over her mouth, preventing her screams from sounding through the still mountain air.

CHAPTER NINETEEN

ETHAN WANDERED THROUGH THE CABIN, surprised that it was larger than it had looked from the outside. The great room had high, angled ceilings and a giant stone fireplace. Along the back wall was a bold, knotty-pine staircase, which led to a large loft overlooking the room. A moderately-sized but comfortable kitchen sat off to the right.

A hallway stretched toward the back of the cabin, and he began his investigation there. He flicked on lights as he went, relieved that the cabin had power. A door on the left revealed a smaller bedroom, which had possibly doubled as an office. Next was a bathroom. At the end of the hall, a door opened into a large, open, wood-paneled catch-all room that ran almost the entire length of the cabin.

The wood-plank floor was covered with large area rugs, and a couple sets of bunk beds sat along the back wall. A cloth-covered pool table sat near the shuttered windows on the left. Several enormous log poles lined the center of the room about every ten feet, obviously designed to support the weight of the overhead loft.

He flipped off the lights and headed back out into the hall. The entire cabin had been shut up, with closed and latched shutters on all the lower windows, and the furniture covered. Cambry had said her father had been here recently, but it didn't look like he'd planned to come back anytime soon.

If he'd hidden the technology here, had he planned for it to stay here awhile? And where would he have hidden it? With furniture draped, it was possible there was a desk and computer hidden from view in one of the rooms. Maybe uncovering some furniture would give some answers. As soon as Cambry got back, he'd get her help.

He made his way down the hall and had just stepped into the great room when the front door banged open and three large, armed men dressed in camo gear and dark ski masks burst through the doorway.

As he stood poised to defend himself, he quickly assessed the situation. The lead man continued toward him, the 9mm trained on him, while the two other men parted and went to do a sweep of the cabin.

Guns for hire. Without their weapons, Ethan might have been able to outfight or outsmart them, but clearly, fighting wasn't an option. That didn't bode well for him. Or for Cambry.

Cambry!

Panic surged through him. Cambry had gone after Willoughby. Was she still out in the woods? Had she seen the men and hid, or was she walking into an ambush? Ethan held still, but his mind worked frantically. He had to get to Cambry before these men did. If he could narrow the odds a bit, take on one of them at a time . . .

The men had yet to speak, but as Ethan watched, the man with a 9mm trained on him made eye contact with the other two, motioning them toward the hallway leading to the back of the cabin. They nodded and then moved around Ethan to check out the back rooms.

Ethan saw his chance. The instant the man in front of him chanced a glance toward the loft overhead, Ethan charged him. He rammed his shoulder into the man's sternum and sent him crashing to the floor.

The blow winded the man, and Ethan took off running. But just as he reached the door, two more armed men charged inside. He collided with them, knocking one of them off his feet.

With only one man between him and freedom, Ethan rushed forward, only to be tackled from behind. Ethan hit the floor with a thud. Soon the weight of several men pinned him to the ground. He fought for all he was worth, but it wasn't long before he realized it was a losing battle.

"Get him up," a gruff voice ordered.

The weight of the men on his back eased, and he was grabbed by his arms and hauled roughly to his feet. He came face-to-face with a man whose features and skin color indicated South American descent. He had dark hair and ever darker eyes, and a puckered, ugly scar ran along his cheek from almost mouth to ear. The man's eyes flashed as they met his, and he jerked his head slightly toward the cabin door.

"Take him out front and wait."

The men on either side of Ethan obeyed, and he was half walked, half dragged down the cabin steps. When they stopped in the clearing, Ethan scanned the area for any sign of Cambry. He saw a dozen or so men, but no Cambry. He breathed a sigh of relief. With any luck, she was deep enough in the woods that she wouldn't be found. She could head down the mountain and go for help.

"Agent Ethan Reece, I presume."

The voice caught his attention, and he looked over to see a husky, broad-shouldered Caucasian man walking toward him. His chest was shoved out, his hands clasped behind his back, and an arrogant smirk stretched across his face.

Ethan's jaw tightened. It was a face he instantly recognized.

Isaac Benton.

Benton looked at his men holding Ethan's arms. "Pat him down."

Ethan was quickly relieved of his off-duty gun and the cell phone in his pocket.

"What do you want, Benton?"

Benton's smirk grew. "So you already know who I am. Then you probably know what I'm doing here."

"Stealing technology and selling it to the highest bidder, with no care how it's used or who it hurts? That is what you do, isn't it?"

Benton shrugged. "As long as it pays the big bucks, I don't care. And this new technology Saville developed? I want it. That's where you come in."

"Why do you think I can help you?"

"Don't act so naive, Reece. We know all about you. Former special ops. Now FBI. And undercover to find out where your former girlfriend hid the technology."

Ethan's heart stopped. His cover had been blown.

How? By whom?

Making sure his expression remained impassive, he shrugged. "So you've done your homework. What difference does that make?"

"Because I believe you've learned enough from your ex-girlfriend to tell me what I need to know."

Ethan felt a muscle jump in his jaw as he clenched his teeth. "Sorry, Benton. Can't help you."

"Can't?" Benton lifted an eyebrow. "Or won't? Maybe all you need is the proper incentive."

Benton turned toward the darkening woods, and Ethan followed his gaze. A moment later, three figures emerged from the trees. The first was a large, burly man with dark clothes, a dark ski cap, and a high-powered rifle in his hands. The other man, just as big and threatening, had a smaller person in a death grip by the back of the neck and was half guiding, half shoving his hostage into the clearing.

Ethan's heart sank. It was Cambry.

"Why, if it isn't Ms. Saville," Benton mocked, his sneering smile turning her direction.

Ethan caught Cambry's gaze, and her eyes widened at seeing him restrained and surrounded by armed men. He gave her what hoped was a reassuring look and then turned back to Benton.

"Let her go, Benton," he said. "She's not going to be able to help you."

Benton ignored him and walked toward Cambry. "Why don't you let me determine that for myself, Reece."

"What do you want? Why are you doing this?" Cambry demanded as he stopped in front of her.

"If your father weren't so stubborn, Ms. Saville, I'd already have his technology. But he had to be difficult and hide it somewhere. Maybe if he hadn't resisted, he wouldn't be laying in a hospital bed."

Her face paled. "You tried to kill my father?"

"Well, that wasn't the plan, but things happen. Why don't you just tell me where the technology is? I might even let you go."

To her credit, Cambry stood, unflinching, and stared right back into his intent gaze. "I don't know where it is."

"Really?" he asked, his voice filled with sarcasm. "Why do I find that hard to believe?"

"It's the truth," Ethan interrupted. "We've been looking for it too."

Benton turned to glower at him. "I find that hard to believe, Agent Reece. You mean to tell me that you've been undercover as Ms. Saville's doting boyfriend for a week and still don't know its whereabouts? I don't know if that makes you a lousy undercover agent or just easily distracted by a beautiful woman."

Cambry gasped, and Ethan's gaze flew to her face. Her expression registered shock and disbelief while his own stomach plummeted to his toes.

Benton snorted. "Oh, I'm sorry. That was supposed to be a secret, wasn't it, Agent Reece?"

When Cambry only continued to stare at Benton in astonishment, Benton gave her an impatient look. "Look, let me spell it out for you, Ms. Saville, so we can move on. The FBI's been looking for your daddy's technology. When you wouldn't tell them where it was, they sent in an undercover agent to get close to you and find out. Who better than an ex-boyfriend and childhood friend?"

"Benton, that's enough," Ethan bit out, the words coming from between clenched teeth.

"Hey, I'm just getting that out of the way," Benton said almost conversationally. "There. Now can we get on with this?"

***

The FBI had sent Ethan in undercover to find out what she knew?

Cambry felt as if the ground was tilting beneath her feet, and the only thing that kept her from falling was the man holding her arm in a bruising grip. She was aware of Benton's return to her side, but she was unable to tear her gaze from Ethan's tortured, guilt-ridden gaze.

Pain and betrayal swelled in her chest, the hurt so heavy she struggled to breathe around it.

It couldn't be true. Could it?

She thought back on everything that had happened in the days after her father's attack. The police. FBI. Being named as a person of interest. But then the FBI had backed off. She'd thought it was because they figured she really didn't know anything. But maybe they'd backed off because . . .

Her vision started to blur as tears burned her eyes.

Because they were sending in Ethan.

A collection of memories flooded her mind. Ethan standing down Detective Dalton in her driveway. What was it Ethan had said? Something about local law enforcement no longer having jurisdiction in her case. How would Ethan have known that unless he'd learned that from the FBI? Then there'd been the questions he'd kept asking, as if he'd been pressing her for information. And the argument at Alisa's that morning when he'd insisted she take the thumb drive to the FBI.

All that had seemed innocent at the time, but when she looked at it from the different perspective . . . It looked bad. Really bad.

"Ethan?" she managed in a strained voice. She stared at him, her eyes pleading with him to deny it.

A muscle bunched in his jaw, and he stared back at her, his expression haunted. "Cambry, I'm sorry . . ." His voice trailed off, and he said nothing more.

The tears she'd been holding back started to flow down her cheeks as deceit and betrayal seared a hole in her heart.

She'd trusted him. Believed him when he said he'd wanted to be there for her. To help her through this. She warned herself not to get involved, and what had she done? She'd fallen in love with the man all over again only to learn the reason he'd been here was to investigate her.

It had been an act. All of it. The concern. Lunches out. Dinners in. How could she have been so stupid?

Benton's angry face flashed in front of hers. "You can have it out with loverboy later, lady," he snapped. "Tell me what I want to know! Where is your father's technology?"

She choked back her tears and shook her head. "I don't know."

Benton's eyes narrowed, and he took a threatening step toward her. "Maybe you just need help remembering."

Before Cambry could react, Benton jerked a switchblade out of his jacket and snapped it open. He plunged a hand into her long hair and wrenched her head backward, holding the knife against her throat.

Terror seized her, stealing her breath. The feel of cold steel against her skin made her tremble, and she fought to control the shaking as she stared into the evil and anger lurking in Benton's eyes.

"Benton, no!" Ethan yelled.

She heard Ethan struggling against the men holding him, but all she could do was stand frozen in terror. The man was seriously desperate. He wouldn't kill her, would he? Not if he thought she might still be able to give him what he wanted?

Ethan's menacing growl reached her ears. "I swear, Benton, if you hurt even one hair on her head, I'll—"

"You'll what?" Benton asked, looking over his shoulder at Ethan as his knife remained pressed against Cambry's throat. "Someone in your position isn't capable of following through on such empty threats. How about you tell me what you know, and I'll consider letting Ms. Saville go?"

Silence.

"No?" Benton challenged.

A stalemate seemed to have been declared. Nobody moved. Benton's blade twitched against her throat, and it was all she could do not to swallow.

A low rumble sounded behind her. Her eyes darted to her right, but she didn't dare move to see what had made the noise. A distant ATV? Before she had time to consider that, the vibration intensified into a deep, throaty, lethal-sounding snarl.

Benton spun. Luckily, his knife moved away from her throat instead of against it. Then the man holding her jerked and let out a hair-raising scream. In the next instant, she was free.

Cambry whirled to see what was happening. She was just in time to see Willoughby release the man's calf and sink his massive jaws in a second time. The man let out another scream.

Chaos erupted.

Men shouted and started running. A gun fired. Then another. Cambry dropped, hoping to avoid the shots. Willoughby yelped, let go of his victim, and took off running into the woods.

A flash of motion caught her attention, and she looked over to see Ethan snap his head back, delivering a solid blow with the back of his head to the face of the man behind him. The man howled and went sprawling as he clutched his bleeding and clearly broken nose. Then Ethan spun and drove his fist into his other captor's gut, knocking the air out of him.

In spite of everything, Cambry was impressed.

That's when she realized she had the same opportunity for escape. All the men were distracted. She didn't need to think twice. Scrambling to her feet, she took off running for the woods. She knew Ethan had spotted her break for freedom because she heard him yell, "Run! Keep going!"

Cambry didn't look back. As dark as it was amongst the towering pines, she kept running. Branches slapped at her face and arms as she darted around trees and skidded along the scattered leaves and pine needles. A knobby tree root caught her toe and almost sent her sprawling. She heard shouts from behind her, and the sound of pounding footsteps seemed to draw nearer by the second.

Her lungs felt like they were going to burst as she pushed for even greater speed—dangerous, she knew, because of the growing darkness around her. It was almost impossible to see anything, but the alternative was to be caught.

She'd take her chances in the woods.

A large fallen tree appeared in her path, and she scrambled to climb over it. A sharp branch ripped at the skin on the palm of her hand, but she barely noticed as she slid over the other side of the tree. As her feet hit the ground, she stumbled, fell, picked herself up, and kept running.

The footsteps grew closer. She tried to push herself faster, but she was tiring. Her legs were on fire. Her chest hurt. Her breathing grew ragged. She was slowing, her pursuer closing in.

The sound of a gurgling stream nearby gave her a sense of direction. If she could lose her pursuer, she could follow that stream, and it would lead her down the hill to the little town.

Letting her ears guide her, she rounded a large tree stump. Then the ground fell out from under her and she was falling. Her feet connected with ground again moments later, but the pitch was steep. Before she could do anything, she was sliding downhill.

She bumped and tumbled down the edge of a steep incline until she was able to get her feet pointed back downhill. Frantically, she grabbed at bushes as they flashed past in an effort to stop her descent down the tree- and bramble-covered slope.

A thorny bush caught at her shirt and yanked it up as she skidded past, causing what felt like half the forest to slide up her back, scratching, scraping, and rubbing her skin raw. A tree rushed toward her, and she twisted her body sideways to try to grab one of its low branches. Pain exploded in her side as her she raked across something sharp—possibly a rock or an exposed root—and felt skin rip.

Then she was falling again. The sheer drop-off was probably only a few feet, but it felt like a dozen. She hit the ground with such force that her breath was driven right out of her lungs. The woods around her stilled, and she lay there, dazed and breathless. Dark spots danced across her vision, and for a moment she thought she was going to lose consciousness.

When the threat passed and she was finally able, she sucked in a lung-ful of air. She immediately thought better of it when the pain in her side flared to life. She pressed her hand to her side, and when she withdrew it, she stared numbly at the dark red substance that covered it.

A noise to her left made her jump. She jerked her head toward the top of the slope she'd just tumbled down, and a dark shadow stepped up to the edge. A fresh jolt of adrenaline surged through her, lending her strength and allowing her to ignore the pain and roll to her feet. She lurched forward in two awkward steps and started to run.

She didn't get far. Her determination, mixed with fear and adrenaline, wasn't enough. Within seconds, the man had scrambled down the slope after her and caught up with her in only a few long strides. A burly arm clenched around her and jerked her to a halt.

She tried to scream, but the man quickly slipped a hand over her mouth. Another man skidded to a stop beside them.

"Do it!" the man with his hand over her mouth ordered. "If she gets away again, it'll be our hides."

The second man whipped something from his jacket pocket and fumbled with it for a moment. When he lifted his hand, a stray beam of waning sunlight flashed off a thin tube. A syringe.

She fought harder, and the man holding her swore. "Hurry up!"

That was all the urging his cohort needed. He yanked up her sweatshirt sleeve and drove the needle into her arm. She jumped at the sharp pinch. She continued to fight against the man's constrictive grip, but the woods around her started to blur, and her mind went fuzzy. Her will to struggle faded as the drug invaded her system.

Finally, unable to fight it a moment longer, her body went limp and everything went dark.

CHAPTER TWENTY

ALMOST AS QUICKLY AS THE fight had started, it was over. Half a dozen men rushed to help secure Ethan moments after he'd broken free. As they swarmed and trained their guns on him, Ethan knew there wasn't anything else he could do.

At least Cambry had managed to escape. With any luck, she'd duck the guys who'd taken off after her and she'd soon be clear of this mess. She was smart. She'd know where to go to get help. He sent up a prayer for her safety, and also for Willoughby's. If it hadn't been for that dog . . .

When Willoughby had let out that chill-inducing primitive growl, it had scared even Ethan, and he knew what a pushover the dog could be. Hopefully none of the bullets had hit him as he'd taken off running into the woods, seeming to understand that his part in creating a distraction was over. Hopefully he'd find his way to safety too.

As a few men went to help the guards that Ethan had pummeled, Ethan shot them a gloating look. The man still clutching his broken nose only looked away, his ego dented and body hurting, and the other man was busy rubbing his sore rib cage.

Good. If he was going to go down, he was going to go down fighting.

There was the distant crackle of radios, and then men started to emerge from the woods. Benton was at the front of the group. Ethan's breathing quickened as he waited to see if Cambry might be with them.

But before Ethan could see everybody in the group, Benton hustled back toward them and gestured at the group of men surrounding Ethan. "Get him inside! I want him secured immediately."

The men jerked Ethan in the direction of the cabin, but he did his best to resist, desperately searching the group coming out of the woods. He was almost to the front steps when he saw the last man carrying Cambry's limp body in his arms.

"Cambry!" he shouted, struggling to break free.

He was very nearly able to wrench himself free, but Benton saw the struggle and waved another of his men over. "Fredrickson! Get over there and help. I don't want him getting away!"

Ethan was quickly brought back under control and taken inside. When they reached the door that led into the game room, they shoved Ethan roughly inside. Before he could turn around, the door was slammed shut behind him, the noise echoing in the cavernous room. Then he was alone.

Knowing there'd be an armed guard standing on the other side of the door, Ethan stepped farther into the room. He'd only given the room a cursory glance earlier, but he looked more carefully at it now. The room—running almost the entire length of the cabin—had several windows, easily large enough for a body to get out. But when he went over to inspect them, he discovered the winterizing shutters were all bolted shut from the outside. No escape there. There was a built-in entertainment system along the far wall, but it was devoid of anything but a few hunting magazines. No TV, electronics, or phones.

Apparently the times Cambry's father had come up here, he hadn't been concerned about the lack of technology.

Before he could consider another possible means of escape, the door swung open. Benton stood in the doorway, flanked by two of his more brawny thugs. Ethan was immediately on alert.

"Where's Cambry?" he demanded. "What have you done to her?"

"I haven't done anything to her, Reece. Not yet, anyway. If you cooperate and tell me what I want to know, she'll live. If not . . ." He pulled out his gun and cocked it.

When Benton felt like he'd made his point, he nodded at the two men. They hurried forward and grabbed Ethan, dragging him to one of the log support beams in the center of the room. They jerked his arms behind him and bound his hands with rope around the pole.

Once he was secured, Benton gave him an arrogant smirk and sauntered closer. "So, Reece. Let's have a little chat, shall we?"

***

A good while later, Benton and his men emerged from the room. He glanced over his shoulder at them. "You guys take a break. Tell Fredrickson and Myers that I want Ms. Saville brought down here and put in the room with Reece, whether she's regained consciousness or not. We'll see if we can use her to get what we want out of Reece. When she wakes up, we can start on her."

"What about Reece?"

"Leave him tied to that pole."

The men nodded and hurried away. Benton headed the opposite direction and walked into the kitchen where Garrison was leaning back against the counter, his arms folded over his stout chest.

"So what did you get out of him?"

"It's a work in progress," Benton answered irritably. "Did you find anything here in the cabin?"

Garrison shook his head. "Nothing. We've checked every room, every cupboard, every closet. There's nothing here. Not even a computer or files from work." He nodded at the leather backpack on the counter beside him. "We got Ms. Saville's bag out of the car. We didn't find anything in it either."

Benton walked over to the backpack and upended it, scattering the contents onto the counter. Lipstick, pens, notebook, brush, tissues, candy bar, lotion, paperback book . . . Everything except what he wanted.

"I'm running out of time! If I don't find that technology before the meeting with Navarro . . ."

Garrison pointed out the obvious. "Our best chance at getting what we want is with those two." He gestured with his head toward the back of the cabin. "They know something. I can feel it."

They were interrupted by the arrival of one of the men. "Saville's been taken to the room as you requested. She's still out."

After the man left, Garrison pushed off from the counter. "Well, I'll leave you to your interrogation. I've got a few calls to make."

***

Cambry struggled to open her eyes. It seemed to take all her strength just to accomplish the task, and when she did, the dim light overhead stabbed into her head like a thousand needles. She quickly closed them again, feeling her stomach roil. She swallowed hard and fought the urge to throw up.

When the nausea subsided somewhat, she tried to bring her hand up to her throbbing head, but her limbs felt too heavy.

What had happened? Where was she?

When her mind finally started to clear and the roaring sound in her head began to fade, a new sound replaced it—a soft, gentle voice that sounded warmly familiar.

"Cambry? Cambry, can you hear me?"

More slowly this time, Cambry opened her eyes. The dim light coming from somewhere nearby still made her head ache, but at least the throbbing wasn't as excruciating as it had been. She turned her head cautiously to see she was lying on a bottom bunk in the dimly lit, wood-paneled game room.

Suddenly, it came rushing back. Benton. Benton and his men had been at the cabin. A foggy image of a restrained Ethan came to her, and then other images started to appear. There'd been a struggle. Willoughby.

She moaned and put a hand to her head. Thank goodness he'd managed to run off. Hopefully he'd find his way down the mountain to civilization.

But what had happened to Ethan? She'd just heard his voice a minute ago, hadn't she?

Slowly and cautiously, she started to push herself upright. Pain exploded in her side, making her breath catch in her chest. Straining her sensitive eyes against the light, she reached down and pulled up the hem of her battered shirt. A large, blood-soaked gauze pad was taped to the skin just above her jeans and ran up almost to her ribs.

More memories started to filter in. A fall down the mountain. A syringe. How long had she been out?

Gritting her teeth against the pain, she sat up the rest of the way and searched the dimly lit room. Through blurred vision, Cambry finally made out Ethan's form across the room. He wasn't moving around, so she guessed he was probably tied to the support pole he was leaning against. At least he was alive.

"Cambry, are you okay?" she heard him ask, his voice thick with concern.

She nodded groggily. "Yeah, I think so." She put her hands on the mattress and started to push herself up, but Ethan quickly protested.

"No, Cambry, don't stand up! Just take it easy for a few minutes."

Ignoring his warning, Cambry stood and took two shaky steps before she suddenly realized she should have listened. The room began to spin, and her legs gave out. She made a desperate grab for the bunk bed ladder, holding tightly to the rungs as she let herself sink to the ground. Once she felt the cold wood floor against her legs, she leaned her forehead heavily against a rung and closed her eyes to the spinning room around her.

She forced herself to take several deep breaths and tried to focus on pushing her pain and nausea aside. When she started to feel a little better, she opened her eyes again and looked drowsily over at Ethan.

Now that her vision was clearing, she could see that his hands were indeed secured behind him around the pole. His shirt was dirty and untucked from his jeans, his bottom lip was split and bleeding, and a large, ugly, bluish-purple bruise was beginning to form on his left cheek.

Her stomach lurched at the sight. How much had he been through while she'd been unconscious? It was apparent from the pained, weary look in his eyes that he'd been treated roughly and that he was hurting. But he seemed to be trying extremely hard to mask his own pain in his concern for her. That touched her deeply.

"Who are those guys?" she asked quietly, finally finding her voice.

"Isaac Benton. Ties to Al-Qaeda. Not a good man." He grimaced. "As you heard, he's behind the attack on your father. The other guys are probably just hired muscle. I got the impression they don't have much to do with intelligence. I've spent the last little while trying to convince Benton that we don't have your father's technology, but obviously he doesn't believe me. And he's starting to lose patience."

"Yeah, I can tell from that bruise on your face."

It was quiet for a long minute. Then Cambry remembered what Benton had told her. And what Ethan hadn't denied.

Her eyes started to burn, and she blinked back tears. "Is it true? You've been undercover, investigating me this whole time?"

He swallowed, and his voice barely a whisper, he answered. "Yes."

The confirmation felt like a blow. It wasn't until she felt something wet drip onto her hand that she realized her tears had started to flow.

"So it was all an act?" she managed. "Wanting to be my friend? That story about feeling guilty for what happened five years ago?" She paused. "That kiss in my kitchen?"

A look of distress etched further into his features. "Cambry, none of it was an act. I swear. This whole thing has just been so complicated. When my boss called me into his office and asked me to see if you knew where your father's technology was while I was home for my dad's surgery, I was against it. But there was some question about whether or not you were working with Benton—"

Cambry stared at him in shock. "The FBI thought I was working with Benton? That I attacked my own father?"

"I promise, I never thought that, not even for a second. But these agents didn't know you, so they trusted me to find out what was really going on. And we have. Benton's been behind the whole thing."

"Well, yay for you for coming to that conclusion," she said, her voice dripping with sarcasm. "I'm so glad you figured out that I didn't try to kill my father and commit international espionage with a group of terrorists. How great to know you have so much faith in me."

"Bree, don't." Ethan's voice sounded anguished. "It's not like that. If you had any idea how much I've hated deceiving you in this . . . I never wanted to hurt you."

"Well, you did," she informed him on a painful, hitched breath. "What did you expect was going to happen? That you were just going to report back, give the all clear, and then we'd go on with our lives with me never being the wiser?"

Ethan had the decency to look guilty. "I hoped."

She shook her head and let her eyes drift to the ceiling. "Unbelievable."

"I'm sorry, Cambry," Ethan said quietly. "You have no idea how sorry. Yes, I had a job to do, but I had every intention of seeing if we could still mean something to each other long before my boss told me to see what you knew. What made it even more complicated was . . ."

When he didn't finish, Cambry glared at him. "Was what?"

He dragged in a breath. "Was that I hadn't counted on falling in love with you all over again."

Cambry's chest tightened painfully. "Great way you have of showing it."

"I know." His jaw tightened. "Please don't push me away, Bree. Give me a chance to prove to you that I really do love you. That I'm worthy of your trust. I know it could take a while to restore that trust, but I'm in this for as long as it takes."

She lifted her gaze to his, and she saw soul-deep pain reflected in his expression. He really did mean what he was saying. And he was hurting just as badly as she was.

But that didn't mean she could forgive him. Not for a betrayal this big.

Heartbreak and anger warred for dominance inside of her, and her lips started to tremble.

All she wanted to do was curl up in a corner, bury her face in her knees, and cry, but she would never let him see how much his betrayal had hurt her. When they managed to find a way out of this and go home, she would cry then. Lock herself in her silent house, climb into bed, and cry for a week. Alone. She would refuse to let anyone else see how weak she'd been to let this man back into her life and then subsequently destroy her.

She looked over to see Ethan watching her expectantly. She lifted a hand to her throbbing head and closed her eyes. "I'm sorry, Ethan, but I don't know what to say. Up until a few hours ago, I thought we might be rebuilding something, you and me. But suddenly everything is different, and I don't know how to feel about that."

"Besides hurt and angry."

She dropped her hand and glared at him. "Don't you think I have every right to be? I thought you were spending all that time with me because I was your friend, not because I was the focus of an FBI agent's undercover investigation."

"I just explained to you that wasn't the case," he said in exasperation. "Look, Cambry, I know you're mad, and yes, you have every right to be. But we've got bigger problems to deal with right now, so maybe we should just agree to put off this discussion until after we get out of here. And we *will* get out of here," he said, his voice low and determined. "Trust me in that."

Ethan was right, Cambry realized reluctantly. Somehow they had to get out of here, and that would take two calm and collected minds.

Closing her eyes, she shifted and then winced at the pain in her side. "Any ideas how? I doubt we'd be able to unlatch the shutters from inside."

"I agree. The windows aren't an option."

Cambry tried to come up with an alternative means of escape, but the fog in her brain seemed to thwart her efforts. "I wish I had my handy sonic screwdriver," she mumbled, trying to inject a little levity to the situation. "I think I left it in my other jeans' pocket."

Ethan's grin flashed in the semidarkness at her *Doctor Who* reference. The iconic tool had been used by The Doctor for any number of things, including picking locks. Somehow the reference managed to ease the tension just a little.

"Yeah, too bad you didn't bring it along," Ethan said. "In a more realistic attempt to escape, I've been working on getting out of these ropes. There's a rough spot at the bottom of this beam that I'm using to try to saw through them, but it could take some time."

"Need some help?"

He shook his head. "Not much you could do unless you have a pocketknife hidden somewhere."

"Sorry."

"Yeah. Didn't think so. Just rest. Getting out of these is just the first step in our soon-to-be-hatched escape plan."

The silence stretched out between them as Ethan continued to work at the ropes. Cambry sighed heavily and let go of the ladder, feeling worn out. "I know we should be putting our heads together to hatch that plan, but my mind's not cooperating. I think I'll just lie down for a few minutes," she said as she lowered herself carefully to the floor, gritting her teeth against the shooting pains in her side. "My mind is still too fuzzy to be creative."

She pressed her cheek against the floor, relieved at how the cool wood made her hot cheeks and throbbing head feel better. Not trying to fight off the pull of sleep any longer, she let her eyelids droop and her mind drift.

***

Ethan continued sawing at his ropes, encouraged when he felt another strand snap. Almost there.

He looked over at Cambry's motionless form, still prone on the wood floor, and realized how quiet she'd been for the past few minutes.

He stopped sawing. "Cambry?"

"Hmm?"

He let out the breath he hadn't realized he'd been holding. "I just thought . . . Were you asleep?"

"No, just thinking."

"About what?"

There was a smile in her voice when she answered, "About how great an omelet sounds right now. Is that weird? We're being held captive, and I'm thinking about eggs."

Ethan chuckled. "I think you're entitled. You hungry?"

Cambry turned her head toward him, settling her opposite cheek against the floor. She cringed at the pain even that small movement caused. "Maybe a little," she admitted. "I wonder what time it is."

Ethan glanced toward the light from the moon spilling in from between the shutters. "Probably eight or nine. You were out for a while."

It was obvious she still felt foggy from whatever drug they'd given her, but he doubted the hard, uncomfortable floor was the best way to help her recover.

"Cambry, why don't you get back up on the bottom bunk?" he suggested. "At least there you'd be up off this cold floor."

She shook her head slightly and mumbled, "No, the cold floor feels good. I'll be okay here."

Ethan's brow furrowed. The cold floor felt good? That didn't bode well. It was freezing in the room.

Tearing his gaze from Cambry, he looked around the room while he continued to saw at the ropes. He could feel more individual strands fraying and breaking, and it wouldn't be long before his hands were free. But he wasn't sure what he would do then. He needed to come up with a plan. With the windows secured and an armed man standing guard on the other side of the door, Ethan knew those methods of escape were out. He spotted a door in the far corner of the room behind the pool table. It obviously didn't lead outside since it was on an inner wall. So what was it? A bathroom?

Before he could ask Cambry about it, he heard the sound of footsteps approaching in the hallway. Moments later the door banged open. Cambry jerked partially upright, and Ethan stiffened when he saw Benton standing in the doorway.

"Ms. Saville. How nice to see you awake," Benton said with sardonic cheerfulness.

"What do you want, Benton?" Ethan demanded, trying to draw the attention away from Cambry. He pulled at the ropes, encouraged when they gave a little. "Come to take another shot at me?"

Benton looked over at him, his expression calculating. "No, I think we've finished having fun with you for a little while. I thought I'd come have a little chat with your lady instead."

When Benton strode toward Cambry, fear tightened Ethan's chest. He pulled harder on the ropes. "Benton, leave her alone. She doesn't know anything!"

"Why don't you let me be the judge of that?"

Two of Benton's men, including the one with the ugly scar running down his cheek, suddenly appeared in the doorway. Benton gestured to Cambry. "Take Ms. Saville upstairs." The men nodded, and Benton turned toward the door as one of his men started for Cambry. Ethan gritted his teeth as he twisted his wrists back and forth and strained for all he was worth. The last strand of the rope broke free, and Ethan leaped to his feet just as Benton's thug grabbed Cambry by the arm and hauled her to her feet. She cried out in pain, the sound searing a hole straight through Ethan's heart.

Free of his restraints, Ethan charged across the room. A look of surprise crossed the men's faces, but the man with the scar leaped into action and intercepted Ethan. He grabbed Ethan and shoved him face-first up against the wall, pinning Ethan's arms and bodychecking him to keep him from moving.

"Let her go!" Ethan yelled as he watched the other thug drag Cambry out the door.

"Not a chance, Reece!" Benton thundered, stepping close and shoving his face near Ethan's. "You wouldn't tell me what you've learned, so I'll just have to get it from her! Maybe that's something you should think about."

When Cambry's pleas for freedom faded down the hall, Benton backed off and looked at the man holding Ethan. "Do we have more rope to secure him?"

The man shook his head. "That was it. Want me to find something else?"

"Don't bother," Benton said. "The room's secure. Just keep the guards stationed at the door and around the outside perimeter."

Nodding, the man watched Benton leave and then released Ethan. The man was gone a moment later.

Ethan had no way of knowing how long Cambry had been gone, but it felt like an eternity as he paced and ran his hands raggedly through his hair. The all-too-painful reminders of Benton's determination were still evident on his own body—his bruised cheek, split lip, and sore ribs—and he worried that Benton wouldn't go any easier on Cambry. In fact, with her being a woman, surrounded by all of Benton's men . . .

Ethan stopped and shook his head. No, he couldn't even think it. What was worse, he knew that Benton was capable of just such a nightmare. And that made Ethan worry even more.

He finally sat down on the bed, giving his sore body a moment to rest. Their best option was to escape. He'd already checked out that mysterious door in the corner of the room, but it was only a utility closet containing a water heater and nothing else. No tools or anything else that could help them escape.

He bowed his head and prayed for what felt like the hundredth time, pleading for their safety and a way to escape. He knew there had to be a way out of here. They just had to wait for their chance and be prepared to take it when it came.

A door slammed, and Ethan jerked upright. He strained his ears, listening. But no other sounds came. Had it been a door to one of the rooms? The front door? Or maybe even a car outside?

Ethan stood, unable to sit for a moment longer, and resumed his pacing. At last he heard footsteps coming down the hall. Then the door opened and a different man appeared, pulling Cambry along behind him. She looked even more pale than when she'd left, and there was an unusual lack of fire in her eyes. But at least she was alive and apparently unharmed.

As Ethan started toward her, the man yanked a .45 caliber automatic from his waistband and leveled it at Ethan. "Get back or I'm not letting her go."

Ethan lifted his hands and backed away. The man waited until Ethan had backed up against the bunk bed, then he shoved Cambry into the room. She stumbled, and Ethan quickly rushed forward to steady her.

She collapsed gratefully into his arms, burying her head against his chest. Ethan looked over at Benton's thug just in time to see him disappear through the doorway and pull the door shut behind him.

CHAPTER TWENTY-ONE

TEARS BURNED IN CAMBRY'S EYES as she clung to Ethan, not even caring that he'd recently betrayed and deceived her. Right now, he was on her side, and his strong arms around her had never felt so good. She felt him drop his head and press a gentle kiss to the top of hers.

"You okay?"

His voice sounded shaky, unsteady. She was glad she wasn't the only one who felt that way.

She nodded but couldn't speak. The last two hours had felt like two hundred, and she'd never been so terrified in her life. She trembled against Ethan, and his arms tightened around her.

"It's okay, I'm here. I'm right here."

He stroked her hair and held her close, speaking in soft, soothing tones. All she could think about was that thumb drive at Alisa's house and the copy on the disc safely in her messenger bag at home. When she and Ethan had stopped by her house so she could change, she hadn't even taken the time to pull the disc out. Why would she? It was safer tucked away in her bag in the back of her closet until she could decide what to do with it.

She didn't want to admit to Ethan just how close she'd come to confessing to Benton about the still unknown contents on that disc and thumb drive. He'd probably think her weak. But she'd known that the second she told him where to find it, Benton would probably kill her. Both of them. If she could just stick it out a while longer, maybe they could find a way out of this.

A muscle in her side twitched, and the pain from her fall flared to life. She clutched at her side and drew a shuddering breath.

Ethan sensed her discomfort and took a step back. "Let me take a look at that gash." He guided her to the bottom bunk in the corner and helped her sit. When she pulled up the hem of her shirt to reveal her blood-soaked bandage, he grimaced.

Sinking to his haunches beside her, he reached for the bandage. "I'm going to pull back some of this tape so I can see underneath the gauze."

When he did, she sucked in a startled breath. The wound looked red and angry, the skin around it starting to turn an alarming array of colors. It had apparently been haphazardly closed with a couple of butterfly bandages while she was unconscious.

"So what happened up there?" he asked, trying to distract her as he continued to inspect the wound.

Cambry flinched as he touched the discoloring skin around the gash. "They grilled me about the technology and where it was. I kept telling them I didn't know anything, but of course they didn't believe me. Ow!"

Ethan pulled his hand away from her side. "Sorry." He studied the cut for a moment longer and then exhaled. "This looks deep enough to warrant stitches, but there's not a lot we can do about that right now."

"What about infection?"

His expression was grave. "Yeah, I have concerns about that too. I doubt anybody took the time to clean it properly."

Ethan did his best to secure the gauze back over the gash, then he patted her knee and rocked back on his heels. He straightened and turned to sit beside her. "I want you to lie down and take it easy for a while."

"What about getting out of here?"

Ethan sighed. "While you were with Benton, I checked out the place. The window shutters are impossible to open from the inside, and the room's well guarded. Our best bet is to sit tight and wait for an opportunity to present itself."

The anguish she felt at having to sit back and wait must have shown because Ethan muttered something and drew her carefully into his arms.

"It'll be okay," he whispered, holding her tightly. "I'll get us out of here. Trust me."

She nodded against his shoulder, finding herself too weary to do much else.

"So what happens next?" she asked quietly.

Ethan released her but reached for her hand, intertwining his fingers with hers. "Normally, they'd try to wear us down. No food. No water. Leave us to worry and wonder about what's going to happen to us. They'd use whatever intimidation tactics they can. But Benton's pressed for time, so that changes things. If it comes down to your life, though, Cambry, you do whatever you can to survive. Understand?"

Ethan's expression was fierce, and what she saw in his eyes sent a chill down her back. She nodded. It was all she could do.

Their conversation drifted off, and Cambry felt herself start to lean more heavily against him. Fatigue made her eyes droop.

"Lie down and get some sleep," Ethan said softly, brushing her hair back from her face. "It's well past midnight, and we could both use the rest."

"'Rest is for the weary, sleep is for the dead,'" she managed with a slight smile, her eyelids already heading south.

Ethan chuckled, a deep, comforting sound that reverberated through his chest and warmed her insides. "You can't be that bad off if you're still managing to quote *Doctor Who*."

When she lay down, he pulled the solitary blanket on the bed up over her. "Get some rest. I have a feeling we're both going to need it."

"Where are you going to sleep?" she mumbled.

His eyes drifted to the bunk above them and the ladder. "I'm not sure I can make it up onto the top bunk," he admitted. "But don't worry about me, I'll just doze here next to you."

He scooted back into the corner of the bunk next to her feet and leaned his head back against the wall. Before long, they were both asleep.

***

Sunlight filtered in through the window shutters near the bed, causing Cambry to stir. She opened her eyes and blinked a couple of times. Her arm stung from its awkward position curled beneath her.

She lifted her head off the pillow and spotted Ethan half sitting, half slumped on the bed near her feet, his head propped against the bunk bed's framework and his eyes closed. The ugly bruise near his eye was darkening into a sickening purple.

As if he'd sensed her watching him, his eyelids fluttered open. His sleepy gaze swept around them before settling on her.

"Hi," he murmured, sitting up and rubbing at his stiff neck. "Did you sleep okay?"

"As well as you did, it looks like."

Ethan opened his mouth to reply, but the door suddenly swung open, silencing them both. Cambry stiffened when she saw Benton standing in the doorway.

"Rise and shine!" the man called out, his voice echoing harshly through the empty room. He walked in, followed by a dark-haired man who was carrying a plate of food. Cambry eyed the food hungrily, and Benton smirked. "Hungry, Ms. Saville?"

He took an apple from the tray and tossed it into the air. "Here's the deal. You two tell me what I want to know, and you can eat. If you don't, well, all this food will go to waste."

Ethan slid out of the bunk and got to his feet. "Benton, you're wasting your time. We don't know where the technology is."

Benton's face hardened. "Wrong answer."

Turning to his man behind him, Benton placed the apple back on the plate and made a motion with his head. The man nodded and left, taking the food with him.

"I can see this is going to take a little more convincing." With anger flashing in his eyes, he flicked a hand toward the open door, and two burly men appeared. They crossed the room in determined strides and grabbed Ethan.

"Boys, take him upstairs and see if you can change his mind about what details he's willing to share."

Cambry sat up quickly, gritting her teeth against the hot flash of pain in her side. "Can't you see that you're wasting your time? Why don't you just let us go?"

Benton turned back to her as his men began to pull Ethan out of the room. "I think you should be more worried about what's going to happen if you or your boyfriend here don't start indulging me with some details."

He turned on his heel and started back across the room when Cambry had a sudden inspiration. "Hey! Don't I even get to go to the bathroom? You can't expect us to be willing to share any details with you if we're not even treated halfway decently!"

Ethan twisted his head around to look at her in a silent warning. Cambry ignored his menacing *Don't you dare try anything stupid* look and watched as Benton stopped in his tracks and turned back. He seemed to deliberate over her request and then turned to another man in the hall. "Wait five minutes and take her to the bathroom."

The man nodded, and Ethan was tugged the rest of the way out of the room. The door slammed shut behind them, and she was alone. The silence set her on edge.

It's not stupid to try to get out of here, she grumbled silently, thinking of the warning look Ethan had given her. She couldn't stand idly by and wait for the inevitable. If she was careful and creative enough, she could put this time to good use.

As Cambry swung her legs over the side of the bed, she gasped at the resurgence of pain in her side. If anything, it was worse than the night before. She sat on the edge of the bed, breathing shallowly through her nose, and tried to focus. She couldn't let Benton's men see her hurt. They would use whatever advantage they could.

When the pain subsided somewhat, she braced her palms on either side of her and pushed herself up. By the time the door opened and the man walked in, she felt capable of walking without flinching. The man took her arm and led her from the room, giving her a shove through the bathroom doorway.

It was all Cambry could do to keep herself from crying out in pain.

"You have two minutes," he snapped before pulling the door shut between them.

Alone once more, she turned to the medicine cabinet. Being as quiet as she could, she opened it and looked inside. Disappointment set in when she saw that it held only a sample-sized tube of toothpaste and a couple of toothbrushes. She shut the cabinet and turned her attention to the drawers. They were empty.

Her heart sank. She hadn't known what she'd hoped to find or what she could have possibly done with anything that might be there, but the fact that she didn't even have anything to try to formulate a plan with was dispiriting.

She saw to her needs quickly, splashed some water on her face, then opened the door.

The guard glowered at her. "It's about time. Let's go."

He grabbed her arm, towed her down the hall, and pushed her back into the room. The door shut with a thump, and all was quiet.

Trying to distract herself from thoughts of what Benton and his brutes were probably doing to Ethan, she walked back to the bunk beds and sat down. She pictured where else she might be right now. It was Saturday. She'd probably be at home, eating a late breakfast. Maybe a breakfast burrito. With a couple of Pop-Tarts. Her empty stomach rumbled in protest.

Unbidden tears slid down her cheeks. Early last week, her life had been fine. Normal. Then her father was attacked. Since then she'd been accused, harassed, stalked, and now kidnapped. To top it all off, the man she'd thought she was falling back in love with had deceived her. Tricked her into thinking he was her friend—and maybe even more—for the sake of their country. His duty to the FBI.

Pain swelled in her heart until her chest was so tight that it was difficult to breathe. How could she ever get past that? The Ethan she'd known had been loyal. Steadfast. She'd always been able to trust him with everything.

Except her heart. He'd shown her twice now that she'd been a fool to trust him with that.

Pulling the solitary blanket up over her, she turned her face into the pillow and closed her eyes, feeling utterly miserable. She was hungry, tired, and hurting, but most of all, she was scared. Scared for herself, scared for Ethan, and scared for anyone else who might become involved in this.

Without even the energy to kneel, she prayed from where she lay. She pleaded for her and Ethan's safety, along with the safety of Ethan's family and Alisa, that nothing would lead Benton to any of them. And for this ordeal to be over soon. She prayed long and hard, until finally a peace settled around her.

Fresh tears sprang into her eyes. She wasn't alone. And somehow everything was going to be okay. The realization eased her turbulent emotions.

Letting her drooping eyelids fall shut, she gave in to the pull of sleep.

CHAPTER TWENTY-TWO

THE CLOMPING OF BOOTED FEET on the stairs jerked Cambry awake. She sat up, feeling achy and stiff all over. The sun was bright outside the window, telling her that quite a bit of time had passed since she'd fallen asleep. She heard the footsteps reach the bottom of the stairs and turn down the hall. She tensed. Somebody was coming.

As the footsteps drew closer, she drew the blanket around her chilled shoulders. Why couldn't Benton's GI Joes figure out how to turn up the heat? It was freezing.

The door opened, and two of Benton's men appeared in the doorway with Ethan supported between them. Cambry ignored her own aches and pains when she saw the ragged condition Ethan was in. His face was alarmingly pale, his hair was tousled, and there were two new bruises on his face.

Rising, she watched as the men shoved him roughly inside and slammed the door behind him. Ethan stumbled forward and nearly fell, but Cambry reached out and caught him, doing her best to support him as he regained his balance. Whatever he had done to her, however he had deceived her, she would never wish this kind of abuse on him.

"Are you okay?" she asked, shaken by Ethan's condition.

He gave a slight nod but winced when Cambry slipped her arm around his waist to help him to the bed. "I will be. Just . . . give me a minute, okay?"

She quickly let him go. "I'm sorry. What did they do to you up there?"

"Whatever Benton told them to," he said grimly, trying to straighten up without flinching. "But don't worry. I'm sure I look worse than I feel."

She helped him to the bed where he sank gratefully onto the mattress. When he looked up at Cambry, his eyes were a little more focused.

"What was up with that stunt you pulled about being more cooperative if you were taken to the bathroom?"

She gave him a look. "Besides needing to go to the bathroom?" She shrugged. "I wanted to see if there might be anything in the cupboards or medicine cabinet that could help us get out of here. Unfortunately, there wasn't."

He shifted, grimaced again, and put an arm across his ribs. At her look of concern, he shook his head. "Just some bruised ribs, I think. Not the worst I've faced."

"I'm not sure that's comforting."

He opened his mouth to respond, but then his gaze moved over her, and he frowned. "You look paler than when I left. Are you okay?" He pressed a hand to her cheek, and his frown intensified. "You're starting to run a fever."

That explained why she felt so chilled. She tightened the blanket around her shoulders and shifted away from his hand. "I'll be fine. You worry too much." Changing the subject, she asked, "Have you had any brilliant ideas about how to get out of here yet? If you have, I'd love to hear them."

He glanced toward the door. "I'm still thinking," he said in a low voice, making sure he couldn't be overheard. "I thought about creating a distraction, but that didn't work so well for us earlier, even though Willoughby tried."

His mention of her dog made her throat grow tight. "I hope he's okay. I thought I heard him yelp. Do you think one of the bullets hit him?"

"I don't think so," Ethan reassured her, squeezing her hand. "The way he took off running, he couldn't have been that hurt. He was smart enough to try to give us a chance to escape. He's smart enough to find his way to safety. We just need to do the same."

"But there's no way we're getting out of here through the door. Too many men inside the cabin."

"I know. Our best chance would be to slip out through a window after dark and escape into the woods, but I don't think there's any way we're going to get out through those shutters without making a lot of noise."

Cambry frowned. "If we can't go through the door and we can't go out through a window, what other options do we have?"

One side of Ethan's mouth quirked up in a smile. "You don't have some secret wardrobe in here with a passageway to Narnia, do you?"

Cambry froze.

Passageway.

Why hadn't she thought of it before?

"I was kidding," Ethan drawled.

She bit back a laugh, excitement practically bubbling over. In hushed tones, she explained. "I don't know why I didn't think of it before! There's a door to a crawl space in the water heater closet. And there's an external entrance to the crawl space as well."

Ethan's eyes widened. "The crawl space has internal *and* external access?"

Cambry nodded. "The original door to the crawl space is on the north side of the cabin, but when my father decided to build the wraparound deck, he didn't like the idea of getting into the crawl space by crawling under the deck, so he had a new entrance cut into the floor of the closet."

"Are both doors still usable?"

"I think so. The one in the closet just lifts up. The outside one could be a challenge because it's under the deck, but I'm sure we could army crawl out."

"The external door's not locked?"

"It shouldn't be. Nobody would have been able to see the door under the deck. It's just a metal cover, kind of like a door on a locker, only it doesn't have hinges. You keep it shut by putting a combination lock on it, but when my father built the deck over it, he didn't bother securing it. It's probably still just sitting wedged in the hole of the foundation."

Ethan got up and walked quietly over to the closet in the corner. Cambry followed, watching as Ethan eased the door open and peered inside. Hunching down on the balls of his feet, he grabbed a corner of the old woven rug in front of the water heater and flipped it aside. Sure enough, there was a hinged door beneath. Being as quiet as possible, he slid a couple of fingers into the silver dollar–sized hole on one side and pulled. It lifted easily.

"Here, hold the door up while I climb down and take a look."

Cambry did as he asked, and Ethan lowered himself into the hole. When his feet touched ground, he lowered his big body into the tight space and looked around. His low whisper drifted up to her. "Do you know if your father stored anything under here that would block us from getting to the external door?"

"He didn't. It should be clear."

Ethan stood up and silently hopped back up through the hole. Then he eased the trap door shut and covered it back up with the rug. "Which way to the external door?"

Cambry gestured toward the right front of the house. "Not far that way. We'll just have to keep our hand on the wall until we feel the cutout in the foundation and then push out the metal cover."

Ethan considered as he left the closet and quietly shut the door behind him. "Let's wait until dark and then slip out. Hopefully we can get through the patrols around the cabin without being detected. Unfortunately, all we can do until then is wait."

Before she could think about that, the sound of approaching footsteps made her whirl. The instant the door was thrown open, Ethan moved in front of her, shielding her from their visitors.

She cringed as Benton's angry voice filled the room. "Last chance, you two. I want to know where that technology is, and I want to know *now*."

Cambry heard the lethal tone in Benton's voice and knew the man was out of patience. Clearly something had happened since Benton's thugs had finished beating Ethan. Maybe he'd heard from his buyer. Or something was happening with his deal. Whatever it was, he was beyond reasoning. Everything they'd suffered to this point would be nothing compared to what he'd do to them next.

She clenched Ethan's polar fleece sweatshirt in her fists and rested her forehead against his back, wishing they could both disappear.

"There's nothing to say, Benton." Ethan's voice was cold and hard. "You're wasting your time."

Benton moved partially into Cambry's view, and she could see that his jaw was clenched and his motions were tense. He looked like a crazy man on the verge of losing it. He moved a couple of steps closer, his booted footsteps making her feel light-headed with fear.

"How much more of this do you think you both can take?" Benton ground out. "Without food or water, you're not going to last long."

When Ethan didn't answer, Benton took another angry step forward, his eyes blazing with fury. "I've dealt with people like you before, people who will do anything to hold on to their secrets, no matter the cost. But believe me, I *will* get what I need. And I'm tired of playing around."

At Benton's nod, two men rushed forward, grabbing Ethan and hauling him aside, leaving Cambry exposed and vulnerable. Benton lunged for her and grabbed her by the hair. Needles of pain drove through her scalp as he yanked her forward and shoved her to her knees. She cried out at the impact, but the sudden pressure of a cold, hard muzzle of a gun against her temple cut the sound short.

"So what's it going to be?" Benton demanded through clenched teeth. "Do you tell me, or do I kill you right now?"

She swallowed even as she began to shake. She didn't dare move for fear that it would be all the invitation Benton needed. "Please," she whispered, tears starting to course down her cheeks. "I don't know where my father hid the technology."

"Listen to her!" Ethan yelled, his voice desperate. "A man like you would have done your research, so you'd know she and her father were estranged. They haven't talked in six years!"

"Except that when she found him, he was still conscious and talking!" Benton snapped over his shoulder at Ethan. "I want to know what he said. And Ms. Saville will tell me now, or she's going to die."

Cambry felt the gun shift, heard it cock. A noisy sob escaped her throat, and she clamped her eyes shut. Desperation and fear made her limbs numb.

She'd held out on the police. The FBI. Even Ethan. But the game was up. She either told this man now, or she wasn't going to live to see another tomorrow.

She opened her eyes and looked over at Ethan, silently pleading with him to tell her what to do. Did she tell Benton? Was she supposed to? Was it okay for her, a civilian, to give in to a terrorist if her life was threatened? Or was she dead either way?

***

Rage surged through Ethan's body as he met Cambry's terrified gaze. She hadn't been trained for this kind of situation. But he had. The only way they were going to get out of this alive was to give Benton something. A morsel. Buy them some time, give them some distance. But just enough to convince Benton they were still valuable. If he thought they could still be of use, he'd keep them alive.

"She doesn't know anything," he spoke up. "But I do. I have a disc."

That caught Benton's attention. His finger eased off the trigger, and he looked up at Ethan. "What disc?"

Ethan met Benton's hard glare without flinching. "I found it in her father's files."

The lie wasn't important. The details about how he'd managed to acquire it wouldn't matter as long as Benton knew where to get it now. And it would keep Cambry and Alisa Munro out of this.

Greed gleamed in Benton's eyes. "And the technology?"

"Working on that." Ethan considered his next words. "The disc contained multiple encrypted files, and I'm having the files decrypted as we speak. It's possible the technology is in one of those files."

"And where is the disc now?"

Ethan let out a breath. When Cambry heard this, he knew whatever chance they'd had at a relationship was over. But he had to do it. It was their only chance to get out of this alive.

"I delivered it to the Denver field office yesterday. They're working on the decryption."

Cambry's startled gasp went straight to his heart. He forced himself to meet her confused gaze. He saw the instant that it registered—that the only way he could have managed to get the disc was if he'd snuck it out of her bag.

Pain, betrayal, and heartbreak burned clearly in her eyes. That's when he knew it was over between them. Over before it had started.

Benton lowered the gun with a satisfied smirk. "See? Was that so hard?" He gave Cambry a shove, sending her sprawling to the floor. He turned to the darker-skinned man with the scar standing beside him. "Let's go. It appears we have a disc to retrieve."

The man with the scar nodded toward them, an evil glint in his eyes. "What about them?"

Ethan felt Cambry's terror as Benton looked back and forth between them. Finally, Benton grunted.

"Tell the men to keep them under lock and key in case I find out he's lying. If he is, we'll be back."

Without another glance, Benton turned and hurried out the door, his men behind him.

The sound of the door slamming echoed off the walls, reverberating through the silence. Ethan looked over at Cambry, who sat motionless on the floor. She looked so lost and hurt and vulnerable. He knew that his final announcement of betrayal had destroyed her.

He didn't know what to say, but the truth seemed to be as good a place to start as any. "I snuck it out of your bag," he said, his voice low and solemn. "We couldn't wait any longer."

She didn't move.

"Cambry, I'm sorry."

Nothing.

He walked over to where she sat and reached out to put a hand on her shoulder.

"Don't." The word held a lethal warning.

He dropped his hand.

Without looking up at him, she bit back a grimace as she got awkwardly to her feet. She swayed slightly once she was upright. Concerned, he reached for her again, but she stopped his movement with a scathing look.

Wordlessly, she turned and walked over to the bed. She lay down and rolled over to face the wall, her body language clear. She didn't want anything to do with him.

Her rejection felt like a slap. He didn't know what he'd expected though. He'd ruined whatever slim chance they'd had for a future once and for all. His shoulders slumped as he turned and walked to a cloth-covered chair in the corner by the pool table. He eased himself into it and hunched forward, his elbows on his knees. Staring miserably at his hands, he listened to Cambry's quiet sobs, each one making his heart break even further.

Moisture gathered in his own eyes. *You did the right thing,* he reassured himself.

Telling Benton about the disc had just saved their lives. It bought them the time they needed until nightfall when they could escape. And many of the men would go with Benton, bettering their chances of escape. But that would be little consolation for Cambry right now. She hated him.

Not that he could blame her. Right now he hated him too.

***

Benton grabbed his keys from the counter and hurried to the front door, expecting Garrison to follow. For now, Garrison did.

"I need that disc," Benton said as they stepped out onto the front porch. "Or at least a copy of it. Get on the phone with your source inside the Denver field office and tell him what's going on. He can get it, right?"

Garrison nodded. "He's resourceful. He can get it."

"Then what are you waiting for?" Benton said, hurrying down the cabin's steps with his keys in hand. "Let's go."

Garrison ambled down the steps after him. "My source is skittish. He won't talk to you. Wait here, and I'll call you when I have it."

"All I've done is wait," Benton growled. "Even if I have to sit at some roadside café while you meet with your source, I'll be close by to put things into motion the second you have it."

"Fine." Garrison pulled out his own set of keys and strolled to his car. "I'll let you know when I have it."

That seemed to satisfy Benton. The man gave him a short nod, got in his car, and peeled out of the dirt lot.

Garrison shook his head at the retreating taillights. Trusting fool.

He slid into his SUV and pulled his cell phone out of his pocket. Holding it up to the dome light, he checked for a signal. It was weak, but it was there. He dialed the number and held the phone to his ear and waited for Crowder to pick up.

When a sleepy voice answered, Garrison said, "Yeah, it's me. Sorry for the wake-up call, but I have a job for you."

CHAPTER TWENTY-THREE

ETHAN MUST HAVE DOZED OFF because he jerked awake in his chair when the door opened. He blinked, surprised to see that the room was starting to get dark. A man he didn't recognize stood in the doorway. He was dressed in a black, long-sleeved shirt and jeans and didn't look as threatening as the other men he and Cambry had encountered.

Ethan darted a glance in Cambry's direction, but she didn't stir from her position on the bed. He guessed she was still asleep.

The man spotted him in the corner and took a step inside. He had a plate in one hand and a bottled water in the other. Ethan watched cautiously as he approached.

"I was told to bring you this," the man said in a low voice. He surprised Ethan by merely setting it on the pool table before turning around and walking out of the room. The door shut quietly behind him.

Ethan sat unmoving. Was this a trick?

As he mulled that over, he concluded Benton didn't stand to gain anything by killing them at this point.

Judging from the waning light coming through the windows, only a few hours had passed. Even if Benton had somebody on the inside—which Ethan suspected he did after the way his own cover had been blown—he wouldn't have had time to get back to Denver, find a way to steal a disc that was currently in the FBI's possession, and get it to somebody who could decrypt the files any faster than they could.

No, Benton would still want them alive in case something came up.

Ethan eyed the offerings hungrily. There was a rather skimpy looking sandwich, an apple, and the bottled water. It wasn't much for two people, but it was something.

Getting up stiffly from his chair, he picked up the plate and bottle and carried them over to the bed where Cambry was sleeping. He sat down beside her, balancing the plate on his knees, and reached for her shoulder.

"Cambry."

No response. He gave her a gentle shake. "Cambry, wake up."

She made a noise low in her throat and rolled over. When she opened her eyes, they were sleepy and unfocused.

Hoping this might be a start at getting back into her good graces, he held up the plate and water. "Hungry?"

She blinked a few times and pushed a loose tumble of hair back from her face. Her skin was flushed and her eyes a little glazed. She stared at the items and frowned.

"Benton's way of saying thank you for not having to waste bullets on us?" The sarcasm in her voice was obvious, but her voice was hoarse and strained. "Or is he just trying to poison us so he doesn't have to be at the scene of the crime?"

He didn't know if her crankiness was because she was still furious with him or if she was just taking it out on him because he was the only one there.

"I considered that, but he doesn't stand to gain anything by poisoning us. He can't possibly have the disc yet, and even if he did, he'd be running into the same problems decrypting it that Alisa did. He'll be back for us. Fortunately, we'll be long gone by then." He unscrewed the lid on the water bottle and held it out to her. "Here. Drink some of this. Slowly, though. Just sip it."

"Thanks," she mumbled reluctantly.

Ethan monitored her slow intake and then took the bottle. "That's enough for now. Let your body get used to that before you have more."

Nodding, she lay back down and pulled the lone blanket back up over her shivering body.

His brows drew together in concern. "How are you feeling?" He reached out to check her temperature, but she shoved his hand away, her resentment obvious.

"I'm fine," she rasped. "Just leave me alone, okay?"

"Sorry, no can do." He reached out again and pressed the back of his fingers against her flushed cheek and then her forehead. She was burning up.

Worry balled up in the pit of his stomach. "We've got to get you to a doctor," he said, fighting to keep his tone neutral. He set the plate and water down on the floor next to the bed. "Let me check your side. I think it's infected."

It took a little convincing, but when he finally managed to take a look under the haphazardly taped gauze, his concern deepened. The cut was swollen and draining, with red streaks radiating out from the cut, which was hot to the touch.

There was no doubt about it. It was deeply infected and needed to be treated by a doctor.

He thought about going to the door and asking whatever guards might be stationed there about the possibility of some medical supplies, but he decided that would be asking for trouble. He didn't think it would take much for them to decide to use him or Cambry for a little sport.

A glance up at the darkening windows told him it would be nightfall soon. Only a few hours. They would have to wait it out until then. All he could do was make her comfortable until then. With any luck, he could get her to eat something to build up a little strength for their escape.

Turning back to her, he brushed her hair back from her face. She didn't bother opening her eyes. "Cambry, it's almost dark out. As soon as it's late enough, we'll get out of here, but you need to eat something. Here," he said, pulling off a corner of the sandwich that he thought would be a manageable size. "Eat this."

She shook her head, the movement barely noticeable. "I'm not hungry."

His voice gentled. "Honey, that's the fever talking. You need to get some calories in your system or we'll never make it through those woods tonight."

Her eyes opened, and she looked at him for a moment, as if weighing her options. He could see in her expression that she was still angry and hurt. Taking anything from him probably felt like accepting an apology, and she was a long way from that, he could tell. But his logic won out in the end, and she took the piece of the sandwich.

Getting her to eat even that small amount was a challenge, and when she finished, no amount of coaxing could get her to eat any more. Knowing the rest of the sandwich would only go to waste if he left it for her, he finished it off but pocketed the apple. He was able to get her to drink some more water, but the simple task of eating seemed to have drained her. Fatigue took over, and her eyelids drooped.

"Get some sleep," he whispered, running his fingers through her hair. She didn't push him away this time, and soon her breathing deepened. She was asleep.

Ethan stared down at her for a long time as he continued to run his fingers through her tangled curls, the protectiveness he felt nearly overwhelming him. She wasn't doing well. She needed antibiotics and medical attention. Soon.

Turning so he could sit beside her and stretch out his legs, he leaned his head back against the wall and closed his own eyes wearily. It had already been a long day, and Cambry wasn't the only one who was feeling the effects of Benton's treatment. His ribs ached, and his cheek and jaw were sore from where he'd been punched numerous times during his interrogation. The sooner they got out of here, the better.

Cambry stirred, and Ethan opened his eyes and looked down at her. She seemed restless, uncomfortable. He reached over to rub her arm in an attempt to soothe her. He breathed a sigh of relief when she quieted at his touch.

What a mess. It was going to be hard enough to get out of here, but he feared it was going to be even harder to fix his relationship with Cambry. He'd known this undercover investigation would come around to bite him in the backside. How on earth was he going to convince Cambry to trust him now?

He feared he might never be able to. This damage could very well be permanent.

Closing his eyes, he decided he'd deal with that later. For now, he needed his rest too. Night would come soon enough.

***

Ethan dozed fitfully over the next few hours, grateful that Benton's departure had made things quiet. The room grew dark, and Ethan felt a mixture of relief and anxiety. On the one hand, he'd never been so glad to see approaching darkness since he didn't know how much longer he could sit around watching Cambry's health dwindle. On the other hand, he knew that everything with their escape had to go just right. He didn't want to think of the consequences if things didn't.

His trained ears listened as sounds in and around the cabin quieted. Still he continued to wait. When his best estimate told him it had to be after midnight, he decided it was time. He put a gentle hand on Cambry's arm.

"Cambry, honey, wake up."

Her eyelids flickered open. She looked up at him, disoriented, then realized where she was and slowly sat up. "How long was I asleep?" she asked, her voice sounding gravelly and unused.

"A few hours." He reached out to palm her cheek. "It's time we get out of here. You ready?"

That put a little life in her expression. "More than. Let's go."

She winced as she twisted to put her feet on the floor, and Ethan kept an arm around her as she stood. When he felt confident she was steady, he released her and picked up the water bottle. A little water remained, and he handed it to her.

"Drink the rest of this."

He was relieved when she didn't argue.

When it was gone, her gaze drifted to the shuttered windows. "Do you think everyone's asleep?"

"I don't know about asleep, but the activity has died down. This may be our best chance at getting away undetected. We'll need at least a fifteen- or twenty-minute head start since we'll be on foot. Once they discover we're missing, they'll come after us in force."

"Then let's go. I can't wait to be away from here."

They silently crossed the room to the closet, and Ethan opened the door and pulled back the rug. He lifted the door to the crawl space and without hesitation lowered himself through it. Then he held up his hands and helped Cambry down.

"You sure you know your way to the exterior door?" he whispered as she scrunched down so he could close the door above them. "I don't want us to be wandering around down here in the pitch dark."

"Yes. It's just a short distance ahead on the right. Follow me."

Cambry started crawling forward, so he followed, using her soft shuffling sounds to gauge the distance between them. It wasn't long before she slowed and then stopped. He heard her let out a relieved breath.

"Found it. It should just push out."

He stopped beside her and ran his hands over the wall until he felt the metal door. "Let's each grab a side so we can do this as quietly as possible," he whispered.

The door wasn't wedged all that tightly in the hole, so it didn't take much to dislodge it. They quietly lowered it to the ground outside. Ethan could see the hint of moonlight in the distance, and it defined the shadows enough so that he could make out the edge of the wraparound deck about ten feet away.

Various shrubs and plants grew along the edge of the deck to shield the unsightly underside, and he knew that would work to their advantage.

It would hide them from watchful eyes until they had the opportunity to crawl out and make a break for the woods.

"Is your side okay?" he asked, able to see the faint outline of Cambry beside him.

"I'll manage."

He helped her out through the hole in the foundation and then crawled out next to her. They listened for long minutes, and Ethan was able to pick out the sounds of boots on dirt as one guard moved slowly past them toward the back of the house. Then everything was still for a long time.

Ethan leaned over to put his mouth near her ear. "Sounds like only one guard," he whispered in barely audible tones. "I think we're okay to go, but let me go first."

He sensed more than saw her nod. Almost soundlessly, he crawled toward the edge of the deck. Cambry followed. After what seemed like forever, both he and Cambry lay on their stomachs behind the bushes, peering out into the clearing surrounding the cabin.

Ethan watched and listened, waiting to determine a patrol pattern. It wasn't long before the one lone guard strolled out from around the back of the cabin and walked toward the front. He felt Cambry stiffen anxiously beside him, but he put a hand on her wrist and squeezed, his touch reassuring her.

When the man disappeared around the corner, he whispered, "Ready?"

He felt her nod, so he crawled forward between the shrubs, trusting her to follow. He paused, looking left and right. When he was confident they were alone, he moved through the bushes and stood. Cambry was instantly at his side. He helped her to her feet and then put a hand on the small of her back, guiding her forward.

"Hurry!" he urged in a low whisper.

Ethan's heart pounded as they ran across the clearing. He expected to hear shouts at any moment from a guard, but thankfully everything remained silent except for the sound of their footsteps.

Cambry stumbled, and Ethan reached for her just in time to keep her from going down. Without speaking, he urged her along beside him again, and moments later they disappeared into the cover of the woods.

***

Garrison pulled into the deserted lot of a dilapidated park. He parked and checked his watch. It had been almost two hours since he'd roused

Crowder from bed. He should be here by now. Shadowy movement caught his eye, and Garrison spotted the hint of a figure near the old jungle gym, far away from the streetlights.

Garrison climbed out of his car and crossed the weedy turf to the jungle gym.

"What do you have for me?" came Crowder's voice through the darkness.

"Agent Reece brought in a disc with encrypted files to the field office on Friday morning. We're pretty sure it contains Saville's missing technology. The computer nerds are working on decrypting it. I want a copy."

"*You* want a copy?" Crowder arched a brow. "Or Benton wants a copy?"

Garrison's jaw clenched. "What do you think?"

Crowder studied him for a long moment. "You going to make your move on this one?"

"It's time." Garrison grunted. "The man's getting greedy and careless. His organization is falling apart."

"And you're going to take over."

"Yes. Navarro doesn't care who sells the technology to him as long as he gets it. There will be a place for you, if you want it."

"For the kind of money you'll be offering, I'm in."

"And the disc?"

"I can get it." He lifted a shoulder in a casual shrug. "No problem. I'll be in touch in a couple of hours."

Garrison's mouth twitched. "I'll be waiting for your call."

***

Benton took the large Styrofoam container from the diner counter, slid a couple of bills across the counter to the waitress, and left the building. He crossed the nearly empty parking lot to his car, jumping when a voice came from the darkness.

"Took you long enough."

He looked up to see Garrison leaning against the driver's door, his arms folded across his barrel chest.

"Lousy service," Benton grumbled. "What did your source say?"

"He'll have it in a couple of hours."

Benton felt the tightness in his chest loosen. "Good. Hopefully there won't be any complications." His brow furrowed as he looked around them once more. "Where's your car?"

"Around the other side of the building."

The sound of his cell phone ringing brought a terse word to Benton's lips. He fished his phone out of his pocket. Pressing the button, he held it to his ear and barked, "What?"

He instantly recognized the voice of Meyers, his head of security. "Sir, Reece and Saville are gone."

Benton's eyebrows flew upward. "What do you mean, they're gone?"

"What?" Garrison's head came up at that piece of news. "Tell him to hold on. Let's get in the car and put it on speaker."

Benton grabbed his container of food and got behind the wheel. Garrison was in the passenger seat just as quickly. Benton pressed the speaker button and held the phone up so they could both hear.

"So what happened?" Benton started again.

Meyers's voice filled the interior of the SUV. "When we went to check on them a few minutes ago, they weren't there."

"Where did they go?"

Meyers hesitated. "They escaped through a crawl space door in the water heater closet."

Garrison leaned over to the phone. "And your team didn't notice the door when they scouted the room?"

Meyers had the decency to sound embarrassed. "The door was concealed under a rug. Somehow we missed it."

Benton's hand tightened around the phone. "Organize a search party and find them before they get too far away. We may still need Reece and Saville. If they make it back to civilization, we'll never have a chance to get near them again. And get on the radio and call in our chopper. I want some overhead help. The chopper's ready, right?"

"Yes, sir."

"Start searching on foot first, and the chopper can join in the search when it gets there," Benton ordered. "Any idea how long ago they escaped?"

"No, sir."

Benton let out an exasperated breath. "They could be anywhere by now. We'll just hope they don't get far in the shape they're in. Get as many vehicles out as possible, and tell your men to go over those woods with a fine-tooth comb. If you find any tracks or signs they've left behind, I want to know. Is that understood?"

"Yes, sir," came Meyers's reply.

With a growl, Benton clicked the phone off and slid it into his jacket pocket before he could throw it. "How did this happen?" he snapped.

"Your men are idiots, that's how it happened," Garrison grumbled back. Benton glared at him. "Don't start with me."

"You asked." Garrison reached for the door handle and let himself out of the car. "Deal with your search. I'll deal with the disc."

Garrison shut the door and disappeared into the darkness.

With his hands shaking in anger, Benton shoved the key into the car's ignition. But then he realized he didn't have anywhere to go. It wouldn't do any good to drive back up into the mountains. He couldn't do anything his security team wasn't already doing. Besides, it was a good hour and a half drive. If Garrison's source delivered the disc as projected, he wouldn't have enough time to get back here. He was better off hanging out here and waiting.

Sighing in resignation, he reached for his Styrofoam container. His car wasn't his first choice of places to eat, but at least he could do it in silence and let his anger keep him company.

CHAPTER TWENTY-FOUR

CAMBRY DUCKED UNDER THE TREE branch Ethan held back for her and then stepped over a clump of fallen branches. She wrapped her arms around herself. It was cold, but she knew it could have been much worse. Their part of the state had been enjoying a warm fall, and snow hadn't yet appeared in the mountains. She couldn't imagine making this trek through a foot of snow.

She trudged along behind Ethan, feeling worse with each passing minute. Her side blazed with every movement, and her head throbbed. All she wanted to do was lie down and rest.

"How long have we been walking?" she asked quietly.

Occasionally, the hoot of an owl or a rustle in the woods alerted them to the fact that they weren't alone, but so far there had been no indication that Benton's men were following them.

"Maybe an hour," Ethan answered as he concentrated on navigating the hilly terrain.

Cambry's heart sank. "An hour? That's it?" she asked, unable to keep the despair from her voice.

Ethan turned to glance over his shoulder at her. "Sorry to break the news, but yeah."

Tears brimmed in Cambry's eyes, and she slowed her already sluggish stride. Unable to force herself to continue, she veered out from behind Ethan and headed for a large, fallen tree. When she reached it, she collapsed onto it. This was a nightmare. Were they ever truly going to get out of this?

It wasn't long before Ethan realized Cambry was no longer behind him. When he turned and spotted her, he walked back and sat down beside her. Sensing she was discouraged and hurting, he slid an arm around her shoulders and pulled her close.

"Come on, Cambry, we can't quit now," he said gently. "This will all be over soon. I promise."

"I don't feel so great," she admitted, leaning her head against his shoulder.

His shoulder shifted beneath her cheek, and he pressed the back of his hand to her other cheek.

"You're still really warm," he confirmed. "Look, I know you feel lousy, and I wish there was something I could do about that, but I'm sure somebody has noticed we're missing by now. We have to keep moving."

"I know." Her voice sounded strained even to her own ears. "But can we rest for just a minute? I'm so tired."

Ethan nodded. "Okay. We'll rest for a minute."

Cambry allowed herself to relax against him. She knew she should be furious with him for lying to her and deceiving her, but right now she was just thankful for a warm body to lean against.

She made an effort to slow her breathing, and in the quiet, she almost felt at peace. Ethan shifted beside her, and she glanced over to see him rub a hand across his rib cage. Obviously, she wasn't the only one hurting.

"So where are we going?"

"We need to make it to the town and get help. But we need to make sure not to cross the road too soon. Benton's men will look there first. It can't take more than a few hours to hike."

If we're heading in the right direction.

She must have voiced the concern out loud because Ethan sat up and took her face firmly in his hands. His gaze, filled with determination, met hers. "Cambry, I swear to you, I am not going to get us lost or let Benton's men catch us. We've come too far and gone through too much to get to this point. All you have to do is trust me."

She stiffened. Trust? It seemed like such an absurd thing to ask of her now, after she'd learned just how much of her trust he'd betrayed since he'd arrived back in Denver.

He read her reaction, and his face fell as he let out a bone-weary sigh. "Look, Cambry, I said I was sorry. You have no idea how sorry I am. We're going to talk this out once we're back home safely, and I'm going to make it up to you. But for now, just know that you *can* trust me on this, okay?"

She stared at him in silence. What else could she do? He was her only way of getting out of these mountains. And she did trust him in this, she supposed. She just couldn't trust him with her heart.

Her mouth tightened, and she nodded. "Okay. Let's go."

Ethan's voice stopped her. "Before we do, would you mind if we said a prayer?"

Surprised, Cambry looked into Ethan's earnest expression. Instantly, she felt contrite for not having thought of it herself. When she nodded, she let Ethan help her move from the log, and together they knelt. Ethan offered the prayer, asking for guidance and direction and that they would get to safety soon. His humility and strength brought tears to her eyes, and when he closed with *amen,* an overwhelming feeling of warmth and protection washed over her. It gave her the strength to keep going.

Ethan helped her to her feet, and her legs felt a little less shaky. When he moved off, she followed.

He set a brisk pace, but somehow she managed to keep up. She had no idea how far they'd walked until Ethan suddenly stopped. As he looked over his shoulder, the moonlight touched his face. She caught his distant, distracted expression. He appeared to be listening.

"What is it?" she whispered. "What's wrong?"

He held up a hand, silencing her. A few seconds later, she heard it too. It was the unmistakable, rhythmic sound of an approaching helicopter.

Cambry gasped. "Benton must have discovered we were missing."

Ethan grabbed her hand. "Run!"

Cambry forced her legs to move. They whirled and took off into the dense cover of trees in the opposite direction of the approaching helicopter. Glancing back over her shoulder, Cambry could make out the helicopter's brilliant searchlight darting among the trees in the not-so-far distance. At the helicopter's current speed, it wouldn't be long before it was on top of them.

Ethan realized it too, and his eyes darted around their surroundings, searching. Then he tugged on her hand and pointed to his right. "This way!" he shouted, pulling her toward a denser gathering of trees and a shallow ravine.

Cambry stumbled along after him, fighting to stay on her feet as they dodged rocks and jumped over fallen tree branches. They paused at the top of the shallow ravine, and Cambry looked up frantically at the approaching helicopter.

The darting searchlight loomed even closer, illuminating the area just to the left of them. Cambry could feel the wind from the helicopter's blades rush over her, and the trees around them started to sway. Paralyzed with fear, she could only tighten her grip on Ethan's hand.

Ethan tugged at her, jerking her attention back to him. "Quick! Down into the ravine!" he yelled over the rhythmic beating of the blades.

She made her resistant legs move, and together they scrambled and skidded down the six or so feet of embankment into the empty ravine, causing a shower of loose dirt and rocks to fall down around them. They landed with a thump on the uneven ground at the bottom, and Cambry's knees nearly gave out from the impact.

She gasped as prickles of white-hot pain seared through her side. Frantically, she grabbed for Ethan's arm to keep herself upright. With the help of the adrenaline flooding through her, she was able to recover quickly. She turned to her right, preparing to flee along the bed of the ravine, but Ethan's hand nearly crushed hers as he pulled her back alongside him. Then he hastily threw his arm across her, shoving her backward against the wall of the ravine bed in an effort to shield them from the helicopter's approaching searchlight.

Cambry stood, numb with fear, as the searchlight darted closer. Glancing quickly to her left, she saw Ethan flatten himself even further against the ravine's wall. She clenched her eyes shut and sent a prayer heavenward. At the angle the helicopter was flying, it was possible that the embankment of the ravine and the dense population of trees along the banks would shield them from view. She could only hope and pray.

In the next instant the helicopter's searchlight flooded over them, illuminating them and their surroundings with the brightness of midday. Cambry's heart lunged into her throat, choking off her breath.

Just as suddenly, things went dark. Letting her breath out in a rush, she opened her eyes. She blinked several times before her eyes readjusted to the darkness. When they did, she was able to spot the helicopter growing smaller in the distance as it continued on with its search.

The noise diminished, the trees around them slowly stopped swaying, and the air finally stilled. Cambry could once again hear Ethan beside her.

Almost afraid to trust her own voice, she whispered, "I don't think they saw us."

"Not this time," Ethan said, his taut muscles relaxing somewhat. "But they'll be circling back and continuing to look until they find us, so we'd better get out of here. Let's find a spot where it'll be easier to climb out of this ravine and then search for cover."

With a quick nod, Cambry pushed off from the cold dirt embankment and took a step, but Ethan quickly put a hand on her arm to stop her. He gestured for her to be quiet again. Not daring to move, she held still and listened. Seconds later she heard it. Car doors slamming. Loud voices shouting instructions.

Benton's men were closing in.

"Let's go!" Ethan urged, grabbing her hand once more.

They ran together along the bottom of the ravine, away from the approaching men. They hadn't gone far when Ethan spotted a section of the bank that had washed away and a fallen tree that dipped into the ravine.

Ethan pointed at it. "I'll help you up."

Cambry hurried to the tree and grabbed for a branch. With Ethan's steadying hands, she was able to use the branches to scramble up the side of the embankment. Seconds later, Ethan was standing behind her on the bank.

After a few moments of consideration, Ethan put a hand on the small of her back and urged her forward. "Up the hill," he said, motioning to his right. "Maybe there's somewhere to hide up there."

Cambry stared at the steep incline. It was treacherous at best. "You've got to be kidding," she whispered in disbelief. "I can't make it up there!"

"It's steep, but it's not very far." Ethan gave her arm a quick, reassuring squeeze. "You can do it. Just follow me."

Still skeptical, Cambry cast about for her courage and followed Ethan up the incline. The going was slow as they searched for toeholds and firm footing, and soon the ground turned rocky. Cambry struggled to maintain her footing. In the darkness, she didn't see the single root sticking up from between two rocks until it snared her foot. She let out a startled cry as she pitched forward and fell hard on her knees, the sharp edges of the rocks cutting into her tender skin.

Ethan turned and shuffled back down toward her to help her. "Are you okay?"

She nodded, even though pain burned like fire in her side. "I'm alright."

Reaching for his hand, she leveraged herself to her feet. Just then the flicker of flashlights through the trees near the bank of the ravine caught their attention. Ethan's gaze darted toward the approaching men and then back to her.

"We've got to move. It's just a little bit farther. Can you keep going?"

She sure wasn't going to wait around to be found by Benton's men.

They were quiet as they concentrated on scrambling the rest of the way up the slope, and Cambry breathed easier when they neared the top and the ground began to level out. Ethan pulled her toward an overgrown thicket along the ridge about twenty yards away, and she did her best to follow.

They maneuvered around fallen branches and avoided prickly shrubs that seemed to reach for them as they fought their way past. But Ethan kept leading them farther into the dense foliage, and Cambry didn't question him.

Ethan suddenly stumbled over a log partially hidden beneath the underbrush. He put a hand down to catch himself and then paused. He ducked beneath an overhanging limb, took a few cautious steps to the left, and peered intently into the darkness.

"Ethan, what is it?" Cambry whispered. "What do you see?"

"I think it's a cave!" he replied in an excited whisper. "The mouth is really overgrown with bushes and shrubs, but it's there! If it's big enough for the both of us, we can hide in there, and Benton's men wouldn't find us. Come on, let's check it out."

Cambry fought her way toward him through the snaring branches and came to a stop beside him, where he was moving the dense foliage aside to get a better look. Then she saw it too. It was indeed the opening to a small cave, so overgrown with bushes and branches that its mouth was impossible to see unless you were looking for it.

When Ethan succeeded in parting the foliage without breaking the branches that would shield them from Benton's men, he gestured for Cambry to go inside. She got down on her hands and knees to crawl through the hole. She had to squint to see anything because only the faintest of moonlight reached past the overgrowth into the cave.

"It looks like an old mine shaft," Cambry said in a hushed whisper as Ethan scrambled in after her. "Probably abandoned ages ago."

"Colorado's mining history is the last thing on my mind right now," he admitted gruffly as he turned in the confined space and replaced the branches and foliage shielding the cave's entrance. "All I care about is that we should be safe in here."

When the entrance was covered to his satisfaction, Ethan turned back to her in the near darkness. "I think our safest bet is to stay here for the night while Benton's men are combing the area. Besides, we could both use the rest."

Cambry nodded wearily. "I won't argue with that."

Ethan swung around in the cramped space and leaned back against the cool dirt wall. When he was situated, he shifted and pulled something from his pullover's pocket. In the dim light, she saw he was holding an apple.

She smiled. "Dinner?"

"Or something. I saved it from earlier."

Together they shared the fruit and then settled back against the cave wall. Ethan pulled Cambry to his side. She went willingly, letting her head droop against his shoulder.

"Sleep," he murmured. "I'll keep an ear out for trouble."

"Shouldn't you get some sleep too?"

"Thanks to the military, I'm used to sleeping in shifts. When I'm sure Benton's men have moved on, I'll sleep."

It was quiet for long minutes as they listened to the sounds of the mountains outside their hiding place. She surprised herself by nestling further into him, letting his warmth and strength seep into her. She was going to need it. They had a long road ahead of them tomorrow.

Closing her eyes, she felt the pull of exhaustion drag her under.

***

Garrison's phone beeped, pulling him from the catnap he was taking in his car in the early dawn hours. He pulled his cell from his pocket and read the text from Crowder.

Behind the warehouse. Half hour.

The warehouse was an abandoned car parts place outside of town, a location where they had met before. At this early hour, he'd have no problem getting there on time. Rubbing a hand over his face to wipe away his weariness, he started the car and headed out. As anticipated, he made it in time. He pulled around back, and his headlights reflected off the back end of Crowder's car. Stopping beside the vehicle, Garrison climbed out.

"Did you get it?" Garrison asked.

Crowder pulled out a tiny thumb drive from his jacket pocket. "The analysis team is running decryption programs on multiple systems, so it was easy to slip in and make a copy on one of the systems while the team was distracted."

"I'm assuming the analysis team hasn't found Saville's file yet?"

"No, but they do have an interesting new theory. There's a picture on the drive, one of Saville and his wife and kid taken at a cabin. The techs have been analyzing it to see if any data is buried in the image file."

Garrison frowned. "Meaning?"

"They're specifically looking for steganography. It's a way to hide encrypted files within an image. In this case, possibly that family picture."

"You think Saville hid his research files inside a picture?"

Crowder nodded. "An image file is so large that hiding an embedded file within the pixels of the picture would be easy enough to do."

Garrison reached for the drive and looked at it speculatively. "How long until they know if it's there?"

"Hopefully not long. But there's a catch. If there is an embedded file, the next step is to find out what program Saville used to do the steganography. From what the analysts were saying, you need to have the exact program that was used to embed it. Once you find the program and run the file, it'll likely ask you for a password."

Garrison shrugged. "I'll take it to a friend of mine who's off the grid. He can run it through a brute force password cracker."

"From my experience, that could take minutes, or it could be days."

"We'll hope for minutes. Benton said Navarro is on his way here, and the deal goes down at midnight. If I don't have the file, he's gone. I need this file *today*."

"I understand. Go to Saville's house and look for the software while we're working on the picture. One of the analysts said it wouldn't be in a box like other programs you'd buy. It's typically something downloaded from the Internet and will be small enough to fit on a thumb drive or disc. Do a check on his computer for the most recent programs he's run. If it's not there, find a way to get into his office and look through his work computer. It's possible he ran the program at his office or has it stored on an external drive there."

"I'm on it." Closing his fist around the drive, Garrison pulled a large envelope from his jacket and handed it to Crowder. "Consider this an installment. There'll be more when you unlock that data."

Crowder took the envelope. "Pleasure doing business with you. I'll keep you posted."

Garrison got back in his car and headed back the way he came. He knew where Dan Saville's house was. With any luck, the software would be there, and he'd be on his way to making a fortune.

CHAPTER TWENTY-FIVE

Ethan was pulled from his tense, dreamless sleep by unfamiliar sensations: a chill in the air, his aching body, and something digging into his lower back. He opened his eyes. It only took him a moment to realize where he was. Mountains. Hiding out from Benton's men. Cave or mine shaft, though which was still open for debate.

With a low groan, he shifted his position on the cold dirt floor to move away from the sharp rock jabbing him in the back. As he did, he felt the weight on his left arm. Glancing down, he saw that Cambry was still asleep against him. Good. She was going to need her strength for what was to come. Hopefully Benton's men had exhausted their search of this area and had moved on.

They were going to have to keep to the woods, stay alert, and make good time. The town couldn't be more than a couple hours' walk. He had a good sense of direction. It had been something he'd picked up over his years in the military, and he felt confident he was taking them in the right direction. But to do that *and* avoid Benton's men . . . It made things more difficult.

Looking toward the bush-covered entrance of their accommodations, he could see the faintest glimmers of dawn outside. They should get going. Hiding in near shadow would be far easier than trying to hide in full daylight. With any luck, they'd make it down the mountain by the time the sun was up.

After that he and Cambry could start to deal with everything else—alerting the FBI to Benton's involvement in their kidnapping, finding out what was on that disc he'd turned over to Agent Lawford two days ago . . . and finding a way to keep Cambry from shutting him out of her life forever.

He shook his head. She was still angry, and he couldn't blame her. This whole thing had turned into such a nightmare. But he couldn't think about that now. His first priority was to get them both down off this mountain undetected and in one piece. Then he could take the steps necessary to make amends.

Deciding it was time to get moving, he put a hand on Cambry's shoulder and gave her a gentle shake. "Cambry, time to wake up."

Cambry's eyes opened, and she groaned when she took in their surroundings. "I was hoping it had all been just a really bad dream."

"No such luck," he said with the hint of a smile. "How do you feel?"

She shifted and winced. "Stiff and sore. And still so tired. Can't we rest a little while longer?"

He reached out and touched her cheek, and his smile faded. Her skin felt hot and dry beneath his hand, and he realized her fever had continued to climb overnight. His mind sorted through his options. They couldn't stay. She needed medical attention. But she was clearly exhausted. How were they going to trek down the mountain with her feeling so lousy?

He was simply going to have to help her. They couldn't wait.

"I know you're not feeling well," he said, his tone patient, "but we've got to get moving so we can get help. Do you think you can try?"

She nodded but winced when she shifted. She closed her eyes for a moment and then reopened them, looking apologetic. "I think I'm going to need some help up. Every movement makes my side hurt."

"Did you hurt it again last night when you fell?"

"I don't know. Maybe." She grimaced. "It's hard to know when my entire body hurts."

"Let me take a look at it before we go."

She lifted the hem of her hoodie so he could see the bandage just above her waistline, and what he saw in the dim light made his throat constrict. The once-white bandage had been soaked through with blood, and tiny rivulets had slithered from beneath the soaked bandage to the top of her jeans and had dried there overnight. Either something during their escape or her fall on the mountain had forced the wound open. Staring at the blood-soaked bandage, Ethan knew it was no wonder she was exhausted. Not only was she hurting from her reopened wound, but she'd lost so much blood.

"How bad is it?" Cambry asked softly.

One corner of Ethan's mouth twitched in his attempt at humor. In a terrible British accent, he quoted, "It's just a flesh wound."

Cambry glared at him.

"What?" he demanded with a soft laugh. "You can quote *Doctor Who,* but I can't quote *Monty Python?*"

She rolled her eyes.

With another smile and a shake of his head, he turned his attention back to her side. Knowing that pulling the gauze away would only cause more damage, Ethan left it alone. "It definitely needs medical attention. There's nothing I can do for it out here. The sooner we get back to town, the better." He glanced toward the cave entrance. "The sun's not up yet, but it's light enough that we can find our way."

"Let's do it." She nodded and gamely started to move. "I'll do anything to have this nightmare over."

As she headed for the cave entrance, Ethan marveled at her resilience. Nobody could ever call her a wimp. His Cambry was, hands down, one of the toughest people he'd ever known. He'd known men in combat who shut down in the heat of battle. Cambry would never be one of those people. It made him love her even more.

When he was convinced that it was safe, they crawled out of the cave. The cold morning air hit him in force, and he shivered involuntarily. He'd forgotten how cold mornings in the mountains were.

Ethan got to his feet, his body stiff from the cold. He did a couple of torso twists, and the motion sent a twinge through his ribs. He smiled wryly. He felt almost as beat up as he knew Cambry did. Together they were quite a pair.

Turning back, he held his hands out to help Cambry up. She slid her hands into his without hesitation and let him pull her to her feet. She flinched as she straightened and took a stumbling step closer.

His hands tightened around hers. "You okay?"

She looked up at him, and he realized how close they were standing. Her face was so close that he could see the flecks of bronze in her golden brown eyes. A familiar sense of attraction washed over him, and the very rightness of her hands in his sent such a feeling of longing through him that it almost brought him to his knees.

He couldn't lose her. Wouldn't. Not to Benton, not to Benton's men, not to injury or illness, and definitely not to the undercover assignment that had spiraled out of his control. He would make things right between them if it was the last thing he did.

Sensing the change in mood, Cambry stepped back and pulled her hands from his. "We should get going."

"Bree—"

"Don't." She held up a hand, wariness in her eyes. "Let's just . . . not. Okay?"

All he could do was nod. When she started walking, he scrubbed his hands over his face. Getting back in her good graces just *might* be the last thing he did at this rate.

"Which way do we go?" she asked without looking back.

He hurried to catch up with her. "We need to continue on over this ridge heading east and hope we don't cross the road where Benton's men are likely staked out. We weren't far from the road last night, and that makes me nervous."

Cambry looked over at him in surprise. "What makes you think that?"

"Remember hearing the men's voices and slamming car doors? Those men wouldn't have been off-roading aimlessly through the woods and happen to stop where they did. That's just too much of a coincidence. There must be a road nearby. It's a good idea to follow it from a distance."

"Makes sense."

He looked off toward the east. The mountains looked forbidding in the early morning light, but he could do this. He had to. Besides, Cambry was putting on a brave face and giving what little energy she had left to this. He had to do the same.

For both their sakes.

***

Cambry stopped walking and bent over, resting her hands on her knees and clenching her eyes shut against the dizziness that had been threatening for the past hour. They'd been walking for about two hours, as best as she could guess, and she kept telling herself they were making good progress. But her optimism was beginning to fade.

Biting her lip in determination, she started walking again, forcing herself to concentrate on just one step at a time. Her stomach growled hungrily, but she tried not to think about it.

On second thought . . .

Steak. Burger and fries. Apple crisp. She continued to think about her favorite foods, using her hunger as motivation to keep going. Once she was back in Denver, she could have any or all of those. The thought of eating at least kept her feet moving.

Just then Ethan turned to check on her, and she was grateful that he hadn't caught her moment of weakness. They continued on, but Cambry found it hard to keep up with Ethan's brisk strides. The distance between them grew. She knew she should be moving faster, but somehow she couldn't make her legs obey.

When she couldn't go even one step farther, she sat down in the meadow grass with a graceless thump. She had just closed her eyes and was contemplating lying down when she heard Ethan call her name. Then she heard his quickening footsteps as he hurried back to where she sat.

"What's wrong?"

She opened her eyes to see him lower himself to his haunches in front of her, his face creased with concern.

"I can't keep walking, Ethan," she admitted, hating the weakness she heard in her own voice. "I need to rest. I'm so tired."

He pushed the curtain of hair out of her eyes so he could meet her gaze. "I know you're tired, but I don't think the town is much farther. And there's no way I'm going without you."

Her composure started to crumble. "Ethan, I can't—"

"Fine," he said abruptly. "I'll carry you."

His voice was more determined than Cambry had ever heard it. "How are you going to do that? I'm sure you're tired too."

"I'll manage," he said. "I carried packs across the desert in Afghanistan that weighed more than you."

She managed a smile. "You don't even know how much I weigh."

He snorted. "I can guess. Come on. Can you manage piggyback?"

When she nodded, he helped her to her feet and then squatted in front of her. When he wrapped her arms around his neck, she let out a gasp of pain.

"What?" Ethan asked quickly, looking over his shoulder at her.

"Stretching my arm up like that hurts my side," she admitted.

"Then just hold on with one arm and keep the other down. I'll keep a good grip on your legs."

Without waiting for her response, he patted her thigh in a gesture for her to hop up, and she did. He hooked his arms under her knees and started walking again, his pace easy. She wrapped her arm around his neck and tried to stay as still as possible.

It wasn't long before his steady strides lulled her, coaxing her eyelids shut. She rested her cheek against the base of his neck and drifted.

She didn't know how long they'd traveled when Ethan's lack of movement stirred her. She lifted her head and peered around Ethan's head to see why they had stopped. Hope flared in her chest when she spotted a paved road up ahead through the dense trees. And on the other side of it, buildings. They were barely visible through the dense trees, but they were there.

"Is that the town?" she whispered, hardly daring to hope.

"Yes." Ethan's eyes darted left and right, looking for any sign of Benton's men staking out the area.

He set her down carefully and reached for her hand. Together they crept closer to the tree line. They studied the collection of log buildings, including the ma-and-pa grocery store, gas station, and a couple other businesses with signs they couldn't make out.

"So what do we do now?" she asked. "Do we flag down a ride?"

He nodded. "We need to get back to Denver somehow, but we don't want to be standing along the side of the road and happen to have Benton's men drive by and see us."

"But by the time we hear a car, verify that it's not one of Benton's guys, and rush down to the road to flag them down, the car would be gone."

"I know." He was silent a minute as he considered their options. "Okay, here's what we're going to do. I don't see a lot of cars parked in front of buildings, and there aren't people out walking. We're going to make our way down this hill and cross the street as soon as the coast is clear. Then we'll hide behind one of the buildings until we can decide what to do next."

She followed Ethan as he started forward, watching for signs of activity. Feeling like a deer in hunting season, she stepped out of the tree line with Ethan. All was quiet.

They skittered gingerly down the edge of the mountainside until they were standing on the paved road.

Ethan peered up and down the road for signs of oncoming traffic. "I think it's safe to cross."

Cambry didn't argue. She let Ethan retain his grip on her hand as they hurried across, and they didn't slow their pace until they reached the edge of the graveled parking lot. Ethan gestured to a tall sign, which they hadn't been able to see before because of the trees, standing near the first building. It gave the name of a café, and it was clearly being patronized by early risers, if the several cars out front were any indication.

There was a large truck parked in front of the building. Its wire-cage bed was stacked high with firewood, and Ethan remained cautious as they crept closer to see who or what might be on the other side of the truck.

Cambry's heart gave a little leap when she spotted salvation. "Ethan, look!" she exclaimed excitedly. "Next to that blue pickup over there. That's a state trooper's car!"

The tension in Ethan's face eased somewhat. They'd just taken a couple of eager steps toward the car when the sound of tires crunching on gravel brought then up short.

Cambry whirled. What she saw sent fear straight to her heart.

A Jeep. Men dressed in camouflage uniforms.

Benton's men had found them.

CHAPTER TWENTY-SIX

ETHAN LUNGED FOR CAMBRY. HE grabbed her arm, nearly crushing it as he jerked her back behind the café's Dumpster and pulled her into a squat beside him. He peered out around the side as the Jeep with Benton's men steered through the parking lot and pulled to a stop in front of the café. The man in the passenger seat spoke into a handheld radio as his gaze swept the surrounding buildings.

"What's happening?" Cambry asked in a scared whisper.

"They're parked in front of the café. They look like they're reporting in."

Cambry started to ask more, but Ethan held up a hand to silence her. He watched as the man finished talking and then climbed out of the Jeep. The men circled the parking lot, glanced through windows of parked cars, and finally walked up the wooden steps to the café's front door.

Ethan lost sight of them then, but he heard a bell on the door jingle as Benton's men went inside. Cambry must have heard it too because she felt comfortable enough to speak again.

"This is just *great*," she hissed. "What are we going to do? We haven't come all this way only to be caught again."

Ethan felt a muscle twitch in his jaw. "We're not going to be caught again," he said from between clenched teeth. "What we're going to do is sneak over to that state trooper's car and climb into the backseat. Let's just pray it's unlocked. Benton's men already looked in the back of it, so I doubt they'll check it again. Then hopefully the trooper won't realize we're in there until after Benton's men are gone."

"But why should that matter?" Cambry asked. "They wouldn't mess with a state trooper, would they? They're all going to jail for a long time for kidnapping as it is."

Ethan's mouth firmed. "Men like Benton think they're above the law. If his men report back that we've been picked up by a state trooper, he'll set up a barricade farther down the mountain and ambush the trooper. We need to do this as quickly and as inconspicuously as possible."

Ethan gestured for her to follow, and together they moved around the side of the Dumpster. When he was able to see Benton's men through the windows of the café, he settled in to wait. Out of the corner of his eye, he saw Cambry rub her arm. "Sorry I jerked you like that. I didn't mean to hurt you."

"I know. It's okay."

Ethan continued to watch the café for long moments. Then they got a break. The driver of the Jeep gestured to the other man to help him check the back, and they moved away from the windows and disappeared deeper into the café.

"Come on," he whispered urgently, grabbing her hand. "They're in the back. Hurry!"

They made a quick dash for the trooper's car. When they reached it, they collapsed into a squat on the far side.

"Did they see us?"

Ethan straightened a little and peered toward the café through the windows of the trooper's car. "I don't think so. Let's see if the car's unlocked."

Cambry reached for the handle and lifted. The door swung open. Just then they heard the bell on the café door jingle.

With a renewed sense of urgency, Ethan gave Cambry a shove. "Hurry, get in!"

Cambry threw herself into the backseat and slid onto the passenger side floor so Ethan could scramble in after her. He pulled the door toward him without letting it click shut for fear the noise would draw attention.

He squeezed his considerably larger frame into the cramped floor space behind the driver's seat and waited. They huddled on the floor, listening, until the sounds of feet crunching on gravel finally receded. Finally, they heard the sound of an engine starting.

Ethan straightened to peer out the back window. "They're both in the Jeep," he whispered. "The one guy's talking on the radio. Now they're backing out . . . and they're gone."

Cambry let her breath out in a rush. "Are you sure?"

Ethan watched as the Jeep accelerated out of the café parking lot and sped away up the road. "Yeah, they're gone. But let's stay put for the time being in case more of Benton's men are lurking about."

Just then the bell on the café door jingled again. Ethan whipped around to see who was coming, but he breathed a sigh of relief when he saw that it was the state trooper. He straightened and slid onto the back-seat of the car as the trooper walked up to his door, and the motion caught the man's attention.

Instantly, the trooper was on alert. "Hey, what are you doing in my vehicle?" the trooper called out, his tone serious and commanding.

Ethan pushed open the back door and climbed out, startling the trooper and causing him to reach for his holstered weapon. Ethan immediately held up his hands.

"Please, we need your help," he said. "My girlfriend and I were kidnapped. We escaped and made our way down the mountain, but she's badly hurt and in need of medical attention."

The trooper dropped his hand from his holster and hurried over. Ethan moved aside as the trooper stepped around the open car door and leaned into the backseat. He immediately spotted the blood along the side of Cambry's hoodie and helped her up onto the seat.

After seeing the blood-soaked bandage and asking several questions about Cambry's injury, he agreed that it was better to leave the bandage in place until they got her to a hospital. The officer turned his attention to Ethan, taking in the bruises on his jaw and near his eye.

"How are you doing? Any cuts or broken bones?"

"No, I'm okay. Just some bruised ribs, I think."

The officer nodded before turning back to Cambry. "Just hang in there, Miss . . . ?"

"Saville," Cambry answered. "Cambry Saville."

The officer's eyes widened. He turned to Ethan. "You wouldn't be Special Agent Reece, would you?"

Ethan looked at him in a mixture of surprise and confusion. "I am. Why?"

"There's an APB out for you two. Issued yesterday."

Ethan caught Cambry's startled gaze. "Somebody must have realized we were missing." He turned back to the trooper and glanced at his badge for a name. *Harris.*

"Officer Harris," he said, "could you radio in and get me in contact with Special Agent Lawford in the Denver field office? I want to explain to him what's happening and have him contact my superior in Baltimore."

"You got it." He paused, looking thoughtful. "How long has it been since you two have eaten?"

"A while," Ethan admitted.

Harris gave Ethan's shoulder a pat. "I'll tell you what. Climb in there next to your girlfriend, and I'll go get you two some food. You can eat it on the way to the hospital."

Ethan felt some of the tension drain from his body. "That would be great."

Cambry's weary voice interrupted their exchange. "What about Benton's men? They could come back any second, and if they find us—"

"Don't worry," Harris hurried to reassure her. "I'm going to radio in right now and put Agent Reece in touch with his agency while I'm getting food. Once they hear what's happened, we'll have troopers and FBI agents up here within the hour, searching the woods for those men."

Ethan slid into the backseat beside Cambry as Officer Harris got behind the wheel and picked up his radio. As he radioed in, Ethan reached out and cupped Cambry's cheek. "We're going to be okay, Cambry," he said quietly. "You just rest and let us take care of everything."

Cambry nodded and closed her eyes, too tired to fight sleep any longer.

The trooper turned to Ethan and held up the radio. "Here's your call."

Ethan got out and went around to the front passenger seat. He took the radio from Harris and was soon talking to Agent Lawford. The call didn't take long. Ethan explained what had happened and what Benton was up to, and Lawford told him they'd send out agents in force to search for Benton. He also reassured Ethan that he'd phone Special Agent Natoni in Baltimore and get him up to speed. With a promise to meet them at the hospital, Agent Lawford hung up.

Ethan kept an eye out for Benton's men until Officer Harris reappeared from the café with two large to-go bags. "I wasn't sure what you liked, so I just got an assortment. Help yourself to whatever looks good."

"I don't know how to thank you," Ethan said as he took the bags.

Harris smiled. "Don't worry about it."

Getting out of the front and climbing in next to Cambry again, Ethan's stomach rumbled as the smell of the hot food filled the car. He turned to Cambry, who was slumped over with her head against the window, and gave her shoulder a gentle shake.

"Cambry, wake up. You need to eat something."

Ethan's gentle prompting roused Cambry from her sleep. She took the container of scrambled eggs and spooned a few into her mouth. Ethan dug in as well. When his container was empty, he turned to see that Cambry's food had been only partially touched.

He frowned at her. "Eat a little more, Cambry. You need it."

Cambry shook her head as she leaned back against the seat and closed her eyes. "I'm too tired to eat anything else. I just want to sleep."

Ethan's heart ached for her as he took the Styrofoam container off her lap and guided her head to his shoulder. "Go ahead and sleep," he murmured. "I'll wake you when we get to Denver."

Cambry muttered something incoherent and, a moment later, was fast asleep. Ethan sighed and turned to look out the window at the passing scenery. She wasn't pushing him away now, but that was because she was exhausted, sick, and clearly in need of a comforting arm. Would she be as inclined to have him near when this whole ordeal was over?

Deciding to put off those thoughts until later, he leaned his head back against the seat and let his mind drift. Before he knew it, he too was asleep.

***

Ethan was startled awake by a sudden stop. He tried to blink away the haze over his eyes and the fog in his mind. Where was he and why was he in a car? A weight on his arm proved to be Cambry sleeping against him, but he was fuzzy on the details.

Before he could figure it out, his car door opened, and hands were reaching in for him. He jerked upright, preparing to defend himself and Cambry.

"Whoa, Agent Reece, slow down. I was just trying to wake you."

Ethan made out Officer Harris standing over him, holding his hands up in front of him.

"We're at Denver General," Harris explained. "I radioed ahead and told the ER staff we were coming. They're on their way out now."

Ethan looked over to see that they were indeed in front of the hospital's ER doors, and several people in scrubs were coming out to meet them.

Brushing aside the hands of the doctor who started to look him over, Ethan gestured to Cambry. "Check on Cambry first," he told the man. "She's got a nasty gash that's infected. She's worse off than I am."

"Don't worry, Agent Reece," the doctor replied. "We're going to take care of you both."

Ethan heard the other passenger door open, and he turned to see another doctor leaning in to assess Cambry's condition. She barely stirred as the woman looked her over quickly and turned to call for another set of hands.

"Where do you hurt?" the doctor hovering over Ethan asked, studying the bruises on his face.

Ethan barely heard as he continued to watch the physicians assess Cambry's injuries, straining to hear what they were saying. "What?" He glanced back at the doctor. "Oh, um, my ribs are a little sore, but other than that, I'm okay." He turned back to Cambry, but his attention was diverted when the doctor prodded his ribs, causing Ethan to flinch.

The doctor frowned. "I think you might have broken a rib or separated some rib cartilage. We should get some X-rays to be sure."

"No, I'm okay, really," he said as he brushed the man's hands aside and climbed stiffly out of the car. "I just want you guys to focus on Cambry. She's not doing well."

The doctor scurried in front of him and stood firmly in Ethan's path. "Agent Reece, I know you're concerned about your girlfriend, but we need to take care of you too. We have enough staff to help you both."

Ethan saw the doctors lift Cambry carefully out of the car and put her on a gurney. Turning to the doctor in front of him, Ethan's brow furrowed in a mixture of frustration and determination. "Look, I know that you're just trying to help me, and I appreciate it. But believe me, I'm fine. I just want to stay with my girlfriend."

The man studied him for a long moment before nodding and stepping back. "Just promise me that you'll let someone take a look at those ribs before you leave, okay?"

Ethan nodded and hurried around the back of the car. He took a few stiff running strides to catch up with Cambry as she was wheeled toward the sliding glass doors. Before they went through, Ethan turned to look for the state trooper. He spotted Officer Harris standing next to the car, so he gave the trooper a wave of thanks, which was acknowledged with a smile and a wave.

They were taken into a curtained-off room, and as the doctors bustled around them, Ethan reached for Cambry's hand.

"What about you?" she managed in a tired voice. "Did somebody say something about a broken rib?"

Ethan snorted. "I was in the marines. We're tough. Separated rib cartilage or busted ribs don't slow us down. Besides, you can't do anything for either, other than wrap it."

"That's not true, is it?" Cambry asked the nurse taking her blood pressure.

The nurse gave her a reassuring smile. "He's right, I'm afraid."

Ethan squeezed Cambry's fingers. "See? Don't worry. A week or two and I'll be as good as new."

"Agent Reece?" A nurse appeared in the opening in the curtain. "You have two FBI agents out here asking to talk to you."

At Cambry's startled expression, Ethan squeezed her hand again. "It's probably Agent Lawford and his partner wanting to know about Benton. I'll be back in a minute."

He walked out into the hall and spotted Agent Lawford and Agent Arehart standing in the corridor looking anxious.

"Glad to see you in one piece," Agent Lawford said. "When your parents called in a missing persons report yesterday afternoon, the police notified us. We were expecting the worst."

"My parents called in a missing persons report?" Ethan felt a rush of guilt as he realized that he hadn't even stopped to consider that his parents would have worried about him.

"I called Special Agent Natoni in Baltimore," Lawford continued. "He knows you're safe now, but you might want to give him a call and fill him in."

Agent Arehart spoke up. "How's Cambry?"

"A little rough," Ethan admitted. "She's got a gash in her side from falling down a hill, and now she's running a pretty high fever from infection. I don't want to leave her alone for too long."

"I understand," Arehart said. "Tell us what happened on that mountain so we know what we're up against."

Ethan detailed the events, including Benton's knowledge of his undercover assignment and how he'd exposed that to Cambry.

"That means we have a leak," Agent Arehart said with a frown. "Any idea who or from what department?"

"No, but somebody inside Benton's circle used connections to dig into details that weren't widely known. Whether that leak is from the Denver office or somebody higher up who has contacts in other offices, I don't know. Any sign of Benton?"

"Not yet. But just so you're aware, I've tasked two agents to stick close to you and Cambry until Benton and his men are caught. And a couple more are stationed outside your parents' home. We don't want to take any chances."

"I appreciate that," Ethan admitted. He knew Cambry wouldn't like the idea of agents following them around, but he felt better knowing she'd be protected.

"In the meantime," Arehart continued, "we'd like to talk to Cambry's friend who worked on the decryption. We could use her help."

"Her name's Alisa Munro," Ethan said, wondering how Cambry would feel about involving her friend but knowing they didn't have any choice. "You'd better let me call her though. She doesn't have any idea who you are. What's going on with the decryption?"

"We're focusing on the picture," Agent Lawford said. "We think it has a file embedded in it, and it may be Saville's technology."

Ethan's brows lifted. "The picture could be the key?"

Lawford explained about steganography and embedded files and how they would need the same program Dan Saville had used to encrypt and embed the file, which would also likely require a password. A password that Cambry could hopefully help them figure out.

"I don't mean to sound callous," Lawford continued, "but we're still racing the clock on this. How soon can we talk to Cambry? There might have been something else her father said that could help us. And if there really is an embedded file, we're going to need to find the steganography program he used, which means looking on his computers. We can't do that without permission and help from her."

Ethan pushed a hand raggedly through his hair. "The problem's going to be Cambry's willingness to cooperate at this point. When Benton revealed that I'd been undercover . . . She didn't take the news well. I don't think she trusts me anymore. I don't know how much she's going to want to talk to me, or anybody else in the FBI, for that matter."

Agent Lawford offered him a sympathetic look. "I'm sorry. What can we do?"

"Nothing." Ethan shook his head. "Just let me try to talk to her."

"Okay. But do everything you can to convince her."

Ethan nodded.

"We'll get out of here and let you see to Cambry," Arehart said. He ran an assessing gaze over Ethan, taking in the bruises on his face and the arm Ethan had pressed over his ribs. "No offense, but it looks like you need some medical attention too. You look a little worse for the wear."

Ethan grimaced. "It's been a bad couple of days."

Agent Lawford put a careful hand on his shoulder. "You and Cambry get better. In the meantime, we'll work on that file and call you as soon as we know anything." He frowned then. "Do you still have your cell phone?"

"No, Benton's men took mine. I'm sure it's long gone."

"We'll get you something immediately," Lawford told him, pulling his cell out of his pocket and hitting a speed dial button. "Let me talk to my supervisory agent. We're going to need to be able to stay in touch with you."

As Lawford's call connected and he started talking, Ethan turned to Agent Arehart. "Would you mind if I used your cell to call my folks? I want to tell them we're okay."

"No problem." Arehart pulled his phone out of his pocket and handed it to him. "Take all the time you need."

Agent Arehart walked down the hall to give him some privacy, and Ethan made the call. His mom started to cry when she heard his voice, but he reassured her that he and Cambry were both okay. He gave her a glossed-over account of what had happened and told her they were at the hospital. She was ready to rush over, but he talked her out of it. He reminded her that Dad shouldn't be exerting himself so soon after his surgery, and he told her they weren't planning on staying at the hospital for long anyway.

Even as he said that, Ethan wasn't sure that it would be true. He wondered if they might keep Cambry for a day or so, but he figured he'd cross that bridge when he came to it. More than anything, Cambry needed some quiet and some time to rest, and he knew she'd work too hard at putting on a brave face if his parents were there. That would just delay the healing process.

His mom handed the phone off to his dad, and they talked for a few minutes. He was both touched and concerned by the emotion he heard in his dad's voice.

"I'm okay, Dad, really," he said. "Cambry's pretty cut up from a fall down a mountainside, but the doctors are taking care of her. I'll be back to the house sometime today."

"We'll look forward to it. You two take care."

Ethan hung up and walked around the corner to find Lawford and Arehart waiting for him. When he gave Agent Arehart back his phone, Agent Lawford promised to be back with a new phone for him. They left, and Ethan hurried back into Cambry's exam room.

As he stepped through the curtain, he saw a pretty woman in her late forties with hazel eyes and chin-length blond hair sitting on a stool beside Cambry, irrigating the nasty-looking gash on her side. She looked up as Ethan walked in.

"Agent Reece, right?" she asked. When Ethan nodded, the woman gave him a friendly smile that put him at ease. "I'm Dr. Turek."

Ethan walked over to Cambry and took her hand. She seemed to be drifting in and out of awareness. "You okay?"

"I feel a little out of it," she admitted.

"I gave her some pain medication," Dr. Turek explained. "It's finally starting to kick in."

"How is she?"

"She's severely dehydrated, so we're pushing IV fluids and antibiotics. Her fever is pretty high, but once we get this infection under control, it should go down. This gash, though, is going to be a challenge."

"Why?" he asked, frowning. "What's wrong?"

"It's deep enough to warrant stitches, but because it's already been more than twenty-four hours, it has started to heal. The best I can do is use a few butterfly bandages to keep it closed until it finishes healing. It's going to leave a nasty scar."

The news didn't seem to bother Cambry. Or maybe she was just too out of it to consider it. She turned to him with glassy eyes. "Can you do me a favor?"

"Anything."

"Is there any way you could find out how my father's doing? I'd like to know if there's been any change, or if . . ."

Her voice trailed off, and Ethan knew she was wondering if the worst had happened. He put his hand on her arm. "I'll see what I can do. Will they talk to me about his condition if I'm not immediate family?"

Dr. Turek spoke up. "I don't mean to intrude, but is this something I can help you with?"

"My father's in the ICU at Denver West," Cambry explained. "He's been in a coma this past week."

"I'm so sorry," Dr. Turek said. "I know the director there pretty well. I'll call him as soon as I'm finished here and see what I can find out."

"Thank you."

Ethan's knees started to protest standing, so he headed for the chair next to Cambry's bed. He reached for Cambry's hand through the bed rail.

"Dr. Kopp told me you refused care when he tried to check you over outside," Dr. Turek said to Ethan. "You sure you're okay?"

Ethan nodded as he scrubbed a hand over his face, trying to wipe away his weariness. "I am. Just some bruised ribs. Nothing I haven't seen in action."

She lifted an eyebrow. "Army?"

"Marines. Until a year ago."

She smiled. "Good for you. Still, you look exhausted. We should hook you up to an IV and get some fluids into you too. I'll bet you're as dehydrated as Cambry." When Ethan started to protest, she huffed a little laugh and shook her head. "Be a brave marine and say yes. Besides, I won't make you lie in a bed or stay in a different room. You can keep sitting right there in that chair while the IV works its magic. Maybe even take a power nap. Deal?"

Ethan wavered and then nodded. He wasn't going to be any help to the FBI if he collapsed later today.

"Good." Dr. Turek pushed a call button on the wall. Before long, another IV stand and bag were brought in, and a nurse hooked him up.

With his fingers curled around Cambry's, he slouched down in his chair and let his body relax. He surprised himself by falling asleep.

A gentle hand on his shoulder woke him a while later, and he recognized the nurse who'd hooked him up to his IV. When he looked around the curtained-off room, Dr. Turek was nowhere in sight, and Cambry was sound asleep.

He sat up in his chair, taking care not to pull on his IV. "How long was I asleep?"

"Maybe an hour. You looked like you needed it. I only woke you because this was dropped off for you by an FBI agent. He said you were expecting it."

She handed him an envelope. He opened it and tipped it over. A sleek new smartphone slid out into his hand.

Nice. Maybe there was something to be said for a terrorist confiscating his stuff during a pat-down.

The battery was charged and active, and a look at the settings told him the phone was programmed with his previous number. He was impressed. Lawford had gone above and beyond.

He looked back up at the nurse. "Is Agent Lawford still here?"

"No, he dropped it off and left. You do have two rather intimidating agents standing guard though." She jammed a thumb over her shoulder, and Ethan leaned over to look through the partially open curtain.

Two men in dark suits stood across the room as discreetly as possible. The hint of a leather strap inside the men's suit jackets told Ethan that they were wearing shoulder harnesses. Good. Without a gun himself, he felt more comfortable knowing they were armed.

"I'm supposed to take Ms. Saville to a private room upstairs," the nurse said, drawing his attention once more. "Do you feel up to walking with us? Or should I have somebody bring you a wheelchair?"

"I can walk. Does this mean Cambry's going to be staying awhile?"

"Dr. Turek wants to keep her overnight just to be safe," she said as she went about unhooking tubes and wires, getting Cambry ready to move. "She'll be by later to check on Ms. Saville when she's settled in her room."

Relief flooded Ethan's body. Cambry really needed the medical care and downtime. He could take care of everything on the outside. All she had to worry about now was getting better.

He got slowly to his feet and winced. As much as he'd love to collapse in a bed and sleep for a week, Benton was still a threat. He needed to help the FBI track down the man and put him away once and for all.

Ethan held on to Cambry's bedside rail with one hand for support, pulling his IV tower along beside him as they got into a large elevator. The dark-suited agents followed. The private room that the nurse led him to was clean and quiet, and Ethan nodded his thanks at the two agents, who immediately moved to flank the doorway.

The nurse settled Cambry, told him she'd be back in a little while to disconnect his IV, and left. Ethan settled into the chair beside Cambry's bed. He was still tired, but the IV fluids seemed to be helping. He glanced up at the clock on the wall. Lawford was probably getting antsy. As soon as his IV was done, he was going to head to the field office and see what he could do to help.

Movement out of the corner of his eye caught his attention, and he looked over to see Cambry starting to wake up. "Hey," he said softly, scooting his chair closer. He was pleased to see that her eyes looked less glazed than they had downstairs.

"What have I missed?"

"Well," he said. "I talked to my parents and let them know we're okay. They both said to give you their love."

"Are they okay?"

"Yes. No sign of Benton or his men. Agent Lawford put a couple of agents in front of their house just to be safe. And you have two standing guard outside your room at this very moment. Benton's men won't get a second chance to come after you."

"That's a relief." She closed her eyes and lifted a hand to rub her forehead. Feeling a tug, she looked down at the IV in her arm. She made a face. "Ugh. I hate needles."

"Don't complain. I have one too." He raised his arm to show her his. "They said I was probably dehydrated, so they hooked me up. I do feel better, so I won't complain."

It was quiet for a minute. Then Ethan remembered to tell her what he'd learned. "Dr. Turek called Denver West to check on your dad after I fell asleep. She told the nurse to tell me that he's been showing some signs of improvement the past two days. He's been giving brief responses to commands, and the doctor says he's hopeful that your father is emerging from the coma."

Cambry brightened a little. "That's great. Maybe he'll just wake up and tell us where the technology is himself."

"I'm afraid we don't have time to wait and see," Ethan said, his voice grave. "As it is, the nurse is supposed to be by in a few minutes to unhook me so I can get out of here."

Cambry's brows drew together. "Where are you going?"

"I've got to go to the field office and help Agents Lawford and Arehart."

Predictably, Cambry's mouth tightened.

Raking his hand through his hair, he let out a frustrated breath. "Cambry, can we please talk about this?"

"About what exactly?" Her eyes flashed. "About how you pretended to be my friend? About how, all this time, I was just a job to you?"

"I've already told you that wasn't the case," he argued. "Even before my director gave me this assignment, I had every intention of coming home and trying to make things right not only with my parents and sister but between us. I hoped we could at least be friends again."

"So your idea of trying to be my friend meant spying on me, stealing my disc, and convincing me to trust you so I would tell you everything I knew?"

He rubbed his hand across the back of his neck. "I know it sounds bad when you put it that way, but ultimately I wanted to protect you. My Special Forces unit and the FBI have been after Benton for a long time, and I knew what the man was capable of. So when I learned about the dangerous position you might be in with Benton, I took the assignment. I care about you, and there was no way I was going to trust another agent with making sure you stayed alive while we worked to put Benton away. So, yes, I was told to find out what you knew and to find Benton, but that's where my objectives ended. Everything else between us has been real."

"How can you expect me to believe that after everything you've done?"

"Because it's true!" he shot back in exasperation. "And one more thing. That kiss in your kitchen you accused me of doing to manipulate you—

that had nothing to do with my job. That was me falling in love with you all over again. None of what was growing between us was an illusion, Cambry. I need you to believe that."

She stared at him in stunned silence. A mixture of emotions—hurt, confusion, indecision—flashed across her face.

Before she could say anything, he leaned forward in his chair and reached for her hand. "I know I hurt you, Cambry, but please give me a chance. I made a huge mistake walking out of your life five years ago, and I'm not about to do it again. I want to be in your life. Hopefully for the rest of it. And I'm going to do whatever it takes to regain your trust. Let me prove to you that what we started to rebuild between us wasn't just me doing my job."

Cambry was quiet for a long time, but he could tell his words had touched at least something deep inside of her. "I don't know, Ethan," she said at last. "My heart is telling me to believe you, to forgive you and move on, but my head is saying something completely different."

He looked at her earnestly. "What can I do? How can I make this right?"

She shook her head. "You can't help me with this, Ethan. I'm going to have to work through this on my own. Figure out how I feel. Convince myself to try to trust you again. And I have to admit that's not going to be easy."

He squeezed her hand. "I understand. I'll give you the time you need, but please don't push me away. Let me help you get healthy, and let's work together to make sure Benton doesn't finish what he started."

After a long moment, she nodded. "Alright."

That one word took an enormous weight off his chest. "Thank you," he said, leaning over her and pressing a gentle kiss to her forehead.

The door opened, and the nurse came into the room. She smiled when she saw Cambry was awake and asked a few questions about how she felt. Then she took out Ethan's IV, and a few minutes later, they were alone again.

"There's something you need to know," Ethan began, approaching the topic cautiously. He told her what Agent Lawford had said about the encrypted and embedded file, the steganography, and the need to find the program and the password.

"Agent Lawford was hoping to get in touch with Alisa. He's hoping she can help us with the steganography. Could I get her number from you?"

He was grateful when Cambry didn't protest, and Ethan typed the number into his new phone.

"So what happens if they confirm there's a file embedded in the picture?" Cambry asked. "That's when they need to use the software to retrieve the information?"

"Which would probably be on one of his computers, yes," Ethan said. "And Agent Lawford said we'll need your permission to search for it. Maybe get you to talk to Jim at Saville Enterprises so we can get permission to get into your father's office and look for it there."

She considered that. "And even if you do find it, there's still the matter of trying to learn what password he used," she pointed out.

Ethan nodded and then gave her an apologetic look. "Agent Lawford is hoping to talk to you later. He thinks there's still a lot you can do to help. Starting with finding out if there's anything else your father might have said that could help."

Cambry's eyes grew distant as she stared off into the room, obviously thinking back to that night. Her brow furrowed, and she seemed on the verge of remembering.

"What?" Ethan asked, watching her intently. "Do you remember something?"

Finally, she shook her head and rubbed her fingertips over her right eye. "I don't know," she admitted with a grimace. "There's . . . something. He did say the word *password*, but I can't remember."

Ethan put a reassuring hand on her shoulder. "It's okay, Cambry, don't push yourself too hard. It'll come. Just give it a little time."

She dropped her hand to her side in frustration. "But that's just it. We're out of time. And so is Benton, apparently. That's why he came after us, right? And why there are now two FBI agents standing guard outside my door? He's desperate, and that makes the FBI desperate. If I could just think . . ."

After several moments, she turned to him, remorse in her eyes. "I *am* sorry," she said. "If I'd just told you what had happened when you first came, we wouldn't be in this position. It's just"—she ran a hand through her long locks in frustration—"my father told me not to give it to anybody, not to let 'them' find it. I didn't know who he was talking about, and I didn't know who to trust."

"I understand." Ethan's expression softened. "No one's blaming you. You just concentrate on getting better, and we'll get to work on this steganography thing. We'll let you know what we find."

Ethan got to his feet, and the sound of his chair legs scraping was loud in the otherwise quiet room. "I'm going to get out of here—see what I can do to help." He held up his newly acquired cell phone. "You can reach me at my regular number if you need to, but I'll be back soon to check on you, okay?"

She nodded, and he stood beside the bed for a moment, debating. Then he leaned forward and pressed a lingering kiss to her forehead. She looked up at him, and he could see the question in her eyes—What happens now? He forced himself to step back. They could talk more about *them* later. Right now she needed to rest.

"I know I have a lot to make up for, Cambry," he said, his voice sounding a little rough, "but I promise I will."

Her expression softened a little, and that gave him hope. She was mad and feeling betrayed now, but he was going to make sure she had his continual love and support. She'd get past those feelings eventually, and he planned to be there when she did. He wanted to be a permanent part of her life, and he knew that, deep down, she felt the same way. He just needed to give her a little time.

"I'll see you in a while," he said. When she nodded, he turned and left the room, shutting the door silently behind him.

***

Garrison approached the elegantly paved seating area outside the restaurant, the red awnings snapping in the brisk fall breeze above him. He weaved between the mostly vacant cloth-draped tables. It was still too early for a lunch crowd.

Benton sat at the far end, working on a plate of food set before him. Garrison joined him and pulled out the ornate iron chair, ignoring the scraping sound it made on the pavers beneath his feet.

"You said we needed to talk?"

Benton nodded. "Turns out Saville and Reece are at the hospital getting medical attention. Unfortunately, they're also under heavy guard. I don't know how we're going to get to them now."

"We may not need to. I have a copy of the files," Garrison said, "but it won't do us much good until they're decrypted. We can let the FBI do that for us. All we have to do is wait."

Benton's brows drew together. "Time's running out."

"I'm expecting a call from my source at any moment."

"It had better be good news," Benton growled. "If I don't have the technology by tonight, Navarro walks. This is the deal I've been waiting for. If you mess this up for me—"

"If *I* mess it up for you? Since when did all this suddenly fall on me?" Garrison's brows lowered, and his eyes flashed dangerously.

"Your source, your results." Benton glared back, refusing to be cowed. "Have that file to me in the next few hours or you're finished."

A low simmering anger built in Garrison's chest. His fingers twitched at his side, urging him to reach for the Glock shoved into his waistband and finish off the arrogant man sitting next to him.

Patience, the voice of reason in his head soothed.

Drawing a deep breath, Garrison tamped the anger back down. He stood up and leaned forward, putting his palm on the linen tablecloth and bringing his face level with Benton's. "Don't threaten me," he said in a low, controlled voice laced with warning. "You won't like the consequences."

A flicker of alarm surfaced in Benton's gaze, so brief that Garrison almost wondered if it had ever been there. But he knew it had. He'd made his point.

Straightening, he said, "I'll call you as soon as I have the technology." He turned on his heel and left.

CHAPTER TWENTY-SEVEN

WHEN CAMBRY WOKE TO SUNSHINE spilling across her bed, she blinked in the brightness. Glancing up at the clock, she saw that it was just after one. The best she could tell, Ethan had been gone for a couple of hours.

She let out a troubled sigh. Her talk with Ethan had left her feeling more confused than ever.

Her heart told her that any man who could leave her Reese's gifts, kiss her until her knees went weak, and made mistakes like using furniture polish on her hardwood floors when cleaning up after her dog couldn't possibly be a hardened, uncaring man. He'd just been a man caught in the bad circumstances of a serious job. But her head warned her that she'd fallen in love with the man before and he'd walked out on her. And this time he'd lied to her and used her. Not exactly a desirable track record. She'd be a fool to set herself up for heartache a third time.

But he said he loved her. And for some crazy reason, she believed him—and still loved him too.

Okay, fine. She'd admitted it. She still loved him, despite everything he'd done to hurt her this past week and five years before. But did that mean she should risk giving him another chance? That he was worthy of one?

Her thoughts were interrupted when her door was opened and a nurse appeared carrying a lunch tray. Her stomach rumbled in anticipation. She ate quickly, then she dozed a bit and channel surfed. Nothing on TV interested her, and she soon became restless.

With nothing to distract her, her mind went back to the conversation she'd had earlier with Ethan. She hoped Alisa wouldn't hate her for giving Ethan her number and involving her in this. But if anybody could help, that person would be Alisa.

Had they found an embedded file? Were they looking for the software? No, they couldn't do that without her, she remembered. Legally, they couldn't just barge into her father's home or office and start looking for files. He'd done nothing illegal, so there were no grounds with which to acquire a search warrant. They needed her. She supposed they could approach Jim at the office for permission, but that wouldn't get them into her father's home.

And then there was the matter of the password. A password that maybe her father had given her some clue about, and she only needed to piece together what he'd told her to figure it out.

Bottom line, the FBI needed help. They needed *her*.

Experimentally, she shifted in her bed. No aches and pains. The pain meds made her feel pretty good, actually. Capable of functioning.

The realization made her sit up straighter. She was capable of functioning. Didn't that mean she could ask to be discharged? Actually, now that she thought about it, she didn't think anybody could force her to stay.

She started to formulate a plan. She was still tired, and her brain was a little foggy, but all she was doing was lying here. She could do that anywhere. And the FBI agents working on this case sounded like they could use her help.

The more she thought about it, the more resolved she became. If she could help bring this nightmare to an end, she was willing to do whatever it took. And right now, that meant getting herself out of this hospital.

Her mind made up, she reached behind her and pushed the nurse call button on the wall.

***

Cambry sat back in the chair next to her hospital bed with a grimace. Now that she was alone in her room, she didn't have to hide the fact that she was exhausted . . . and feeling rather defeated.

She pushed her long, damp curls out of her face and blew out a breath. The shower that she had taken—the test Dr. Turek had given her—had felt wonderful. She'd scrubbed her skin clean, shampooed her hair, and used nearly the entire travel-sized bottle of hospital-issued conditioner to detangle her rebellious curls. And she'd done it without help, as per doctor's orders. That meant she could get out of there.

She'd managed to change into the jeans and T-shirt she'd conned Emma into bringing her and was now attempting to put on her socks.

She'd never hated socks so much in her life.

When had slipping socks onto her feet become such a chore? She'd been trying for the past ten minutes to get them on, to no avail. She may as well have been trying to climb Mount Everest. Every time she moved, the burning in her side became sheer agony. And apparently, there was more moving and twisting required to put on socks than she'd ever considered.

Steeling herself once more, she gritted her teeth, pulled one sock open, and bent over. She had just hooked her big toe when her room door swung open. She glanced over and got a glimpse of jeaned legs and big sneakers. Men's sneakers.

She groaned inwardly. She knew those sneakers.

"What are you doing?"

With a wince and a sigh, she eased herself back upright and met with the disapproving look on Ethan's face.

"I'm trying to put my socks on," she said, her tone laced with annoyance. "What does it look like I'm doing?"

The door swung shut, and Ethan stalked the rest of the way into the room. "I see that," he said irritably. "My question is *why*?"

"I called your sister and had her bring me some clothes. I'm getting out of here."

His expression darkened. "No, you're not. The only thing you're going to do is get back into that bed."

She shook her head and gave up on the socks. "I'm not going to, Ethan. I'm sorry. You guys need my help, and I can't lie around in some hospital bed when there's something I can do to help."

"Bree, you're exhausted. You can hardly move without your side hurting, and you can't even put on your own socks." He gestured to the abandoned socks on her lap. "And you're still fighting that fever."

She shook her head in protest. "No fever. Feel."

Ethan reluctantly pressed the back of his fingers to her forehead and then to her cheek. He frowned. She suspected it was because he didn't like that he'd lost that part of the argument.

"Okay, maybe your fever's gone for now," he conceded, "but that doesn't mean it's gone for good. I know for a fact that Dr. Turek pumped a lot of antibiotics and drugs into your system. As soon as those wear off, you're going to feel terrible again."

"But that's the thing. When the drugs wear off, I can take more. I have prescriptions. It'll be fine."

Ethan glared. "No, it won't be fine. You'll just be masking the symptoms, not making them better. What you need is a few days in bed. The antibiotics and meds aren't going to do you any good if you're wearing yourself out."

"Ethan, please," she reasoned. "What's the difference if I go to the FBI office, or wherever they need me, and rest there while I do what I can to help?"

Ethan fell silent, and she could see he was considering that. Finally, he asked, "What does Dr. Turek think about you leaving?"

"She's not thrilled, but she's letting me go."

"Fine," Ethan said at last. "But I'm going to be there to make sure you don't overdo it. You'll take your medications when you're supposed to and rest like you need to, and the instant I think you're overdoing things, that's it. I'm going to take you home. No arguments. Got it?"

"Yes, Dad," Cambry drawled, rolling her eyes. She picked up her socks and bent over, slowly attempting to slide her foot into the sock. She missed—again.

With a huff of exasperation, Ethan took the sock out of her hand. "Give me that," he said, his tone gruff but not unkind.

Cambry relaxed as he put her socks on her feet, then he reached for her tennis shoes and put those on her as well. When he was done, he gave her knee a gentle pat that seemed at odds with his frustration. He stood and offered her his hand.

She put her hand in his and let him ease her to her feet. When she turned to get the shoulder bag on her bed, Ethan reached for it.

"Let me get that."

"Thanks."

"So Emma brought you the bag of clothes?"

Cambry nodded. "I called her instead of your mom because I can tell your sister, 'Thank you, now get out, and I'll talk to you later.' Your mom . . . not so much."

A chuckle rumbled in his chest. "I can see that." He lifted the bag to slide it onto his shoulder, and as he did, his jacket bunched. Cambry caught a glimpse of a dark leather strap over his T-shirt. She pushed his jacket aside curiously.

"Shoulder harness. The FBI issued me a new gun," he explained.

She felt a jolt of alarm. "Is it loaded?"

"Yes." He paused as if to let that sink in and reassure her that he was more than willing and able to protect her. Then he put his hand on her back and guided her toward the door. "Come on. I have my rental car out front. I went and picked it up from my parents' house."

Cambry walked beside him through the doorway and immediately spotted the two FBI agents standing guard outside her door. It was a little unnerving. She'd never had something like a bodyguard before. When she and Ethan stopped at the in-house pharmacy to fill her prescriptions, the men remained close by.

The four of them walked out to the parking lot, and when they got to the car, Ethan popped the trunk. "When the agents went to check out your father's cabin, it was empty. But they did find this." He pulled out her leather backpack and handed it to her.

The relief of having something of hers returned after their ordeal made her feel a little emotional. She looked inside and was surprised to see her things still in it, including her phone.

"Your things had been dumped out, but the guys gathered up what they could find. Is it all there?"

"Whatever isn't can be replaced," she said. "At least I have my phone. I would have hated the hassle of getting a new one and getting all my information back on it." She looked up at Ethan. "Thank you."

He smiled. "Don't thank me. I'm just the delivery man. Oh, and one of the agents drove your car back to your house. It should be in the driveway."

"Tell them I said thanks."

When they got in and Ethan started the car, she looked over her shoulder to see the agents backing up from a parking spot nearby and coming up behind them.

"That's a little disconcerting," she said as she buckled her seat belt. "Are they going to follow us around all day?"

"Yeah. Does it make you uncomfortable?"

"A little," she admitted.

He put his hand over hers. "They're just keeping you safe."

"I know. I guess it worries me because it means Benton is still out there somewhere, probably looking for us."

Ethan's expression darkened, and his voice became a low growl. "That man's not coming anywhere near you, I promise."

The intensity in his eyes made her shiver. This was a side of Ethan she didn't know, and it unnerved her a little. She was sure his combat and special ops training were to thank for his cool head and unflinching demeanor when Benton had had them in her father's cabin. But to see Ethan in action, with a gun strapped to his side and FBI agents with him, was just a little unsettling. It made her wonder what else she didn't know about this man she hadn't seen in five years. Had other things about him changed as much?

The short drive was made in comfortable silence. When they pulled into the parking lot at the FBI field office, Ethan and Cambry went inside to find Agent Lawford waiting for them at the security desk. He led them upstairs and down a wide hallway to a set of double doors. A small black plaque to the right of the doors read *Computer Analysis Lab.*

She balked. "Don't I have to have some kind of security clearance to get into a room like this?"

Agent Lawford shook his head. "It's a secured room but not a classified one. You'll be fine. Besides, this isn't classified data we're working with. It's research that belongs to your father."

When he opened the door, Cambry followed him inside and looked around with interest. The windowless room was huge, with off-white walls and fluorescent lighting. Long tables held twenty to thirty computers, and half a dozen analysts were working, rolling in their chairs from one computer station to another.

"Cambry!"

She looked over to see Alisa clomping toward her on a zebra-striped cane with dozens of tiny rhinestones that caught the light like a spinning disco ball.

"That cane's a little blinding," Cambry said with a laugh as Alisa grabbed her and hugged her. "It's all about making a statement with you, isn't it?"

"Of course," Alisa replied. "I'm so glad you're okay. When Ethan told me what happened, I was so worried. It's good to see you up and about."

"Though she really shouldn't be," Ethan cut in, a note of displeasure in his voice.

"I'm okay, really. Just a little tired," she said. "When did you get here, Alisa?"

"A couple of hours ago. Ethan came to my house and explained everything. He said there might be something I could do, so I headed over."

Ethan and Agent Lawford stepped aside to discuss something, and Cambry leaned closer to her friend and lowered her voice. "I'm so sorry to get you mixed up in all this. That's why I didn't go into detail when we talked."

Alisa touched her arm. "It's okay. You should have told me what was going on. Maybe if I'd know exactly what you were looking for, I would have honed in on the picture. Being on a drive with a bunch of encrypted files, it would have waved a big red flag at me. It's not uncommon to use steganography to hide sensitive material, and the fact that it was there would have made me take a closer look at it."

"Does that mean you found something in the picture?"

"Yes, there's definitely a file embedded in it."

"That's something we wanted to talk to you about," Agent Lawford broke in, moving back to her side.

When he opened his mouth to go on, Ethan interrupted him. "You can talk after Cambry sits down. Can we bring in a soft chair for her?"

"Sure," Lawford said. "There's a leather armchair in the office across the hall. Do you want to help me get it?"

Ethan gave Cambry a warning look. "Don't do anything until I get back."

"Like what?" she asked with a laugh. "It's not like I'm at the gym."

When he left with Agent Lawford, Cambry turned back to Alisa. "Can you say *overprotective*?"

"I think it's adorable," Alisa said with a grin. "I want one."

Cambry rolled her eyes. "You can have mine."

Alisa laughed. A few moments later, she sobered. "You sure you're okay? You look exhausted."

"Between you and me, I am pretty tired," she conceded. "But I was sick of sitting around in a hospital bed. I figured I'd do just as well taking it easy at home or helping here in spurts."

"I understand, but sometimes the weeks after having an experience like you had can produce some unexpected results."

Cambry frowned. "What do you mean?"

Alisa pressed her lips together and hesitated, and there was a flicker of something in her eyes—a memory of old pain. "I've never told you the whole truth about what happened to me before I left the CIA and came back to Denver," she began haltingly.

Cambry's eyebrows rose. "You told me you'd been in a car accident and were thrown from the car. That's not what happened?"

"In a sense." Tension started to form around the corners of Alisa's mouth. "It wasn't a car accident, per se, but I was thrown from a car. By somebody."

Cambry gasped.

"It's not something I talk about," Alisa said, shaking her head, "but it was a run-in with a criminal my cyber team was investigating. We caught him, but he managed to escape. I picked up a digital trail when he tried to access an overseas bank account that we'd seized. He seemed to be searching for something.

"Before we could find out what he was looking for, though, he found *me*. It's a long, frightening story, but the short of it is, he and another guy kidnapped me, and together they beat and tortured and interrogated me for two days about the whereabouts of the items in the bank vault we'd raided."

"Alisa," Cambry whispered in horror, feeling the blood drain from her face.

Alisa drew a steadying breath. "I had no idea what they were talking about, since I wasn't involved in that part of the investigation. When they finally decided I didn't know anything, they drove me to a deserted part of town, threw me from the speeding car, and disappeared." She lifted her zebra-striped cane. "I broke a lot of bones and had a half dozen surgeries. It took me eight months of therapy to learn to walk again. That's when I quit the CIA and came back here."

"Are the men in prison?"

Alisa's mouth drew into a taut line. "No, we never found them."

Cambry felt a chill slither up her spine.

"Why do you think I have such tight security at my house?" Alisa asked. "But the reason I'm telling you this is that, for a long time afterward, I had a hard time coping with dark places. I had nightmares . . ." She stopped and shook her head, as if trying to rid herself of the memory. "It wasn't until I swallowed my pride and started talking to a therapist that I learned to cope."

"Alisa, I'm so sorry," Cambry said, pulling her friend into a hug. "Why didn't you ever tell me?"

"Like I said, it's not something I talk much about. But I want you to know that I've been through this. I understand what you're going through. If you need to talk, or if you start having a hard time with any of it, you call me, okay? I may be able to help or at least point you to people who can."

"Thanks, Alisa," Cambry said, squeezing her friend's arm. Cambry was about to say more, but suddenly it felt like a puzzle piece had clicked into place. "Wait. Not to make light of what you just told me, but I think I just had an epiphany. Those buff guys in green landscaping T-shirts at your place—the ones that never seem to actually be doing any gardening—they're not really gardeners, are they?"

A slightly embarrassed look slid across Alisa's face. "Guys from the security company. My idea of low key."

Cambry's jaw slid open as she stared at Alisa for a long moment. She bit back a laugh. "I see," she managed at length.

"Please don't tell anybody." Alisa gave her a pleading look. "The fact that I hired bodyguards is not exactly something I want spread around. If anybody found out, the first thing they'd want to know is why. And I'm not about to explain."

The door beside them swung open, and they looked over to see Agent Lawford and Ethan maneuvering a leather armchair through the doorway. After putting it in the corner, out of the way, Ethan gestured her toward it.

Once she was sitting, Ethan pulled a bottle of soda from his jacket pocket and opened it. "Here, drink this," he said, shoving it into her hand. "You look like you could use a boost."

"Thanks." She took a slow sip.

Agent Lawford shrugged out of his jacket and tossed it over the back of a chair he'd dragged over for himself. She noticed he was also wearing a shoulder harness over his white dress shirt. Glancing a little apprehensively around the room, she wondered how many of the other agents were carrying guns.

"So here's what's happening," Agent Lawford said as he and Ethan sat down beside her. "Since we've confirmed there's a file embedded in the image, we need to find the software your father used, and that's where we need your help."

"Anything. What do you want me to do?"

"We need to get into your father's house to look for it, and also into his office. Could you talk to whoever you need to so we can get into his office?"

"Jim would be fine with it," she said. "And I have my father's keys back at my house. The nurse gave me what he had on him when he was admitted to the hospital."

"Great." Lawford rose. "We can focus on the file while the field agents track down Benton and his men."

"Wait a minute," Ethan protested, standing up alongside Lawford. "Cambry, I don't want you running all over the city. It's too much."

"Ethan, I'm fine," Cambry insisted, getting to her feet, as well. "A drive by my house to get the keys, then a drive to my dad's house isn't going to kill me. I'll be sitting in a car, for crying out loud. How tiring can that be?"

He put his hands on his hips and fixed her with a stern look. "You'd be surprised."

Cambry looked at Agent Lawford and Alisa. "Can you two excuse us for a moment, please?"

When they stepped away, Cambry looked back at Ethan. "Will you stop treating me like a two-year-old!" she hissed at Ethan, doing her best not to be overheard. "I'm perfectly capable of going for a drive! You, of all people, know how tough I am. It took you until you turned eleven before you could even pin me in a wrestling match, remember? So don't start thinking I can't handle myself because I can!"

She finished her tirade by poking Ethan hard in his chest for emphasis. She instantly wished she hadn't. In the past five years, Ethan had clearly put on a lot of muscle.

As she shook out her finger and glared up at Ethan, she watched a slow smile curve across his face, even bringing the dimple in his right cheek into play. Then, to her surprise, he gave a low chuckle and reached for her finger, bringing it to his lips. He pressed a gentle kiss to its tip.

"The only reason I didn't pin you before I was eleven was because I was being a *gentleman*," he emphasized the word, "like my dad taught me to be. But by the time I turned eleven, I started getting flak from my friends. My pride kind of won out then."

She jerked her finger away and gaped at him in indignation. "Are you saying you *let* me win all those years?"

"Yes."

When that was all he said, she let out an aggravated growl. "Ethan, I hate you!"

"No you don't," he said with another soft chuckle. "Come here." Sliding his arms around her, he pulled her close and leaned over to kiss the top of her head. It caused an eruption of butterflies in her stomach.

"I'm not treating you like a two-year-old," he said quietly against her hair. "I'm just worried about you and want to make sure you don't overdo it. My dad would agree with me that it's the gentlemanly thing to do."

She bit back a smile. "*Now* you want to be a gentleman?"

Another low rumble of laughter vibrated against her ear. As she lingered in Ethan's arms, she realized their bantering had chipped away a little of the shield around her heart.

How did he do that? It was pretty hard to stay mad when her Ethan of old made an appearance. But letting some of the anger drain away and convincing herself to completely trust him again were two very different things. It wasn't going to come easy. If at all.

Letting out a deep breath, she pulled back and looked up at Ethan. "You said you want to keep me safe. What better way to do that than to keep me with you? Besides, it's just a drive to two places. If I get tired or start to feel lousy, I'll let you know."

He exhaled in resignation. "Fine. Come. But no exerting yourself, understand?"

Trying not to look so victorious, she nodded as humbly as she could. "Yes, Ethan."

"Stop that," he growled, reaching for her hand. "You know I hate it when you patronize me."

They were soon on their way to Cambry's house to pick up her dad's keys, accompanied by Agents Lawford and Arehart, three field agents, Alisa, and another computer analyst.

After getting the keys from Cambry's house, Agent Lawford decided they should split up. He sent Agent Arehart, the computer analyst, and a couple other agents to Dan's house to look for the file while the rest of them continued on to Saville Enterprises.

The drive to Saville Enterprises didn't take long, but it gave Cambry enough time to call Jim. She briefly explained what had happened, and he was just as worried about them as Janette and Dean had been. When she told him what the FBI agents were hoping to do, he assured her that was fine.

As soon as they reached the building and walked inside, Jim was waiting for them at the security desk. His face creased in fatherly concern as he hurried over and pulled her into a hug.

"Are you sure you're okay? You said something about being in the hospital?"

She gave him a reassuring smile. "I'll tell you what happened, but is it okay if these agents get started?"

"Oh yes, please." He waved Alisa and the agents on toward the elevators.

Remembering her manners, she gestured to Ethan. "Do you remember Ethan Reece?"

"Of course I do." Jim grinned and shook Ethan's hand. "You two were practically joined at the hip. It's good to see you again, Ethan."

They went upstairs to Jim's office, and Cambry shared a shortened version of what had happened. He expressed his concern and told them to let him know if there was anything he could do to help.

Cambry thanked him and told him they would, then she left with Ethan. Her father's office was a hub of activity when they arrived. Alisa was working on the computer, and two agents were looking through drawers, file cabinets, and shelves for any external storage devices that might hold the program. Agent Lawford was on the phone, speaking to somebody in harsh tones.

As soon as he saw them walk into the room, he barked something into the phone and ended his call.

"What's up?" Ethan asked.

"That was one of the computer security specialists at the field office. He was looking through the system logs and saw that somebody copied the files we have onto a removable drive early this morning."

Ethan's eyebrows rose. "Who made the copy?"

"That's what we're trying to find out. We have agents going through the keycard entry logs to see who accessed the lab. Whoever made that copy has got to be our leak."

Cambry felt her body go numb with realization. "Whoever made the copy gave it to Benton, didn't they?"

"I assume so," Lawford answered. "Which would explain my next piece of bad news. Agent Arehart called. Somebody beat us to your father's home office. The place was a mess. It had clearly been searched."

Ethan blew out a breath and rubbed the back of his neck. "Benton must be working with whoever this leak is and knew the next thing we needed was the steganography program to retrieve the file from the image. He's keeping Benton apprised of our progress."

"Appears that way. What worries me is that we don't know if the person who broke into the house found what he was looking for."

"And if we're wasting our time looking here," Cambry said.

"Don't worry," Alisa said from her post at the computer. "If it's here, it won't take me long to find it."

"Let's hope so." Cambry turned to Ethan. "Since there's nothing I can do right now, I'm going to go check in with Shanice and see what work has been piling up for me."

Ethan gave her a stern look. "You're not working, Cambry. That wasn't part of the deal."

Cambry sighed, already beyond weary of this debate. "I'm not working, Ethan. I'm just going to talk to Shanice, have her put whatever work she has for me on my desk, and then rest on the couch in my office for a little while because I'm tired." She cocked an eyebrow at him. "Or do you have a problem with that too?"

He had the decency to look embarrassed. Turning to Agent Lawford, he said, "I'll be back in a few minutes." Then he led her out into the hall.

"I'm sorry," he said softly as they walked down the hall toward her office. "I didn't mean to come off sounding so bossy. I'm just—"

"Worried about me," she finished for him. "Yeah, I know. But there's such a thing as overkill, Eth. And after everything that happened between us, I need some time to think about things. Give me some space, okay?"

The worry lines around his eyes deepened. "I will. But you know that sooner or later we're going to have to talk about this, right?"

"I know. Just not now, okay?"

He squeezed her hand and gave her such a look of tenderness that something shifted in her heart.

"Okay," he said at last.

Ethan saw her to the reception area, where Shanice came rushing around the desk to hug her. Apparently, word was spreading about what had happened.

Cambry reassured Shanice she was fine, just tired, and Shanice shared her good news.

"My son phoned me this morning. Willoughby showed up at a lodge in the foothills, and the owners took him to the vet for some small cuts on his feet. The vet scanned him for a microchip and called my son when the information came up. My son called me, and I drove out to get Willoughby. He's fine, and back at my house, making up for lost meals and eating me out of house and home again."

"Oh, I'm so relieved!" Cambry said, blinking back tears. "I'll get him later tomorrow, if that's okay."

"*I'll* get him tomorrow," Ethan corrected. "I don't want you going anywhere else. You need to rest."

Shanice assured him that would be fine. As she took a call, Ethan collected the paperwork Shanice had set aside and carried it to Cambry's office. He set the small stack of papers on the desk and then ordered Cambry to the couch.

"Do you have a blanket around here somewhere?"

Cambry felt the corners of her mouth twitch. "Eth, it's an office, not a bedroom. Besides, I'm not going to sleep. I'm just going to rest for a while." She started to lift her feet up onto the couch but winced when she felt a twinge in her side.

Ethan was at her side instantly. "Careful," he warned, reaching down to help her lift her feet up onto the couch. Then he pulled off her sneakers and set them on the floor. The simple, thoughtful gesture both surprised and touched her.

"Don't think I'm being nice," he said when he caught the emotion on her face. "I just took off your shoes to make sure you don't leave this office and start trying to do business with coworkers down the hall."

She laughed. "Figures you'd have an ulterior motive."

When he left to go back to the agents, she settled into the corner of the couch. She *was* tired. And more sore than she wanted to admit. But Ethan's gesture had been so thoughtful that she wondered if the walls around her heart had just lost another brick. Before long, she wasn't going to have any defenses left. He was definitely making this hard.

And he wanted to talk. What was she supposed to say? That she loved him but didn't trust him not to break her heart again? It was the truth. But he hadn't run. He was clearly working hard to prove that he was serious about rebuilding her trust. And he'd said he loved her. How could she not give that serious consideration?

Closing her eyes, she let her head fall back on the arm of the couch. If nothing else, she had a quiet office and time to think. That's just what she would do.

CHAPTER TWENTY-EIGHT

Tired of lounging on the couch and thinking about the complication that was her relationship with Ethan, Cambry got up and padded over to her desk in her socks.

It wouldn't hurt to take a quick look through the papers Shanice had given her, she decided. Besides, the work would keep her mind off things. She was starting to go a little crazy knowing Benton and his men were still out there, planning—or doing—who knew what.

She sat down in her desk chair and turned on her computer. As the hard drive whirred and beeped to life, she thumbed through the stack of paperwork. To her relief, there was nothing too stressful in the pile. It would be just enough to give her something to do until Alisa found the program.

The quiet tick-ticking of the clock across the room was familiar and somewhat comforting, and for a time she was able to forget about everything else.

A knock on her door startled her, and she glanced down at the paperwork spread out in front of her, realizing how incriminating this looked. If that was Ethan on the other side of the door and he walked in to find her like this, she was in big trouble.

Before she could react, her door opened, and Kurt stepped inside.

"Cambry, it's just me. Are you okay?"

She felt her shoulders sag in relief. "Kurt. Hey. It's good to see you."

"It's good to see you too," he said as he came in and shut the door behind him. "I just heard what happened."

"It's probably spreading like wildfire. Who did you hear it from?"

"Jim told me. He said you'd been hurt and that you were in the hospital this morning. And *kidnapped*? What on earth . . . ?"

As she started to explain, Kurt pulled a chair over to sit beside her and listened with concern. "Cambry, you could have been killed," he said, reaching out to take her hands. "I'm so glad you're okay."

The concern of a longtime friend was almost her undoing. Tears gathered in her eyes, and Kurt immediately pulled her into a gentle hug. She allowed herself to close her eyes and rest her head on his shoulder, enjoying the brotherly hug. It was exactly what she needed, she realized. A guy friend to hold her with no expectations or complications.

Why can't it be this way with Ethan? she thought as a couple tears escaped and slid down her cheeks. Why did everything have to be so complicated? Kurt eased back and looked at her. When he saw her tears, he wiped them away with the pad of his thumb. "Cambry, what can I do?"

"I'm sorry," she said, fighting to get her emotions back under control. "It's just been a hard few days."

"Knowing you, you've been keeping all your feelings under wraps," he reprimanded. "You did the same thing when you were interning here years ago. You're allowed to be human, you know."

"I know. Things are just . . . complicated."

He frowned. "There's something else, isn't there? Other than the kidnapping." He studied her for a long moment before understanding flashed into his eyes. "It's Ethan, isn't it?"

She remembered times like these when her parents were separating, and she and Kurt had talked for hours. He'd always been a good listener. Deciding she needed that right now, she let out a breath and started talking. She told him how she'd found out Ethan had been undercover to find out what she knew about her father's missing technology and how she now couldn't be sure if anything that had happened between them had been real or just an act to get her to trust him.

"I thought I was falling in love with him again," she admitted softly, staring down at her hands. "He says what he feels for me is real, but after he spent the past week lying to me, I'm not sure I believe him."

Kurt's hand under her chin guided her eyes to his. "You deserve better than that, Cambry. How can you be with a guy who lies to you and will say anything to do his job? He's not the guy for you."

A teasing smile tugged at the corner of her mouth. "And you're saying that you are?"

"I'm saying you should consider the possibility."

His words stunned her into silence.

Before she could untangle the words in her brain, he leaned in and kissed her.

She sat, frozen, not knowing what to do or how to react. He didn't smell right. Feel right. Her heart didn't flutter, and his lips felt cold and unfamiliar against hers.

He wasn't Ethan.

Her heart wrenching in her chest, she pulled back and fought the awkwardness of the moment. Finally, she composed herself enough to give him an apologetic look.

"Kurt, I'm sorry, but I just don't feel that way about you," she said gently.

Kurt straightened, and a look of pained rejection filled his eyes. "Well, I think you should consider it," he said a little stiffly. "I realize you're tired and have just been through a traumatic experience, but I'm willing to give you the time you need. Within reason, of course." He trailed a hand down her arm and squeezed her fingers. "Just think about it."

The door opened abruptly, and Cambry jumped a little. She looked over to see Ethan standing in the doorway, one hand still on the doorknob. He wore a formidable scowl on his face.

"Am I interrupting something?"

Kurt got to his feet. "No, we're finished." He looked pointedly at Cambry. "For now. Let's talk later, okay?"

When Kurt disappeared into the hall, Ethan shut the door behind him with a forceful thump. "What do you see in that guy, anyway?"

Cambry bristled. "He's a decent guy. You don't even know him."

"Wanna bet?" Ethan's eyes flashed as he stopped in front of her desk with his hands on his hips. "You know I'm great at reading people. Let me tell you what I know about your friend Kurt. He's self-absorbed, money and power hungry, and educated but not particularly wise. How could you even like a guy like that?"

"Yeah. Well, we've already established that I have poor judgment when it comes to men," she snapped.

She knew she'd driven her point home when Ethan visibly flinched.

She picked up the papers on her desk and started to straighten them.

He watched what she was doing and glared at her. "You're supposed to be resting."

"I couldn't sit still any longer. Why are you here?"

"Lawford just got a call from one of the agents tracking Benton," he said. "He got a more complete list of Benton's assets, and it turns out that

Benton owns a five hundred–acre ranch just outside of Denver that he sometimes rents out as a corporate retreat. A dozen agents were just tasked to go to check it out."

Interest in Benton's possible capture overcame Cambry's annoyance. "Do they think he's there?"

"We'll find out, I guess."

Cambry finished aligning her stack of papers and set them beside the keyboard. When she looked back up, Ethan was studying her with concern. "What?"

"Your hands are shaking."

She looked down at them. "Are they?" To her dismay, she noticed they were. Ethan pressed the backs of his fingers to her cheek.

"You don't feel feverish. You okay?"

She let out a shaky breath. "I think my pain meds are just wearing off. It's probably time to take my next pills."

"I'll get them. You sit down."

She went over to the couch and sat, and Ethan rummaged in her bag for her prescriptions. He was at her side a moment later with her pills and a bottle of water from her tiny fridge. She put the pills into her mouth and chased them down with the water, giving a grateful sigh.

"All right?"

She nodded as she closed her eyes and rested her head against the back of the couch. "I think I'm just going to rest for a few minutes until they kick in."

"Want me to stay?"

"I'd like that."

He sat beside her, slid an arm around her shoulders, and pulled her into his side. She dropped her head to his shoulder and felt his lips tentatively touch her forehead.

"Sleep," he said. "I'll make sure you're safe."

***

"Garrison, you've got to move." Crowder's voice was laced with an urgency that Garrison couldn't miss, even over the phone. "There are at least a dozen agents gearing up to head for Benton's ranch."

A flash of alarm made Garrison's fingers tighten around his phone. "They're what?"

"They found out about Benton's ranch. If you don't get up there right now and send the men packing, they'll be caught red-handed when the agents arrive. You can beat them up there if you hurry."

Garrison ended the call and whipped his car around, ignoring the blaring horns. His gear and equipment were at Benton's ranch. He couldn't afford to lose any of it. Plus, his laptop had his contacts in a password-protected file that he knew would be at the mercy of the FBI.

Garrison headed out of Denver, driving as fast as he dared. It seemed to take forever to reach Benton's ranch, but when he turned down the road leading to the ranch, he saw that it had only been forty minutes. He'd made good time. All he had to do was get in there, throw his things into his bag, and run.

He drove down the dirt road in record time and careened into the parking area in front of the lodge. Getting out of the car, he rushed up the steps and flung open the door. All was quiet. Just as well. He wouldn't have to give any explanations.

He shoved his keys into his jacket pocket, feeling them clank against the thumb drive Crowder had given him. He shrugged out of the jacket and tossed it over the back of a leather armchair in the great room before rushing down the hall and into his room.

Grabbing his duffle bag from the closet, he unzipped it, put his laptop in, and started throwing in only what he needed or what could be linked back to him.

When he had everything, he snatched up the bag and hurried from the room. His footsteps echoed through the empty lodge. As he reached the great room, he grabbed his jacket and threw it on. His hand automatically went into his pocket for his car keys. His fingers closed around them, but nothing else.

His brow furrowed as he pulled out the keys, transferred them to his other hand, then put his hand back into his pocket. Where was the thumb drive? It had been there when he'd taken his coat off. Confused, he bent down to look on the floor around the chair. Nothing. He dropped to his knees and looked under the chair.

"Looking for this?"

Garrison's head jerked up, and he saw Benton standing in the entrance to the great room. He was looking rather smug as he held up the thumb drive.

Garrison blinked. "How did you get that?"

Benton sauntered closer. "I know you think I'm weak. Incapable of doing the dirty work myself. But you—you underestimate me."

Garrison stood, took two hasty steps toward Benton, and attempted to snatch the drive out of the man's hand.

"Uh-uh, not so fast," Benton said. "You didn't think I was capable of figuring out what you were up to, did you? But you've been the one meeting with your source, putting me off, stringing me along. That's when I realized just how much power that gave you. And the opportunity to pull off the perfect coup." He lifted a shoulder and gave a reckless smile. "Or not so perfect, since I found out."

"Give me the drive," Garrison growled.

Benton's lips pulled back in a snarl. "Not a chance. Tell me, is the technology on this drive decrypted yet or are you still waiting for it?"

Garrison clenched his fists. "You're supposedly in charge of this operation. Don't you know?"

Anger flickered in Benton's gaze. "I trusted you to get the information. Not keep it for yourself." In a quick move, he pulled a gun from the back waistband of his jeans and leveled it at Garrison.

"What do you think you're going to do with that?" Garrison scoffed. "Is it even yours or did you take it off one of the men? Speaking of which . . ." He looked around the empty lodge. "Where *are* your men?"

"I sent them back to the airport with my stuff. We'll be long gone before anybody even learns we were here. You, on the other hand, will be here. Dead, but here."

Garrison snorted. "You've never shot anybody in your life. You always leave that to me."

Benton's eye twitched. A telling gesture. The man was a decent actor, Garrison gave him that. But he wasn't ruthless. That fact was catching up with him.

"Get down on your knees," Benton said, his tone harsh, but the hand holding the gun shook almost imperceptibly.

Garrison eased himself down to his knees, lifting his hands placatingly. "You won't kill me," he said, biding his time as Benton strolled closer. He was almost within reach. "Who would do all your dirty work? Kill those who cross you? Use their sources to get what you want? If I'm gone, you're in a world of hurt, man."

"That's what you think." Benton moved steadily closer until he was an arm's length away. "I climbed this ladder before you were here, and I'll keep climbing after you're gone. You're finished."

"Think again."

In a flash of movement, Garrison grabbed the gun, twisted it in Benton's hands, and yanked it from the man's grasp. Then with a knee to the chest and a leg sweep, Garrison put Benton on the ground.

As Benton gasped for breath, Garrison moved over him. He leaned over and snatched the thumb drive from his former boss.

"Thanks," Garrison said as he straightened back up. "Do you remember what you said to me earlier today at the restaurant? You warned me not to mess this up for you, that because it was my source, you'd hold me accountable for my results. Well, I'm taking my source and walking. And you're right. I did the work, so the reward is mine."

He held up the drive and smiled coldly. "You know me well enough by now to know that I'll stop at nothing to get what I want. Nothing."

Staring back into Benton's anxious gaze, Garrison steadied the gun and squeezed the trigger.

The sound of the Glock firing shattered the mountain's stillness.

CHAPTER TWENTY-NINE

CAMBRY WAS DOZING AGAINST ETHAN when a buzzing cell phone brought her head up off Ethan's shoulder. He shifted to pull his phone from his pocket and then put it to his ear.

"Reece."

She sat up and stretched a little as he exchanged a few words and then finished with, "We'll be right there."

"What's going on?" Cambry asked.

"Lawford. He says Alisa thinks she found the software."

"Yes!" Cambry said, feeling suddenly more awake. She stood up carefully. "Let's go."

He stood up beside her, giving her a skeptical look. "Are you sure you're feeling up to it?"

"My little power nap helped," she admitted. "I'll be fine."

They hurried to her father's office, where Ethan became all business as he ushered Cambry over to a chair near the desk. "Where did you find the program?"

Alisa's enthusiasm was palpable. "I checked his local system and then checked the history on it. I saw that it had communicated with the network server, so I looked through the logs on the network server to see where it had communicated. Then I went to the location and had to find the hidden share on a network drive. And there it was."

"Did anybody actually follow that?" Cambry asked dryly.

Ethan chuckled. "Not me. But at this point, I don't care. What now?"

"Now we need a password." Alisa turned to Cambry. "Any idea what your dad would use?"

Ethan put his hand on her arm as he hunched down beside her. "Your father was trying to tell you something the night you found him," he reminded her. "Think, Bree. What did he say? I remember you telling me he said something like *nickname*. Could he have been trying to tell you that his nickname was the password?"

"That makes sense," Alisa chimed in from her place in front of the computer, her fingers hovering over the keyboard. "What was his nickname?"

Cambry gave a helpless shrug. "He could have gotten a nickname in the five years since I last talked to him, but I wouldn't know. Maybe somebody should go talk to Jim."

"I'll go," one of the agents said, heading out of the office.

Cambry turned back to Alisa. "I remember a few casual nicknames people called him back when I was in high school, but I have no idea if any of them stuck."

Alisa asked her what they were and typed them in one by one. None of them worked.

"What about when you were little?" Agent Lawford asked. "Did you call him anything that he liked? That he was fond of?"

"When I was really little, I used to call him Papa Bear."

Alisa tried that without success.

Cambry sighed in frustration. "I just don't know. Isn't there a password-hacking program you could use?"

"Sure." Alisa nodded. "But they're not always fast or successful. It's better to try what we can on our own and then resort to that if we hit a wall."

"What about some other nickname?" Lawford prompted. "Maybe yours? Did he call you something?"

She thought about that a minute. "He used to call me Cambear," she said, and Alisa typed that. That didn't work either.

"What else?"

Cambry groaned. "I don't know. Nothing else comes to mind."

They all sat in silence for long moments, considering what to do next. As Cambry tried to think of anything that could help, her mind went back to the night of her father's attack. She replayed, in careful detail, everything he said. There had to be something.

His urgent, gravelly voice echoed in her head.

Password. Nicknames.

She sat up in surprise. He'd said *nicknames*. Plural. Why hadn't she remembered that? What had he been trying to tell her?

As Cambry's mind churned, a long-ago memory crept into the back of her mind. Lazy Saturdays with her father at the office. Sitting in his swivel chair, twisting back and forth as she played games on his computer.

She suddenly went still. *The games.*

Her father often brought her in to work with him on those lazy Saturdays when she was little. He'd let her hang out with him as he caught up on paperwork, leaving her mom free to run errands. While he worked, she'd sit in that chair and play games on his computer. The games had been their thing. Scrabble, online checkers, crossword puzzles—all games he'd saved in a special folder on his desktop for their Saturday morning office outings, as he'd called them. During the week, he'd take his turns at whatever games they were currently playing, and then on Saturday morning, she'd open the password-protected folder and take her turns.

She'd asked him once why he required a password to open the folder, and he'd laughed and said he couldn't very well leave a file of games readily available for a receptionist or colleague to stumble across. "It would make me look like I haven't been working very hard," he'd answered.

And the password for their games folder had been their nicknames intertwined—his capitalized, hers lowercased, the common word *bear* separated from the rest by the caret symbol. His nickname wrapped around hers like a giant bear hug, he'd always said with tenderness in his voice. He'd come up with the nickname password combination, and it had made her feel special.

Dismissing the pinch in her heart caused by the long-forgotten memory, she tried to think. Was that what he'd been trying to tell her? That the password was that long-ago intertwining set of nicknames?

With shaking hands, she snatched a pen and notepad off the desk and started scribbling frantically.

PcAaPmA^bear

Her urgent movements caught the attention of those around her, and Ethan and Alisa leaned in to try to see what she was writing. She ripped the sheet of paper from the tablet and thrust it at Alisa.

"Here, try this."

Alisa read it and then looked up at her with an eyebrow arched.

"Long story," Cambry said. "Just try it."

With a shrug, Alisa turned back to the computer and typed in the characters from the paper. She hit Enter, and they all waited breathlessly as the computer processed.

Then the password box disappeared and a pop-up flashed onto the screen, asking where the file should be saved.

"Yes!" Alisa cried out. "That was it!"

Resounding cheers filled the office, and Cambry couldn't help the feeling of warmth creeping into her heart. Maybe Jim was right. Maybe her father *had* been working at changing. Why else would he have used such a nostalgic password for such an important file that he'd never even planned on her seeing? The only explanation she could come up with was that the password had been dear to his heart.

That spoke volumes.

Alisa continued to type, and by the time the cheers had died down, she had a file open on the screen. "And there it is," she said, as if she'd just found the Holy Grail. "The research file. Safe and sound."

"So what do we do with it?" Ethan asked.

Agent Lawford spoke up. "Because it officially belongs to the military as per its contract, Jim and Cambry can get in touch with the contract holders and deliver it to them as soon as it's safe. We'll need to keep it closely guarded until Benton is caught, though, or more people could get hurt in his attempt to acquire it."

A new voice entered the conversation. "That won't be a problem."

They looked up to see Agent Arehart walking into the room with a handful of other agents. His gaze landed on Cambry and Ethan. "Benton's dead."

"What?"

"How?"

Agent Arehart put the questions off for a moment, turning to look at Alisa. "I take it you found the file?"

Alisa beamed. "We did. Opened it, saved it. We're good."

"Great. At least something has gone right this afternoon."

"But . . ." Cambry started, looking at Ethan and the other agents in confusion. "If Benton's dead, isn't that something else that's gone right?"

"You'd think." He tugged at the knot of his tie in agitation. "When we got there, we found him dead. Shot. And the place was otherwise deserted."

Ethan's expression tightened. "And now we're looking for whoever shot him."

"Exactly. So, the big question is who killed him. And why."

Ethan considered that. "A power play? Somebody planning on taking over the organization?"

"Possibly." Arehart looked at Cambry and Ethan. "You were essentially on the inside of Benton's organization for a couple of days. Did anyone stand out? Somebody that argued with Benton or was at odds with him?"

An image of the mean-looking man with the scar along the side of his face flashed into Cambry's mind. She gave an involuntary shiver. Looking over at Ethan, she said, "The man with the scar. He scared me as much as Benton did. Maybe more."

Ethan nodded. "I remember him." He turned to Lawford. "When I told Benton about giving the disc to the FBI, he turned to this guy and said, 'We have a disc to retrieve.' That would indicate he was a right-hand man."

"I agree. If we showed you some pictures of the men we know to be in Benton's organization, could you ID him?"

When Ethan and Cambry nodded, he pulled out his phone. "Let me call in and see if I can get somebody to run the files over so you can take a look."

Agent Arehart spoke up. "We could VPN into the FBI computers and look at them from here. If we could remember how to do that," he finished with a sheepish smile. "I've personally never had to do it before."

"Or I could hack in," Alisa spoke up enthusiastically. "With your permission, of course," she added when Agent Lawford gave her a stern look. Then, when she saw he was not amused, she backed down. "Or maybe not. You can't blame me for asking. CIA hacker, remember? It posed an interesting challenge."

Cambry laughed softly. "Alisa, I think you'd better quit while you're ahead."

"Right. Shutting up."

The other computer security analyst guided them through the VPN process, and before long they were looking through pictures of Benton's known associates. They paged through several before a familiar face made Cambry's heart clench. She pointed to the man with the deep scar along the side of his face.

"That's him."

"Richard Garrison," Agent Lawford read. "Looks like he's been with Benton's organization for several years."

"What do we do now?" Cambry asked.

Agent Lawford pulled out his phone. "I'll call it in and let the supervisory agents know who we think we're looking for. They'll pool their research and task agents to track him down. If he's the one who shot Benton, he's got something planned. Maybe he's even planning to meet with the buyer and finish the deal on his own."

Cambry shuddered. She remembered well the evil glint in the man's eyes. There wasn't a hint of compassion there. If this Richard Garrison was rogue, he was capable of anything.

***

Garrison answered his phone as he steered out into traffic.

"They just found the program on the office network and retrieved the file," came the voice of his source inside Saville Enterprises.

"When did this happen?"

"About a half hour ago. I just managed to slip away. The office is crawling with agents."

"And a password?" Garrison asked.

The man hesitated. "I don't know. I wasn't there when they found the file."

A horn blared, and Garrison swerved back into his own lane. "Look, I'll call you back in five minutes."

He clicked off the call and then dialed Crowder.

"It's me," he said when Crowder answered. "I heard they found it."

"Yeah. I can't get it for you though. Security's too tight. But I did get the name of the steganography program Saville used. You could download the software to decrypt the file yourself. The only problem is you would still need his password."

"What is the password?" Garrison asked.

"That's what I'm telling you," Crowder said. "I don't know. Apparently, Ms. Saville figured it out for them, but I wasn't there. If I asked somebody for it, it would make them suspicious. That's attention I can't risk. Sorry. You're on your own."

After Crowder told him the name of the program, Garrison hung up and looked at his watch. He was meeting with Navarro in a few hours. He didn't have time to be creative. Yes, he could download the software himself, but he needed that password. His best hope was to grab Ms. Saville and make her tell him what the password was. Then he'd kill her.

His plan firmed in his mind, he picked up his phone once more and called his source inside Saville Enterprises back. "Yeah. It's me again. We're going to grab Ms. Saville and get the password from her. Here's what I want you to do."

CHAPTER THIRTY

"So what happens now?" Cambry asked Ethan as they stood in a corner of her father's office and watched the gathered agents start to drift away.

"There's no reason for anybody to stay here," Ethan said. "The file's been found, and we'll take it to the office for safekeeping until this threat from Benton's men is over."

"And what do *we* do?"

Ethan gave her a look that brooked no argument. "*You* are going home. Then I'm going to help these guys go after Garrison and Benton's other men."

"Isn't your part in all this over? I thought you were only supposed to spy on me, not go after Benton and his men." The second the words were out of her mouth, she wished she could suck them back in. She hadn't meant them to sound accusing, but to her dismay, they did.

A look of guilt and hurt flashed across his face.

"I'm sorry," she said, feeling contrite. "I didn't mean—"

"Yes, you did. Some little part inside of you meant exactly what you said."

He shook his head and moved closer, his large body only inches from hers. His expression was frustrated, weary, and more than a little hurt as he met her gaze. He lowered his voice so nobody would overhear them, but still it was filled with strained tension when he answered.

"Look, Bree. I know I hurt you. I get that. Don't you think this is killing me too? I had planned to come here to make things up to my family and to see if you and I could still have a future. But all my good intentions were trampled by this job."

He looked down and plowed a hand through his hair. When he looked back up at her, he blew out a troubled sigh and said, "You know what, Bree?

I've lived under a mountain of guilt for the past five years for the way I walked out on you, and ultimately, I came here to make amends. But I can't keep hanging on to the past. I know the circumstances of this last week don't exactly reestablish your trust in me, but you know how I feel. Don't use this as a reason to keep punishing me for what I did five years ago."

He glanced over his shoulder and saw Agent Lawford motioning for him to join him. Turning back to Cambry, he said, "I've got to go." Then he walked away, his shoulders slumped as he shoved his hands into his jeans pockets.

His words had surprised her. Was that really what she was doing? Using this latest offense to punish him for how he'd hurt her five years ago?

She considered that in brooding silence. No, she didn't think so. She had reason to be angry and hurt for what he'd done to her this past week. He'd intentionally deceived her.

But he'd also explained and said he was sorry. Was she really going to throw away the possibility of something more over something he'd begged forgiveness for?

Her gaze drifted back over to him as he continued to talk with Agent Lawford and another agent. He'd put his work face back on. He was professional and determined to do what needed to be done to track down this latest threat. But knowing him as she did, she could still make out the hurt and anguish held tightly in check.

It was clear he'd been telling her the truth. He was hurting over this as much as she was.

You know you could fix this by simply forgiving him, the voice of reason put in.

She sighed. She knew that's what she needed to do. The hard part was doing it. For so many years she'd been holding on to her hurt and anger, both at him and at her father. Now both those men wanted her forgiveness. Why was she having such a hard time doing that?

Deciding she was more than ready to get home and be alone for a while, she picked up her backpack and headed for the door.

"Where are you going?"

Ethan's gruff tone made her look his way. He was watching her over his shoulder with his arms folded over his broad chest. She had to admit he looked a little intimidating. "You said you were leaving, so I'm going to go back to my office and shut down my computer."

He nodded, his expression unreadable. "Take somebody with you." His eyes scanned the room and landed on the man standing half in the doorway. "Dixon. Can you see Ms. Saville to her office and back?"

"No problem," the man said.

Cambry resisted the urge to roll her eyes. She was a big girl. She could walk across the building to her office without one of the FBI's trained pit bulls following her. Besides, she knew the people here, and even though it was almost dinnertime, there were still coworkers around finishing up for the day. She would be safe.

Feeling disgruntled, she allowed the man to walk with her. They hadn't quite reached the end of the hall when another agent came around the corner and spotted Agent Dixon walking beside her.

"Oh, good," the man said, addressing Agent Dixon. "Carlson is looking for you. He said he needs your ID number for the security sheet downstairs now, before the guard shifts change."

Agent Dixon glanced hesitantly at her. Cambry waved him on. "Go. I'll be fine. My office isn't far."

"You're sure?"

When she nodded, he hurried off with the other agent. Cambry shook her head as she continued on. She appreciated them watching out for her, but having a guard walk with her inside her own office building was ridiculous.

She'd just turned down the hall and was in sight of the east wing's reception desk, where Shanice was tidying things up for the day, when Kurt came around the corner and saw her.

The memory of their conversation earlier—and his unexpected kiss—made her a little uncomfortable.

"Hey, Cambry," he said with a smile that looked a little forced. "Jim's looking for you. He said he's been trying to call your cell phone, but you weren't answering."

Confused, Cambry fished her phone out of her pocket and thumbed it on. She grimaced when nothing happened.

"Sorry," she said as she slipped it back into her pocket. "I haven't had a chance to charge it today, and the battery's dead. What did he need to see me about?"

"Something about the military contract, I think. He said it was urgent."

She drew in a deep breath and let it out. "Okay. Let me just turn off my computer so I can head home after I talk with him."

"I'll talk to Shanice and have her do it for you," he offered. He looked around. "Where are your men in black?"

Cambry laughed. "I hadn't thought of them that way, but I guess they kind of are." She shrugged. "I had an agent with me a few minutes ago, but he had to go do something."

"Well, it doesn't hurt to be careful," he said. "Let me walk you to Jim's office."

Cambry couldn't really tell him no, even though she wanted to. After that kiss in her office, she felt awkward around him. Fortunately, they passed several people in the halls who were heading out for the day, and some stopped to chat about one project or another. It kept her and Kurt from having a chance to talk privately.

When they reached the corridor leading to Jim's office, Cambry thought she was home free. But then Kurt put a hand on her arm and stopped her.

"Do you mind if we talk for a second, Cambry? Preferably somewhere we won't be interrupted every other minute?"

She opened her mouth to answer, but his expression tightened. "It'll only take a minute."

Before she could protest, he took her hand and led her into the stairwell.

"Didn't you say Jim needed to see me right away?"

"This will just take a second," he insisted, opening the door and ushering her through.

Anxiety tumbled in her stomach. This was *so* a conversation she didn't want to have. She expected Kurt to stop just inside the door on the landing, but he led her down the stairs, his arm tightening around her hand until her fingers started to tingle.

"Kurt, you're hurting me," she protested, trying to pull her hand free. "Where are we going? We could talk right here, you know. Nobody's around."

He didn't answer. Just kept leading her down.

When they reached the next floor's landing, she decided she'd had enough. "Kurt, *stop.*" She dug in her heels and refused to move another step. "If you want to talk, talk. Right here."

He whirled on her, his face contorted in anger. "Cambry, stop being difficult! I want to go downstairs to talk. What is so hard about that?"

She shook her head. "Not happening. Tell me right here or I'm going back upstairs."

The muscle in his jaw jumped. Then he threw his arm around her shoulders and practically dragged her down the next few steps. "We're going downstairs whether you want to or not."

A frisson of fear slid down her spine. "Kurt, what has gotten into you?" she said as she tried to struggle out of his grasp.

The second they set foot on the next landing, Kurt shoved her backward against the stairwell wall and shoved his face near hers. Then, to her shock and horror, he pulled out a handgun and pressed it to the underside of her jaw.

"You're going to come with me," he snarled, the muscles in his face contracting in barely contained anger. "Or I'll shoot you just like I did your dad."

Cambry felt the blood drain out of her face. "You did what?"

A sneer curled his lips. "You heard me. I came to get the technology from your father that night, and he refused to play ball. He could have made a lot of money. But I guess since he's already a multimillionaire, that wasn't enough."

"You wanted to steal his research?" she squeaked. "What about Benton?"

"I met the man a couple of years ago at a conference and knew he was going places. There's only so much power a chief financial officer has. So I started looking for different . . . opportunities."

She balled her hands at her sides. "To work with a terrorist? And become a murderer? That's not exactly a step up."

Kurt's eyes narrowed. "Do you think I want to be stuck in some office, dealing with finances all my life? I'd always planned to move up in the corporate world, but I got stuck here. The economy's not what it used to be, and big companies are laying off executives just as often as little ones. There are too many people vying for the big positions. So when I was offered the chance to work for Benton, I jumped at it. Now I'm making more than I ever dreamed, and I have international contacts at my fingertips."

"Benton's dead, you know," she said, trying to keep her voice steady as the muzzle of the gun shifted against her skin.

"I know, but he's not the only game in town. His replacement will take this organization to even higher places."

"But it's blood money, Kurt," she tried once more. "Is that really what you want to do with your life?"

"It suits me just fine." He grabbed her by her shirtfront and hauled her away from the wall. "Now let's go."

As she stumbled forward, he wrapped his arm around her shoulders again and shoved the gun against her ribs. She fell into a stunned silence as he hurried her down the rest of the steps.

When had Kurt become so greedy and power hungry that he was willing to align himself with terrorists? What had happened to the man she used to think of as a big brother?

Think, Cambry, think, she ordered herself as they neared the bottom floor. *You've got to get away from him.*

They stopped in front of the door leading to the back of the lobby, and Kurt gave her a threatening look. "We're going to walk quietly, and if you make contact with anybody, I'll shoot you, then I'll shoot them. Understand?"

Cambry nodded.

Kurt slid the gun inside his suit jacket, still pointing it in her direction, and gestured for her to open the door. She did, and together they went through. She took a step toward the front of the lobby, but Kurt jerked her back.

"Not that way," he hissed, giving her a hard nudge toward the back emergency exit down an empty hallway to their right. "That way."

Her voice shook as she asked, "Isn't there an alarm that will go off?"

He snorted. "This isn't some retail store. It'll be fine. Now move."

CHAPTER THIRTY-ONE

ETHAN FINISHED TALKING TO AGENT Lawford about their next move in tracking down Richard Garrison and glanced at his watch. *Shouldn't Cambry be back by now?*

As he turned, he spotted Agent Dixon coming back into the room. Cambry wasn't with him. Confused, he frowned at Dixon. "Where's Cambry?"

"Isn't she back yet?" Dixon looked around the room. "I had to run downstairs to sign in for security, and she told me to go on ahead."

Ethan's muscles tensed as he took two threatening steps toward the agent. "You left her alone? After I specifically asked you to see her there and back?"

Agent Lawford put a hand on his shoulder. "Don't worry. She probably just stopped to talk to somebody. Let's go see if we can intercept her on her way back."

Ethan slid his gaze away from the anxious-looking agent and forced himself to take a breath. Lawford was probably right. She'd probably gotten stopped by somebody on her way. No need to take it out on the young agent.

Ethan and Agent Lawford headed out, but to Ethan's increasing concern, they didn't see her on their way to her office, and when they got there, her computer was still on.

With his heart in his throat, he jogged down the hall to the reception desk where Shanice was just shutting down her computer for the night.

"I'm looking for Cambry. Have you seen her?"

Shanice's eyebrows lowered. "I saw her coming down the hall a few minutes ago, but Kurt stopped her, and they went back the other way. Why? What's wrong?"

Ignoring her question, Ethan pulled out his phone. With shaking fingers, Ethan punched in Cambry's cell number and held the phone to his ear. It went straight to voice mail.

Shaking his head, he disconnected the call. "I don't like this," he said to Lawford.

"Why? Is this Kurt guy a problem?"

"He's the company's CFO, and something about him has always rubbed me the wrong way. The idea that she would make a detour with him just feels . . . off."

Ethan turned back to Shanice. "Could you call and see where Kurt is?"

Without hesitation, Shanice picked up the phone and hit a speed dial number. After a few moments, she shook her head and hung up. "That was his cell, and there's no answer. I know he and Cambry weren't heading to his office because it's back that way." She pointed down another hall.

"So where were they going?" Lawford asked.

"I don't know," Ethan said, "but Arehart's still in the building. Call him and tell to get everyone looking."

"On it." Lawford dialed and put his phone to his ear.

As he and Lawford rushed to the elevator, Ethan's sixth sense told him Cambry was in trouble and that they didn't have any time to waste.

***

Cambry winced as Kurt hauled her backward through the emergency exit and then swung her around so the door could shut behind them. She blinked in the semidarkness. The sun had already set, and the dim lighting on the back of the building did little to illuminate the area.

She looked around and realized they were in the equipment loading area behind the building. The place was deserted, and the parking lot where most employees parked was around the side of the building, well out of sight. Nobody would see her leaving the building.

Kurt grabbed her arm and rushed her down the steps to the asphalt loading area. When he steered her around the half wall separating the driveway from the alley, he shoved her forward. She stumbled and almost fell, throwing her arms forward to catch herself.

"She's all yours," Kurt said cryptically.

Another set of arms grabbed her, and she looked up at Kurt's partner in crime. Her eyes widened.

It was Richard Garrison.

The man's inky eyes looked even more ominous and threatening in the darkness. The scar along his cheek stretched as his lips curled into an evil smile.

"Ms. Saville. How nice to see you again."

She straightened painfully, her side feeling like it was on fire. She pressed a hand to it and felt something wet. Glancing down, she saw blood on her palm. Her eyes went to her shirt. Blood was seeping through the fabric, telling her she'd reopened the wound.

Pressing her hand back over the area to try to slow the bleeding, she looked back up at the man standing before her. With more courage than she felt, she said, "I wish I could say the feeling was mutual."

If possible, his expression darkened. He pulled a gun from the waistband of his jeans and cocked it. The threatening sound ricocheted in the alley around them.

Fear lodged in her throat, but she jutted out her chin and forced herself to meet his gaze coolly. "The FBI is already on to you, Garrison. They know you killed Benton to stage a coup. You might as well give yourself up."

Garrison's chuckle was anything but pleasant. "Give myself up? You've gotta be kidding. I stand to make six figures on this deal. Benton was an idiot. He couldn't run this organization without people like me, and after a while I got sick of taking orders from him. The only thing that stands between me and my money now is a password."

A cold chill settled in her stomach. "Password?"

"Don't try to play dumb with me, Ms. Saville. You know the password, and I want it."

"It's not going to do you any good without the software," she said, trying to stall for time. Surely by now Ethan would have noticed she hadn't returned from her office. She clung to the hope that he was looking for her. Right now it was all she had.

"I have the steganography software and the file. All I need is the password."

She hesitated.

"Surely it's not worth dying for, Ms. Saville." His tone was low and menacing. "You're a beautiful young woman with a bright future. Don't risk that by being stupid."

Cambry stared into his eyes and shivered. "If I tell you, you'll just kill me anyway."

Garrison leveled her with a look. "What makes you think I'd do a thing like that?"

"Because you're as insane as Benton, and you'd kill anyone who stood in your way."

"You know what, Ms. Saville? You're right." He grabbed her long hair, snapping her head back, and pressed the gun to her head. As he held her immobile, he turned to Kurt and snapped, "Start the car."

As Kurt rushed to do his bidding, Cambry noticed for the first time the dark SUV parked at the edge of the loading area near the corner of the building. Her heart slammed in her chest as Garrison pulled her hair to steer her in its direction.

"Where are we going?" she asked.

"For a little ride where no one will hear you scream."

Kurt started the car, and Garrison forced her forward. When they neared the vehicle, Kurt jumped out and came around to open the back door. He had a roll of duct tape in one hand.

"Do it," Garrison snarled when Kurt hesitated.

The order seemed to shake Kurt from his momentary bout of ethics. He hurried behind her, clasped her hands together, then started wrapping the tape around her wrists. She flinched as the tape twisted and pulled at her skin. After a few wraps, he tore the strip and smoothed the edge down.

"Get in." Garrison grabbed her upper arm and jerked her toward the open door.

Fear raced up Cambry's spine as her gaze darted around the parking lot, desperate for a passerby to notice and do something to stop this madman from taking her away. There wasn't a soul in sight.

Frantically, she tried to remember what she'd learned about self-defense years ago in mutual. She couldn't remember much, but she remembered being told never to get in the car. If you did, you were dead.

She decided to fight and hopefully attract as much attention as possible. She drew in a deep breath and screamed.

The sound echoed around them, reverberating with impressive force off the cement loading area and building's walls. Garrison quickly clamped a hand over her mouth with such force that she struggled to breathe.

"*Shut up!*" he hissed in her ear, the first frisson of anxiety sounding in his voice. Out of the corner of her eye, she saw him turn to Kurt. "Hurry! Give me a strip of tape for her mouth."

The sound of duct tape being unrolled renewed her will to fight. She twisted her mouth beneath his hand so she could open her jaw and then clamped down on one of his fingers with her teeth. He jerked his hand back, giving her another chance to split the night air with her scream.

Garrison's fist connected with her left cheekbone, and pain exploded through her skull. Spots danced in her vision, and her legs went weak. Darkness loomed, and she welcomed it. But then she was jerked upright and shaken. Somehow the motion cleared her head and firmed up her knees.

She was just managing to regain her vision when the strip of duct tape was slapped over her mouth.

Garrison got into her face, his expression twisted in anger. "Enough, lady! Now get in the car."

"Garrison!"

The shout rang out through the night.

Cambry's head was still buzzing from the blow, but she managed to shift her unfocused gaze to the left. There was a figure moving along the edge of the building. The world was blurry, but even so, she could make out the familiar build and movement.

Ethan.

A sob erupted in her throat.

Ethan took cover behind a parked car, but his head and hands were visible over the trunk. That's when she realized he had a gun.

"Garrison, let her go!" Ethan's voice contained a hard, threatening edge that was unmistakable.

She felt quick movements from Garrison as he shifted to look around their surroundings. He eyed the idling car as if considering his options, then looked at Kurt standing beside the passenger door, arms raised to show he wasn't holding a weapon.

Garrison seemed to realize how precarious his position was. He wasn't going to be able to get into the car and drive away, and Kurt wasn't either. Realizing his options were limited, Garrison threw a burly forearm around her neck in a choke hold and dragged her back against him, shoving the cold, hard muzzle of his gun against her head.

"Shoot me and the girl dies too!"

There was a flurry of motion behind Ethan, and Cambry spotted several armed agents moving into position behind and around Ethan. The gun was pressed tighter against her temple.

"Give it up, Garrison!" Ethan called back. "You're surrounded! You're not getting out of here, so you might as well let her go. If you do, you won't be harmed."

Garrison snorted and dragged her backward a couple of steps. "Yeah, the word of a fed!" he shouted. "There's something I can get behind!"

"You have our word." This time it was Agent Lawford's voice she heard. "You won't be harmed if you let Ms. Saville go."

A couple more steps backward and they were even with Kurt. Kurt's face was pale, and little beads of sweat were starting to form on his brow.

There was a look of desperation in his eyes as he saw other agents taking up position around the cement half wall of the parking area. The barrels of several rifles were lifted and resting on the ledge.

Kurt swallowed. "Maybe we should do what they say."

Garrison shot him a look of pure loathing. "Forget it. We'd be dead before she took two steps."

Panic skidded across Kurt's features. "I think we should trust them. Come on, Garrison. What choice do we have?"

Their gazes met in a silent clash of wills, both men unmoving.

Then Kurt's jaw clenched, and new resolve flashed in his eyes. "Do what you want. I'm taking the deal."

He turned around and lifted his hands, facing the men behind them along the half wall. He took a few cautious steps toward them, moving out of Cambry's line of sight. "I'm taking your deal!" Kurt called out, his voice shaky but resolute.

Garrison tensed against her, his fury unmistakable. "There will be no deals!"

He yanked the gun from her temple and whipped his arm around in a backward arc. To her horror, there were two quick pops followed by Kurt's strangled cry. Then she heard Kurt collapse.

Frozen in terror, she felt Garrison start to turn back around, his gun arm swinging back around toward her head.

"Cambry, down!" Ethan yelled.

Cambry wrenched away from Garrison's grip and dropped to the ground just as a firefight exploded above her. She screamed behind the strip of tape covering her mouth, and she curled into a ball, trying to make herself as small as possible.

She saw Garrison dive for the car, managing to wedge himself between the open passenger and rear doors for a measure of protection as he opened fire on the agents surrounding them.

She shrieked as a bullet whizzed past overhead and struck a target. Garrison bellowed, fired his gun twice more, then hit the ground with a sickening thud behind her. Then all was quiet.

Cambry sucked in shallow, terrified breaths through her nose as she lay still, too scared to move. Just as suddenly, the night came alive again.

FBI agents, some she recognized and some she didn't, rushed in, weapons drawn. She heard the sound of guns being kicked away, then warm, familiar hands were running along her arms.

"Cambry," came Ethan's voice. It was the most amazing sound she'd ever heard.

She blinked a couple of times, and his face, so close to hers, came into focus. Fear and distress warred for dominance across his features. Tight lines of concern were etched around the corners of his mouth and eyes.

She let out a sob from behind the duct tape. Ethan pressed a hand to her cheek to hold her still as he eased the tape off. As the cool night air touched her lips, she sucked in a lungful of air, then another, and another as her panicked sobs made it difficult to breathe.

"You're okay," Ethan murmured as he quickly unwrapped the duct tape from her wrists. Once that was done, he sat beside her and smoothed her hair away from her face over and over again. "You're okay. Slow down your breathing. Deep and easy. There you go."

Her breathing eventually slowed and evened out, and the dancing spots of lights in her vision finally faded.

Agent Lawford appeared beside Ethan. He looked grim as he opened a portable first-aid kit and pulled out a stack of gauze. "Let's see if we can get that bleeding under control."

She glanced down to see her side covered with blood.

Lawford moved over her and pressed the gauze to her side. Cambry jerked when she felt the pressure then closed her eyes to stem the pain.

"You're going to be okay, Cambry, just lie still," came Ethan's low, reassuring voice, his hand continuing to stroke her hair. "Are you hurt anywhere else?"

"My cheek," she said, the sound of her voice reverberating painfully inside her skull. She swallowed back the threatening nausea, drawing in a steadying breath through her nose.

"What happened?"

"Garrison punched me."

The look of raw fury in Ethan's eyes made her shiver. "Don't worry," Ethan said grimly. "He'll never do it again."

"Is he . . . ?"

When she met his gaze, Ethan's mouth pressed into a taut line, and he nodded.

Cambry shifted as she tried to look over her shoulder, but Ethan put his palm on her head to keep her from moving. "Don't look. That's a memory I don't want you to have."

"And Kurt?"

"Garrison killed him."

Emotion danced close to the surface, and tears blurred her vision. Kurt may have chosen a different road, one that had led to his death, but she couldn't help remembering the friend he'd been to her before. Reaching up for Ethan's hand, she closed her eyes and let the tears run down her face as he murmured soothing words of reassurance.

The nightmare was over. But it didn't feel like it. She suspected her physical wounds were going to take a lot less time to heal than her emotional ones.

"Cambry," Ethan said softly. When she looked up at him, she saw that his expression was full of concern yet reassurance as well. "You'll get through this," he said in an even voice as if he'd heard and understood her fears. "We both will."

She nodded as the sound of distant sirens drew closer. Then an ambulance pulled into the parking lot and stopped close by.

"I don't need an ambulance," she muttered to Ethan as two EMTs jumped out and hurried over to her. "You could have just driven me to the hospital."

Ethan shook his head and smiled. "Not a chance. I don't want blood in my car."

"It's not even your car." She mustered up a little energy to glare at him. "It's a rental. What do you care if there's blood in it? Just tell the EMTs to go away."

Agent Lawford chuckled as he looked at Ethan. "Stubborn, isn't she?"

"Tell me about it," Ethan said as he ran a hand tenderly over her face. "And I wouldn't trade her for the world."

CHAPTER THIRTY-TWO

THE NEXT COUPLE OF HOURS went by in a blur. Cambry was transported to the hospital and subjected to a battery of tests to check for a concussion and broken bones in her face. When the ER doctor finally came into her exam room, he announced with a reassuring smile, "No concussion, no broken bones. You can go home, Ms. Saville."

"Thank goodness," Cambry said, easing herself into a half-sitting position. She lifted the ice pack from her numb cheek and handed it to Ethan.

He winced as he looked at the purpling skin around her eye. "Tomorrow that's going to look terrible."

"At least we'll have matching black eyes."

Ethan chuckled. "Next time let's just buy matching T-shirts."

"Deal." She eased her legs over the edge of the hospital bed. "Who called earlier? You slipped out to talk when the doctor was changing the bandage on my side."

"Agent Lawford. He called to tell me that they took Verlin Crowder into custody. He was one of the assistant special agents in charge—and apparently Richard Garrison's inside man. Garrison's cell phone call log showed dozens of calls this week between the two men. When the director confronted him, he admitted to everything."

"That's terrible."

"I know. It explains so much though—how Benton knew I'd been tasked to talk to you, how Garrison got the copy of the disc, and how he seemed to know about every move we made."

"I'm sorry."

"I didn't personally know the man," Ethan said, "so it doesn't affect me that much. But I can imagine it'll take the agents working this field office a while to get past that. Want to know who else's number we found on Garrison's phone?"

"I hesitate to ask."

"Detective Dalton's."

Cambry's mouth dropped open in surprise. "From the police force? The one who threatened me and stalked me?"

Ethan nodded. "Apparently, the man's been under some scrutiny in previous cases, suspected of taking money to misplace evidence or manufacture some when needed. Garrison knew he could be bought. He told him to put enough pressure on you until you let something slip about your father's missing technology."

"He admitted to that?"

"Yes. The minute he was hauled into the field office and heard what charges he'd be facing."

Cambry shook her head. "Unbelievable. Well, at least he won't be involved in any more police investigations."

"I also talked to my mom," Ethan said. "I let her know what happened, and she's going to stay with you at your house tonight."

A nurse bustled in with a wheelchair, interrupting their conversation. "Ms. Saville, you're all signed out. I'm here to help you out to your car."

Cambry made a face. She wasn't thrilled about being wheeled around like an invalid, but she had to admit she was beyond exhausted. All she wanted to do was go home and sleep for a week. If a wheelchair got her to the car a little faster, she'd take it. Soon they were in Ethan's rental car and headed home.

Cambry fought to keep her eyes open as they drove, but the gentle motion of the car made her eyelids droop.

A hand on her shoulder a short time later startled her awake. She opened her eyes to see that they were sitting in her driveway. The engine was off, and Ethan was leaning over her in the open passenger door.

"Let's get you inside," he said.

Feeling groggy, she unfastened her seat belt and climbed out. Ethan kept a steadying hand on the small of her back as they walked up her front path. When they reached her front steps, she decided they may as well have been Mount Everest.

Ethan picked her up as if she weighed nothing and carried her up the steps. She let her head fall against his chest and nestled up against him with a contented sigh. Something about being in Ethan's arms just felt right.

The front door opened, and she looked up to see Janette standing in the doorway looking both concerned and amused.

"Hi, Janette," she managed sleepily as Ethan carried her into the foyer.

Janette shut the door behind them. "Ethan called and told me what happened. He didn't want you to stay alone tonight."

"Ethan told me. I appreciate it." She looked up at Ethan, touched by his thoughtfulness. "It was sweet of you to think of it."

"Yeah, well," he said, looking a little uncomfortable at her praise. "You need someone here tonight to make sure you take your medications and get around okay. In the future, I can do that, but for now, you're stuck with my mom."

Cambry stared at him in surprise as he carried her up the stairs.

In the future? Did he mean . . . ?

She looked over at Janette just in time to catch his mother's knowing smile.

Ethan carried her into her room and set her down gently on the edge of her bed. "Mom's going to take over from here, but I'll be back in the morning."

He rested his hand on her head for a moment and then let it slide down a handful of tousled curls. With a tender smile, he leaned down and pressed a soft kiss to her lips.

"See you in the morning."

Before she could react or respond, Ethan was gone. She turned to Janette, who was suddenly busying herself in Cambry's drawers to find something for her to sleep in. When Janette finally turned back with a pair of lounge pants and an old T-shirt in her hands, Cambry gave her a pointed look.

"In the future?" She repeated Ethan's comment. "What was that? And why do you look so smug about it?"

Janette fought back a smile. "It would just be nice to finally have you as a daughter-in-law."

Cambry's eyes grew moist.

Janette walked over and sat down next to her on the bed. "Ethan told me what happened this week. And I know how hurt and betrayed you must feel. But I know he loves you, Cambry. The circumstances weren't ideal, I'll give you that, but over and over again, Ethan has stuck by you, worried about you, and protected you. If that hasn't proven how serious he is about wanting to be back in your life, I don't know what will."

Cambry nodded. "You're right. He has. But there's still this part of me that is so scared that he'll hurt me again."

Janette reached for her hands. "Cambry, Ethan loves you. Give him another chance. And if you still love him as much as I suspect you do, forgive him. He's been so hard on himself these past few years—about Adam, about me and Dean and Emma, and about you."

"He told me he's been so wrapped up in guilt these past five years that he hasn't been able to get on with his life," Cambry admitted. "I can't stand the thought of him feeling so tortured about the past."

"Then tell him you forgive him," Janette said. "Sometimes people need to hear that we forgive them before they can start forgiving themselves."

***

Ethan slept in later the next morning than he had in a long time, and he woke up feeling surprisingly rested. He got up and showered then went downstairs to find Emma and her two sweet daughters having a late brunch with his dad.

When Emma spotted him, she got up and hugged him. "I was so worried."

"I'm fine. And Cambry's going to be fine too."

It was over brunch, eating and laughing with his dad and Emma and his nieces, that he knew the decision he'd made the night before was the right one.

He was going to move back to Denver.

He wanted to spend time with his mom and dad, make up for the lack of brotherly teasing Emma deserved, and spoil his two cute nieces rotten.

And he wanted to spend every minute of that future loving Cambry.

Having experienced over the past few days just how fragile life is, he didn't want to live with even one more regret. As soon as breakfast was finished, he let himself into the garage so he could have some privacy to call Agent Natoni back in Baltimore.

To his credit, Natoni didn't act all that surprised when Ethan put in his request for a transfer to Denver. Maybe Agent Lawford had given him a heads-up. Or maybe Agent Natoni had listened to his phone reports over the past week and figured it out on his own. Either way, he'd been prepared.

"I'll be sorry to lose you, Reece," Natoni said. "You're a good agent. But I know how falling in love changes a man. I fell in love with a beautiful woman once too."

"You did? What happened?"

"I married her."

Ethan chuckled. "Well, I think I'm going to do the same, if you don't mind."

"You're crazy if you don't. I'll call the assistant director over Denver's field office and put in a good word for you."

"Thanks. I'll see you in Baltimore in a few days."

When he hung up, Ethan's heart felt lighter than it had in a long time. As excited as he was about the possibility of moving back here, he decided not to say anything to his family until he knew for sure if the transfer would go through.

He spent a few more minutes with his dad and Emma and her daughters before announcing he was going to head over to Cambry's to see how she was doing. He'd just slipped on his jacket and climbed into his car when his phone rang. It was his mom.

"Ethan, we're on the way to the hospital," she said when he answered.

Instantly, his heart was in his throat. "What happened? What's wrong?"

"Oh, no, Cambry's fine. Sorry to frighten you. We just got a call from the hospital. Cambry's father is awake."

CHAPTER THIRTY-THREE

CAMBRY WALKED WITH JANETTE DOWN the silent ICU corridor, trying not to feel uncomfortable amidst the sound of doctors conversing and the whoosh of life-support machines.

Janette must have sensed her unease because she put a motherly hand on her back. "Everything will be fine."

Glancing over her shoulder at the elevator, she said, "I wish Ethan was here. Didn't you say he was coming?"

"He's on his way. Now relax. You look about ready to bolt."

"I feel ready to bolt," she confessed. "What am I supposed to say to him?"

"This isn't an Oscar speech, you know," Janette teased, not unkindly. "You don't have to plan it all out. Just ask him how he's feeling. Then go from there."

Cambry reached for Janette's hand and held on desperately. When they stopped outside the partially open door to her father's room, Janette gave Cambry's hand a squeeze.

"I'll go in with you, but I won't stay."

Cambry nodded, gathered her courage, and walked inside.

She didn't know what she'd expected, but it hadn't been this. Whenever she'd thought of her father over the last few years, the images weren't happy. But something inside her shifted as she looked at him now. He looked startlingly old and fragile as he lay in the hospital bed. She didn't know how it was possible, but her memories seemed to reflect a different man. The harsh lines and planes she remembered on her father's face didn't seem to exist on this man's kinder, softer one. Something in his eyes seemed gentler. Made him more approachable.

For a moment, a happier, more distant memory flashed: Her father laughing as he helped his eight-year-old daughter build a birdhouse that still hung on a tree near their cabin in the mountains. He'd clenched a tiny Crayola paintbrush in his hand—the only brush they'd been able to find—and he'd painted a rather lopsided pink heart above the circular opening on the front.

He hadn't always been spiteful and mean. Once she had loved him.

Before she could reconcile the two sides of this man before her, he looked up, and his expression brightened when he saw her.

"Cambry," he said in a weak but delighted voice.

Forcing her feet to move, she walked to his side. She glanced back at Janette, who nodded encouragingly. Remembering Janette's advice, she asked, "How are you feeling?"

"I'm tired," he admitted, the usually deep, booming voice she remembered reduced to raspy whispers. His brows lowered as she moved closer. "What happened to your eye?"

She self-consciously lifted a hand to the bruise and swelling on her cheek. She knew how bad it looked. This morning when Janette had woken her to take her medicine, she'd gone to the bathroom and made the mistake of looking in the mirror.

"It's a long story," she said, skirting the question. She sat down in the chair next to his bed as he looked at Janette.

"Janette? Is that you?"

"Hi, Dan," she said as she walked over to put her hand on his. "You look terrible."

He gave a quiet snort of laughter at her teasing, which surprised Cambry. He would have never allowed anybody to say something like that in the years before her mom's death. Instead, he reached over with his other hand and patted the top of Janette's.

"I'll forgive you for saying so this time."

Janette took a step backward. "I'm going to let you two talk," she said, moving to the doorway. "Cambry, I'll be out in the waiting room if you need me."

Cambry watched in a panic as Janette disappeared and pulled the door shut behind her. She was stuck. Turning back to her father, she watched him finger the breathing tube in his nostrils. Then he surprised her once more by giving her that gentle look of persuasion he used to give her when she was little and reluctant to talk about what was bothering her.

"Tell me what happened to your face, Cambear."

She fought back a well of rising emotion at his use of her long-ago nickname. "Like I said, it's a long story. But now that you're awake, I should let you know that you're going to be getting a visit from some FBI agents. They have questions for you. The good news is," she said, with what she hoped was a cheerier smile, "we found your research file, and it's under heavy supervision. You no longer have to worry about the men who were after the file."

"Kurt Kunde?"

Her smile faded. "He's dead. And yes, we know he was the man who attacked you in your office building that night."

Her father's eyes closed in grief. "I never thought Kurt would be involved in all this. It was Isaac Benton who contacted me initially. He kept pressuring me, threatening me to sell him the technology. That night Benton had called me at my office and told me he was done playing nice and that he was sending somebody over for the technology. I was horrified when I learned it was Kurt." He shook his head. "I figured it would be Benton's other man, Richard somebody . . ."

"Garrison," Cambry finished for him in a strained whisper. "He and Benton are dead too."

Her father's eyebrows crawled up his forehead. "Both of them?"

She nodded. "And one of the assistant supervisory agents at the FBI's Denver field office was also involved. He's in custody now."

"Sounds like I missed all the excitement," he said. His eyes met hers and held. "You okay?"

The memory of the feel of a gun's muzzle against her temple and the sound of bullets whizzing over her head made a cold chill go down her back. "I will be," she said, hoping that if she said it enough times, it would be true.

Her father lifted his hand and placed it on top of hers—something he hadn't done since she was a little girl. Her throat grew tight.

"I talked with Jim," she said. "He had some interesting things to say about you."

"Did he?" The hint of a smile pulled at his mouth. "That man always has something interesting to say."

She attempted to smile back but failed. "He swears you've changed. I told him I didn't think it was possible, but after seeing you now . . . I'm not so sure."

"Ahh, Cambear." He squeezed her hand even as tears sprung into his eyes. "I have changed. Over the past couple of years, I've had some things happen that were real eye-openers for me. They made me realize that what

I thought was important all those years ago really wasn't. Money, business, work—what's it all for if that's all you have?"

"You used to say that's all a man needed, remember?" Cambry's voice sounded bitter, even to her own ears.

"I was a fool."

That simple statement hung in the air until Cambry was forced to acknowledge it. "What exactly are you saying?" she asked.

Tears of remorse started to run down his cheeks. "I was so wrong, Cambry. About everything. I look back at who I was and what I did, and it's like watching somebody else go about ruining my life. I did horrible things, Cambry. Unforgiveable things. Things I can never undo and never take back. You have no idea how sorry I am."

Something wet dropped onto Cambry's arm, and she was startled to realize she was crying too. Pulling her hand out from under her father's, she leaned over and pulled two tissues out of the box on the nightstand. She handed one to her father and then used the other one herself.

He took it meekly and wiped his cheeks. "Is there any chance we can see each other? Try to get to know each other again?"

She considered his request. He really did seem to have changed. And if she was capable of forgiving the other man in her life, maybe she was capable of forgiving this one too.

She nodded and said, "Let's take it day by day."

CHAPTER THIRTY-FOUR

ETHAN REMAINED IN THE HALL, alternating between pacing and leaning against the wall across from the room where Cambry talked to her father. According to his mom, Cambry had been in there for about twenty minutes. Was she okay? How was this little reunion going?

Just then the door opened and Cambry stepped through it. When she looked up and saw him, she crossed the hall and moved easily into his arms.

He tucked her head up under his chin and pressed a kiss against her hair. "You all right?"

She nodded against him. "I think I've decided to forgive him and move on."

"Wow." He straightened in surprise and leaned back so he could look down into her face.

"I think he's changed," she said cautiously. "At least enough to give him another chance. We'll take things slow and see how they go."

Ethan's chest tightened with longing. "He's a lucky man to be forgiven so readily."

Cambry's expression became guarded. Wary. "Ethan, can we go somewhere and talk?"

"Sure." He said the word with more conviction than he felt. It was never a good sign when somebody wanted to go somewhere to talk.

Cambry looked around. "Where'd your mom go?"

"She left. I told her I'd take you home. You ready to go?"

"Let me use the ladies' room first."

He nodded. "Okay. And actually, while you do that, I'm going to talk with your father for a few minutes. If I'm not out before you, wait for me right here, okay?"

She gave him perplexed look but didn't argue. She turned and walked away, her sneakers squeaking on the linoleum floor.

With nervous steps, he crossed the hall to her father's room and pushed the door open. Dan was dozing in bed. It had been a long time since Ethan had seen him—the last time had been when Cambry had been a sophomore in high school and she'd dragged him along to a company picnic.

Dan's eyes opened, and he spotted Ethan standing in the doorway. One corner of his mouth lifted. "Ethan Reece. It's been a long time. Last I heard, you were in Afghanistan."

"My tour ended about a year ago. I'm with the FBI now."

Dan's eyebrows inched toward his hairline. "Is that so? In Denver?"

"Baltimore."

"Ah. So what are you doing here? You in on this investigation?"

Ethan met her father's gaze without flinching. "Among other things."

"What other things?"

Ethan had to admire the man's keen instincts.

He sat in the chair next to the bed and met Dan's steady gaze. "I'm going to level with you, Mr. Saville. My dad was having knee surgery, so I decided to come home to help him and my mom. And to see Cambry."

"Trying to pick up where you left off?"

Dan's tone was dry and slightly protective. Hearing him sound like he actually cared about Cambry made Ethan warm to the man a little bit.

"That too." Ethan fixed the man with an unapologetic stare. "I also came to investigate Cambry."

Dan sat up a little in bed. "You came to investigate my daughter? Why? What does the FBI want with Cambry?"

Ethan briefly explained about his assignment and about what he'd uncovered once he'd arrived. Then, carefully choosing his words, he touched on their kidnapping and the firefight Cambry had been in last night, resulting in Kurt Kunde's and Richard Garrison's deaths.

Her father looked like he'd aged ten years by the time Ethan finished.

"She's been through so much," Dan said, emotion deepening his voice, "and she didn't say a word about it while she was in here."

"She's a tough woman," Ethan agreed. "The bravest I know."

Dan wiped away tears from his cheek with a shaking hand. "Thank you for protecting her. I don't think I could ever repay you for keeping her safe."

"I know how you could repay me."

Dan's hand dropped to his side. "Name it."

"I want your blessing. I'm going to ask your daughter to marry me."

The room went silent. The two men stared at each other for a long moment. Then Dan's brows angled downward. "I seem to remember you were planning on doing that before. It didn't end so well, I was told."

Ethan's jaw clenched. "I was an idiot. At the time, I thought my actions were justified. My brother had been killed in Afghanistan, and I went a little crazy with grief. I enlisted in the military, bent on revenge. By the time I came to my senses, I was halfway across the world and missing my family and the only woman I've ever loved."

"Does she know you want to marry her?"

Ethan nodded. "I suspect so."

"What about this undercover business? Has she forgiven you?"

That touched a nerve. "She will. She's had a harrowing few days, and she needs some time to come to terms with how she's feeling. We're going to talk after we leave here."

"Talk." Her dad scoffed at that. "Sounds like she's going to give you the shove off, if you ask me."

Ethan bristled. "I won't let her."

"And what exactly are you going to do to change her mind? She's one of the most stubborn people I know."

"I'm just as stubborn," Ethan insisted. "I walked away from her once. I'm not about to do it again. It's taken me five long years to gather the courage to come back here to make things right. And now that I have, I'm going to spend every minute of the rest of my life making sure she knows how much I love her. *Nothing* is going to stop me from being with her. Not my job, not our circumstances—not even you."

Dan glowered at him, but Ethan stared back, refusing to be cowed. Then Dan smiled and relaxed against his pillow. "Good. You still have the backbone I remember. Hold on to that because only somebody who has that is going to be able to go toe-to-toe with my Cambry."

Realizing the man's words had been a test, Ethan's shoulders sagged with relief. He chuckled along with Dan and shook his head. "You really had me going there."

"I always liked you, Ethan," Dan admitted. "I knew you'd be going places. You served your country honorably and are doing the same with the FBI. Now you need to make sure you're good to my daughter."

"I will be." He stood up and shook his future father-in-law's hand. "I'm going to go so you can get some sleep."

"Would you see to it that Cambry comes back to see me tomorrow?" Dan asked, his eyelids starting to visibly droop. "I'd like to talk to her again."

Ethan nodded. "Just don't say anything to Cambry about our chat. I don't want to ask her until she's ready."

"As far as I'm concerned, that's between you and my daughter. I'll just wait for the announcement."

Ethan grinned at that and left. Cambry was waiting for him in the hall.

"What did you say to him?" she asked, her tone brimming with curiosity.

"Let's talk outside," he said, putting a hand on the small of her back and guiding her down the hall into the elevator.

When the elevator let them off on the ground floor, Ethan took her hand and walked with her outside into the beautiful, crisp fall afternoon. "I explained to your father about the FBI's involvement with his research, and I told him a little about what Benton and Garrison put us through."

"How did he take it?"

He gave her a sidelong glance as they started across the campus's grassy area toward the parking lot. "Honestly? I think it took a few years off his life. He really does care about you, Cambry. I'm glad you're giving him another chance."

She looked down at her feet. "I've done a lot of thinking lately, and I've come to the conclusion that everybody deserves forgiveness."

Hope flared inside Ethan's chest. "Everybody?"

"Yes."

"Even me?"

They stopped walking and turned toward each other. His words hung in the air, a barrier waiting to be crossed.

Cambry looked up at him and nodded, her eyes bright with emotion. "Especially you."

Ethan let out the breath he hadn't realized he'd been holding. He gathered her into his arms, and it took him a minute to force his words past the lump in his throat. "Thank you," he whispered against her hair. "You have no idea how much that means to me."

They held each other for a long time until Cambry finally stepped back. She then surprised him by stretching up on her tiptoes and kissing him sweetly. His body tingled and warmed, and he slid his arms around her and pulled her close. He wanted to kiss her this way the rest of his life.

"So what now?" she asked when their lips parted. "Are you heading back to Baltimore?"

"I have to, at least for a while," he said reluctantly. "I need to get back to my job. Fill out reports. Work on my transfer."

Cambry's brows knit in confusion. "Transfer?"

A smile curved across his face. "I asked my supervisor about a transfer to the Denver field office."

"Really?"

The happiness in her eyes went straight to his heart.

"Yes, really. I want to be with my family again, get to know my nieces. I want to feel a part of things again. And I have friendships to renew."

Cambry's expression fell a little. "Friendships?"

He feigned confusion. "Don't you want to be friends?"

"Friends." Cambry looked so crestfallen that he almost let her off the hook. But he couldn't resist stringing her along a little more.

"Sure. We've always been best friends. Don't you think that's worth working on?"

She bit her lower lip. "I guess."

"On second thought," he said, pulling her back into his arms. "I don't want us to be friends."

Now she really looked confused. "You don't?"

He shook his head. "I want us to be more."

"How much more?"

"I want us to be everything."

***

I want us to be everything.

Cambry's world slid to a halt. The wind stopped blowing through the grass. The birds stopped trilling. The distant waterfall in front of the hospital stopped gurgling. All the noises around her faded away as she looked into Ethan's vivid, evergreen eyes.

Was he saying what she thought he was saying? And why did she feel the urge to turn and run instead of hear him out?

"Are you serious?" she asked.

His mouth twitched. "Why do you look so terrified? I think I'm insulted."

"No, it's just . . ." She worried her bottom lip as she thought. "So much has happened the past few days. I think I need—"

"Time." He nodded. "And I'll give it to you. All I want is for you to give me another chance to prove how much I love you."

Her throat grew tight. Trying to keep her expression neutral, she said, "Your mom and dad would love having you here. So would Emma."

He took a step closer. "And you?"

"Me?"

Another step. A nod. "Would *you* love having me here?"

He took another step, stopping mere inches from her. The air around them crackled, jumped. It seemed alive and charged with energy.

At last she nodded. "I'd love having you here too. In fact, there's nothing I'd love more."

CHAPTER THIRTY-FIVE

CAMBRY STARED OUT HER KITCHEN window, watching Ethan as he fought the flames erupting from the barbeque grill on her patio. She clamped a hand over her mouth to smother a laugh.

It had been five weeks since Ethan had flown back to Baltimore, and those five weeks had been some of the longest of her life. In the week after their final run-in with Garrison, she and Ethan had eased back into their old, comfortable friendship, talking and laughing and teasing. She'd spent more time over at his parents' house with him than she had at hers. Being with him, Emma, Janette, and Dean had made everything feel right again.

It had been difficult to have him go back to Baltimore, but they'd kept in contact through texting, e-mails, and nightly phone calls. Even so, none of their long conversations made up for his absence.

When at last he'd called to let her know that his transfer to the Denver field office had come through, she'd been ecstatic. His family had been too, especially when Ethan told them he'd be starting his new job in Denver in three weeks.

She'd told him that day at the hospital after seeing her father that she'd needed time. Time to get to know him again. Time to learn to trust him. But she'd surprised herself to realize she hadn't needed as much time as she'd thought to fall in love with him all over again—and to trust him again with her heart. He'd proven just how preciously he held it beside his.

In the days spent waiting anxiously for Ethan to return, everything about her life seemed to be falling into place. Her health was returning, and the gash in her side was healing. She still had twinges of pain from time to time and a nasty scar, but she was thrilled she could finally do things like reach up into her cupboards without pain.

Her mental scars, however, were going to take time. She still fought with occasional nightmares, but thanks to Alisa's recommendation, she was seeing a trauma therapist who was helping her manage her anxiety.

She also found a new challenge in her job as COO at Saville Enterprises. When her father had first broached the topic about the position, she wondered how things were going to work out. She was only starting to get to know her father again. It was plain to see he'd become a much different man, tolerating the poking and prodding in the hospital with patience and kindness. The father she'd remembered from years ago would have been a snarling beast—insufferable and demanding.

But liking him and liking him enough to work with him were two very different things. She was approaching that aspect of their relationship cautiously.

To her surprise, the first couple of weeks she'd spent working with him had been encouraging. She'd been astonished at the kind but firm way he did business, and the respectful camaraderie he had with his employees and cochairs. He always stopped to chat with people in passing, asking them how their son had done on his English final or how somebody's wife was faring with her charity benefit preparations. He'd clearly taken a sincere interest in their lives, and they loved him for it.

If she hadn't seen the change in him with her own eyes, she'd never have believed it. What had finally convinced her this was going to work, though, was his approach to their working relationship. He worked her hard, but he was respectful and genuinely interested in hearing her opinions and suggestions. Many of the changes she'd proposed were adopted quickly, and he praised her often about how much more smoothly the day-to-day operations were running because of her contributions. The job was exciting and new, and it gave her the challenge she'd been looking for.

With the addition of a wonderful new job and the love of an incredible man, her life had started feeling very much like a fairy tale.

Except for the fire. She looked out the kitchen window again as Ethan continued to battle the flames on the barbeque grill.

When he'd stepped out of the airport a couple of hours ago and reveled in the unseasonably warm October temperatures in the mid-70s, he'd insisted on stopping at the grocery store to buy steaks to barbeque for dinner.

She'd arched a brow at him and given him a skeptical look. "Do you even know how to barbeque steaks?"

"Oh yeah," he'd answered. "Dad and me used to barbeque steaks all the time."

Apparently, that had been a long time ago.

When the flames were finally under control, he looked up and caught her grinning. He glared at her, so she quickly stepped back from the window.

She chuckled quietly and looked down at Willoughby, who was sitting at her feet, staring up at her with his head cocked. He'd managed to keep her from getting too lonely in the weeks Ethan was gone. Thankfully, Ethan was as fond of Willoughby as she was.

"Maybe you should get out there and help him, Willoughby," she told him as his now familiar shoelace-looking drool dangled from his jowls. "You could lean over the grill and drool on the flames. That would put 'em out."

He gave a little wuff of agreement, and she smiled.

Cambry flipped the dish towel over her shoulder and walked across the kitchen to the back door. Willoughby trotted next to her, and when she slid the glass door open, he hopped through the opening. Ethan was too busy scraping the burned edges off the steaks to pay attention to him.

"Everything okay out here?"

"O ye of little faith," he said without looking up from the steaks. "This just adds extra flavor to the meat."

She bit back a smile. "If you say so."

Leaving the door open so Willoughby could go in and out—something he did frequently—Cambry turned and went back to putting away her mixing bowls. She'd just finished when she heard Ethan calling to her from outside.

"Hey, Cambry, I think these are done," he said. "But I can't take them off the grill because your mammoth out here won't leave me alone. Call him in, would you?"

"Willoughby!" she called, giving an accompanying whistle. Moments later, she heard click-clicking of dog toenails on her kitchen's hardwood floor. She finished putting the large bowl up in her cupboard, conscious of Willoughby practically sitting on her feet.

As she shut the cupboard, she looked down at Willoughby's broad head and gave him a nudge with her knee. "Get off me, would you? You're going to trip me."

Willoughby didn't budge.

Growing a little annoyed, she gave him a shove. "You rotten beast, move!"

He shoved back. Then he wuffed. He continued to look up at her pitifully, and that's when she realized she was standing right next to the cupboard where she kept the dog biscuits.

She rolled her eyes. "If I give you one, will you move?" Turning, she fished a dog biscuit out of the bag in the cupboard and tossed it to him.

He immediately chased after the treat, which bounced off his nose, and it was then that Cambry saw the little red velvet bag tied to the back of his thick leather collar with a bright, glittery bow.

What on earth . . . ?

As Willoughby happily munched on his treat, she hunched down beside him and untied the bag from his collar. It was a drawstring bag about the size of her checkbook, and it was lumpy. Pulling the mouth of the bag open, she slid her fingers inside and pulled out several circular shapes wrapped in gold foil.

She started to laugh. They were miniature Reese's Peanut Butter Cups.

Willoughby chose that second to whirl, and he plowed into her, knocking her to the floor and spilling the treats. "Wills, move!" she said impatiently, giving him a hearty shove before he could Hoover up the chocolates.

Deciding from her tone that he'd pushed her far enough, Willoughby trotted off, leaving her to gather up the contents of the bag. She was just reaching for another handful when something else lying on the floor among the Reese's caught her attention.

It was a diamond ring.

Her heart stopped. With shaking hands, she picked up the ring. Three princess-cut stones, the largest in the middle, sat on a white gold band and twinkled in the light from the fluorescent bulbs overhead.

"Do you like it?"

Cambry's head jerked up. Ethan was leaning over the end of the peninsula on his forearms, looking down at her with a soft smile. He looked inordinately pleased with himself.

Hot tears burned her eyes as she looked up at him, her fingers tightening around the ring. "It's beautiful," she whispered.

His grinned widened in pleasure as he came around the corner and held out his hand. He helped her to her feet and then reached for the ring. Cambry's chest felt as if it were going to burst as she watched him slip the ring onto her finger.

The diamonds sparkled and winked at her in the fluorescent lighting, and she looked up at Ethan through her misty vision. "It must have cost a fortune."

His expression gentled, and he lifted a hand to cup her cheek. "Not enough to break me, if that's what you're asking. But on your hand, it's priceless to me."

Cambry felt an odd hitch in her breathing, and it was all she could do not to burst into tears. What was she supposed to say to that?

She looked down at the ring, unable to speak for long moments as she struggled to control her emotions. Ethan shifted beside her and then put a tentative hand on her shoulder.

"Cambry? You okay?"

Not trusting herself to speak just yet, she nodded. Ethan moved around in front of her and put a gentle hand under her chin. He tipped her face up to meet his now-anxious gaze. "Cambry, what's wrong?"

Unable to hold back the tears a moment longer, she let them stream down her face. "I don't know what to say," she whispered.

He flashed her a nervous smile. "Just say that I haven't totally freaked you out and scared you away."

Laughter bubbled up in her chest and erupted as a half laugh, half hiccup. "I'm not freaked out, and you haven't scared me away. I'm just . . ."

"Just what?" he prompted, looking nervous. "Fearful? Apathetic? Happy? Give me an adjective, here, Cambry, because you're making me a nervous wreck."

"Happy," she blurted out with a genuine laugh. "Happy." She sniffled and looked down at the ring once more.

"Oh, thank goodness," he breathed, the relief heavy in his voice. He pulled her into his arms and held her tightly. "You scared me to death. I thought you were going to say no."

"No, I'm not going to say no."

Amusement rumbled in his chest. "So that's a yes?"

She nodded against him. "It's a definite yes." When she pulled away, she reached for a tissue from the box nearby. "I don't know why you want to marry me. I'm such a wreck."

"You're not a wreck," he said, slipping his hand around the back of her neck under her hair. "You're amazing. I can't imagine *not* spending eternity with you. You're my best friend. You always have been. And you're the love of my life too. I love you so much that I plan on never letting you go. I know I've hurt you in the past, but I promise I'll never intentionally hurt you again."

One delicate, reddish eyebrow rose. "Intentionally? Is that a clause or something?"

He laughed. "No. More of a warning. I'm a guy. We do and say stupid things without thinking. But I promise I'll always say I'm sorry."

"I'll hold you to that." She stretched up on her toes to kiss him softly. "And I'll put in a warning of my own. You know me well enough by now to know that I rarely back down from a fight. Maybe you should think about just coming to terms with that and plan on letting me have my way."

His laughter brushed across their lips as their kiss deepened. "Not a chance. After all, we're both equally stubborn. And I did tell your dad I'd be going toe-to-toe with you when it came to things that were best for you."

She pulled away and looked up into his sparkling, green eyes. "My dad? You talked to my dad about this?"

"Mmm, that's a story for another day." He gave her a secretive little smile. "Right now, I just want to kiss my future wife. Think you can help me with that?"

"I think it can be arranged."

She slid her arms around his waist, and he leaned down toward her. As he did, she couldn't help but marvel at how things had turned out between them.

Growing up, she'd never been able to accept that she might marry somebody else someday. It had always been Ethan she saw when she thought of her happily ever after. But she'd lost that dream five years ago when he'd walked away. Her life had seemed empty. Incomplete.

"What are you thinking?" Ethan asked as his lips brushed over hers. "You look deep in thought."

"I'm thinking about those talks we used to have on the swing set out back," she admitted with a nostalgic smile. "How we talked about getting married someday—having a house, a dog, four kids . . ."

The corners of his eyes crinkled. "I remember." He looked pointedly around the room and then down at Willoughby, who came to sit beside them. "Well, we've got the house and dog . . . And after we're married, we can start on those four kids."

Cambry felt warmth spread over her cheeks. "I suppose we could."

Then Ethan's brow furrowed. "Wasn't there something about a Ferrari or a Mustang in there?"

"Fat chance." Cambry laughed, the joy she felt inside practically bubbling out.

Ethan's smile faded, and his expression gentled as his thumb slid over her cheek in a tender caress. "To be honest, I don't care about any of those things. If I didn't have anything else but you, I'd be happy forever."

That darned lump was back in her throat. Blinking back fresh tears, she cupped that handsome face in her hands. "Kiss me," she demanded in a hoarse whisper.

His eyes twinkled. "Yes, ma'am."

When he leaned down to obey orders, she stared up into those beautiful green eyes and marveled at how many things she could see in their depths. She saw the proof of his love, of his friendship, of his caring and trust.

And in that moment before his lips met hers and his eyelids drifted shut, she was surprised to realize that she could see more than just his emotions in his gaze.

She could see her future.

ABOUT THE AUTHOR

ERIN GREW UP IN THE San Francisco Bay area but now lives in southeast Idaho with her husband and five children. She loves playing tennis and staying up entirely too late to read, has a ridiculous amount of hoodies, can be (and has been) bribed with M&M McFlurries, and adores all things Scottish. When she's not writing, she works as a medical transcriptionist—both professions made even better because they allow her to work from home in her pajamas. She has been known to brainstorm aloud, which often garners her odd looks from her kids' friends and, sometimes, grocery store shoppers. Her family, however, has gotten used to it. She is also the author of *Between the Lines* and is currently working on her next novel. (No doubt in the aforementioned pajamas.)